P9-DMT-498

FLESH
&BONE

FLESH

ROT &
RUIN

BOOK THREE

&BONE

Jonathan Maberry

SIMON & SCHUSTER BFYR
NEW YORK LONDON TORONTO SYDNEY NEW DELHI

Also by Jonathan Maberry

Rot & Ruin

Dust & Decay

Fire & Ash

Dead & Gone (An e-book original)

Tooth & Nail (An e-book original)

SIMON & SCHUSTER BFYR

An imprint of Simon & Schuster Children's Publishing Division
1230 Avenue of the Americas, New York, New York 10020
This book is a work of fiction. Any references to historical events, real people,
or real places are used fictitiously. Other names, characters, places, and events are
products of the author's imagination, and any resemblance to actual events
or places or persons, living or dead, is entirely coincidental.
For information about special discounts for bulk purchases, please contact Simon & Schuster
Special Sales at 1-866-506-1949 or business@simonandschuster.com.
The Simon & Schuster Speakers Bureau can bring authors to your live event.
For more information or to book an event, contact the Simon & Schuster Speakers Bureau
at 1-866-248-3049 or visit our website at www.simonspeakers.com.
Also available in a SIMON & SCHUSTER BFYR hardcover edition
Design by Laurent Linn
Zombie Card art by Rob Sacchetto
The text for this book is set in Augustal.
Manufactured in the United States of America
First SIMON & SCHUSTER BFYR paperback edition August 2013
2 4 6 8 10 9 7 5 3 1
The Library of Congress has cataloged the hardcover edition as follows:
Maberry, Jonathan.
Flesh & bone / Jonathan Maberry.
p. cm. — (Rot & ruin ; bk. 3)
Summary: Benny, Nix, Lou, and Lilah journey through a fierce wilderness
that was once America searching for the jet they saw months ago, while
evading fierce animals and a new kind of zombie.
ISBN 978-1-4424-3989-4 (hardback)
[1. Zombies—Fiction. 2. Survival—Fiction. 3. Bounty hunters—Fiction. 4. Brothers—Fiction.]
I. Title. II. Title: Flesh and bone.
PZ7.M11164Fle 2012
[Fic]—dc23
2012000178
ISBN 978-1-4424-3990-0 (pbk)
ISBN 978-1-4424-3991-7 (eBook)

This one's for the librarians everywhere.
(Okay, I'll go sit in the back and read quietly now.)

And—as always—for Sara Jo.

ACKNOWLEDGMENTS

Special thanks to some real-world people who allowed me to tap them for advice and information, lean on them for support, and in some cases shove them into the middle of the action. My agents, Sara Crowe and Harvey Klinger; my editor, David Gale, and all the good people at Simon & Schuster Books for Young Readers; Ashley Davis, Nancy Kiem-Comley, Tiffany Fowler-Schmidt, Rachel Tafoya, Greg Schauer, Rigel Ailur, Bubba Falcon, Jaime Noyola, Bob Clark, Jim McCain, Colin Madrid, and Dustin Lee Frye for technical advice; Michael Homler of St. Martin's Griffin; Dr. John Cmar of Johns Hopkins University Department of Infectious Diseases; Carl Zimmer, author of *Parasite Rex* (Simon & Schuster); Alan Weisman, author of *The World Without Us* (Thomas Dunne Books); Chris Graham, David Nicholson, and John Palakas of the History Channel documentary *Zombies: A Living History*; and the King of the Zombies George A. Romero.

AUTHOR'S NOTE

This novel deals in part with the phenomenon of grief. Benny, Nix, Lilah, and Chong each have a reason to grieve; each has lost something they could not bear to lose. The people they left behind in Mountainside were all traumatized by loss, as are the people they meet out in the Ruin. Grief, in its many forms, is one of the themes that tie all four books of this quadrology together.

While I was writing this book, a great and dear friend of mine died. Leslie Esdaile Banks (aka L. A. Banks), a prolific author of romance, crime fiction, thrillers, and paranormal novels, lost her battle with a rare form of cancer. I've known Leslie since middle school, and we were colleagues in the Liars Club, a group of writers dedicated to promoting literacy and the love of reading. Leslie was a humanitarian, a fierce intellect, and one of the most joyful people I have ever had the great good fortune to have known.

Around the same time my brother-in-law, Logan Howe, also died. He was a good and decent man.

After they died, I found it painful and difficult to accept that the sun shone, the birds sang in the trees, and the world turned without them. Grief is like that. To resist or deny grief does no good. It hurts us to pretend that we are not hurt. Sounds strange, but it's true.

I know that many of the readers of this book have experienced grief, or will. It's human to hurt, but all hurts eventually heal. The best path through grief is to celebrate all those things that made the departed person alive. That's the light to follow. That's what my friends and I did after Leslie died. We cried, but we also threw a party and told tall tales and we laughed. I know—I absolutely know—that Leslie was laughing right along with us.

And . . . talk about it. As Benny, Nix, Lilah, and Chong talk about grief in these pages. Find someone who will listen. There are always people willing to listen. Always.

If you are having trouble dealing with personal loss, please reach out. To parents, relatives, friends, teachers, coaches, or someone at your place of worship. People will listen, and grief is something that we all share. Don't let yourself be alone with it.

PART ONE
A FALL OF ANGELS

The angel of death has been abroad throughout the land;

you may almost hear the beating of his wings.

—JOHN BRIGHT
(FROM A SPEECH TO PARLIAMENT, FEBRUARY 23, 1855)

1

BENNY IMURA THOUGHT, *I'M GOING TO DIE*.

The hundred zombies chasing him all seemed to agree.

2

FIFTEEN MINUTES AGO NOTHING AND NOBODY WAS TRYING TO KILL Benny Imura.

Benny had been sitting on a flat rock, sharpening a sword and brooding. He was aware that he was brooding. He even had a brooding face for when other people were around. Now, though, he was alone, and he let the mask fall away. When he was alone, the melancholy musings were deeper, more useful, but also less fun. When you're alone, you can't crack a joke to make the moment feel better.

There were very few moments that felt good to Benny. Not anymore. Not since leaving home.

He was a mile from where he and his friends had camped in a forest of desert trees deep in southern Nevada. Every time Benny took another step on the road to finding the airplane he and Nix had seen, every single inch forward, he was farther from home than he had ever been.

He used to hate the idea of leaving home. Home was Mountainside, high in the Sierra Nevada Mountains of central California. Home was bed and running water and hot apple pie on the porch. But that had been home with his brother, Tom. It had been a whole hometown, with Nix and her mother.

Now Nix's mom was dead, and Tom was dead.

Home wasn't home anymore.

As the road had unrolled itself in front of Benny, Nix, Chong, and Lilah, and melted into memory behind, the vast world out here had stopped being something ugly, something to fear. Now this was becoming home.

Benny wasn't sure he liked it, but he felt in some strange way that it was what he needed, and maybe even what he deserved. No comforts. No safe haven. The world was a hard place, and this desert was brutal, and Benny knew that if he was going to survive in the world, then he would have to become much tougher than he was.

Tougher even than Tom, because Tom had fallen.

He brooded on this as he sat on his rock and carefully sharpened the long sword, the *kami katana* that had once belonged to Tom.

Sharpening a sword was an appropriate task while brooding. The blade had to be cared for and that required focus, and a focused mind was more agile when climbing through the obstacle course of thoughts and memories. Even though Benny was sad—deep into the core of who he was—he found some measure of satisfaction in the hardships of the road and the skill required to hone this deadly blade.

As he worked, he occasionally glanced around. Benny had never seen a desert before, and he appreciated its simplicity. It was vast and empty and incredibly beautiful. So many trees and birds that he had only read about in books. And . . . no people.

That was good and bad. The bad part was that there was no one they could ask about the plane. The good was that no one had tried to shoot them, torture them, kidnap them, or eat them in almost a month. Benny put that solidly in the "win" category.

This morning he'd left the camp to go alone into the woods, partly to practice the many skills Tom had taught him. Tracking, stealth, observation. And partly to be alone with his thoughts.

Benny was not happy with what was going on inside his head. Accepting Tom's death should have been easy. Well, if not easy, then natural. After all, in Benny's lifetime the whole world had died. More than seven billion people had fallen since First Night. Some to the zombies, the dead who rose to attack and feed on the living. Some to the mad panic and wild savagery into which mankind had descended during the collapse of governments and the military and society. Some were killed in the battles, blown to radioactive dust as nuclear bombs were dropped in a desperate attempt to stop the legions of walking dead. And many more died in the days after, succumbing to ordinary infections, injuries, starvation, and the wildfire spread of diseases that sprang from the death and rot that was everywhere. Cholera, staph and influenza, tuberculosis, HIV, and so many others—and all of them running unchecked, with no infrastructure, no hospitals, no way to stop them.

Given all that, given that everyone Benny had ever met had been touched by death in one way or another, he should have been able to accept Tom's death.

Should have.

But . . .

Although Tom had fallen during the battle of Gameland, he had not risen as one of the living dead. That was incredibly strange. It should have been wonderful, a blessing that Benny knew he should be grateful for . . . but he wasn't. He was confused by it. And frightened, because he had no idea what it meant.

It made no sense. Not according to everything Benny had learned in his nearly sixteen years. Since First Night everyone who died, no matter how they died, reanimated as a zom. Everyone. No exceptions. It was the way things were.

Until it wasn't.

Tom had not returned from death to that horrible mockery of life people called "living death." Neither had a murdered man they'd found in the woods the day they left town. Same thing with some of the bounty hunters killed in the battle of Gameland. Benny didn't know why. No one knew why. It was a mystery that was both frightening and hopeful. The world, already strange and terrible, had become stranger still.

Movement jolted Benny out of his musings, and he saw a figure step out of the woods at the top of the slope eighty feet away. He remained stock-still, watching to see if the zom would notice him.

Except that this was not a zom.

The figure was slender, tall, definitely female, and almost certainly still alive. She was dressed in black clothes—a loose long-sleeved shirt and pants—and there were dozens of pieces of thin red cloth tied around her. Ankles, legs, torso, arms, throat. The streamers were bright red, and they fluttered in the breeze so that for a weird moment it seemed as if she was badly cut and blood was being whipped off her in ragged lines. But as she stepped from shadow into sunlight, Benny saw that the streamers were only cloth.

She had something embroidered on the front of her shirt in white thread, but Benny could not make out the design.

He and his friends had not met a living person in weeks, and out here in the badlands they were more likely to meet a violently hostile loner than a friendly stranger. He waited to see if the woman had spotted him.

She walked a few paces into the field and stared down the slope toward a line of tall bristlecone pines. Even from this distance Benny could tell that the woman was beautiful. Regal, like pictures of queens he had seen in old books. Olive-skinned, with masses of gleaming black hair that fluttered in the same breeze that stirred the crimson streamers.

Sunlight struck silver fire from an object she raised from where it hung on a chain around her neck. Benny was too far away to tell what it was, though he thought it looked like a whistle. However, when the woman put it to her lips and blew, there was no sound at all, but suddenly the birds and monkeys in the trees began twittering with great agitation.

Then something else happened, and it sent a thrill of fear through Benny and drove all other thoughts out of his mind. Three men stepped out of the woods behind the woman. Their clothes also fluttered in the wind, but for them it was because the things they wore had been ripped to rags by violence, by weather, and by the inexorable claws of time.

Zoms.

Benny got to his feet very slowly. Quick movements attracted the dead. The zoms were a dozen feet behind the woman and lumbering toward her. She seemed totally unaware of their presence as she continued to try and make sounds from her whistle.

Several more figures stepped out of the shadows under the trees. More of the dead. They kept emerging into the light as if conjured from nightmares by his growing fear. There was no choice. He had to warn her. The dead were almost upon her.

"Lady!" he yelled. "Run!"

The woman's head jerked up, and she stared across the swaying grass to where he stood. For a moment all the zoms froze in place as they searched for the source of the yelling voice.

"Run!" yelled Benny again.

The woman turned away from him and looked at the zoms. There were at least forty of them, and more were materializing from the darkness under the trees. The zoms moved with the jerky awkwardness that Benny always found so awful. Like badly manipulated puppets. Their hands rose as they reached out for fresh meat.

However, the woman turned slowly away from them and faced Benny once more. The zoms reached her.

"No . . . ," Benny gasped, unable to bear the sight of another death.

And the zombies lumbered past her. She stood there as a tide of them parted to move around her. They did not grab her, did not try to bite her. They ignored her except to angle their line of approach to avoid her and continue walking down the slope.

Toward Benny.

Not one of them touched the woman or even looked in her direction.

Confusion rooted Benny to the spot, and the sword hung almost forgotten in his hand.

Was he wrong about her? Was she one of the dead and not a living person at all? Was she wearing cadaverine? Or was there something else about her that made the dead forgo the feast at hand for the one that stood gaping at them down the slope?

Run!

The word exploded inside his mind, and for a crazy moment Benny thought that it was Tom's voice shouting at him.

He staggered as if punched, and then he wheeled around and ran.

3

He ran like hell.

This was no time to contemplate mysteries. He pounded down the slope faster than a jackrabbit as the mass of the dead growled out a moan of hunger and followed.

A zom rose up out of the tall grass directly in his path. There was no way to avoid the thing, not with all the momentum of the downward run, so he tucked his head and drove his shoulder into it like he was trying to bust through a line of offensive backs on the school football field. The zom went flying backward, and Benny leaped over the thrashing creature.

More zoms came at him, rising up out of the weeds and staggering out from behind tumbled boulders. Benny still held Tom's sword, but he hated using it on zoms. Not unless he had no choice. These creatures were not evil, they were dead. Mindless. Unless he could completely quiet one of them, chopping at them seemed . . . wrong. He knew they couldn't feel pain and wouldn't care, but Benny felt like some kind of malicious bully.

On the other hand, there was that whole survival thing. As three zoms closed in on him in a line he could not bull his way through, the hand holding the sword moved almost without conscious thought. The blade swept upward through one set of reaching arms, and the hands flew high above, grasping nothing but air. With a deft twist of his shoulder, he flicked the blade sideways and a zom's head went flying into the bushes. Another cut left the third zom toppling to one side with one leg suddenly missing from mid-thigh.

"Sorry!" Benny yelled as he burst through the now disintegrating line of three zoms.

But there were more.

So many more, coming at him from all directions. Cold fingers fumbled at his face and tried to grab his hair, but Benny jagged and dodged and dove through them toward open ground.

His foot hit a rock and he sprawled forward; the sword flew from his hand and clattered thirty feet down the slope.

"No!" he cried as the sword vanished in the tall, dry grass.

Before Benny could get up, a zom grabbed a loose pocket flap on his vest and another grabbed his cuff.

"Get away!" Benny yelled as he thrashed and kicked and fought his way free. He scrambled to his feet, but his balance was bad and the slope was steep, so he ran like a sloppy dog on hands and feet for a dozen paces until he could get fully upright again.

More and more of the living dead staggered down the hill after him. Benny had no idea where they had come from, or why there were so many here. Even before Gameland, the zoms had started moving in packs rather than alone as they'd always done before. A month ago Benny, Lilah, and Nix had been under siege by thousands of them at a monk's way station. How and why this flocking behavior was happening was another of the mysteries that no one had an answer for.

"Tom," Benny said, gasping his brother's name as he ran. He didn't know why he spoke the name. Maybe it was a prayer for guidance from the best zombie hunter who had ever worked the Ruin. Or maybe it was a curse, because now everything Tom had taught him seemed to be in question. The world was changing beyond the lessons Tom had given.

"Tom," Benny growled as he ran, and he tried to remember those lessons that could not change. The ways of the samurai, the ways of the warrior.

He saw sunlight glitter on metal ten paces downslope, and Benny leaped at the fallen sword, grabbing it by the handle with his left hand, switching it into a two-handed grip even while his legs continued to run at full speed. Zoms came at him, and the sword seemed to move with its own will.

Arms and legs and heads flew into the hot sunlight.

I am warrior smart, thought Benny as he ran and fought. *I am an Imura. I have Tom's sword.*

I am a bounty hunter.

Right.

You're about to be lunch, you moron, muttered his inner voice. For once Benny could not muster a convincing argument.

Everywhere he looked he saw another withered figure lurching toward him from beneath the shade of the big trees or from between tall shrubs. He knew—he knew—that this was not a coordinated trap. Zoms couldn't think. It wasn't that. . . . He must have simply had the bad luck to run into a swarm of them that was spread out across the whole width of the slope.

Run! yelled his inner voice. *Faster!*

He wanted to tell his inner voice to stop offering stupid advice and maybe instead come up with some sort of plan. Something that didn't involve ending up in the digestive tracts of a hundred zoms.

Run.

Yeah, he thought. *Good plan.*

Then he saw that the tall grass twenty yards down the slope hid the dark cleft of a small ravine. It ran the entire width of the slope, which was bad news, but it was less than ten feet across, which was good.

Could he jump it? Could he build up the momentum to leap across the opening?

His inner voice yelled, *Go . . . GO!*

Benny set his teeth, called on every possible ounce of speed, and threw himself into the air, his feet still running through nothingness as he hurtled over the deep ravine. He landed hard on the far slope, bending his knees just as Tom had taught him, letting his leg muscles absorb the shock of impact.

He was safe!

Benny laughed out loud and spun toward the wave of zoms that still staggered toward him. They were so completely focused on him that they did not notice—or understand—the danger of the ravine.

"Yo! Deadheads," he yelled, waving his sword to taunt them. "Nice try, but you're messing with Benny-freaking-Imura, zombie killer. Booyah!"

And then the lip of the ravine buckled and collapsed under his weight, and Benny-freaking-Imura instantly plummeted into the darkness below.

FROM NIX'S JOURNAL

It is one month and one day since Tom died.

Night before last, while we were all sitting around the campfire, Chong told a joke that made Benny laugh. I think it was the first time Benny laughed since gameland.

It was so good to hear him laugh. His eyes are still sad, though. I guess mine probably are too.

I never thought any of us would ever want to laugh again.

4

BENNY FELL FROM SUNLIGHT INTO DARKNESS AND HIT THE BOTTOM OF THE ravine so hard that his legs buckled and he pitched forward onto his face. Loose soil, tree roots, and small stones rained down on him. Fireworks detonated inside his head, and every single molecule of his body hurt.

He groaned, rolled onto his side, spat dirt out of his mouth, and clawed spiderwebs out of his eyes.

"Yeah, warrior smart," he muttered.

The bottom of the ravine was much wider than the top and thick with mud, and Benny quickly understood that it was not a true ravine but a gorge cut by water runoff from the mountains. During the times of heaviest runoff, the flowing water had undercut edges of the slope above, creating the illusion of solid ground.

If he had kept running after he had leaped the gorge he would be safe. Instead he'd turned to gloat. Not exactly warrior smart.

Warrior dumb-ass, he thought darkly.

As he lay there, his mind began to play tricks on him. Or at least he thought it was doing something twisted and weird. He heard sounds. First it was his own labored breathing and the moans of the dead above him, but, no . . . there was something else.

It was a distant roar that sounded—impossible as that was—like the hand-crank generator that ran the power in the hospital back home. Still half-buried in the dirt, he cocked his head to listen. The sound was definitely there, but it wasn't exactly like the hospital generator. This whined at a higher pitch, and it surged and fell away, surged and fell away.

Then it was gone.

He strained to hear it, trying to decide if it was really a motor sound or something else. There were all kinds of birds and animals out there, weird stuff that had escaped zoos and circuses, and Benny had read about exotic animal sounds. Was that what he'd heard?

No, said his inner voice, *it was a motor.*

Suddenly there was a soft sound from above, and a huge pile of loose dirt cascaded down on Benny, burying him almost to the neck. He began fighting his way out, but then he heard another sound and he looked, expecting to see more of the wall collapsing on him, but what he saw was far, far worse. The leading wave of pursuing zoms had reached the edge of the ravine, and the land had crumbled under their combined weight. Four zombies pitched over the edge and fell into the darkness with jarring crunches, the nearest one landing only six feet away.

Then another zombie—a teenage girl dressed in the rags of a cheerleader outfit—dropped right in front of Benny, striking the ground with a thud that was filled with the brittle crunch of breaking bones. The cheerleader's gray and dusty eyes were open, and her mouth bit the air.

Broken bones wouldn't kill a zom. Benny knew that all too well, and he dug through the loose dirt to find the hilt of his sword.

The zombie lifted a pale hand toward him. Cold fingertips brushed his face, but suddenly a second body—a huge man in coveralls—slammed down on top of her. The impact was massive, and it shattered even more bones.

Benny cried out in horror and disgust and began digging his way out like a mad gopher, clawing at the dirt, kicking his feet free.

Another zom fell nearby, ribs and arm bones snapping with firecracker sounds. The sounds were horrible, and Benny dreaded one of those limp, fetid corpses landing on him before he could get free. Overhead more of the living dead toppled over the edge and plummeted toward him. A soldier slammed into the ground to his right, a schoolkid to his left, their moans following them down as they fell, only to be cut off with a dry grunt as they crunched atop their fellows. Farmers and tourists, a man in swim trunks covered in starfish, an old woman in a pink cardigan, and a bearded man in a Hawaiian shirt—all striking mercilessly down. The impact sounds of moistureless bodies filled the air with an awful symphony of destruction.

Another zom fell. And another.

The cheerleader, broken and twisted now by the impacts, still growled at Benny and clamped gnarled fingers around both his ankles.

Benny screamed and tried to pull his legs away, but the grip was too strong. He immediately stopped trying to wriggle free and sat up.

"Let me go!" he bellowed as he punched the zom in the face.

The punch broke the zombie's nose and rocked its head back, but that was all it accomplished. Benny struck again and again. With pieces of broken teeth falling from between its pale lips, the cheerleader used its grip to pull itself forward, climbing along Benny's legs; and all the time its mouth opened and closed as if rehearsing the feast that was now close at hand. The rotting-meat stench of the creature in this closed space was horrific.

The zom darted out and caught Benny's trouser leg between the stumps of its teeth, pinching some skin as well. The pain was instantly intense. Benny howled. Other twisted and broken zoms clawed along the ground toward him, crawling over one another like maggots on a piece of bad meat.

While he fought, he could almost hear Tom whispering advice.

Be warrior smart.

"Go away!" Benny yelled, half to the zom and half to his brother's ghost.

Benny . . . most people aren't defeated—they lose!

It was something Tom had told him a dozen times during training, but Benny had barely paid attention, because it sounded like one of his brother's annoying logic puzzles. Now he ached to know what Tom meant.

"Warrior smart," Benny growled aloud, hoping that saying it would inspire understanding and action. It didn't. He yelled it again, then followed it with every obscene word he knew.

Don't fight an impossible fight. Fight the fight you can win.

Ah.

That time the lesson got through, and Benny realized that he was reacting rather than taking action. A rookie mistake, as Tom would say.

He hated it when his brother was right. It was even more irritating now that Tom was dead.

As the zombie climbed toward him, Benny stopped punching it and grabbed it by the filthy strands of its matted hair and the point of its withered chin. Then, with a shout of anger, he twisted the cheerleader's head sharply on its spindly neck.

Crunch!

The zom immediately stopped moving; its biting mouth went slack, the cold fingers lost their hold, and the struggling figure sagged down into true dead-weight limpness.

Benny knew that it was always like that when a zom died. Break its neck, or use a steel sliver to cut the brain stem, and the effect was instant. All life, all animation, all aggression was gone. The zom was alive on one side of a thin second and totally dead as soon as that second was spent.

It was a small victory, considering the circumstances, but it put some iron back into Benny's muscles. With another grunt he finally kicked his way out of the pile of dirt and crawled as fast as he could. A spill of dirt plumed down in front of him, and it was the only warning he had as a half dozen zoms toppled over a different section of the ravine. Benny threw himself sideways just in time.

He looked wildly back and saw that at least a dozen of the zoms had gotten to their feet. They would be on him in seconds. He scrambled to his feet too and took the sword in a two-handed grip.

"Come on," he growled, baring his teeth as anger surged up in him.

The first of the zoms came at him, and Benny stepped into its lunge and swung. The wickedly sharp steel cut easily through dry tendon and old bones. The hands of the zom flew over Benny's shoulder, and he ducked under the stumps, instantly straightened, and cut at the neck from behind the monster's shoulder. He got the angle just right and felt almost no resistance as the *katana* cut through the bones of the neck. The zombie's head toppled into the dirt five feet away, and its body collapsed in place.

Now two others were closing in, rushing at him shoulder to shoulder. Benny tried a single lateral cut to take two heads, but his angle was off by an inch on the first one, and even though he took that first head, his sword caromed off the cheekbone of the second zom and did no real harm. He corrected, and with his back-slash decapitated the zom.

He stepped back and gulped air. After running, then falling, and now fighting, he was already exhausted. He shook his head to whip sweat from his eyes.

"Okay, dumb-ass," he told himself, "time to be warrior smart."

He said it aloud, hoping that his voice would have all the strength and confidence he needed. It didn't, but it would have to do.

The dead came forward, and Benny whirled and cut his way through the thinnest part of the circle of them. He jumped over the falling bodies and ran deeper into the ravine. As he did so he reached up and slid his sword back into its scabbard. His main supply of gear was in his backpack at the camp, but he had a few useful items with him. He dug into one of the bulky pockets of his canvas vest and removed a spool of silk cord. It was slender but very strong, and Tom had used it to restrain zoms before quieting them.

Working very fast, Benny snatched up a thick branch, broke it over his knee, and rammed one end deep into the closest wall slightly below waist height. He spun away and repeated the action with the other half of the branch on the opposite wall. Then he tied the silk cord to one stick and stretched it to the other and pulled it taut, tying it off as tightly as he could.

The zoms reached the silk cord and it stalled them for a moment. They rebounded and collided. Some reached for him with some residual cleverness, fingers trying to snag his clothes.

Most of the zoms were still twelve feet away, their progress slowed by the uneven surface and the broken bodies of their fellows over whom they had to step.

Benny had to smack and bash at the reaching hands, but he managed to slip free of their grasp. As he staggered away, he ran a few yards down the ravine, searching for more branches. There were none thick enough. He cursed under his breath but then found a chunk of broken rock about twice the size of a baseball. He snatched it up and turned back to his enemies.

Benny dashed forward and slammed downward with the rock.

"I'm sorry!" he cried as the rock shattered the skull and smashed the brain. The zombie died without a further twitch.

Benny whirled as a second zom fell over the trip wire, and a third. He darted over to them and slammed down with the rock over and over again.

"I'm sorry," he yelled each time he gave final death to one of the ghouls.

The passage was choked with zoms now. Two more fell and he killed them, but the effort of smashing skulls was difficult, and it was very quickly draining his strength.

The silk line creaked as a crowd of the living dead pressed against it.

Benny knew that it could not hold. There were too many of them, and the dirt walls were not densely packed enough to hold the branches. He drew his sword and began chopping at the dead behind the line, lopping off hands and arms, squatting to cut through ankles, rising to take heads. He tried to build a bulwark of bodies that would at least slow the advance of the entire horde.

Then, with a groan of splintering wood, the line gave and the whole mass of them surged forward in a collapsing melee. The zoms Benny had maimed and killed crashed down, and the others flopped down on them. He kept cutting, trying to bury the active zoms under the weight of as many quieted ones as possible.

The sword was incredibly sharp and Benny was a good swordsman, but this was work for a butcher's cleaver. Time and again the blade rebounded from bone and tangled in loose clothing.

Benny's arms began to ache and then to really hurt. His breath came in labored gasps, but still the dead kept coming.

So many of them. So many that Benny ran out of breath

to apologize to them. He needed every bit of breath just to survive. He staggered backward, defeated by the sheer impossibility of the task of defeating so many zoms in such a confined space. Running seemed like the only option left. With any luck the ravine would narrow to a close at some point and a tight corner would allow for handholds to climb out.

He backed away, then spun and ran.

And skidded to an immediate stop.

The ravine ahead was not empty. Out of the dusty darkness came a swaying, moaning line of the living dead.

He was trapped.

5

"COME ON," BENNY SAID AS THE DEAD ADVANCED TOWARD HIM, BUT even to his own ears there was no passion in his tone. No real challenge. No life.

And no way out.

The steep walls of the ravine were too high and the dirt too soft; and the narrow, snaking passage was blocked at both ends by the dead. All he had left were the few seconds it would take for them to climb over broken bodies and heaps of dirt to reach him.

This is it.

Those words banged like firecrackers in his head, loud and bright and terribly real.

There were too many of them and no real way to fight through; and even if he did, what then? He was still trapped down here in the dark. He had already killed ten of them and crippled another dozen, and in a stand-up fight he believed that he could cut at least five or six more of them down in the time he had left. Maybe as many as ten if he could somehow keep moving.

Sounded great, sounded very heroic, but Benny knew the irrefutable truth that swinging a sword required effort, and each time he delivered a killing blow he would spend some of the limited resources he had.

Zoms never tired.

Even if he killed thirty of them, the thirty-first or thirty-second would get him. They had the patience of eternity, and he was living flesh. Fatigue and muscle strain were as deadly to him as the teeth of the dead.

The knowledge of that, the shocking awareness of it, did not spark him into action. It did exactly the opposite. It took the heart from him, and with that went all the power in his muscles. He sagged back against the mud wall. His knees wanted to buckle.

Benny looked into the faces of the zoms as they shuffled closer to him. In those last moments he saw past the sun-bleached skin and desiccated flesh; past the rotting death and milky eyes. For just a moment he saw the people they had been. Not monsters. Real people. Lost people. People who had gotten sick, or who had been bitten, and who had died only to be reborn into a kind of hell beyond anything anyone should suffer.

But they eat people! Benny had once said to his brother, yelling the words during an argument on their first trip to the Ruin.

Tom had replied with five of the most damaging words Benny had ever heard.

They used to be people.

God.

"Nix," he said, feeling a wave of wretched guilt because he knew how much his death would hurt her. And how much it would disappoint her; but there did not seem to be anything he could do about that.

All of the zoms were close now. A knot of dead-pale faces fifteen feet away. Monsters coming for him in the dark, and yet the faces were not evil. Merely hungry. The mouths worked, but the eyes were as empty as windows that looked into abandoned houses.

"Nix," he said again as the dead came closer and closer.

Each face that Benny saw looked . . . lost. Blank and without direction or hope. Farmers and soldiers, ordinary citizens, and one man dressed in a tuxedo. Beyond him was a girl in the rags of a dress that must once have been pretty. Peach silk with lace trim. She and the zom in the tuxedo looked like they had been about Benny's age. Maybe a year or two older. Kids going to a prom when the world ended.

Benny looked from them to the sword he held, and he thought about what it would be like to be dead. When these zombies killed him and ate him, would there be enough of him left to reanimate? Would he join their company of wandering dead? He looked around at the ravine. There was no visible way out of this pit. Would he and all these dead be trapped down here, standing silently as the years burned themselves out above?

Yes.

That was exactly what would happen, and Benny's heart began to break. The helplessness was overwhelming, and for a horrifying moment he watched his own arms sag, allowing the sword to dip in defeat before the battle had even begun.

"Nix," he said one last time.

Then a single spark of anger popped like a flare in his chest. It did not chase away Benny's pity and grief—it fed on it.

"Tom!" he yelled. "You left me! You were supposed to be there. You were supposed to keep the monsters away."

Despite the anger, his voice was small. Younger than his years.

"You weren't supposed to let me see this."

Tears ran like hot mercury down his cheeks.

The dead reached for him.

THEN SUDDENLY THE AIR ABOVE HIM WAS SHATTERED BY A HIGH-PITCHED scream of total terror.

Benny whirled and looked up.

The zoms—their fingers inches from Benny's face—looked.

There, wavering on the edge, fighting wildly for balance at the brink of destruction . . . was a little girl. Maybe five years old.

Not a walking corpse.

A living child.

And all around her were the ravenous living dead.

Benny stared at the child in absolute horror.

A hundred questions tried to squeeze through a crowded doorway in Benny's dazed brain. Where had she come from? Why was she here?

The little girl could not see Benny down in the pit.

"Get away from here!" he yelled as loud as he could, and the little girl's scream froze as she twisted to look down with wild eyes. "Get away from the edge!"

"Help!" she screeched. "Please . . . don't let the gray people get me!"

She backed away from the zombies, who closed around

her, and Benny screamed out a warning a half second before her retreating foot came down on empty air. With a shriek so loud that Benny was sure every zom for miles could hear it, the girl pitched into the pit. Her tiny hands darted out and caught the crooked roots under the lip of the edge and she hung there, legs kicking, her scream unrelenting. The zoms in the pit moaned and reached for her.

The zombies choked the narrow ravine, and Benny knew that if he held his ground, their sheer numbers would crowd him to the point where he could no longer swing the *katana*. Attack was the only option, and that meant carving a pathway through them, impossible as that seemed. It was reckless and crazy, but it was the only choice left to him.

Suddenly Benny was moving.

The *katana* snapped up and flashed outward, and the head of one zom fell to the dirt. Benny spun away from the corpse and cut once, twice, again and again, lopping off dry arms and heads. He ducked and chopped, taking off legs and sending zoms crashing to the ground. If his weary arms ached, he ignored them completely. Rage and urgency filled him.

The undead fell before him, but they did not fall back. Retreat was an impossible concept. They crowded forward on both sides, their attention shifting back and forth between the prey above and the prey at hand.

"Mommmeeeeeee!" shrilled the girl. "The graaayyyy peeeepuuuull!"

He slashed back and forth to clear some room and then attacked the nearest zom with a jumping front kick to the chest that sent it staggering backward into two others. The three of them went down. Benny ran straight at them, running over their bodies, his feet wobbling uncertainly as he stepped on thighs and stomachs and chests. He pivoted and slashed again as a massive zom in the burned rags of a soldier's uniform came lumbering at him. Benny crouched and aimed a powerful cut across its legs. It was a move he had seen Tom do several times, a fierce horizontal sweep that literally cut the legs out from under an attacker. But when Benny tried it, he aimed too high, and his blade struck the heavy thighbone and stuck fast!

The jolt tore the handle out of his hands and sent darts of pain shooting up his arms.

Even with the sword blade notched into his femur, the big zom came relentlessly on.

Above Benny, the little girl screamed. Her fingers were slipping through the roots. Cold hands reached down from the edge and up from the pit.

"No!" Benny drove his shoulder into the soldier zom's stomach and ran him backward into the mass of walking corpses. As the creature fell off balance, Benny grabbed the handle of the *katana* and tried to pull it free, but the blade would not move.

"Help!" The scream had an even sharper note of panic, and Benny looked up to see the little girl's fingers slither through the last of the roots. With a piercing howl, the child fell.

"Helllllp!"

Once more Benny was moving before he realized it, slamming into the zoms with crossed forearms and then throwing himself under the tiny body, turning, reaching—praying.

She was so small, no more than forty pounds, but she had twenty feet to fall, and the impact slammed into Benny's chest like a thunderbolt, crushing him to the ground and driving the air painfully from his lungs. He went limp with her atop him, and instantly she began kicking and punching at him to try and escape.

"Stop it . . . c'mon, ow! OW! Stop!" cried Benny in a hoarse bellow. "Stop it—I'm not one of them!"

Panic filled the girl's eyes, but at the sound of his voice she froze and stared at him with the silent intensity of a terrified rabbit.

"I'm not one of them," Benny croaked again. His chest felt smashed, and pain darted through his lungs and back.

The girl looked at him with the biggest, bluest eyes in the world, eyes that were filled with tears and a flicker of uncertain hope. She opened her mouth—and screamed again.

But not at him.

Zoms were closing in on all sides.

With a cry of horror, he rolled onto his side, huddled his body over the girl's, and kicked out at the legs of the closest zombie. Bone cracked, but the zom did not go down, and Benny saw that it was one of the burly farmers. The thing had been rawboned and sturdy in life, and much of that strength lingered in death.

Benny kicked again, knocking the lead zom backward. He scrambled to his feet and pulled the girl up, shoving her toward a bare patch of wall, away from the grasping hands of the army of the dead. Behind them, the ravine ran on for forty yards and vanished into the shadows around a bend. In front of them were dozens of zoms; and far back in the crowd was the soldier with Tom's *katana* buried in its thighbone. There was no way on earth Benny could retrieve it.

"They're going to eat us!" wailed the girl. "The gray people are going to eat us!"

Yes, they are, Benny thought.

"No they're not!" he growled aloud.

He backed away, using his body to push the girl deeper into the ravine. "Go," he whispered urgently. "Run!"

She hesitated, lost and confused, the fear so overwhelming that instead of running, she closed her eyes and began to cry.

The moans of the dead filled the air.

Benny had no choice. He turned away from Tom's sword and the lost possibilities of survival it promised, then snatched up the little girl, pressed her to his chest, and ran.

FROM NIX'S JOURNAL

The first time I was out in the Rot and Ruin, after I escaped from Charlie Pink-eye and was hiding with Benny, we saw something impossible. A jet. One of the big flying machines from the old world, from before First Night.

It was in the sky, flying west, almost in the direction of home. Then it turned and flew back toward the east.

I know that if I'd been alone when I saw it, I wouldn't have believed it. And no one would believe me if I told them. But Benny saw it too. And Tom.

We knew we'd have to go find it. I mean, how could we not?

That's why Tom started the Warrior Smart program. To get us ready for whatever we'd find. So far it's saved our lives more times than I can count.

Now . . . finding the jet is the only thing that matters.

7

As he ran, Benny could feel the little girl's fluttering heart beating against his chest. It called up an old memory—the oldest memory he owned, a memory born in horror on First Night. It was a memory of being held just like this when he was a toddler less than two years old, being held tightly in Tom's arms while his brother ran away from the thing that had been their father. And the weeping, screaming figure of their mother, who had used the last moments of her life to pass Benny through a window to Tom and beg him to run.

To run.

As Benny ran now.

Through darkness and horror, with death pursuing and no certain knowledge of a way out of the moment.

For most of his life Benny had misunderstood that memory, thinking that Mom had been abandoned by Tom, that his brother had been a coward who fled when he should have stayed to rescue her, too. But then he learned the truth. Mom was already dying, already becoming one of the living dead. She had pushed both her sons out of the window, saving them from the terror inside. And Tom had honored that sacrifice by keeping Benny safe—that night and all the other nights and years that followed.

Now Tom was gone too.

He, too, had died to save others. He, too, had sacrificed himself so that life could continue even in a world ruled by the dead.

The little girl Benny carried wept and screamed, but she also clung to him. And he to her. Even though she was a total stranger to him, Benny knew that he would die to save her.

Was it like this for you, Tom? he wondered. Was this what you felt when you carried me out of Sunset Hollow on First Night? If you were really the coward I used to think you were, you would have run off and left me. Wouldn't you? You would have saved yourself. Alone, without having to carry me, it would have been easier for you to slip away. But you didn't. You carried me all the way.

Was it a memory? Or now that Benny stood at death's fragile door, was it easier for Tom's ghost to whisper to him from the darkness on the other side?

Benny, whispered Tom, *I didn't die to save you.*

"I know that, Einstein," Benny growled back as he ran.

No—listen! I didn't die to save you.

A zom fell into the ravine directly in front of them, and the little girl screamed even louder. But Benny leaped over the awkward form before the zom could struggle to its feet.

I lived to save you, said Tom. *I lived.*

"You died, Tom!" Benny snarled.

Benny . . . back then, on First Night, I didn't die to save you. I did everything I could to stay alive. For both of us. You know this. . . .

"But—"

Don't die, Benny, murmured Tom from the deeper shadows

in Benny's mind. The sound of Tom's voice was comforting and terrifying at the same time. It was wrong and right.

"Tom," Benny said again as he wheeled around a sharp bend in the ravine. "Tom . . . ?"

But Tom's voice was gone.

The ravine sloped down, becoming deeper, and soon he realized that even the gnarled tree roots clinging to the edge of the cleft were too far above his head. He'd hoped for just the opposite, figuring once they were well clear of the zoms he could pass the kid up and let her pull herself out, then scramble up himself. That plan was hopeless now.

They rounded another bend, and Benny slowed from a run to a walk and then simply stood there. Ten feet away was a solid wall of dirt and rock. The entire ravine had collapsed beneath the weight of a massive oak tree whose root system had been undercut by runoff. There was no way through it, and the sides were far too steep to climb. He and the little girl were trapped. He had no sword, no carpet coat. Only a knife, and that would not stop the mass of dead things following them.

"Now what, Tom?" he demanded, but there was only silence from the shadows in his mind. "Really? Now you're going to shut up?"

Nothing.

Benny glanced down at the girl. Could he lift her high enough so that she could grab one of the roots and climb up? It would be her only chance, but doing it would use up the last seconds he had and give him no chance at all. Even so, he thought, he had to try. Better to die trying to save a life than share a hideous death down here in the fetid darkness.

He listened for some trace of Tom's voice, but there was still nothing.

The first of the zombies rounded the previous bend. Five of them, with more behind. One of them broke from the pack and started running along the ravine.

Oh no, thought Benny, *a fast one. Oh God!*

It was horribly true. Lately some of the zoms they encountered were different. Faster, able to run. Maybe even smarter.

Benny set the girl down and pushed her behind him; then he drew his knife. It was hopeless, but he had to try. For the child, he had to try.

The zom raced toward him almost as fast as a healthy human could run. Its teeth were bared and its hands were outstretched to grab. Thirty feet, twenty.

Ten. Benny gripped his knife with all his strength.

Tom . . . I need you now, man.

And then a voice cried, "BENNY!"

Everyone turned and looked. Benny, the girl, the zoms; even the fast zombie slowed to a confused walk as it cast around for the source of the shout.

Suddenly something pale and lithe dropped into the ravine. There was a fierce war cry and a flash of silver at the end of a long pole, and then the head of the fast zombie leaped into the air and bounced off the wall.

"Lilah!" cried Benny.

The Lost Girl had found him.

A moment later another form dropped from the edge of the ravine above. Smaller, rounder, with masses of curly red hair and freckled hands that clutched the handle of a well-worn wooden sword with deadly competence. A long jagged scar ran from her hairline down her cheek almost to her jaw, but it did not mar the beauty of her face. Instead it made her look like a warrior princess out of an old legend. She looked at the zoms and then at Benny, and she grinned.

"I can't leave you alone for a minute without you doing something stupid, can I?" asked Nix Riley.

FROM NIX'S JOURNAL

Ever since Tom died Benny seems to think that he has to BE Tom.

Is that normal grief? Or should I be worried?

I asked Chong, but for once he didn't have any answers. I think he's worried too.

8

"Took you long enough," said Benny, wiping sweat from his eyes. "I was getting bored down here."

He tried to make it sound cool and casual. It didn't.

Nix snorted and started to say something else, but then she caught sight of the tiny figure cowering in the shadows behind Benny.

"What—? Oh my God! Where—where—where—?" Her words disintegrated into a baffled stammer.

"Long story," said Benny.

Nix bent over the girl, who was sniffling at the edge of full-blown tears. She touched the girl's cheek and smoothed her hair. "Hello, sweetie. Don't be afraid. Everything's going to be okay now."

A few yards away, Lilah looked over her shoulder to see what was going on, and her eyes bulged.

"Annie?" she murmured.

Even with everything else going on around them, hearing Lilah say that name came close to breaking Benny's heart. Annie was the name of Lilah's little sister. Annie had died years ago trying to escape from the zombie pits at Gameland, and Lilah had been forced to quiet her when she reanimated.

Benny could only imagine what was going on in Lilah's head—seeing another little blond-haired girl, here in a pit filled with zombies. It was weird enough to Benny; to Lilah it must be totally surreal.

Another fast zom dashed along the ravine—a huge woman with wild black hair and a line of bullet holes stitched across her enormous bosom.

"Zom!" barked Benny, and Lilah blinked once. The shock on her face was gone in an instant as she turned back to deal with the running zom. The black-pipe spear she carried flashed out, and the bayonet blade cut through dry flesh and tough muscle. Lilah's face was stone, but Benny wasn't fooled; her mind had to be churning on this mystery, and it was evident in the renewed force with which she smashed and hacked.

Nix looked over the little girl's head at Benny's empty hands. "Where's your sword?"

"It's stuck in a zom."

"Stuck in a—?"

Benny pointed at the soldier zom far back in the crowd.

"God. We'll never get it!" she gasped.

"We have to," Benny snapped.

The wall of zoms pressed forward even as Lilah cut away at it.

"We can't," growled Lilah. "There are too many."

Nix cupped her hands around her mouth and yelled upward. "Chong!"

Instead of an answer, a coil of rope fell from above and landed heavily on Benny's head, nearly knocking him to his knees.

"Heads up!" came the yell a half second later.

9

BENNY PULLED THE ROPE OFF HIS HEAD AND LOOKED UP TO SEE CHONG'S
head and shoulders leaning over the edge of the ravine, his
long black hair hanging straight down.

"Hey, Benny," he yelled. "Lilah said you were out here
practicing your brooding, and—"

"Chong!" Benny barked. "Shut up and tie that rope to a
tree."

The smile vanished from Chong's face. "Already done. But
c'mon, man, hurry up down there. It's getting weird up here.
There have to be fifty zoms on the other side of the ravine."

"Yeah, well, there are one or two down here, too," Benny
grumbled.

"Then why'd you go down there?" asked Chong.

Benny ignored the comment and turned toward Lilah. The
bayonet blade at the end of her spear was smeared with black
goo. "Let me have your spear and I'll hold them off while you
and Nix—"

Lilah's snort of derision was eloquent. "Go away," she said
in her ghostly whisper of a voice.

"Nix," Benny said, turning to her, "give me your bokken.
I'll guard your back while you take the kid up."

"Oh, please. She's too little to climb, and I'm not big enough to carry her while I climb. You take her up, Benny. Lilah and I will guard your back."

"No freaking way. This is my job."

"Your job?" Nix rolled her eyes. "If you'd stop trying to be the samurai hero for a moment, you'd realize that we're trying to save your life!"

"No, I have to get my sword and save—"

Nix got right up in his face. "I'm not asking you, Benjamin Imura."

Benny very nearly snapped to attention. Nix never called him Benjamin except when she was very mad at him, and she never used his first and last name unless she was going to kick his butt about something.

He flicked a look at the wave of zombies and back at Nix, who stood five feet tall in shoes and had to lean back to look up at him. Even the little girl seemed to glower at Benny, and she had no reason to, since he'd just saved her life. Maybe it was a girl thing. He was dimly aware that there was some important message about female power to be learned here, but now wasn't the time to philosophize. Even Nix's freckles seemed to glow with anger, and her scar turned from pale white to livid red.

He wanted to yell at her, to push her out of the way, to take her bokken and return to the fight—but instead he swallowed his frustration and backed off.

Benny pulled on the rope, which was indeed securely tied. The best and safest way to do this would be to rig a sling around the kid and haul her up; and though they were all good with knots, there simply wasn't time. However,

Benny could see that the collapsed end of the ravine was not sheer. Much of the debris had tumbled down to form a slope, but that slope was far too steep to walk up. With the rope, though, he might be able to do it. He cut a look at the little girl.

That's your job, spoke that inner voice. *Stop trying to be a hero, and get her out of here.*

"Right," said Benny under his breath. He knelt by the girl. "Hey, sweetie, I need you to listen to me and do exactly what I say, okay?"

The child gave him an owl-eyed stare but said nothing.

"I'm going to climb out of here with this rope, and I need you to hold on to me. Like playing piggyback. Do you know that game?"

She paused for a moment as she looked up the dark dirt wall. In the gloom it seemed to stretch on forever.

"It's okay. I'll keep you safe."

Behind him he heard a dull thud that he recognized as the impact of a wooden sword on dried flesh and bone. Sharp and hard, accompanied by a soft grunt of effort. Nix had joined the fight. It was not a comforting sound. It did not mean that they were winning. It meant that there was too much for Lilah to handle alone. It meant that the dead were coming. More and more of them.

Benny squatted and turned his back to the girl. "Wrap your arms around my neck and hold on, okay?"

The little girl suddenly wrapped her arms tight. "Benny!" cried Nix. "Hurry!"

He snatched up the rope and began to climb.

At first it was easy. Tough, but not beyond his strength.

Seven months of training with Tom had given him muscle and tone; another month of living wild in the Rot and Ruin had built his endurance. He was stronger than he'd ever been, and even with the fear that swirled around him like polluted water, he felt powerful. It was how he imagined Tom had felt all the time. Strong enough to do whatever he needed or wanted to do.

Those thoughts brought him about halfway up the wall.

Then, within the next three labored steps, the light-as-a-feather child suddenly felt like she weighed more than Morgie Mitchell after the harvest feast. Benny's foot slipped on the moss-slick wall, and the little girl screeched in his ear like a frightened starling. Her tiny arms locked tighter around his throat, and suddenly Benny could barely breathe.

"Not . . . so . . . tight . . . !"

But she was too terrified to understand. She was halfway up a wall, hanging on for her life. It was going to take a crowbar to pry her off.

Benny took another step and winced as his muscles began to ache. His thighs burned, and grasping the rope felt like holding red-hot coals.

"Come on!" yelled Chong, and Benny looked up to see his friend stretch a bony arm down to him. Chong had a lot of wiry strength, but at the moment his proffered arm looked like it belonged to a stick figure. And it was still too far away.

Chong gaped. "Wait . . . what's that on your back?"

"What . . . does it . . . look like . . . you brain-dead . . . monkey-banger?" gasped Benny.

Chong didn't even try to answer that. Instead he leaned farther out, straining to reach down for Benny.

"No!" Benny yelled. "The edge is—"

There was a soft *whuck* of a sound, and then Chong was tumbling head over heels toward them, and he and a hundred pounds of loose dirt tried to smash Benny and the girl back down into the zombie pit. The little girl deafened him with a shrill wail that was loud enough to crack glass. Benny threw his weight sideways, running across the wall as Chong tumbled past, yowling like a kicked cat. Below him, Chong landed with a thump and a sharp exhalation of pain. Curses floated up through the shadows. Lilah's and Nix's were louder than Chong's.

Benny's feet slipped on the loose soil that now covered the wall like a coat of oil. The rope tried to slither through his fists, but Benny knew that if he fell, the impact would probably cripple or kill the little girl.

Hold on! cried his inner voice.

He held on, gritting his teeth against the strain and the pain.

With a grunt he took a step upward, slamming his foot into the soil to find solid ground. Using legs and back and arms, he pulled upward. The little girl was still throttling him, but Benny lowered his chin to help open his airway. He took as deep a breath as he could and hauled again, taking another step. And another.

It felt like all he was doing was inching his way up. The wall seemed impossibly high.

And then he rose from shadows into bright sunlight. Benny blinked, his eyes stinging, but he'd never been happier to see a bright, sunny sky than he was at that moment. He pulled, and pulled, and climbed and collapsed onto the grass of the torn ravine edge. He crawled forward along the rope, landing chest first on the ground with a gasp like a drowning man taking his first gulp of air.

"Climb off," he wheezed, and the girl scrambled like a monkey over his back and shoulders and head.

"Benny!"

The cry came echoing up from the darkness, and instantly Benny staggered to his feet. His limbs trembled and his hands were puffed and red, but he was safe. Across the black gash of the gorge a hundred zombies stared at him with eternal hunger and endless patience. No more of them fell into the gorge, and Benny thanked God for that.

"Nix! Climb out. I'll pull. Hurry!"

As soon as he felt her take up the slack, Benny began pulling hand over hand. The rope burned his palms and his muscles screamed, but he planted his feet wide and put everything he had into it. Nix's wild red hair appeared at the edge of the ravine, and then her beautiful face, tight with effort and fear.

Nix climbed out and wiped sweat from her eyes.

"Is Chong hurt?" asked Benny.

"Not as hurt as he's going to be when Lilah gets out of there. She's furious with him for going down into the ravine."

"He fell in. It wasn't intentional," Benny said, coming immediately to his friend's defense.

"Yeah, well, she's not happy with you, either."

"Swell." Benny tossed the rope into the hole. "How about you? You mad at me too?"

She gave him a wicked grin and punched his chest. Which hurt.

Chong came puffing and wheezing up into the sunlight. He did not weigh much more than Nix, but Benny was beyond exhausted, and it felt like hauling a bull out of the pit.

"I'm sorry," Chong began, but Benny cut him off.

"Grab some rocks."

"Rocks?"

"Rocks. Anything we can throw. We have to give Lilah some cover. Go!"

Chong understood at once and ran to collect fist-size stones.

Benny tossed the rope down again. "Lilah! Listen to me."

She didn't answer, but he heard her grunts as she fought.

"We've got some rocks. When I say 'go,' drop a couple of zoms with leg cuts to stall the others and—"

Something flashed past him, missing his head by inches. Benny recoiled from it and saw that it was Lilah's spear. Before he could even speak, the line went taut and Lilah came swarming up the side of the wall, as fast and nimble as an acrobat. She grabbed his shirt as she came out of the hole and used his weight to catapult her body over the edge. She pitched forward, rolled effortlessly, and came to a rest on the balls of her feet. She pivoted and looked at Benny, who lay flat, and Chong, who crouched a few feet away with one arm raised to throw a rock. Benny and Chong gaped at her, unable to manage a single coherent comment between them.

Lilah reached around behind her and removed an item that she'd thrust through one of the straps of her vest, then tossed it onto the grass in front of Benny's goggling eyes.

Tom's sword.

Lilah stood above them, tall and beautiful, her white hair whipping in the fresh breeze, her clothes streaked with gore, her hazel eyes glowing with fire.

She turned slowly to Nix and in her ghostly whisper of a voice said, "I hate boys."

FROM NIX'S JOURNAL

Warrior Smart.

That's what Tom called the training
program he put together to get us ready
for our trip into the Ruin. He said that
he based it on a few different things.
First were the martial arts he'd been
involved with ever since he was a kid.
Before First Night there were thousands of
different kinds of martial arts. Karate,
tae kwon do, kung-fu, aikido, judo. I
don't know much about them. Tom used
to study something called jujutsu (which
I've seen in books spelled a bunch of
different ways: jiujitsu, jujitsu, etc.). Tom
said that jujutsu was an old Japanese
system that his family had practiced for
hundreds of years. He said that the name
means "art of nonresistance," and a lot
of it involves using the opponent's attack
against him.

Tom also included some of the things
he learned while he was in the police
academy. And a lot of stuff he learned
since, including tracking and hunting,
which he mostly learned from bounty
hunters like Solomon Jones, Old Man
Church, and the Greenman.

The training was hard, and sometimes we all hated Tom because he never cut us a break.

Now I understand. Sometimes I wish he'd been even harder on us.

10

NIX SAT WITH HER BACK TO THE TWISTED TRUNK OF A BRISTLECONE TREE that loomed over the clearing forty yards from the edge of the ravine. She hugged the little girl to her chest as the child continued to scream and cry. Benny wondered if the kid's mind had snapped. Those screams were hammering cracks in his own sanity.

Lilah squatted in the tall grass a dozen feet away and stared at the child with hollow eyes through which sad shadows flitted. Benny had once heard Tom refer to that kind of look as a "thousand-yard stare." When Chong made to sit down next to her, Lilah drew her knife and stabbed the point into the earth between them.

"I can see that you need some quiet time," he said, and scuttled quickly away.

Eventually Nix's soothing tones and comforting embrace worked their magic on the girl, and she settled down to sniffles. Nix smoothed her hair.

"Sweetie . . . can you tell me your name?" she asked.

"E-E-E . . ." The girl tried to get it out, but every time she tried, she hiccuped a sob. "Eve," she finally managed. Tiny jewels of tears sparkled on her face.

"Okay, Eve," said Nix in a voice that reminded Benny of Nix's mother. Soft and soothing, and full of the certainty of whatever was going to happen next. A parent voice. "Where did you come from?"

Eve looked at her with huge eyes and then looked over her shoulder, as if she could see her own memories. Her words came out all in a rush. "I was running after Ry-Ry, and I lost my way 'cause there were angels in the woods, and then the gray people were there and I ran some more and I tripped and fell. Where's my mommmmeeee?"

Nix pulled her close again, and the child's face vanished into a swirl of soft red curls. "Shhh, it's okay, Eve. Everything's going to be okay. We'll find your mommy."

Benny looked down at the child clutched in Nix's warm arms. He was far less certain about that.

He wasn't certain about anything. He thought about the sheer number of zoms that had come out of the forest.

Don't forget the first rule about the Ruin, whispered Tom's voice. *Out here everything wants to kill you.*

Benny closed his eyes, and even now, separated from the madness of the ravine, he wasn't at all sure if the voice was a memory or a ghost.

Or something worse than both.

Please don't let this be me, Benny thought. *Please don't let me be going crazy.*

The sun shone and the birds sang in the trees and Benny tried hard not to scream.

11

IN A QUIET TONE SO THAT ONLY BENNY COULD HEAR HIM, CHONG murmured, "Some day, huh?"

Benny jumped, and Chong shot him a puzzled look.

"What are you so twitchy about?"

For a moment Benny wondered if Chong could read his thoughts.

"Sorry," said Benny when he was sure his words wouldn't come out choked and twisted. "Yeah. Weird day."

Chong sneaked a glance over at Lilah and sighed softly. "You know, I think I liked being down in that hole better. All the zoms wanted to do was eat me. I think Lilah would enjoy skinning me alive."

Benny followed his gaze and half smiled. "It's not you, man."

"What?"

"She's not mad at you. I mean, she is . . . but not any more than usual."

"I fell in, and you know how she is with the whole thing about me being a clumsy town boy and—" began Chong, but Benny cut him off.

"It's the kid. I . . . think she looks like Annie."

Chong winced as if Benny had punched him in the stomach. "Oh, man . . ."

"Yeah."

Benny understood Lilah's pain. He and Tom had quieted the zombies that had once been their parents. Tom had helped him through it, though; and later, when Tom passed, Benny had been spared the horror of quieting him. Tom never reanimated. However, Lilah had been all alone with Annie. She had no older sibling to help her through it. Benny was wise enough to understand that no matter how bad his own experiences were, there were some people who had it worse.

As if reading his thoughts, Chong said, "I'd give a lot, you know? To make it different for her."

"Yeah, man. I know."

It was something Benny deeply understood, and he wondered if there was anything he wouldn't give to change some of the things that had happened. To Nix's mom. To Nix. To Tom.

To his parents.

He and Chong each drifted down the silent corridors of their personal pain as the sun burned its way through the hard blue sky. A pair of spider monkeys chattered in the trees. Benny looked at them because it was easier than looking at Eve, who still wept in Nix's arms. He sighed, feeling immensely useless.

In town there was always someone around to help with children. The whole town looked after everyone's kids. It was the way it had always been, at least in Benny's experience. No one would ever let a little kid go wandering off on their own.

Nix kept stroking the sobbing child's hair and murmuring words that Benny could not hear.

Eve was a little girl. Five years old. Helpless.

As Annie had been helpless.

Benny felt the weight of the sword slung over his shoulder. Tom's sword. His sword now. The sword he had very nearly lost.

He felt his face flush as he thought about how Nix had chased him out of the ravine and Lilah had recovered the sword. That was wrong. It wasn't the way things were supposed to work.

He felt eyes on him and turned to see Chong giving him a considering appraisal.

"What?" Benny demanded.

"What's on your mind? You look like you're trying to squeeze out a thought."

"Nothing," said Benny.

Chong sighed.

"Actually, there is something," Benny said tentatively.

"What?"

"When I was in the ravine, I thought I heard something."

"Like the sound of you peeing your pants?"

"Hilarious. Like a motor, like the hand-crank generator at the hospital. Did—did you guys hear that?"

Chong shook his head. "I didn't. I was asleep." Then, without meaning to, he said something very unkind. "Maybe you imagined it. You know, stress and all."

Benny stared ahead, and for a few moments he did not actually see a thing except shadows drifting across the front of his mind.

"Yeah," he said very quietly, "crazy, huh?"

Nix hugged Eve and kissed her hair. Then she encouraged

her to drink from a canteen. Finally Nix caught Benny's eye and gave him a tiny nod.

Benny and Chong came over, but they did not sit too close, warned off by a quick flare of Nix's eyes. Benny sat cross-legged next to Chong and waited as Eve looked shyly at them from within the protection of Nix's arms.

"Eve—?" began Nix softly.

"Mmm?" Eve answered in a tiny voice.

"Do you live around here?"

Eve sniffed and shook her head. "They chased us and . . . we had to run away."

Ouch, thought Benny.

"Who did you run away with?" asked Nix. No need to ask who they ran from.

"Mommy and Daddy and Ry-Ry and me, we had to run away 'cause the angels came and set fire to the trees, and then the gray people came through the fence and ate all the sheep and cows and tried to eat—" She suddenly stopped and looked around, her eyes filling with new tears. "Where's my mommy?"

"Shhh, shhh, it's okay, it's all right," soothed Nix, "we'll find her."

Benny marveled at Nix's patience. As sympathetic as he was to Eve, he could not stand the tears, the crying, the panic that emanated from the girl. It made him want to scream and run and hit things. Dead things. Or . . . anything. Trees, a rock wall. His fists were balled tight, and his whole body remained rigid as he tensed against a possible new wave of weeping.

"Sweetie," said Nix to Eve, "where was your mommy when you last saw her?"

Eve's face went blank as she thought about it. She glanced over Nix's shoulder to the slope that rose above the jagged mouth of the ravine, then turned and scanned the entire terrain. "I was playing in the creek," she said. "Mommy was doing the washing. And Ry-Ry was making breakfast and—"

Benny nodded. He leaned forward and said, "Eve . . . does your mom have black hair?"

Eve blinked at him like a confused turtle. "No. Mommy has yellow hair." She said it as if everyone knew that.

Chong bent close and whispered, "Why'd you ask that?"

Benny shrugged. "Probably nothing. I thought I saw a woman in the woods right before the zoms started chasing me."

"Was she—?" began Chong, and left the rest unsaid.

"I thought so," Benny said, "but the zoms didn't go for her."

"Cadaverine?" suggested Chong.

"Maybe. I don't know, it was all so fast."

Chong nodded sadly. They both remembered Tom's admonition about strangers. "A newly reanimated zom hasn't had time to rot, so they'll look like a living person right up to when they take a bite out of you."

"Where was your camp?" Nix asked the little girl.

"I don't know. When the gray people tried to get me, I ran and ran. We have to find Mommy and Daddy and Ry-Ry."

"Who's Ry-Ry?"

"A girl," Eve said, as if that was obvious to anyone. "She was taking us to a new home where we could all be safe from the gray people and the angels."

Lilah abruptly stood. "I'll find them," she said, and

stalked off to begin preparing her gear for a hunt.

"Where's the spear lady going?" asked Eve.

"She's a very good hunter," said Nix. "She'll find your mommy and the others."

"What about the gray people?" Eve asked in horror. "They'll get her!"

Nix smiled. "No, honey. They gray people won't get Lilah. She's smart and really strong, and she's quieted a lot of them."

"Quieted?"

"Put them to sleep."

"Pretend sleep or forever sleep?"

"Um . . . forever sleep," Nix assured her.

Chong leaned close to Benny again. "This is fascinating," he said quietly. "If there are other settlements out here, then they're probably like islands or distant countries used to be in the days before the world was mapped. So isolated that their own phrasing and references—all the slang and jargon that we've used since First Night—is going to be different."

"But . . . the way-station monks travel all over, don't they?"

Chong shrugged. "Sure. Like the Irish monks did during the Middle Ages and the Jesuits did a few centuries later. The Shaolin did it in China, too. Traveling, recording, spreading information, and making connections among the learned. Kind of a theme with traveling monks."

"The way-station monks don't travel to spread their religion, though."

"Not every monk or priest is an evangelist, Benny. Some were scholars and historians. Though, shocking as it is, you're right about one thing. If we find people using the same post–First Night slang, then it's probably going to be because of the monks."

"Gosh, Encyclopedia Chong. Thanks for throwing me a bone."

"It's a small bone. Chew it well."

Benny elbowed him in the ribs, but he did it discreetly. He didn't want to scare the kid.

Eve eventually fell asleep. Nix waved everyone away so as not to disturb the child. Benny drifted off to stare at the zoms in the ravine.

Chong saw Lilah sitting on a fallen log, sharpening the blade of her spear in preparation for setting off to find Eve's parents. Not feeling in the mood for another rebuke, he sank down with his back to a slender pine, closed his eyes, and began wandering slowly through the library of his mind. That was how he viewed it. A library, with shelves of books and rows of file cabinets in which his thoughts and memories and experiences were neatly filed.

The only mental file cabinet that was not as neatly and precisely ordered was the one labeled LILAH.

That one leaned with an awkward tilt, its sides were dented, and none of the drawers rolled smoothly out.

Lilah was the storm that swirled around Chong's life, and he dwelt in its calm eye, awed by the power and beauty of it, but not at all sure he understood it. Chong was relatively sure he would die of old age before he ever understood her completely.

He conjured the image of her in his mind. She was easily

the most beautiful girl he had ever seen. Tall, lithe, with long, tanned limbs, eyes the color of honey, and snow-white hair. Since Tom's death, it had fallen to Lilah to be the de facto leader of their expedition. Even though she'd never been to Nevada—or in a desert—she understood the logic and science of survival. From age eleven to sixteen she had lived alone in the Ruin, alternately running from zoms and bounty hunters and hunting them. Chong believed that Lilah could survive in any environment on earth in which she found herself. And although he could understand the skills she possessed on an intellectual level, he knew that he lacked her basic survival instincts.

His reverie ended abruptly with a sharp kick in the middle of his thigh.

"Ow!" he yelped, and loaded his tongue with the vilest insult he could construct for Benny . . . only it wasn't Benny.

When Chong opened his eyes, it was Lilah standing over him. She had her leather hunting pouch slung slantwise across her body and the spear in her hand.

"Wake up," she said.

"I am awake."

Lilah dropped the spear in the grass and sat cross-legged, facing him.

"I am leaving," she said.

"You just got here."

"No, I am going to find Annie's parents."

"Eve's," he corrected.

Her eyes flashed with irritation. "That's what I said."

"Okay," said Chong.

Lilah sat there with an expectant look on her face.

"Yes?" asked Chong.

"Well—?" she said.

"Well . . . what?"

"I said I was leaving."

"I know. Did . . . you want me to go with you?"

She laughed. "This is a hunt."

"I know."

"I will be moving fast. Tracking."

"Yes," he said. "I know."

"You're a—"

"A town boy. Yes, I know that, too." He smiled. It was a fact she reminded him of a dozen times each day. "And this town boy would slow you down, get you eaten by zoms, and otherwise bring about the downfall of what's left of humanity."

"Well . . . yes." Lilah studied him, clearly unsure of how to respond. Humor was the bluntest tool in her personal skills set.

"Then if it's all the same to you, I'll stay here and manfully defend this tree."

Lilah narrowed her eyes. "That is not a funny joke."

"No," he admitted. "Just mildly silly."

They sat for a moment, she looking at him and Chong pretending to look at nothing.

"I am leaving," she said again.

"Okay," he said.

She lingered, waiting.

"What?" he asked again.

"I am leaving," she replied, leaning on the word.

"Okay. Good-bye. Be safe. Come back soon."

"No," she said.

"Good hunting?"

Lilah growled low in her throat, grabbed his shirt with both hands, and hauled him toward her. Into a kiss that was fierce and hot and instantly intense. After several scalding seconds, she shoved him roughly back.

She got to her feet and snatched up her spear, then looked pityingly down at him. "Stupid town boy," she muttered, then turned and jogged into the forest.

Chong lay sprawled, eyes glazed and face flushed.

"Holy moley . . . ," he gasped.

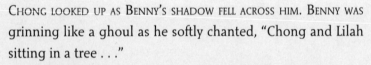

13

CHONG LOOKED UP AS BENNY'S SHADOW FELL ACROSS HIM. BENNY WAS grinning like a ghoul as he softly chanted, "Chong and Lilah sitting in a tree . . ."

"Although I'm a moral person," began Chong as he climbed to his feet, "I would have no compunction about killing you in your sleep."

"Just saying . . ."

Chong squatted down in front of Nix, who held a sleeping Eve. The little girl twitched every now and then, as if flinching away from shadows in her dreams.

Chong reached out to stroke Eve's silky hair. "I'll sit with her for a while if you want."

"You sure?" asked Nix.

"Sure, you know me and kids."

Nix nodded. Unlike Benny, who was often clumsy around kids and old people, Chong was completely comfortable with them. His inner calm seemed to work magic on the little ones, and he told the best stories. Chong knew all of Aesop's fables, Mother Goose, Oz, and Narnia, and a huge number of silly, funny stories culled from the countless books he'd read.

With a grateful sigh, Nix handed Eve to Chong, who took

her with such care that the little girl never even stirred. Chong crossed his legs and sat back against the tree.

Benny touched Nix's arm. "Want to take a walk?"

She nodded, and they set off at a slow stroll toward the forest and then turned just before the line of junipers and walked north in the shade.

The forest itself was a strange holdover from before First Night. It had once been an elaborate golf course that someone had plunked down in the middle of an inhospitable desert. Wind-driven turbines had been erected to pump in water from some distant place in order to keep the grass green; but after First Night, the wind turbines began to fail. Benny and his friends had passed a line of them on the way here. Of the fifty they counted, only three still turned sluggishly, and they must have been enough to allow some trees and plants to flourish. But there was clear evidence that the more water-hungry vegetation was dying and the more desert-hardy junipers and pinyons were taking over. Soon only the desert plants would be left, and another of man's structures that had been imposed on the land would be reclaimed by nature.

They walked in silence through the green trees, leaving the stench of the crowd of zoms behind. A few small white butterflies fluttered past. A black-tailed jackrabbit sat shoulder-deep in the grass, munching on a stem, and paused to watch them with a nervous eye, but soon went back to its foraging. All around them the desert birds flitted and sang. Benny loved birds and pointed out some of his favorites to Nix.

"That one there's a sage grouse," he said. "And see, on that branch? That's a horned lark. And I think I saw a meadowlark earlier and . . ."

His voice trailed off as he realized that she wasn't listening. She wasn't even giving him the usual courtesy nods and grunts people give when they're pretending to listen. Nix was deep inside her own thoughts, and Benny was on the other side of that wall. He lapsed into silence, and they walked without talking for ten minutes.

"I asked Eve about where she came from," Nix said eventually.

"Oh?"

"A lot of it is confusing. She's little, and she doesn't understand most of what's happened, and I think she's a bit out of it, you know? Like, in shock? Some of the things she says don't make much sense. I think she's confusing stuff from dreams, or maybe nightmares, with things that are actually happening."

Benny nodded toward the zoms on the other side of the long ravine. "That's not too hard to understand. Sometimes I can't believe it myself. Sometimes I think I'm going to wake up and smell Tom's cooking, and then I'll go down to breakfast. Scrambled eggs with peppers and mushrooms. Your mom's corn muffins. Fresh-pressed apple juice and a big glass of milk." He sighed.

Nix nodded but didn't comment on that. "Eve said she used to live in a house up in a town called Treetops. I don't know if that's real or something she made up."

"That's actually not a bad idea. Zoms can't climb."

"She said that one night the trees all caught fire and everyone ran. And here's the really strange part: She said that it was angels who came and set fire to the trees."

"She mentioned angels before. Is that another name for zoms?"

"I don't think so. She said the angels came riding in on what she called 'growly horses.' Isn't that strange?"

"Yeah."

"According to her, the angels had wings on their chests."

"On their chests?" Benny grinned at the thought. "Wouldn't that make them fly upside down?"

"It's not funny," said Nix. "Eve was really scared of them."

They stopped and picked some tart early-season elderberries.

As Benny ate, he thought about the idea of wings on the chests of angels, and it made him think about the woman he'd seen in the field right before the horde of zoms attacked him. What was it embroidered on the front of her shirt? Could that have been angel wings?

He told Nix about her.

"You sure she wasn't a zom?"

"Yeah. Weird, huh? Oh, and I heard a strange sound while I was down in the ravine." He described the motor noise. "Did you hear anything like that?"

"A motor?" Nix brightened. "I didn't hear anything, but . . . could it have been a jet?"

Benny thought about it and reluctantly shook his head. "No. It didn't sound anywhere near big enough."

Nix looked crestfallen, and Benny felt bad. Although he was out here in the Ruin to look for the jet too, it was clear to everyone that the search for the jet was Nix's mission. Her quest. Benny wanted to find it, as did Lilah and Chong; but Nix needed to find it. Benny thought he knew why she was so obsessed by it, but he didn't dare say it to her. Not now, anyway.

He let her sort through her own emotions for a moment. She chewed her lip thoughtfully, then grunted. "Hmm. Motors . . ."

"What?"

"I don't know, but it makes me wonder what sound those 'growly horses' made."

He paused with a handful of berries halfway to his mouth. "Wow," he said quietly.

"Wow," she agreed. "Mr. Lafferty said once that just because the EMPs blew out all the motors, there was no reason why someone couldn't repair some of them. I mean . . . we did see that jet."

"Yes, we did."

"So . . . maybe the growly horses are some kind of . . . I don't know . . . car or truck or something."

Benny nodded. "Not sure I want to find out."

Nix looked away and didn't answer. Then, seemingly out of nowhere, she asked, "Do you regret it?"

"Regret . . . what?"

"This," she said, gesturing to the forest. "Leaving town, coming out here. Are you sorry we came?"

Benny tensed. He loved Nix, but he knew that she was not above setting verbal traps for him to put his foot into. She'd done it enough times, and he'd stumbled numbly into them more times than he could count. It wasn't a very likable quality, but it wasn't any kind of deal breaker for them. He was pretty sure there were things he did that annoyed her, too.

So he relied on one of his favorite stalling tactics. "What do you mean?"

"What I said," Nix replied, parrying deftly. "Are you sorry we came?"

Benny stuffed his mouth with berries to buy another second to think, and he rather hoped another ravine full of zoms would suddenly open up in the ground directly in front of them.

When that did not happen, he swallowed and braced himself and said, "Sometimes."

"Why?"

"We haven't found the jet," he said. "And until today we haven't even seen any people. We don't know if we're going in the right direction. We're low on supplies, and now we've run into a horde of zoms." He paused, wondering how far off the cliff of "said too much" he'd already gone. He tried to fix it, but the wrong words came out. "I guess it isn't what I expected."

"I thought so," Nix said, and Benny did not at all like the way she said it.

They walked in silence for another full minute.

"Okay," he said when he could no longer bear it, "what's going on?"

"With what?" she asked, not looking at him.

"With us."

"Nothing," she said tightly. "Everything's fine."

"Really?" he asked. "Is it?"

Nix stared ahead as they walked, watching the bees and the dragonflies.

"Look at me," he said.

She did not.

"Nix . . . what is it?" he asked gently. "Did I do something, or—?"

"No," she said quickly.

"Then what is it?"

"Does it have to be anything?"

"Pretty much, yeah. For the last couple of weeks you've been weird."

"Weird?" She loaded that word with jagged chunks of ice.

"Not *weird* weird, but, you know . . . different. You spend all your time talking to Lilah or not talking to anyone. We hardly talk anymore."

She stopped and wheeled on him. "And you spend all your time moping around like the world just ended."

Benny gaped at her. "No, I don't."

"Yes, you do," she insisted.

"Well, okay, maybe I've been dealing with some stuff. My brother just died, you know."

"I know."

"He was murdered."

"I know."

"So maybe I need time to sort through that, ever think about that?"

Nix's eyes blazed. "Are you going to lecture me about dealing with grief, Benjamin Imura? Your brother died fighting. My mother was beaten to death. How do you think that makes me feel?"

"It makes you feel like crap, how do you think I think it makes you feel?"

"Then what are you harping on—"

"Who's harping?" he said defensively. "Jeez, Nix, all I did was ask what was wrong. Don't bite my head off."

"I'm not biting your head off."

"Then why are you yelling?"

"I'm not yelling," she yelled.

Benny took a steadying breath and let it out slowly.

"Nix, I do understand what you're going through. I'm going through it too."

"It's not the same thing," she said very quietly. An elk poked its head out from behind some sagebrush, studied them for a moment, then bent to eat berries from another bush.

"Then why won't you tell me what it is?"

She glared at him. "Honestly, Benny, sometimes I think you don't even know who I am."

With that she turned and stalked away, her spine as stiff as a board. Benny stood openmouthed until she was almost back to the tree where Chong sat with Eve.

"What the hell was that all about?" he asked the elk.

The elk, being an elk, said nothing.

Dispirited and deeply troubled, Benny thrust his hands in his pockets and walked slowly over to the edge of the ravine to stare at the faces of the living dead. They looked at him with dead eyes, but in some eerie way Benny felt that they could see him and that they somehow understood all the mysteries that were sewn like stitches through the skin of this day.

FROM NIX'S JOURNAL

A lot of the stuff Tom taught us has nothing to do with zoms. Once, right after we started training, Morgie asked Tom why we bothered, 'cause after all, Charlie and the Hammer were dead. This was before we left town, before we met White Bear and Preacher Jack.

Tom said that we should never assume that we know what's out there. He said, "People in town refer to everything beyond the fence line as the great Rot and Ruin. We assume that it's nothing but a wasteland from our fence all the way to the Atlantic Ocean three thousand miles away. But we saw that jet, so there is something out there. We don't know what it is, or whether whoever's out there will be friendly. Or generous. Or open to us joining them. A smart warrior prepares for all eventualities."

Tom also said, "Even before First Night there were all kinds of people who wanted to be on their own. Isolationists, religious orders, militant groups, back-to-nature groups, communes, military bases, remote research stations, and more. Some of these people will do anything to protect their privacy or their way of life. To them . . . we're outsiders and intruders."

14

FOR LILAH, READING TRACKS ON THE GROUND WAS AS EASY AS READING words on a page. Her sharp eyes missed nothing, and as she moved deeper into the desert forest, she began cataloging the marks she found. Eve's were easy to spot, and they wandered out of the east along a crooked path.

As for the rest, Lilah slowed from a run to a walk as she studied them.

The forest was denser than she'd expected. She knelt and pawed at the sandy soil and quickly found darker, wetter soil beneath. She sniffed it.

There was water here. An underground stream or some other source beyond what the wind towers pulled in. Eve had mentioned a creek; and the footprints seemed to be coming from the densest part of the forest. That made sense. People tended to camp near water. Especially in a climate like this.

Lilah bent forward onto all fours and studied the ground. In some spots, like this one, there were many footprints, and they varied. Several men, a few women. From the spacing and gait, it was clear that these were humans. Most of the shoes, even the crudely made ones, were in good repair, and there was none of the aimless shambling typical of zoms.

Not that she didn't find signs of wandering zoms. They were out here too.

Lilah straightened, eyes alert.

So far they had seen no zoms on this side of the ravine, but the footprints didn't lie.

She turned and glanced back the way she'd come as if she could see little Eve sitting there with Nix and the others. The girl must be charmed, she thought, to have made it safely from where her parents were camped to where Benny had rescued her. She had no bites on her, no marks to indicate that zoms had tried to hurt her.

That was a great relief to Lilah, one she had not shared with Chong. If Eve had been bitten . . .

If she was infected and needed to be quieted . . .

Lilah did not know if she could do that.

Not to a little girl who looked so much like Annie.

Not again.

She adjusted her grip on the spear and moved on.

A few minutes later she stopped again and knelt down by a different set of tracks. Not human footprints, and not the scuffling marks of zoms. No, these were straight lines of serrated tracks, like wheel marks.

But . . . wheels belonging to what? If they were made by a cart or wagon, then there was no sign of what pulled it.

She cleared away some loose debris and studied the patterns. The impressions were cut deep into the ground. Whatever made them was heavy, and it had four wheels. She thought of the many abandoned cars and trucks she'd seen over the years, and these marks didn't fit. For one thing, the wheels were too close together.

It was a mystery.

Lilah moved on.

The ground became increasingly moist. Soon she smelled water on the breeze, and then within a few minutes she heard the soft burble of a stream. The footprints and the wheel marks all came from that way.

Five minutes later Lilah stepped out onto the banks of a narrow, shallow stream that ran out of the northeast and jagged off due south. The water was clear and clean, with the kind of mineral taste that confirmed her suspicion that the source was an underground river. She drank handfuls of it and refilled her canteen.

Despite the potential for zoms and the mystery of the tracks, Lilah felt relaxed, content in her skills and in her solitude. She welcomed any opportunity to be alone. Being alone was when she felt most like herself. She felt powerful and normal. For months now, Lilah had felt anything but normal. Except when she went ahead to scout out a path for Nix, Benny, and Chong, she was seldom alone. That bothered her.

Benny and Nix often said things like, "It must be great not to be all alone anymore." And, "You'll never have to be alone again."

On a practical level, Lilah could understand that they meant well. That they thought she had been rescued from loneliness. To a degree, she had.

Mostly, though, the ties between her and her new friends, the responsibility of protecting them, caring for them, felt like tethers holding her down. She did not want to care for anyone. The last person she'd cared for was Annie.

She knew that she was not like other people. Not like

Benny, Nix, or Chong, even though they were all her friends. Their life experience was completely alien to her, as hers was no doubt bizarre to them.

Lilah had been two years old on First Night. Her mother was pregnant with Annie, and they were caught up in the mad exodus from Los Angeles as the dead rose. A handful of survivors managed to find a safe house hundreds of miles from the city, but that house was soon under siege by zombies. None of the other survivors realized that the pregnant woman had been bitten. Just as her mother gave birth to Annie, the infection took her and she died, only to reanimate moments later as a monster.

It was the first time Lilah had witnessed anyone being quieted, though there was nothing quiet about it. Her mother screamed like a feral beast as she tried to attack the men; and the survivors screamed in fear as they bludgeoned her with anything they could grab. Lilah screamed too. She screamed so long and so loud that she permanently ruined her vocal cords, leaving her with a ghostly whisper of a voice.

Over the next few days, the survivors tried, one by one, to escape and find help. None ever returned. The last survivor was a quiet little man named George. He stayed. He cared for Lilah and Annie. Raising them, teaching them, loving them as if they were his own children.

As she moved through the dry desert shrubs, Lilah thought more and more about her early life with George and Annie. They had been her whole world. However, during one of their moves to a new farmhouse, George met a group of armed men who claimed to be part of a movement to reclaim the Ruin from the dead.

That was a lie.

The men brutalized George and kidnapped the girls, taking them to the zombie pits at Gameland. There, Lilah and Annie were forced to fight for their lives against zoms while corrupt men and women wagered on who would survive. Lilah fought hardest against her captivity, and the Motor City Hammer and his thugs frequently beat her. She still had the scars from their fists, belts, and switches.

After Annie died, Lilah spent the next five years alone, living in a cave she filled with weapons and books. Until Benny, Nix, and Tom found her and brought her back to Mountainside.

Tom said that he had met George out in the wild, and had even helped him look for his two lost girls. Then rumors began circulating that George had gone crazy and committed suicide. Tom Imura thought it was a lie, believing that Charlie and the Hammer had murdered him and faked his suicide. Not that it mattered. George was dead.

All those men were now dead. Charlie. The Hammer.

And . . . Tom.

Just thinking his name made her eyes sting.

Tom and the others had brought Lilah back to their town. She went to live with the Chongs, who had a big house with plenty of room. Mrs. Chong took it upon herself to teach Lilah how to act "like a young woman," with all the bizarre rituals that went with that. Lilah's total lack of tact, deference, modesty, and hesitation was a jolt to the Chong household. After a while, some of the family manners and deportment she'd learned while living with George came back. Grudgingly.

Many times during those months, Lilah found the

confinement of a house and the obligations of social interaction to be too much hard work. It became claustrophobic. It was frightening, because every day there were a hundred times when the things she said and did mattered to other people. Things she said caused as much pain as if she'd punched someone. It was confusing to her. So many times she packed her meager belongings—just clothes and weapons—and prepared to sneak away in the dark of the night.

She never did, though.

Partly because she wanted to belong to a family. The loss of George and Annie was so strong, even after all this time. It was as if the bounty hunters had literally carved away a piece of her body; she could feel the loss every day.

But there was another reason she stayed.

During her years of lonely isolation Lilah had read every novel she could find, from *Sense and Sensibility* to *The Truth About Forever*. She understood the concept of romance, of love. Of emotional and physical attraction. She was strange, she knew that, but she was still a teenager. A young woman.

Even so, she was unprepared for the moment when she discovered that Lou Chong had developed "feelings" for her. It was an absurd concept. He was a town boy. Not a hunter, not a fighter. He wouldn't last a single night alone in the Ruin.

And yet.

Lilah did not want to have feelings for Chong.

She would rather have been with Tom Imura.

She even approached him once, on a winter night when no one else was around. She'd come right out and told him, "I love you."

In the novels she read, that usually did it. The hero was swept off his feet by the honesty and directness of the heroine's bold announcement.

What Tom said was, "Wow, Lilah. That's a hell of a way to open a conversation. I thought you came over looking for Benny or Nix."

"They are out," she told him. "I waited until they left."

"Ri-i-ight," Tom said. They were standing in the kitchen. Tom had a cup of coffee in his hand. Outside it was thirty degrees and lightly snowing. "And you stood out there in the storm?"

"It is only snow."

"Right," he said again. "Okay, so here's the thing, Lilah. I know that you like people to be direct with you, so that's exactly what I'm going to be. I don't know if this is going to hurt your feelings, but I think it's absolutely necessary for us to put all our cards on the table. Do you understand that expression? Cards on the table?"

She nodded. "The truth, with nothing hidden."

"Good. Then here's the thing. I'm twice your age."

"What does that matter—?"

"Shhh, let me talk. Let's do this the right way, okay?"

Lilah had not replied to that. The moment had not become what she had expected. In books, the hero sweeps the heroine up into his arms and they kiss. Lilah had never kissed anyone except Annie and George, and those were cheek kisses. Not the fiery kisses she'd read about. The kinds of kisses where the world tilts on its axis and the heroine feels like she's going to faint. Lilah did not know what that really meant, but she wanted to find out.

What Tom said was, "Lilah, you are my friend. You're a very pretty girl, no doubt about that. You are strong, and intelligent, and lovely, and you care about people. All of those are amazing qualities. If I was Benny's age, I have no doubt that I would be one of a hundred boys who would fall head over heels for you. But that's not going to happen, for a couple of very good reasons. First, I'm an adult and you're a teenager, so there are all sorts of legal and moral issues right there, and I'm not the kind of guy who's ever been interested in crossing those lines. Not now and not ever."

Lilah said nothing to that. It was a stupid reason, and she was sure that she could kick it aside.

"Second, even though it's a self-appointed role, I'm charged with protecting you. That means I have to advise you against making the wrong kinds of choices. If you came to me and told me that you were in love with someone else, some other adult, I'd give you the same advice: Don't do it."

She ignored that, too. There were no protectors when she lived alone in the Ruin, and she did not believe she needed anyone to make decisions for her. She had to fight to keep a dismissive sneer off her face.

"And third, and most important of all—I don't love you like that, Lilah. I don't now and I won't."

"Why not?" Lilah demanded, her tone fierce, her posture aggressive.

Tom set his coffee cup down and looked out the window at the falling snow for a long time. When he turned back to her, his eyes were filled with more sadness than Lilah had ever seen in anyone's eyes.

"Because I'm already in love with someone, Lilah," he said

softly. There were thorns and broken glass in his voice.

"With who?" demanded Lilah.

"With Nix's mom. With Jessie Riley."

Lilah blinked. "But . . . Nix's mother is dead. Charlie Pink-eye killed her."

"Yes," agreed Tom. "Charlie beat her so badly that she was dying when I found her. I held her while she died, Lilah. I felt her go. I felt her heart stop. I felt her last breath on my lips."

A single tear broke and fell down Tom's cheek.

"I loved Jessie Riley with my whole heart."

"I—" began Lilah, but Tom shook his head.

"No." He wiped the tear away with his fingers and looked at the wetness for a long moment. "I had to use a sliver to keep her from coming back."

"Oh . . ."

"You know," Tom said softly, "this year, during the spring festival, I was going to propose to her. Benny and Nix don't know that. There's a silversmith in Haven who was making the ring."

He sniffed and took a breath.

"Jessie had my heart, Lilah. And . . . when she died, I think that part of me died with her." He shook his head. "I don't think I'll ever love anyone else. Not like that."

"In books," Lilah protested, "people heal. They get over it."

"Other people, maybe," Tom said. "But—those books were written before First Night."

It was the last thing he said about it. Lilah stayed for a cup of coffee, but they sat at the table and looked at things inside their own heads and said nothing to each other. Her coffee was cold and untouched when she left the house, and they never spoke of it again.

Somewhere, somehow, during the long weeks after that conversation with Tom, Lilah's heart changed. She let go of her desire for Tom, though in a different way she loved him more than ever. She always would.

Now Tom was dead.

She walked on along the stream, pushing herself to focus on her mission.

However, she wondered if, now that Tom was gone too, there was someplace where he and Mrs. Riley were together again. Lilah's understanding of her own spiritual beliefs was largely unformed, but she wanted Tom and Jessie Riley to be together. Tom had earned that.

If that could be true, then maybe there was a place where George and Annie were together. He'd be lying under a tree, peeling an apple, and she'd be laughing as she chased butterflies in a sunlit field where there were no living dead and no evil men.

It was why Lilah did not fear death. So many of the people she loved were waiting for her there.

Lilah kept walking along the muddy bank of the stream, but she slowed and then stopped completely. The path ahead of her was invisible now. It was not hidden by shadows, and it had not petered out as loose soil gave way to hard rock. No, it was simply that Lilah couldn't see a thing through the hot tears that boiled from her eyes and burned their way down her cheeks.

15

BENNY AND CHONG STOOD AT THE EDGE OF THE RAVINE. MORE THAN AN hour had passed since Lilah had gone looking for Eve's family, and half an hour since Benny's inexplicable fight with Nix. Now Nix sat sleeping against the tree with Eve in her arms. Benny did not tell Chong about the argument. He was still trying to figure a way to explain it to himself and so far had made no headway at all.

Benny sighed.

"Something wrong?" asked Chong, distractedly peeling a fig while staring into the ravine.

What could possibly be wrong? wondered Benny sourly. I either think I'm hearing voices or I'm actually being haunted. And I got so depressed down in the ravine that I almost gave up fighting for my own life. How's that for "wrong"?

"Tell me something, O mighty sage," Benny said at length. "Do you ever have too many thoughts in your head?"

Chong started to say something funny and biting, but stopped himself and studied Benny for a slow three-count. He turned back to study the faces of the dead.

After a long time he said, "All the time, man. All the darn time."

They were silent for many long minutes before either of them spoke again.

"Earlier . . . you said you saw a woman?" asked Chong. "What was that about?"

Benny told him. And about how she appeared to blow on a silent whistle, and how the zoms did not attack her. By the time he was finished, Chong had a half smile on his face.

Benny sighed. "Go on, say it."

"You are monkey-bat crazy."

"Thanks."

"A whistle?"

"Yeah."

"Like . . . what? A dog whistle?"

Benny grunted. He hadn't considered that possibility. Mr. Lafferty, who owned the general store, had a dog whistle. You couldn't hear that sound either.

"Maybe," said Benny. "That's what it kind of looked like."

"For calling zoms?"

"I never said she called the zoms. I'm telling you what I saw."

"Okay," said Chong.

"Okay," said Benny.

They watched the zoms.

"Real question," said Chong, "so don't hit me."

"Okay."

"How was it down there? Was it bad?"

"It was bad."

"Are . . . you okay?"

Benny shrugged.

"Did you see any fast ones?" asked Chong.

"A couple."

"Jeez."

"Yeah."

All their lives there had been only one kind of living dead. Slow, mindless, shuffling zoms. It was the way it was—a zom was a zom was a zom. Then last month, while Benny and Nix were on the way to Gameland, they had encountered zombies who moved faster. Not really as fast as a healthy human, but at least twice as fast as any zom Benny had ever heard about.

That ugly fact was just one of several things about the zoms that was changing the world as Benny knew it. The people back in town had only survived this long because they began to understand what zoms could and could not do. Knowledge of them did not make the dead less of a threat, but it increased the chances of survival in a world where zoms were everywhere.

Now that was changing. Now nothing that had previously been known about them could be relied on. Some zombies were faster. The few advantages people had over zoms seemed to be crumbling.

What if the dead started thinking? There were seven billion of them, and barely enough humans to fill a small city.

They stood in the silence of their own thoughts for a long time. The zombies watched them with unblinking eyes. Birds sang in the trees on Benny's side of the divide, but there was movement in the sky above the zoms. Benny shielded his eyes from the glare and peered at a dozen large black birds drifting in slow circles high above the far side of the field. Chong noticed him looking and cupped his hands around his eyes too. He turned and saw even more of them over the forest behind them.

"Turkey vultures," observed Chong.

"I know."

They watched the dark, ugly birds glide without sound on the thermal currents above the endless miles of pinyon pines.

"There are a lot of them out today," Chong said. "Seem to be everywhere."

Benny looked at him. He could feel the blood drain from his face.

"Oh, crap . . ."

"Yeah. Carrion birds don't eat zoms . . ."

". . . so what are they circling?" Benny finished.

It was one of the great mysteries of the Ruin that vermin did not feed on the zoms, even though they smelled of decay. No one understood it, and as Mr. Lafferty at the general store once said, "Kind of a shame, too, 'cause in about a month we'd have had a zillion fat crows and no zoms at all."

Chong said, "Something's dead out there."

"I'd better get Nix," said Benny.

16

LILAH ANGRILY FISTED THE TEARS FROM HER EYES AND GLARED AROUND AS IF ready to bash anyone who happened to be a witness to those tears. She detested weakness of any kind. It was something she could barely tolerate in her friends and would not allow in herself.

Especially after what had happened a month ago. After Tom led them out of town, their group had gotten separated. Chong, torn by guilt for having inadvertently caused Nix's face to be slashed, and generally feeling like the town boy he was, had run away, requiring that Tom go and find him. That night, while Nix, Benny, and Lilah waited for Tom's return in a deserted monk's way station, the place was overrun by a sea of zoms. Thousands upon thousands of them; more zoms than anyone had seen in one place since First Night. In the moments before the attack, Lilah had been arguing with Benny, and he accused her of deliberately ignoring and mocking Chong's feelings for her. That hurt, because it was entirely true. Lilah cared for Chong, but he was the weakest and least hardy of their team. He was not suited for the Ruin; not at all. When the zoms attacked, Lilah panicked and ran. It was the first time she had ever panicked since that terrible night when she had escaped from Gameland and was forced to quiet Annie. She'd thrown down her spear and run blindly into the dark. Even now she could not remember what her thoughts had been in those moments. Or even if she'd had any thoughts. All she remembered was running through the blackness, inside and out.

Awareness came back to her much later. She found herself curled on the ground, totally vulnerable and totally lucky to be alive. The zoms had not found her; but a strange mountain loner named the Greenman had. He hadn't attacked her—just the reverse; he showed her kindness and patience, and helped her discover where she'd left her strength. He also spoke with her about love, about responsibility, about guilt, and about the choices everyone makes.

Lilah had wept several times that day. And she wept even more bitterly that night, when the monster Preacher Jack shot Tom Imura in the back. It did not matter that Preacher Jack and Gameland both died that night. Tom Imura had died too. Lilah had clung to his hand as the last strength went out of it. Even now, a month later, thinking about it was like being punched in the heart.

She stood there in the forest and wept again. For Tom.

And for Annie.

God, how that little girl, Eve, looked like Annie. So much. Too much.

It was unfair.

It was cruel.

She sniffed and wiped her eyes and took as many deep breaths as she needed to in order to stop her chest from hitching with sobs. The forest waited for her. The day seemed to pause for her.

"Annie," Lilah whispered to the forest. "Oh God, Annie, I miss you."

She begged the forest to answer her. She begged for the ghost of Annie to speak inside her mind, like the ghost of Tom Imura sometimes did.

And suddenly the forest stopped being empty and silent.

She spun and faced the northern reach of the forest as noise filled the air. She frowned. This was not a forest sound. It was a sound she had only ever heard once, back in Mountainside.

It was the sound of a machine.

No . . . machines. At least two, coming from different directions.

The sounds rode the breeze toward her from different directions. Motor sounds, clearly mechanical, like the hand-crank generators in the town's hospital.

Lilah ducked behind a tumble of rocks, going low and still, melting into the landscape as the motor sounds grew from a growl to a roar.

The leaves of the forest wall parted, and Lilah beheld something that shocked her. Something she'd believed belonged only to a world that no longer existed.

Two men came out of the woods, one on either side of the stream. They moved fast, but they were not running, nor were they astride horses, and suddenly she understood the nature of the cart tracks she had seen. These men sat on the backs of machines.

They were riding four-wheeled motorcycles.

FROM NIX'S JOURNAL

Can Zoms Think?

Tom said, "As far as we know, zoms have no memory of their previous lives. They don't respond to their name or anything like that. They appear to be mindless, but that can't be true. Some zoms can turn a door handle. All of them remember how to walk, climb stairs, and get back to their feet after they've been knocked down. They know how to use their hands for things like grabbing, tearing, pulling, or holding something or someone. Most of them can recognize the difference between a blank wall and one with a window or door, because they try to get through those. And all of them remember how to bite, eat, and swallow."

But . . . do they remember anything else? Maybe something that we don't know they remember?

That thought sometimes keeps me up at night.

gunshots make a lot of noise, and we don't know how many more zoms are in the forest."

Chong nodded. "Lilah can take care of herself; and she won't appreciate you second-guessing her like this."

"A warning isn't second-guessing," replied Benny. "She doesn't know what's out there."

"Neither do we," said Chong. "I mean, let's have a little perspective here. A few vultures is a mystery, not a certain catastrophe."

"Maybe," Benny said dubiously, but he did not ask Nix for the gun. For her part, Nix did not seem anxious to give it over. She stroked Eve's fine blond hair and studied the sky.

Chong opened his mouth to say more, but instead he froze and stared past Benny and Nix. For the second time in a little over five minutes, Chong's face lost all color, and he suddenly whipped his bokken out of its canvas sheath.

Benny and Nix spun too, their reflexes honed by months of training with Tom and weeks of dangerous travel in the Ruin. Benny's sword flashed in the sunlight, but then it jolted to a halt as his whole body became rigid.

"Oh my God," breathed Nix in a terrified whisper.

There were no zoms behind him.

Zoms—even a lot of them—might have been something they could handle.

This was different. This was much worse.

Instead, standing fifty yards away, huge and powerful and incredibly deadly, was a lion.

18

LILAH STARED SLACK-JAWED AT THE MOTORCYCLES.

She had read about such vehicles in books, had seen abandoned ones on the roads, their bodies rusted and their driv-
ers gone to wander the world as living dead. She had never
imagined she would see one still in operation—let alone two
of them. Yet here they were, mud-smeared and battered, but
clearly in working condition. How had these men gotten
them to work? How had they kept them working this long
after First Night? Where did they find fuel that was still chemi-
cally sound after fourteen years? Unless it was in tightly sealed
containers, most forms of gasoline broke down over time.

Lilah ducked down behind a bush. The motorbikes
zoomed past her, and as they went she winced at the stink of
the thick exhaust fumes. It was a terrible and unnatural smell.

Each of the men carried a weapon slung across his back.
The one on the left bank wore a heavy fire ax in a sling; the
other man had a big two-handed sword in a leather scabbard.
Lilah thought that such a weapon must have been looted
from a museum or private collection. She'd seen bounty
hunters with similar ancient weapons. They were clumsy in
the age of guns before First Night, but practical in the world

of the dead, because a sword is quiet and does not need to be reloaded.

Lilah left her place of concealment and began following the vehicles, running as quickly as caution would allow. Half a mile melted away, then a mile. More. Lilah enjoyed running, and she could travel at a jog trot all day long. Even so, the four-wheeled vehicles quickly outpaced her and vanished into nothing more than a distant engine whine.

She kept going, following their tire tracks for two more miles, and then she heard the engines again. They were stationary now, their grumbling motors idling somewhere around a bend in the stream. She faded into the woods and circled to come up on the stream from the far side, using a line of broken boulders as cover.

Then she heard more engines, and she slid into a hollow formed by several tumbled rocks. Five more of the four-wheeled vehicles came racing out of the woods and went splashing along the shallow streambed to join the others. One by one the engine roars coughed and fell silent as the motorcycles were switched off. In the ensuing silence she could hear the chatter of at least a dozen voices, and as she watched, she saw people moving through the forest on foot, alone and in small groups of two or three.

Lilah wormed her way forward to get a better look.

The gathering was a mix of men and women of all ages—but they were all dressed alike in black pants and shirts, with bloodred ribbons tied around their arms, legs, waists, and necks. On each person's chest, whether rendered in chalk, paint, or fine stitchery, was a similar design of stylized wings. Angel wings.

Lilah immediately thought back to what little Eve had said.

I was running after Ry-Ry, and I lost my way 'cause there were angels in the woods.

Every person's head was shaved bald, and their scalps were covered in complex tattoos. Most of them had patterns of wild-flowers, green vines, autumn leaves, and thornbushes. A few had images of chains and barbed wire inked among the flow-ers. The art ranged from very crude to exquisitely rendered.

All the people were armed, and every one of them showed signs of recent trauma. Bruises, stitched wounds, crusted cuts, and stained bandages.

These were fighters, Lilah decided. She appraised their weapons and saw every kind of knife, hatchet, cleaver, ax, and sword—but not one firearm.

As more people came out of the woods, the others greeted them with joyful smiles, handshakes, and hugs.

Lilah moved away from the rocks and silently threaded her way through a stand of leafy shrubs so she could reach a high stone ledge that rose above and behind the group of people. She moved like a ghost, and no one saw or heard her. She flattened out and went utterly still with a clear view of the gathering through a tiny break in the overhanging foliage.

Two of the gathered people produced glass bottles filled with a viscous red liquid. They uncorked the bottles and moved through the crowd, dribbling the fluid onto the ends of the red ribbons. The breeze carried the foul smell of it to Lilah, and she wrinkled her nose. It was not the same as cadaverine but definitely something similar, and it probably served the same purpose.

The crowd suddenly stiffened and turned as two additional figures stepped out into the sunlight at the edge of the stream. A woman, with a brute of a man walking a pace behind her. The gathered mass of fighters bowed with great reverence to her.

Lilah heard many of them speak a name as they bowed. "Mother Rose."

The woman—this "Mother Rose"—was the most beautiful person she had ever seen, like one of the goddesses from the books of ancient myths that Lilah had read. She was tall, with haughty features and eyes that seemed to radiate their own dark light. Unlike the others, she had all her hair, and it fell in gleaming black curls around her face and shoulders. This woman's personal power was such that all the others, even the men who towered above her, seemed to shrink in her presence.

Behind Mother Rose was a man Lilah knew had to be a bodyguard. He was enormous, a giant who could not have been an inch less than seven feet tall. He had skin the color of mahogany and a shrewd, intelligent face on which was no single trace of compassion or humanity. It was a killer's face, and Lilah knew what killers looked like. The giant stood apart, just inside the darkness of the forest. He leaned on the haft of a long-handled sledgehammer. There were knives sheathed at both hips, and around his neck he wore a necklace of withered human hands. Lilah counted nineteen of them. Somehow she did not think that these hands had been cut from the wrists of zoms.

"Blessings to you all, my reapers," Mother Rose said in a soft southern drawl. "May you always walk the shortest path to the darkness."

"Praise be to the darkness," they responded.

Reapers, mused Lilah. Her hands tightened on the shaft of her spear.

One of the men Lilah had seen on the bikes, the one with the two-handed sword, knelt and kissed one of the streamers that was tied to Mother Rose's ankle. It did not seem to matter to him that this streamer had trailed in the dirt and mud.

"What have you found, Brother Simon?" asked Mother Rose.

"The gray wanderers you flushed toward the clearing are still there," said the man. "Jack and I—"

"Brother Jack," corrected Mother Rose.

Brother Simon nodded, took a breath, and continued. "Brother Jack and I put the call out all along the western slope. There are at least three or four hundred grays heading downland now, which means that those trails will be totally blocked. Sister Abigail has her reapers on the north flank, and Brother Gomez is in a nice blind down at the southern end. If any of Carter's people slip the grays, they'll have to take one of those two routes, and they'll walk right into our people."

Mother Rose nodded.

"I think Carter and his people are still heading southwest," continued Brother Simon.

"Good," said Mother Rose, nodding her approval. "That means the heretics will walk right into Saint John."

At the mention of that name, Lilah saw many of the people stiffen, their smiles becoming tighter, forced.

"It would be better for Carter if he let us catch them," said one of the reapers, a woman with red poppies tattooed on her face. "They'd at least have a chance to join us instead of immediately going into the darkness."

Many of the others nodded. Mother Rose's smile was less forced and entirely unpleasant. Lilah did not like that smile. Not one little bit. It was the way she imagined a shark might smile.

Mother Rose said, "Saint John is the favored son of the Lord Thanatos."

"Praise be to the darkness," replied the gathered reapers immediately upon hearing the name.

"Saint John has his own path to the darkness," continued Mother Rose, "and it is for him alone and not for us to understand."

"All blessings to Saint John," said Brother Simon. "All blessings to the beloved of Lord Thanatos."

As the others echoed his words and bowed low, Lilah saw Mother Rose cut a quick look at her bodyguard. Was that a smile they shared? Or a sneer? Lilah was not well practiced at reading faces, but she had spied on Charlie Pink-eye and his crew many times, and she could recognize deceit when she saw it. Whoever this Saint John was, Lilah guessed that he should be worried about how much Mother Rose truly respected him.

And what was that name Mother Rose had mentioned?

Thanatos.

Lilah frowned. The name tugged at a memory. Not someone she'd ever met, but something she'd read. She didn't push at it; instead she relaxed her thoughts and let the memory float to the top.

Thanatos. One of two aspects of death from ancient Greek culture. Her frown deepened because as she remembered it, Thanatos was the nonviolent death god. The one who came to relieve suffering. And yet all these people were heavily armed. Lilah decided that whoever this "Carter" person was, she was glad she was not in his shoes.

Below, Brother Simon clamped his jaws shut, clearly struggling with something else that he wanted to say, or perhaps feared to say.

Mother Rose saw this and touched his face. "What is it?"

"A few of the scouts have sighted a, um . . . girl with a slingshot among Carter's refugees." He spoke as if prying the words from his mouth. "The descriptions match Sister Margaret."

Everyone gasped and took involuntary steps away from Brother Simon, as if they expected lightning to strike him for some great sin. Suddenly the giant dropped his sledgehammer and caught Brother Simon by the throat, lifting him effortlessly until the reaper stood on the very tips of his shoes.

"We do not speak that name," he growled. Brother Simon's face turned red and then purple as the giant squeezed his hand.

Mother Rose leaned past the giant. "Are you sure, brother?" she asked in a voice that was as cold and hard as a knife blade.

"Y-yes," croaked Brother Simon in a strangled little voice.

The giant glanced at Mother Rose, who studied the choking reaper with narrowed eyes. She touched the giant's arm, a soft brush of fingertips over the landscape of his bulging muscles.

"Brother Alexi . . . ," she said, and the giant released Brother Simon, who collapsed to his knees, gasping and honking as he fought to drag in a breath. The giant, Alexi, picked up his sledgehammer and returned to his station just behind Mother Rose.

The woman reached out and touched Brother Simon's cheek. "Tell me," she said.

"I—I have it from five separate scouts, your holiness," stammered Brother Simon, his throat still raw. "The description matches, even to the markings." As he said this, he touched the pattern of flowers tattooed on his scalp. "Wild roses and thorns."

"Sister Margaret is dead," said Mother Rose in a harsh whisper. "My daughter abandoned her family and her god. She runs with heretics and blasphemers. She is dead." Mother Rose spat this last word. "The gift of darkness is not for her. I hope that her flesh lives on forever. Lost, alone, and damned."

The reaper placed his forehead on the dirt by Mother Rose's feet. "Holiness, forgive this foolish sinner for causing you pain." His body shook with sobs, and Lilah could not tell if his tears were from grief, regret, or fear.

The scene below held for a moment longer, and then Mother Rose bent to the man, kissed his head, and drew him to his feet. "There is no sin in telling the truth, beloved Brother Simon," she said. "Be at peace with the knowledge that the darkness waits to enfold you."

Brother Simon's mumbled reply was too faint for Lilah to hear. He faded back into the crowd. A few of the other reapers touched him lightly on the shoulder.

Lilah sneered at this. When the others thought that he was going to be punished, they'd all stepped back and disowned him; but in the light of Mother Rose's forgiveness, they crowded around to share in the blessing he'd been given. That was not faith, not as Lilah defined it. It was cowardice. These reapers, dangerous as they may be, were ruled by fear as much as by devotion to their strange faith.

Lilah hoped she would not need the knowledge, but she filed it away nonetheless.

A female reaper bowed. Mother Rose said, "Speak freely, Sister Caitlyn."

"Before I heard the darkness call me—"

"All praise the darkness," intoned the others.

"—I lived in Red Rock, near Las Vegas. I worked as a hunter for a group of refugees, and I know the desert and these woods as well as anyone. There are game paths all through here, and from the trail-sign I've seen, I think it's clear that the, uh, person who used to be your daughter is leading Carter's people along those trails. Rumors say that she's lived out here since leaving the grace of the church. If so, then she must know every one of these trails. There are some that aren't easy to spot."

"You think she can help the heretics slip past us?" asked Mother Rose, one eyebrow arched.

Sister Caitlyn flushed, but she lifted her chin. "I know I could do it, and there are some experienced hunters with Carter. The desert is not as empty as people think. There are always places to hide."

Mother Rose nodded. "Thank you, Sister Caitlyn. Your service to our god makes smooth your pathway to the holy darkness."

The young woman bobbed her head. "Holiness, if the person who was your daughter is leading Carter's people south, then I think we have to accept that she's told them about Sanctuary."

Every single one of the reapers gasped in horror.

19

"DON'T MOVE," WHISPERED NIX.

Benny had no intention of moving. He wasn't sure he actually could.

The lion stood in the tall grass, head raised, wind ruffling its thick mane. Its golden eyes were fixed on them. It snarled silently, baring more of its teeth but making no sound. Even the birds in the trees had been stilled by the presence of this great cat.

Nix clutched Eve to her chest, and the little girl moaned softly in her sleep; a defensive, troubled moan.

"Don't provoke it," cautioned Chong.

"Really wasn't planning to," murmured Benny.

"God," said Nix in a hoarse whisper, "there's another one!"

Benny turned to his right and there, just beyond the bristlecone tree, stood another lion. A big female. Easily three hundred and fifty pounds. Tawny and lithe, her whole body rippled with muscular tension.

Benny opened his mouth to try and say something—anything—but before he could, there was movement to his left. A third lion.

And beyond that, another.

Benny felt icy sweat run in lines down his back. He had his *katana* slung over his shoulder, and Chong wore his bokken in a sling at his hip. And Nix had her pistol.

Would that be enough? He doubted it. In fact, he knew for sure that it wouldn't stop more than one of these beasts. Maybe Tom could have managed something, but Tom was dead.

The lions stood watching them. Four pairs of hungry eyes, four cunning minds analyzing the situation, just as Benny was trying to do. He knew that he was losing the battle of wits here as well.

"Benny . . . ?" whispered Chong.

"I'm working on something," Benny lied.

Sure, Nix had the gun, but she was also holding Eve. In order to draw her gun she would have to set Eve down or hand her to someone else. That would certainly wake Eve up, and probably scare her into another fit of loud hysterics. Benny could sympathize. Loud hysterics seemed like the best way to react to this moment.

Tom! What should I do?

Nothing. No voice in his head, no answer.

Benny tried to remember his training. One of the Warrior Smart rules was to always be aware of your resources. And always know your routes into and out of any situation.

Behind them was the ravine filled with zoms. Across the ravine was certain death in the form of a legion of pale flesh-eaters. There were dense forests to hide in, but they were on the other side of the pack of lions.

Crap, Benny thought. *C'mon, Tom . . . now would be a*

really good time for some snazzy battle tactics. How do we get out of this? How do we not die?

But all he heard inside his head were the echoes of his own pounding heart.

20

"Sanctuary is a myth," declared one of the reapers.

"No, it's not," said another reaper. "I heard that the monks there are really scientists."

"I heard that too," said another. "They used to work for the government. Some kind of bioweapons thing."

"No," a female reaper chimed in, "the monks there are supposed to be trying to cure the disease so people can repopulate the world."

"Sinners!" growled a few.

"Before I joined the Night Church," said a man with a Navajo face, "I heard that there are two Sanctuaries. It's supposed to be split down the middle, with the monks on one side and the scientists on the other side. The monks are just taking care of people—like hospice workers used to—and the scientists are trying to cure the plague. The monks are well intentioned but misguided. The scientists are the ones we shouldn't trust."

"That's right," said another of the reapers. "I heard that they had cures for stuff like cancer and all those other diseases, but they kept it all secret because they had deals with pharmaceutical companies. It was all a big moneymaking scam."

Several of the reapers growled agreement with that. Even Lilah had heard some of these rumors. Mostly pre–First Night stuff she'd read in old books and newspapers she had salvaged, but in Mountainside everyone had one kind of conspiracy theory or another. Wriggly Sputters, the town's eccentric mailman, was a walking encyclopedia of such stories, and he frequently said that there was a bunker or lab somewhere out in the Ruin where the government still existed. And in that bunker, the government maintained their power over the other survivors because they had control over cures to every known disease. No one really believed it, but few of the townsfolk stepped up to say that this was total nonsense. Lilah had no opinion on the subject—she cared very little for rumors.

What she heard now, however, was fascinating.

One reaper, a big man with a thick dark beard, laughed at the others. "Oh, please . . . you really think that the government would keep the cure to a doomsday plague to themselves after all that's happened? Why would they let so many people die?"

"Because it's easier to rule a small population than try and control seven billion people," insisted Brother Simon. "C'mon, Eric, that's basic math. They took the best and the brightest and hid them away in these big caves and tunnels, and then they released the Gray Plague. You watch, one of these days they're going to come out and announce a 'cure,' and then everyone who's left will flock to them and hail them as the saviors of mankind. You watch."

"God won't allow that to happen," said Brother Eric.

That quieted the reapers for a moment. It was a hard argument for any of them to knock down.

Brother Simon shook his head. "Sure, that's why we're doing what we're doing. Rather die in glory and join the darkness than live as slaves."

The rebuttal stalled Brother Eric for a moment, and he cut a look to Mother Rose. She gave him a bland smile.

To Simon, Brother Eric said, "Don't believe the myth of Sanctuary. It's a lie told by refugees and heretics to give them false hope and to confuse us."

Before Brother Simon could reply, Mother Rose said, "Sanctuary is not a myth."

They all looked at her in surprise.

"It is a very real place," she continued, "and it is the most dangerous place on earth. Dangerous to everyone living, and dangerous to our own holy purpose."

Eric and Simon and the others shuffled in uncomfortable silence.

"It is a weapon," she said. "A great sword, if you will. A sword by itself is not evil. A sword can be used to slay an enemy, or release a suffering friend into the darkness. A sword can cut ropes that bind the helpless. A raised sword can be a threat or it can be a symbol of leadership." She paused. "Consider our own war with the heretics. Many of them fight us with axes and knives and swords, and we know that in their hands these are tools of evil. And yet, behold the holy weapons you carry. They are sanctified and made pure by the purpose to which they are put. A weapon, my children, is good or evil depending on the intention of whoever holds it."

Lilah surprised herself by agreeing—at least in part—with what this woman said.

The reapers milled around, murmuring and debating this with one another.

Then Mother Rose raised her hand, and every tongue fell silent. "In the actions of heretics the schemes of evil are revealed. We know—we have been told—by the prophet Saint John that in these End Times the struggle to conquer evil will be hard fought. We know this. You, my warrior reapers, have endured fire and blood to send heretics into the darkness. You know, as I know, as Saint John knows, that at the end of our struggles the darkness waits for us. Once we have accomplished our holy purpose on earth, the darkness will embrace us and grant us everlasting peace. There will be no more hunger, no more sickness, no more fear. The darkness is eternal."

"Praise be to the darkness," they intoned.

"But we are all sinners. Everyone who remains clothed in flesh and who pollutes the earth by walking upon it is a sinner. God commanded that all human life should end. He made the dead rise and he opened the pathway to darkness for all who accept this truth."

They stared at her, totally rapt.

"Only two kinds of people are left here in this hell of flesh and pain. The heretics who refuse to accept the truth and the will of our god," said Mother Rose, her voice strident and powerful, "and us—the sanctified soldiers of God. We are the reapers sent among the wayward fields to cut down the infection that is life."

"Praise be to the darkness!" they cried.

"And together we have sent thousands of heretics into the darkness. Thousands."

Lilah could see that most of the reapers were openly weeping, nodding in absolute agreement with everything this woman said.

"And yet we are mortals, we are of the flesh, even if we are filled with the glory of God," she said. "While we remain steadfast to our purpose, we must never forget that we can only glimpse the will of the lord of darkness. We are not arrogant enough to say that we know all of his will."

The reapers said nothing, though Lilah saw some of them frown, as if they were uncertain where this was going.

"We must also be prepared for our holy war to last as long as our god needs it to last," continued Mother Rose, "even if that means that some of us must remain in the flesh."

"But for how long?" begged Brother Simon. "How long until we are all released from the flesh?"

Mother Rose turned fully toward him, and even from her place of concealment Lilah could feel the impact of that woman's stare. It was as hard as a fist and as riveting as a sudden thunderclap.

"As long as God wills it," she said very slowly, spacing each word and filing each syllable to a dagger point. "If he calls us home this minute, we should be ready to open red mouths in our own flesh."

"Praise be the darkness," cried the reapers.

"And if the lord of darkness ordains that we must wither with old age before we are called home, then is that too costly a price for the faithful to pay?"

There was such powerful challenge in her words that every

tongue was stilled, and even Lilah held her breath. Mother Rose stepped close to Brother Simon.

"Answer me, my brother," she said in that cold, cold voice. "If God wills that our holy war last a hundred years, would you spit in God's eye and defy such a request?"

Brother Simon dropped to his knees, weeping and shaking with terror. He struck his own face and tore at his clothes before finally collapsing facedown in the dirt.

"I am the humblest of God's servants," he wailed. "My life is his unto the end of time."

Mother Rose smiled and nodded.

"Thus speak all who truly love the Lord Thanatos," she said, and then turned away.

"Praise be to the darkness!" shrieked the reapers.

Mother Rose raised her hand, and they all fell silent.

"Brother Simon," she murmured, "rise and stand before me."

The wretched reaper staggered to his feet. Blood leaked from his nostrils from his self-inflicted blows.

"The lord of darkness requires much of you," said Mother Rose, then turned to the others. "He requires much of all of you. Will you, by fire and steel, earn your passage into the darkness?"

"Yes!" they screamed. Many of them tore at their own clothes or beat their chests.

Mother Rose raised a hand and pointed a long, slender finger toward the southeast. "Out there, beyond this forest, lies Sanctuary. We cannot let this 'weapon' continue to rest in the hands of heretics and blasphemers. If we do not take control of it, then it will be used against us. Against our god." She paused, and everyone hung on her every word. "Find it. Track down every heretic in these woods. Open red mouths in their flesh, and they will beg to tell you everything about Sanctuary."

"What if none of them know anything?" asked Brother Eric.

"Offer them the choice. Join us or go into the darkness."

The reapers all nodded.

"And if they do know something?" asked a trembling Brother Simon.

Mother Rose's eyes were hooded. "Bring them to me. Anyone who knows where it is. Anyone who knows what it is. Bring them to me, and I will let Brother Alexi coax the truth of this great evil from them, all in the name of Thanatos, all praise his darkness."

Brother Alexi, the towering giant, smiled a cruel smile.

Mother Rose raised her arms wide. "We must take Sanctuary. That, more than anything, is the great task of our time. That is the most sacred of missions assigned to us by God. As long as Sanctuary stands, all that we do, all that we have done, is in jeopardy."

Suddenly every one of the reapers whipped their blades from belts and sheaths. The wicked silver flashed in the sunlight.

"Brother Simon, I charge you to find the team leaders and bring them to me at the Shrine of the Fallen in two hours. The rest of you . . . you know what must be done."

The reapers leaped to their feet, swearing on their lives, their souls, and their salvation. Only the giant remained silent, watching like a granite statue.

Mother Rose studied each of the reapers with her cold, dark eyes.

"To break faith with me is to break faith with God."

The reapers begged her to accept the truth of their promises, and they fell on their faces, scrabbling at the lowest streamers tied to her clothes, kissing the colored cloth, touching it to their closed eyes and to the center of their foreheads. Mother Rose allowed the adoration to go on for twenty full seconds before she held up a hand to stop them. The weeping reapers got to their feet and stood stock-still, their eyes locked on her and that raised hand. Then Mother Rose gave a single dismissive flick of her hand and spoke a single word.

"Go."

The reapers whirled and headed into the woods as fast as they could, howling like demons as they went. On foot and on their motorcycles. In moments they were gone from sight.

Mother Rose waited until even the sound of the motors was gone, and then she exhaled, blowing out her cheeks. The giant set down his sledgehammer and grinned.

"Jeez, you laid it on pretty thick there, Rosie," he said.

"It works every time, Alexi." Mother Rose shrugged. "Besides, you can't dial it down with this crowd or they start thinking for themselves."

"Heaven forbid," he said, and they both laughed.

Brother Alexi came and stood close to Mother Rose. "Are you even sure that Sanctuary exists? We've been to this part of Nevada three times now and we haven't found a trace of it."

"It exists," she said firmly. "I'm positive of it."

"Hey, don't shine me on, sweetie," Alexi growled. "This is me you're talking to, not one of your adoring worshippers."

Mother Rose reached up and stroked his cheek. "I'm serious. I know that it's real, and I know that it's close. Why do you think I've been steering our campaign this way? Why do you think I established the shrine here? Sanctuary is close."

"How do you know? Or is this another of your celestial visions?"

"Don't make fun of me, Alexi," said Mother Rose with just the tiniest bit of coquettishness in her voice. "And no, this is not a vision or anything like that. This is fact. I've known about Sanctuary for three years."

"Okay, but—how?"

Mother Rose paused. "My daughter told me."

"What?"

"Three years ago."

"That's impossible. Margaret took off four years ago and—"

"And she came back," said Mother Rose firmly. "Just the once. She snuck into our camp when we were in Nebraska, the night before we torched Auburn. She said that after she left the Night Church she got really sick. Cholera. She almost died, but then she met some of the Children of God monks, and they took her to a place in Nevada where they cured her."

"Cured her of cholera? What'd they do? Use a time machine and go back to when the pharmacies were still open? C'mon, Rosie, ever since the Fall, if you get something like cholera you die. End of story."

Mother Rose smiled at him. "And yet when she came into my tent she was completely healed. Margaret thought that it was a miracle. She said that there were what she called 'special monks' who had machines and all sorts of chemicals."

"'Special monks'? You mean scientists? Doctors?"

Mother Rose nodded. "She thought that it would change my view of the world, that I'd no longer think there was no hope. She thought that if I knew such things were possible, then I would stop trying to kill everyone."

"Jeez."

"Funny thing is," said Mother Rose, "she was right. Just . . . not in the way she hoped."

"If Margaret snuck into your tent, why'd you let her leave? You could have called a hundred reapers to—"

Mother Rose shook her head. "She's still my daughter."

"So—you let her go?"

"Not exactly."

"Then what—?"

"When I threatened to call Saint John, my darling daughter clubbed me unconscious with my own bottle of wine. When I woke up, she was long gone."

"And you never told anyone?"

"I'm telling you now."

The giant grunted. "Special monks. Jeez. You believe any of that crap?"

"I do. Over the last three years I've kept my ears and eyes open. There have been other people telling similar stories. Unfortunately, these other people were given inoculations and treatments by wandering monks, not at Sanctuary itself. None of them were able to tell me precisely where it is. However, I put enough pieces together to get us this far."

"You really think the reapers saw your daughter?"

She nodded. "I know they did. Sister Cecily already told me. That's why I want to meet with the team leaders. I want Margaret brought to me. Alive and able to talk. She does know where Sanctuary is, and I'm going to . . . encourage her to tell her dear, sweet, loving mother."

"You are one devious broad." He chuckled. "You know Saint John'll skin you alive if he ever gets a whiff of any of this, right?"

"Which is why I have you, dear Alexi." She patted the huge expanse of his chest. "I think it's high time the Night Church had its first martyr."

The giant gave her a cruel leer and hefted his hammer. "I can't wait for the chance to smash that fruitcake into red paste."

"My hero," she said, making a joke out of it and rolling her eyes.

The big man bent and kissed Mother Rose full on the mouth. The kiss was intense and passionate.

Mother Rose pushed him roughly away, but she was laughing as she did so. She took a deep breath and exhaled. "It's coming soon, Alexi, can't you feel it? The war, this killing, it's all going to end, and we are going to own this world."

"What's left of it," he snorted.

She punched him on the chest. "Oh, I think there will be plenty left for us to play with."

They laughed at that, and then turned and walked hand in hand into the forest.

After they were gone, Lilah climbed silently down from her ledge and moved to the spot where the group of reapers had stood. She bent and studied the footprints of each of the people who had just left, identifying them and cataloging them in her mind. Alexi's prints were larger than any prints Lilah had ever seen. He would be very easy to track, though

Lilah knew that if it came to a fight, she would have to use her pistol. There was no way she wanted to tangle with that brute and his sledgehammer. Alexi looked like he could have broken Charlie Pink-eye in half with his bare hands.

She moved along the bank of the stream, backtracking to follow Mother Rose's footprints. They came from the east. Lilah also saw that those prints overlapped several of the tiny prints made by Eve. Mother Rose had clearly come from the east, just as Eve had. As, perhaps, all of these strangers had. Coming from the east, pushing trouble to the west.

Lilah caught movement above her and glanced up to see several vultures circling in the east. If Eve's family was somewhere farther down this creek, then Lilah needed to find them and warn them.

But as she ran, she already believed that it was too late.

21

THE MALE LION STOOD AND WATCHED THEM, BUT HE MADE NO MOVE. The breeze ruffled the dark tangles of his mane but he held his ground, seeming content to be a spectator. It was the females, Benny remembered, who did the hunting. Males, though powerful and aggressive, were lazier. After a science class one day, Nix had dropped a comment about how true this was among humans, too. Benny had wisely avoided replying, but Morgie Mitchell challenged her on it, and the rest of the afternoon was spent at the fishing hole, watching Nix surgically dissect Morgie with her sharp tongue.

Now he watched as one big female took a tentative step toward them. The other two females, both of them considerably smaller than her, crouched and tensed, waiting to pick up their attack cues. Benny remembered something about smaller lionesses in a pack "herding" prey toward the big female, who did the killing. He and his friends had made that job easier for them by standing all in a bunch, with a deadfall behind them and nowhere else to run.

Benny very slowly took his *katana* in a two-handed grip.

"No," warned Chong. "Don't provoke them."

"Dude, they're hungry lions. I'm pretty sure they're already provoked."

The sword did not give Benny much comfort. Fighting lions had never been part of Tom's training. The weapon felt like a dull kitchen knife.

"You got a plan?" he whispered.

"No," croaked Chong. "I'm hoping for an evolutionary jump that will allow me to suddenly grow wings."

It was a dumb time for a joke, but Benny knew his friend was talking to keep from panicking.

Benny tried to view their options like a chess player. The ravine was behind them; the forest was to their left, and to their right was a field of tall grass that washed up against a smaller section of forest, which in turn circled around to join the main woods. However, the smaller lions were between them and whatever meager safety the forest might provide. There did not seem to be any way out.

"Benny," Nix whispered, "why aren't they attacking?"

"Don't encourage them."

"No . . ."

"Zoms," said Chong. "After all these years, they've probably gotten wary of zoms."

"Lions don't attack zoms," said Nix.

"No. As you both pointed out, nothing does." He lightly touched his pocket, and they could hear the clink of his bottles of cadaverine. "We all smell like zombies."

"I'm not wearing any," said Benny. "Neither is Eve."

Chong sighed.

The lioness heard their muted conversation and growled.

"She knows. God," said Nix, adjusting her hold on Eve.

Then a moment later she said, "Chong . . . very slowly, see if you can get a bottle of that stuff out of your pocket. Benny, you get my gun."

"What—?"

"Do it."

Benny lowered his sword as slowly as he had raised it, all the time watching the lionesses. Moving as smoothly as he could, he shifted his weight toward Nix.

Now two of the lions growled.

He froze. Waited. But the lions still seemed uncertain about their prey. Nix and Chong wore cadaverine, and the wind was blowing toward the lions, which meant that the dead-flesh stink of the zoms was being blown their way too.

Great, thought Benny, *zombies might save our lives. Weird.*

He placed his palm around the worn rubber grips of the revolver. He could feel the heat from Nix's body, and there was a slight tremor running through her. She looked calm, but she was clearly as nervous as he was. In a weird way he found that comforting and disturbing at the same time. Benny thought he had begun to understand Nix by the time they left Gameland, but over the intervening weeks he felt she'd changed, and he wasn't sure he quite got this new Nix. She was stronger, much more confident, more decisive, but also more inward and acid-tongued.

"I have it," said Chong, and immediately the carrion stench of fresh cadaverine filled the air.

The closest lion suddenly roared in anger. Chong yelped and dropped the bottle, which bounced and vanished into the grass.

"Oh . . . crap," said Benny and Chong at the same time.

The lioness took a threatening step toward them. Both of the smaller lions lowered themselves into attacking crouches.

"The gun," growled Nix.

Benny took a breath. All he had to do was pull the gun out of the holster, thumb off the safety, point it at the big female, and fire. It could all be done in one smooth move. They'd all practiced it, and even if he wasn't as good a shot as Nix, the target was big.

"Nix—get ready to run," he said. "Ready? Three, two, one!"

He whipped out his hand, gripped the pistol, and yanked as hard as he could.

He was lightning fast, his hand closed perfectly around the pistol butt; he had the strength and the timing exactly right.

But the safety strap was still snapped in place.

The sudden jerk nearly pulled Nix off her feet. She yelped as one hip was yanked upward, and she lost her grip on Eve. Chong dove to catch her, but the action jolted the little girl awake.

Eve saw the lions and screamed.

The lions roared.

The big female suddenly launched herself forward, tearing across the flat ground toward them.

"Nix!" yelled Benny. He let go of the pistol, brought his sword up, and jumped into the path of the charging animal. On either side the smaller lions roared and charged.

I'm going to die.

But then there was a huge *crack!* and Benny felt something burn past his cheek.

The charging lion shrieked and skidded to a stop, shocked

by the sound. Benny couldn't tell if she had actually been hit by Nix's bullet. The other lions froze, looking from the prey to the lioness and back again.

Nix shouldered Benny out of the way as she pointed the smoking pistol at the leader of this pack of killers.

The big female roared in fury.

The smaller lions roared.

Even the male bellowed out a roar of bloodlust and anger.

Only Eve's supersonic shrieks were louder.

The lions began moving forward again, but this time they crept along, angry but wary. Every muscle in their bodies was etched with tension.

In a moment of crystal clarity, Benny realized that even though they might smell like zoms, what they were doing was not zombie behavior. Skilled predators would know this. Would it deter the lions, or would it hasten their own deaths?

Nix wasn't waiting to find out. She fired again, and this time the lioness jerked suddenly to the left, her hunting cry punched into a different shape—high and plaintive. And angry.

Very, very angry.

Once again the lions froze in place.

The two smaller cats were only twenty feet away. A few more leaps and they would have been among Benny and his friends with claws and fangs. However, their attack had been stalled by the sharp noises and the suddenness of their leader's hesitation. They turned to look at her. Benny could see blood on the big cat's shoulder, but if the animal was seriously injured, it didn't show. Still, she did not immediately renew her attack; instead she began pacing in front of them.

Her tail whipped back and forth in irritation, and with each turn she bared her fangs at them.

Nix trembled with mingled fear and effort as she tracked the lion with the gun.

"Benny . . . ," she breathed.

Eve kept screaming.

"Hush!" barked Nix, and her tone was so commanding that it even silenced the watching lions for a moment; and the big female paused for half a heartbeat in her pacing. Eve lapsed into a sniffling, watching, quivering silence, her fists knotted in Chong's shirt.

Nix's lips barely moved as she asked, "What do I do now?"

"Shoot it!" urged Chong.

"I can't. I only have three bullets left. The rest are in my backpack."

Benny swallowed. The pistol was a six-shot revolver, but Tom had taught them to keep only five rounds in the cylinder, with the hammer resting on an empty chamber in case of unexpected jolts. The backpack was hanging on the tree.

"Did you hit it both times?" Benny demanded, squinting to study the animal's fur.

The lion kept pacing, assessing them, eyes narrowed, teeth bared, tail switching with fury.

"No. I missed the first time because someone almost got in the way of my shot."

"Oh," said Benny.

"I got her the second time," continued Nix, "but she doesn't look hurt."

"She's bleeding," Benny said hopefully.

The lion continued to pace.

"She's not even limping. Can't stop four lions with three bullets."

The smaller ones continued to crouch and glare; and the big male was now on his feet. He might not have been part of the hunt, but he looked more than ready to use his mass and muscle to protect his mate.

"Nix," said Chong as he shifted to put his body between Eve and the cats, "try and kill the big one. Use a couple of shots."

"Why?" Benny and Nix both asked.

"It might scare the others off."

Benny thought about the funeral for Morgie's dad. Even though they had just buried a person, everyone hung around the Mitchell house for hours to eat and drink. He had an image of the other lions doing the same right now, and he did not particularly want to be grief snacks for hunting cats that shouldn't even be on this continent in the first place.

"No," he said. "Don't." He didn't explain his reasoning.

"I have to do something," said Nix, and now the tremble he had felt in her body was evident in her voice.

The hunting cat stopped pacing and stood directly in front of Nix. Amber eyes burned into Nix's green ones. There was awful promise in those eyes. Revenge for pain, death to feed her family, satisfaction for frustration.

"Uh-oh," murmured Nix, and she nervously adjusted her grip on the gun. Sweat ran along her arms.

The lioness lowered herself into a crouch, her muscles springing into sharp definition as she prepared for a charge that a popgun was not going to stop.

A Fall of Angels

Benny suddenly stepped forward, putting himself between her and the lioness. "Listen to me," he said between gritted teeth. "I'm going to charge them. Maybe I can get one or two of them. As soon as I go, you run. Go into the ravine if you have to. Zoms are easier than—"

"No!" snapped Nix. "Damn it, Benny, you're not Tom and you can't do this."

"I didn't say I was Tom," he barked.

The lions growled.

Chong said, "Will you two shut up?"

The big cat screeched her hunting cry and attacked. Her massive body became a tan blur and ran directly at Chong and Eve.

"No!" Benny and Nix both screamed. Nix shoved Benny out of the way and snapped off a wild shot.

Then something whipped between Benny and Nix and flew across the clearing toward the lioness. Benny had a splintered second's glimpse of it. A cylinder of bright red paper that trailed a plume of thin gray smoke. It struck the ground between him and the lioness, bounced once . . .

. . . and exploded.

BANG!

The flash was as bright as the sun and as loud as a gunshot. But it was a . . .

Benny's stunned mind scrambled for the word.

. . . a firecracker?

The lion hissed in fear and confusion, looking wildly around to find this new attacker.

Then a second firecracker dropped out of nowhere and exploded before it even hit the ground. The bang tore a howl of anger and fear from the smaller cats, and they scrambled backward, falling, snarling, twisting away.

A third firecracker snapped through the air and burst inches from the lioness's face.

Her shriek was earsplitting.

Another and another detonated in the air around the lioness.

She tore deep gouges in the ground as she spun around and ran flat out for the tall grass. Despite her wounded shoulder, she passed the smaller cats like they were standing still, and even the powerful male ran in the dust kicked up by her passage.

In seconds the four lions had dwindled to specks in the distance and then were gone, totally out of sight.

Benny stood with his sword forgotten in his hand, mouth open. Nix and Chong were as still as statues. Benny heard a soft footfall to his right, and he turned to see a figure stand up out of the tall grass a dozen feet behind where one of the lions had crouched. A stranger whose presence had not been noticed by anyone, human or feline, who had moved with all the silent stealth of Tom or Lilah.

It was a girl. A teenager. Beautiful, tall, and wild.

But it was not Lilah.

This girl was maybe seventeen, with large brown eyes, a small mouth, and a scalp that had been completely shaved to reveal a complex series of tattoos. Wild roses and thorny vines. She had multiple silver rings pierced through the upper parts of both ears, and a silver necklace from which hung an old-fashioned skeleton key. She wore tattered camouflage shorts, sneakers that were worn to threads, and a vest that was buttoned up over, apparently, nothing else. A Marine Corps belt was strapped around her hips, and it supported a leather-handled hunting knife, a whistle, and a lumpy pouch of what Benny guessed were stones. Crisscrossed over her torso were bandoliers—not of bullets, but of firecrackers.

The girl held a slingshot in her hands, and there was a sharp-edged rock seated in its leather pouch.

The rock was aimed at Nix's throat.

"I think y'all better lower that gun," said the stranger. "Right now."

"Well," said Chong with a disgusted sigh, "I guess it's fair to say that this day can't get any worse."

The girl smiled a wicked smile and pulled the bands back so hard that they creaked with tension. "Yes, it surely can."

LILAH RAN ALONG EVE'S BACK-TRAIL AS FAST AS SHE COULD.

With every step, though, she felt her heart slip another notch and sink lower in her chest. The sky above her was filled with vultures.

Where were Eve's parents?

She rounded a bend in the stream and skidded to a stop, whipping the spear up into a combative grip. There, right in front of her, was a clearing in which a camp had been set up. Crude tents and a screen of cut shrubs, a cook fire in a sheltered pit. Clothes and gear.

All of it scattered and torn.

All of it bloody.

Half a dozen vultures huddled around a twisted tangle of rags that had once been a human being.

Lilah held her ground, watching before acting. To rush the scene and chase off the ugly birds would be like sending up a flag to signal her presence. Hunters and killers both watch for disturbances in nature.

She squatted down and tried to look under the carrion birds.

The body on which they were feasting was that of an old man. She could see just enough of its shape and a spill of white hair.

Too old, probably, to be Eve's father.

The rest of the camp was empty. No other bodies. However, it was clear that there had been a fight here. There were blade marks on the surrounding trees, shrubs were trampled, and there was far too much blood to have come from one feeble old man.

Where were the others? Had they fled the fight? Or had they died and reanimated before the vultures could reduce them to scraps of flesh and bone?

No way to tell. Not without a thorough search, and Lilah did not think she had the time for that. Not with all those reapers in the woods.

Time was burning away. She would have to abandon this search and get back to her friends. If this camp belonged to Eve's family, then it was already too late. If not . . . ?

"Chong," she murmured. Chong was a town boy, and those reapers looked fierce. They were engaged in some kind of holy war. Lilah had no intention of getting involved in that, but at the same time, she did not have a clue as to how those reapers would react to Chong, Benny, and Nix. Would they all be left alone as outsiders?

Lilah doubted it. Her instincts were screaming at her to get back.

She backed away from the clearing and made a wide circle around the scene of carnage. As she did so, she caught sight of a ridge of white rocks just past a line of bushy pines. Lilah frowned at them. The rocks were unnaturally bright, almost like they had been painted with whitewash. Were they rocks or a structure?

She ran through the trees toward them, intending to cut past them and head west again.

However, the closer she got, the more her frown deepened, because it became quickly apparent that they were not rocks at all. Nor was it an old building.

Lilah slowed from a jog to a walk, and as she emerged from the trees she stopped stock-still. Her mouth dropped open in shock.

"No . . . ," she whispered.

The thing lay there. Huge. Ugly. Impossible.

The thing was perched precariously on a shelf of rock that overlooked a long drop into a cleft that was thick with dark scrub pines and creeper vines. Someone had taken red paint—or perhaps blood—and written these words on the broad, white side of this impossible thing:

WOE TO THE FALLEN

Nearby, on a mound of dirt, three bodies in ragged military-style uniforms were hung on wooden posts. Zoms. They thrashed against the ropes that bound them.

Lilah turned quickly and looked back the way she'd come, staring at the woods as if she could still see Nix and the others. Indecision tore at her. Should she tell her friends about this, or steer them away from it and never say a word about it?

She thought about what it would do to Nix and Benny. Even to Chong.

Lilah shut her eyes for a moment and ground her teeth

in helpless frustration. It was so much simpler living alone. You never had to hurt anyone you cared about, because there was no one to care about. Telling her friends about this would be exactly like stabbing them through the heart.

She lingered there, thinking it through, wrestling with it, aching with doubt.

Then a voice behind her said, "There's one!"

Lilah instantly leaped to one side, twisting in midair to land facing the way she had come, her spear ready in her strong hands.

Thirty feet down the path she had just come stood a pair of men dressed in black with red streamers tied to their clothes.

Reapers.

Lilah gaped.

Not at the reapers, but at the figures who milled behind them.

Zoms!

There were at least a half dozen of the living dead—men, women, even a child. All newly dead, some of them glistening with blood that had not yet dried.

Lilah's heart sank. Now she knew what had happened to the other people who had camped here. The zoms moaned in freshly awakened hunger. They staggered through the tall grass, hands reaching awkwardly toward her, completely ignoring the two reapers as they shuffled past.

"Hey, girl!" yelled one of the reapers. "Drop your spear and give yourself up to the darkness. It wants you. The darkness wants to open the red door in your flesh. Why fight it? The darkness is beautiful. The darkness is eternal. The darkness is yours if you stop fighting and allow it to enfold you."

The words had a cadence like scripture, but they were from no holy book Lilah had ever read—and in her solitude, she had read most of them. These words were intended to coax, but instead they made the hands that held her spear tighten with anger.

"Come on, kid," said the second reaper. "Accept the truth. The darkness wants to take you. The darkness wants to take us all. It's the will of God."

Lilah had never been much for profanity, but as the men continued to call for her to open herself to the darkness, she responded with a series of phrases she'd learned at Gameland. It shocked the men to silence.

The dead kept coming.

Fifteen feet away now.

Lilah debated pulling her Sig Sauer. She had no doubt that she could put all the zoms down as well as the two men with less than a full magazine.

It would be noisy, though, and Lilah liked the quiet.

Instead she gave her spear a single arrogant twirl and charged straight at the zoms.

And the dead rushed at her on stiff and clumsy legs. All but one. A tall woman whose throat had been slashed rushed ahead of the pack, arms outstretched, mouth wide, racing toward Lilah.

A fast zom.

The running zombie grabbed for her, and Lilah uttered a feral growl as she jumped left and used the short leap to channel power into a vicious cut that took the zom across the upper chest. The heavy blade sheared through one arm, part of the chest, and clean through the dead woman's spine; and the shock of the powerful blow reverberated through Lilah's entire body. The creature instantly dropped into a boneless heap that would never move again.

Lilah's heart was racing as adrenaline flooded through her bloodstream.

The slower zoms had reached her now and attacked in a ragged line. Two reached her first.

Lilah spun and swept the spear low, cutting the first one's leg off at the knee; then she continued the swing and brought the weighted opposite end around in an overhand sweep that crushed the second zombie's skull. Before it even had a chance to fall, Lilah pivoted and used the same metal knob to end the torment of the child zom.

Three down in two seconds.

She kicked out at one zom as it tried to dive for her thigh, its teeth clacking in the air. The kick jolted it to a stop in a half crouch, and she swept the knob up under its chin so hard and fast that its head snapped back, breaking its neck.

"Hey!" yelled one of the men, but Lilah ignored him. She'd seen no firearms on them. They could wait.

A cold hand closed on her shoulder, knotting her shirt in dead fingers as it sought to pull her backward toward its bloody teeth. Lilah went with the pull, but as she did so she spun her body in a violent pirouette. The torsion bent the zom's arm backward so fast that bones splintered and the creature lost its grip. Lilah rammed the shaft of her spear across its throat and drove it into the last of the zoms, knocking them both to the ground. She thrust the blade into the neck of one, severing the spinal cord; then tore the blade free, twirled the spear again, and brought the heavy knob down on the last zombie's skull.

There was a pulpy *whack* and then the trail was still.

She turned toward the two reapers, who stood where they had been, their eyes goggling, mouths hanging open in total shock.

Lilah smiled at them.

And charged.

It had taken her five seconds to destroy the six zoms.

It took two seconds to cut both reapers down.

They reeled away, each of them clutching identical red lines across their throats. They gagged. They tried to speak, perhaps to protest the impossibility of everything that had just happened; but neither of them would ever speak their confusion. They dropped to their knees. One fell forward onto his face. The other toppled backward.

In the trees above them, the monkeys screamed in panic at the smell of death and blood.

Lilah stood above the dead reapers, her chest heaving, sweat glistening on her cheeks and throat.

Her heart sank, though. Without wanting to, she had taken sides in the war between the reapers and the people they called heretics. Which meant it was her war now.

Would it get her killed?

Would it get Chong killed?

She looked down at the two men, wondering if they would reanimate. Or had the zombie plague truly changed?

Then a cloud moved above, and fresh sunlight blazed on the big white thing behind her on the edge of the cliff. She turned and stared at what she had thought was a line of white rocks.

"God," she murmured. This was going to really kill the others.

Between this and the thought that she had dragged her friends into someone else's war, her entire mind was in turmoil.

She never saw the shape that stepped out of the woods behind her.

It, however, saw her, and its lips peeled back from jagged teeth as it charged at her. Not in a slow, shambling gait—death raced at Lilah at incredible speed.

"Do as she says," growled a voice behind them, and Benny, Nix, and Chong wheeled around to see a man come stalking out of the woods beyond the bristlecone tree. He was tall and middle-aged, with black hair tied back in a ponytail and bloody bandages around one thigh and his forehead.

He stopped forty yards away and raised a shotgun to his shoulder, the barrel pointed at Benny's head.

"Riot," barked the man, "take their weapons and gear."

The slingshot girl—Riot—gave a short, harsh laugh. "Y'all heard the man. Drop all the goodies and maybe y'all will still be sucking air come sundown."

Benny did not drop his sword, but instead moved to stand in front of Eve.

"Ry-Ry!" cried the little girl.

Riot looked past Benny. "You okay, squirt?"

"Ry-Ry . . . where's—?" Then the little girl saw the man and shrieked with joy. "Daddy!"

Chong said, "'Daddy'?"

The man's face went white, but his eyes hardened. "Take your filthy hands off my daughter!"

"Whoa, mister!" said Benny. "Everything's cool here and—"

"I won't tell you a second time," growled the man as he took a threatening step forward.

Nix swung the pistol toward him and met his eyes with her own uncompromising stare. "You pull that trigger, mister, and I'll kill you where you stand."

The man snorted. "You're at a long range for a pistol, girl."

"And you're at a long range for a shotgun. Let's see who's left standing to take the next shot."

Benny said, "And you really want to fire a shotgun with a kid here?"

They were all in bad positions. Benny felt the moment becoming incredibly fragile. If someone pulled a trigger, probably everyone would die.

The man's face was flushed, and fury seethed in his eyes as he looked from them to Eve and back again. "Why can't you freaks just let us be?"

"What are you talking about?" barked Nix. "How are we bothering you?"

A third stranger came hurrying out of the woods behind the clearing, and once more Benny realized that he and his friends were boxed in.

The newcomer was a woman wearing a hooded sweatshirt that was smeared with bright blood. She held an ax in her hands, and its blade glistened with red.

Blood, whispered Tom inside Benny's mind. *Zoms don't bleed.*

I know, Benny told him. *So who'd she chop with that thing?*

Behind Benny, Eve cried, "Mommmeeeee!"

Chong tried to hold Eve, but Riot shot a stone at Chong, missing his nose by half an inch. Eve broke free and ran like lightning across the clearing toward the woman.

The woman fairly shrieked. "EVE! Oh my God . . . Evie!"

She dropped her ax and swept Eve into her arms.

"Okay," said Chong, "this is heartwarming and all that, but if they're here, then where's Lilah?"

Benny cut a cautious look around, but there was no sign of the Lost Girl.

The man with the shotgun grinned at the reunion between his daughter and wife, but he kept his shotgun pointed at Benny. They were thirty yards away, and Benny took a step toward him, raising his hand.

"Hey, mister, we're glad to—"

"You freeze right where you are, boy," barked the man in a voice that was hard and flat. An uncompromising voice. "If you reaper scum harmed a hair on my little girl's head, I'll see you dead—and it won't be no ticket to paradise. No sir, it'll be slow and ugly. Tell me I'm lying."

Benny froze, and his smile flaked away like peeling paint in a stiff wind. "No," he said neutrally, "I think you're telling the absolute truth. But you aren't making any sense. I think we need to—"

"I got nothing more to say to you."

"'Reaper scum'?" echoed Chong. "I'm real certain I don't like the sound of that."

"Benny—?" began Nix, but Benny cut in.

Under his breath he said, "Keep your gun on him."

Benny shifted position again, putting himself squarely between Nix and Riot.

"Sarah," said the man with the shotgun, "is she hurt? Did they do anything to her?"

"I'm okay, Daddy," began Eve, but the man growled at her.

"Hush, girl."

The woman—Sarah—did a quick but thorough examination of her daughter, then pulled her into another hug. "She's fine, Carter. They didn't hurt her."

"They didn't have time," sneered Riot. "I told you we'd find her."

"Of course we didn't hurt her," snapped Nix. "We rescued her."

"Oh yeah," mocked Riot, "I'm sure."

"What's the truth of it, Evie?" said Carter. "None of your pretend stories now. Did these people hurt you? Did they touch you?"

Eve shook her head. Her eyes were wide and filled with doubt and confusion.

"It's true, mister," insisted Benny. "She was being chased by zoms, and we rescued her. She's fine."

Riot edged forward, tightening her aim at Nix. "Rescued, huh? Don't buy that bullcrap, Carter. I'll bet my dear ol' mom sent them to grab Eve so they could sacrifice her. That's just the kind of thing she'd like."

"Sacrifice?" gasped Benny. "What are you, nuts or something? It was like I said. Eve was being chased and—"

"We know she was being chased," cut in Riot. "How stupid do you think we are?"

"You really want an answer to that, baldy?" asked Nix coldly.

"Well, ain't you got a smart mouth?" said Riot, grinning a nasty little grin. "I'd love to kick it off your face."

"Try it. I don't mind shooting girls, either."

Riot's grin flickered.

"She's not joking," Benny said, and pointed his sword at her. "Neither am I. Don't try it."

"Ooooh," said Riot, "fierce."

"Get stuffed," said Nix. She focused her attention on Carter. "Eve's fine because of us, mister. I don't know who you think we are, but you're wrong."

"Reapers don't open their mouths unless they plan to lie," warned Riot. "Believe me, I know."

"We're not reapers, whatever they are," said Nix angrily. "We're travelers. We're looking for something."

"Looking for what? The darkness?" demanded Carter in a tone that was heavy with disgust. Riot gave a harsh laugh of agreement.

"Darkness?" echoed Benny, but Nix ignored him.

"We're looking for an airplane," she said. "A jet."

Carter's expression changed from open hostility to doubt. He shot a look at Sarah, who frowned.

"They saw it too," she said. "Carter—they saw it too!"

"You saw it?" demanded Nix, her tone suddenly urgent. "When? Where?"

"Don't say anything," warned Riot, but Sarah ignored her.

"The last time we saw it, it was heading south."

"Last time?" echoed Chong.

"You've seen it more than once?" Nix gasped.

"Sarah, hush," said Carter. "This isn't the time or place."

"But, Carter—look at them. They don't look like reapers. Look at their clothes. No wings. No tassels or anything. And they don't have the mark."

As Sarah said this, she touched her head, but Benny did not understand the reference. *What mark?*

"Enough!" growled Carter.

"Look, guys," said Benny, "I think we should all chill out and talk about this. No one wants to hurt anyone here—"

"Speak for yourself," said Riot with quiet menace.

"—and it sounds like we have a lot to talk about," Benny concluded, pasting on his best "aw shucks, we're all friends" smile. The kind that used to get him a bottle of pop at Lafferty's General Store, even when he had no ration dollars.

Carter wasn't impressed. "If you want to talk, then tell the young miss there to put her gun down."

"The young miss says, 'Bite me,'" replied Nix. "You put your gun down first and then we'll see."

"Not a chance," said Carter, and Riot gave a snigger of agreement.

"Look, how about you both put your guns down at the same time," suggested Chong. "On a count of three, okay? One, two, three . . ."

They ignored him.

"This is stupid," Benny yelled. "Nobody here wants to hurt anyone else."

"Don't bet on it," said Riot.

"Absolutely," agreed Nix.

"They're reapers, Carter," said Riot. "Maybe they even have some quads hidden somewhere."

"What's a quad?" Chong asked, but no one heard him.

"They don't look like reapers," repeated Sarah.

"Then they're new converts," countered Riot. "They could have taken the vow but haven't yet done the ceremony of purity. But it doesn't matter. They had Eve!"

"Yeah, we were keeping her safe," replied Nix. "What were you doing to protect her? Letting her run around in woods full of wild animals and zoms?"

"Yeah, nice try, Freckles," snorted Riot. "C'mon, Carter, don't let her scramble your grits. My mother's people are gonna be here soon. These punks are scouts or something equally squirrelly. Let's put 'em down before we get overrun."

Carter's face was rigid with tension, but there was doubt in his eyes. "Sarah—?"

Eve's mother looked up, and if Benny was expecting her to be the voice of reason, he was dead wrong. "She's right, Carter, we can't take any chances. Don't hurt them, but take their weapons and gear. Then we have to go. We have to get to Sanctuary and—"

"Jesus! Hush your mouth, woman!" screeched Riot.

"Sarah," Carter said with quiet horror. "What have you done?"

The woman clapped a hand to her mouth and her face went dead pale. "Oh God," she said. "I'm sorry . . . I'm so sorry. I didn't mean to . . ."

Carter nervously shifted the shotgun barrel between Nix and Benny, as if trying to decide which of them should die first. Or maybe, thought Benny, trying to decide which one would be easier to kill without losing too much of his own soul. Benny did not believe that this man wanted to fire that gun, but he looked desperate and shoved to the edge of panic. Benny knew full well how panic could inspire the worst possible choices.

Riot's face hardened. "Now we got no choice at all, Carter."

In a voice loud enough for only Benny and Chong to hear, Nix muttered, "Screw this."

"Nix," warned Benny too quietly for the strangers to hear, "don't do anything crazy."

"Wouldn't dream of it," she murmured.

And then she fired at Carter.

24

Lilah had no chance.

She heard the scuff of a footfall on stone behind her, but before she could turn the thing slammed into her. Even then she tried to dodge, but pain exploded along her side and suddenly she was flying through the air.

Blood trailed behind her like the tail of a comet, spattering the leaves and bristles of the shrubs. Her spear spun away into the weeds. Then Lilah struck the ground on the edge of the cracked shelf of rock, and the impact knocked all the air from her lungs.

She lay there, firestorms of pain racing up and down her spine. She clung to the edge of the shelf and to the edge of consciousness. Blood pooled under her. Every part of her was wrapped in pain. She tried to get up, tried to see what it was that had attacked her, but fresh pain detonated in her lower neck and back. She collapsed down with a helpless cry.

The thing wheeled toward her and grunted in awful hunger.

Lilah craned her neck and stared at it. At the impossibility of it.

It was a massive wild boar. Five hundred pounds of muscle and hunger. Brutish, ugly, with a barrel chest, short legs, and wicked tusks.

But that was not the worst part of it.

Flesh hung in bloodless strips from the massive shoulders. Its teeth were caked with rotted meat. It stank of rot and death.

It was impossible.

And yet . . . it was a zombie.

Lilah screamed.

The monster roared with terrible hunger as it charged.

25

Nix's shot galvanized everyone into motion.

Carter flung himself to the ground, twisting and firing as he fell. Nix dropped down to avoid the buckshot, but the pellets went high and wild, chasing birds screaming from the trees.

Sarah clutched Eve to her chest and dove into the tall grass.

Chong staggered backward from the blast and stood teetering on the edge of the ravine, his arms pinwheeling, while below him the zoms let out a renewed moan of hunger.

Benny had to drop his sword to grab him, but he spun fast and flung Chong with unintended force straight into Riot. They slammed down on the ground and vanished into the brush.

For a moment only Benny was left standing.

Then Nix and Carter both rose to their knees, guns coming up. Benny dove for his sword and skidded five feet on his chest.

"Don't!" he cried, but Nix fired again, forcing Carter to dive sideways again.

Benny heard a *thwop* sound, and something whipped

through the air a finger's width from his cheek. He saw Riot lying on her side with the slingshot in her hands. She'd aimed at Chong, who was already on his feet, but the stone missed him and almost hit Benny.

Riot's hands moved with incredible speed as she fished out another stone and seated it into the sling.

"Chong—run!" yelled Benny, but Chong was already in motion, cutting away from them toward the nearest stand of pinyon trees. His only weapon was a wooden bokken, and that was the wrong thing to bring to this fight. Benny was relieved to see Chong dive into the shadowy woods.

Carter got to his knees again and put his shotgun to his shoulder.

"Riot!" he yelled. "Get out of the way."

Benny turned to see that Riot was aiming her next rock at Nix. Benny dove into Nix, knocking her out of the way. Riot's stone hit hard on his hip, and it hurt like hell.

He landed sloppily but got up fast, bringing his sword up.

Riot snarled at him, and there was murder in her eyes as she fished out another stone.

"Don't," he warned.

She drew back the sling—and froze.

Carter and Sarah and Eve froze too, all of them staring at the eastern woods, their eyes wide.

Benny heard it then.

The motor sound he'd heard earlier.

It was back. Louder.

And it was heading their way, closing fast from at least three different points in the forest.

"Reapers!" screamed Sarah.

Riot shot a brief look at Benny and Nix, and then she spun on her heels and ran full tilt into the woods, following the same direction Chong had taken.

"What's going on?" begged Nix, her pistol still held out in a two-handed grip.

Carter began backing away from the forest, edging toward a thin stand of trees due south. Sarah rose, clutching Eve to her chest; the eyes of both were wild with fear.

"Nix!" called Eve, reaching a hand toward her.

For a split second, Carter and Sarah looked at their daughter's face and then across the field to Nix and Benny.

Carter lowered his shotgun.

"Run," he said.

The motor sounds were everywhere now, getting louder and louder.

"RUN!" screamed Sarah.

She and Carter whirled and ran for the trees.

Benny glanced at Nix.

The ravine was behind them and there were woods all around the clearing.

Nix pointed her pistol at the closest of the motor sounds. "What is that?"

"I don't know," Benny said, pushing her arm down. "But let's not find out. Let's go."

They backed up several steps, then together they turned and ran as hard as they could for the forest.

LILAH TRIED TO PULL HER PISTOL AS THE MONSTER RACED TOWARD HER.

But it was too fast and too close.

She tried to get up, but her left side was a furnace of heat and blood. Her leg buckled, and she fell back.

Over the edge of the cliff.

The darkness below swallowed her—body, screams, and all.

27

LOU CHONG RAN FOR HIS LIFE.

It was, he realized with some despair, something he had to do way too often.

Chong was lean and fit, but he was not a good runner. He felt that his body was better suited to climbing a tree with a good book in his back pocket, wading out into slow streams with a fishing pole, or sitting at a picnic table eating apple pie and discussing either fishing or books. Eluding hot pursuit had never been on his list of things to enjoy before he got old. Neither, for that matter, was fighting zoms in a ravine, staring down the mouths of lions, or looking into the barrels of shotguns.

Nevertheless, he ran.

This forest was sparse compared to the denser woods back home in central California. Even so, Chong managed to use the meager vegetation for cover as he put as much distance as he could between himself and the craziness back on the field.

He paused only once, to gape in wonder at the men and women on motorized machines who came tearing out of nowhere.

Jeez, he thought dryly, *Nix is going to love this.*

And not for the first time—or even the first time that day—Chong wished that Tom was still here.

But . . .

The motor sounds faded a bit, and Chong felt a splinter of relief that those newcomers were not chasing him. The others, though . . . Riot, Carter, and Sarah. They could be anywhere out here, and Riot had already demonstrated that she was capable of moving like a ghost through the forest and tall grass.

Moving like Lilah.

Chong wanted to find her more than anything in the world.

In the far distance he could see a ridge of rocks that were eye-hurtingly white, but he decided not to go that way. With his dark jeans and shirt, he'd be like a black fly on white linen.

Instead he headed along a ridge of red rocks that cut through the forest and seemed to curve around to the east. Lilah probably went east to find Eve's parents, so Chong angled that way.

When he was a mile into the woods, Chong dropped into a low squat and listened. He was a very good listener, with sharp senses that he'd honed for months as a tower guard on the fence line between Mountainside and the Ruin. Tom had helped him refine his understanding of the information his senses offered to him. The difference between the rustle of branches in a variable breeze and the sounds of someone—or something—moving stealthily through the brush. The difference between the moan of wind through rusted metal on a deserted farm or abandoned car and the hungry cry of a distant zom. He made his body go absolutely still as he listened.

The motor sounds were far away, and the woods around

him were still. The forest, though, is never silent; nature never totally holds its breath. There are always small sounds—insects and animals, the subtle noises made as the temperature changes throughout the day, causing wood to expand and contract. He listened for sounds that shouldn't be there.

There was nothing.

Until there was something.

Chong tilted his head to try and catch the ghost of a sound. He almost dismissed it because it was in time with the breeze, but then he listened closer. No, not in time with the breeze; just behind it. He nodded to himself. What he heard was the sound a careful person made when they were trying to move with the breeze, but they were doing it slightly wrong. They were waiting for the wind to stir the branches and then moving with the swaying brush; but that wasn't the way Tom had taught them.

"You have to be warrior smart," Tom once told them. "And a smart warrior looks ahead. Watch for the wind as it comes toward you, look into the distance and see how the foliage moves. The wind is like a wave rolling in. If you want to hide in its sound and movement, then time your movement so that you are starting to move as the wind reaches you. Don't chase the wind—let it push you."

Don't chase the wind, thought Chong. That was exactly what he was hearing.

He held his position.

Then he caught a whiff of something. At first he recoiled, thinking that it was the rotting stench of a zom, but he shook his head and took another sniff at the odor on the breeze. It was similar to the spoiled-meat smell of cadaverine or putrescence.

The sounds were louder now. Whoever was sneaking

through the woods was coming his way. Panic jumped in Chong's chest, but he fought it down. He looked around and studied the woods for a couple of good choices for escape routes if the stranger came directly toward him. The best route was to his right, a stony path shaded by chokeberry and bitterbrush shrubs. He edged toward it, ready to bolt.

A man suddenly emerged from the woods twenty feet in front of Chong.

But he was facing the other way. Chong froze and stared at the stranger.

And strange he was.

The man was short and broad-shouldered, with huge biceps like soccer balls, a freakishly overdeveloped chest, and almost no neck at all. He wore the same black clothes as the people on the motorbikes, with red streamers fluttering in the sluggish breeze.

The man started to turn, and Chong slipped soundlessly behind a bush, certain that he hadn't been spotted.

A pair of angel wings had been carefully embroidered on the man's shirt, and around his neck was a chunky steel chain from which hung a slender silver whistle. Chong recognized it at once.

A dog whistle. Benny was right.

What drew Chong's eye, though, and sent a thrill of icy fear through him, was the thing the man carried in his massive fists. A long, twisted wooden handle from which a wicked blade curved like the fang of some great dragon.

A scythe.

Chong remembered the word Riot had used.

Reapers.

His mouth went totally dry.

The big man stood listening to the forest, much as Chong had done. His face was harsh and grim, but then a small smile formed on his thin-lipped mouth.

"No sense hiding," said the reaper as he brought the scythe up and made a slow, deliberate cut through the afternoon air. "Hiding will only make it hurt more."

SHE DRIFTED IN DARKNESS.

Lost.

The Lost Girl.

That was what people called her.

Lost.

For years the travelers in the Ruin believed that she was a myth. Or a ghost.

In the towns, she was a campfire tale. Something used to frighten children.

There were a dozen versions of the Lost Girl story, and in each one of them she died. Sometimes the zoms got her. Sometimes it was crazed loners. Sometimes it was her own bleak despair.

The Lost Girl died, though, in every version of the legend.

When Benny, Nix, and Tom brought her to Mountainside and she learned about those stories, she laughed. They were stupid stories. Silly.

A teenage girl, living alone? With no one to protect her?

No, they all said. Couldn't happen. She would die.

The Lost Girl. Dead according to everyone who spun a tale about her. It was impossible for a girl to survive out in the

Ruin alone. Everyone knew that. There were too many dangers. Zoms and wild animals and bounty hunters. There were crazed loners and cannibals and a thousand different kinds of disease.

Stupid stories, she told herself. Except at night, when she thought about them in the private darkness of her bedroom, in the one place where she was safe enough to be weak. That was when she cried. That was when she believed that she was living on borrowed time—alive only because death had considered her too insignificant to pause long enough to collect.

Except that death collected everyone. Death is like that. Relentlessly efficient.

Borrowed time is no place to live.

Lilah had often feared that they were right.

Now she was sure they were.

That was the only thought that would fit into her head as she lay suspended in darkness.

She remembered the boar. Feral, massive. Four hundred pounds at least.

Both dead and deadly.

But animals can't become zoms. It doesn't work like that.

Unless, somehow, it does.

The Lost Girl should not be alive.

Unless, somehow, she was.

For now.

It felt like she was falling and yet not falling. Pinpricks of pain held her aloft, and for a long time she could not understand that.

Little points of pain all along her body. Except for her hands, which hung down into the black well of nothingness.

Above her, she heard the grunt of the boar and the scuff

of its hoof on the edge of the rocky shelf. Then dirt and loose stones tumbled down, striking her face and chest and stomach and thighs. She heard a rustling sound as the debris fell past her. It sounded like foliage, like pine boughs and vine leaves being pelted by rain.

She forced one eye to open. It was smeared with blood, and what little she saw was filtered through red. She blinked and blinked until tears ran pink from the corners of her eyes. Above her—thirty feet at least—the snout of the dead boar protruded over the edge of the stone shelf. That meant that . . .

Panic flared in her heart, and it brought with it a fresh burst of adrenaline, and with adrenaline came clarity.

She knew where she was.

She was suspended in a tangle of dense trees and tall shrubs, caught in the midst of her fall. Temporarily held, as if fate was waiting for her to wake up and pay attention as death made his call to collect her.

Lilah tried to move, to lift her arms, and suddenly the whole assembly of branches shifted with her. Pinecones rained down on her. Angry birds fled the trees.

How far down was the ground? The cleft was so choked with foliage that she had not been able to see the bottom. It could be six feet below her. It could be sixty. She wished she knew how badly she was hurt. Or where.

In all the tales, in every variation, the Lost Girl died.

Lilah closed her eyes.

"Chong," she said hoarsely.

Or, she meant to say "Chong."

What she said was, "Tom."

Benny and Nix made it to the woods with no time to spare. The motor noise roared as loud as thunder as they dove beneath the canopy of leaves and pine needles.

Nix led the way, and Benny was a half step behind her. He cut a quick look over his shoulder and saw something that made him grab Nix's arm and jerk her to a stop.

"Look!" he said in an urgent whisper.

They crouched down behind a thick bush and stared with slack-jawed amazement at something neither of them had ever seen.

Ten people came tearing into the clearing, all of them dressed in black clothes tied with red streamers, all of them heavily armed . . . and each of them on four-wheeled motorized vehicles.

"Oh my God," breathed Nix, gripping Benny's arm. "What—what—?"

The machines were not cars or trucks, and not quite motorcycles, either. Benny fished for the name and scraped up the initials ATV. He thought they stood for "all-terrain vehicle," and that was probably right, because these machines roared easily over the uneven surface of the field. They each had four fat rubber tires and a kind of saddle for the driver. The machines were spattered with mud, but some colored metal shone through. Different colors for each—blue and green and other shades. A basket or duffel bag was lashed to the back of each, and the handles of swords and axes sprouted from many. The roar of the machines was unnaturally loud—and even in that moment of tension, it struck Benny how quiet his world was and how loud the old world of machines must have been.

The presence of these machines was like a punch to the head.

"Are we seeing this?" he asked.

"Yes," she said in a fierce tone. She turned to him, her eyes alight. "First the jet and now this. Benny—the old world isn't dead. Everything wasn't destroyed."

Benny nodded, but he studied the figures on the machines and didn't like what he was seeing. He remembered the word Riot had used. *Quads.* This had to be what she was referring to.

The quads zoomed across the field and circled the big bristlecone tree. One rider stopped and dismounted, studying the ground. Looking for footprints, Benny realized.

"Nix," he said, indicating the man who had dismounted, "look at them, look at his chest."

She looked where he was pointing, and her mouth turned down into a frown of doubt. On the center of the man's black shirt were angel wings, neatly embroidered in white thread.

"Angels with wings on their chests," Nix murmured as she dumped the spent shells from her pistol.

"Angels came and set fire to the trees," Benny added.

"Uh-oh," she said softly.

"Listen, much as I'd love to find out about those machines and where these people come from, somehow I don't think now is the moment."

"No," she agreed. She checked all her pockets for bullets and found only two.

"That's it?" Benny asked, a note of panic in his voice.

"The rest are in my backpack."

She thumbed the two shells into the gun and closed the cylinder. They both looked at the pistol for a moment.

"Hope we don't need more than two shots," said Benny.

"No kidding." As she holstered the pistol, she glanced back the way they'd come, indecision stamped on her face.

"Look," Benny said, "Carter and those other people said they saw the jet. If we circle around to find Chong, we'll probably find them. Even with everything that just happened on the field, I'd still rather talk to Eve's folks than . . . these guys."

"Yes." Nix brushed a tangle of red hair away from her face. "Damn it."

They rose silently and moved deeper into the forest, going as fast as caution would allow and sticking to paths that were heavy with fallen branches or uneven ground. Benny did not believe that "all-terrain" could possibly mean that.

With minds full of questions and hearts heavy with regrets, they fled from the angels and their impossible machines.

FROM NIX'S JOURNAL

Tom taught us that you can't prepare for every emergency or every threat.

"The trick isn't to practice too many specific danger scenarios, but to learn the skills that are common to all. A smart warrior is always observant, always aware of his surroundings, always aware of his resources, and always ready to adapt to situations as they change."

"Nix," puffed Benny as he slowed to a walk, "maybe we're doing this wrong. Maybe we should go back and try to talk to those people."

She made a face. "Really? That's your plan?"

"I—"

"Or is that what you think Tom would do?"

That stung.

"Now wait a minute—" he began, but she shook her head.

"No," she snapped, "don't you have a clue as to how you're behaving lately? You keep telling me and the others to back off so you can handle things. You were going to charge those lions and—"

"What does that have to do with Tom?" he demanded.

She peered up at him, her green eyes surrounded by a sea of freckles and wild red curls.

"Look," she said, "I know you think that because you have Tom's sword, you have to be the great warrior, but here's a news flash, Benny: You're not Tom. The sword doesn't give you superpowers."

Benny felt his face grow hot. "I never said—"

She pointed back toward the field. "You think Tom

would have just waltzed in there and sorted this out?"

"I know he would. This is the sort of thing he was good at."

"No, he wasn't," snapped Nix. "He was never out this far. He doesn't know these people. We stepped into the middle of something big and nasty that doesn't concern us. It wouldn't have concerned Tom, either. He'd have steered us around this and left these people to sort out their own troubles."

Benny seethed for a moment before he tried to speak. "Tom would never have walked away from that little girl."

Nix's eyes were as hard and cold as green glass. "Tom brought us out here to find that jet, not to solve the problems of everyone in the world."

"So . . . what? Are you saying we should just walk away from Eve?"

"She's with her parents," she said, "and here's another news flash: Eve's parents tried to kill us back there. I'm going out on a limb here, but I pretty much think that means they don't want our help."

"That's because they were looking for her and were probably scared out of their minds, Nix."

"Doesn't change anything."

"And they thought we were reapers."

Nix cocked her head to one side. "It's that bald girl, isn't it?"

"What?"

"You want to go back and talk to that bald girl with the slingshot."

"Oh, for—"

Screams tore through the air behind them. A male voice, but high and filled with terrible pain. The sound was cut off in a way that suggested the worst.

The air was filled with screams and the roar of quad engines.

"Chong—?" Benny gasped. "We have to—"

"No, that's not Chong," Nix said with a firm shake of her head. "Chong made it to the woods before we did. I never saw him run that fast before. He'll be okay."

There were more screams and shouts, male and female voices; and every now and then the blast of a shotgun.

"Sounds like a full-out war," said Benny.

"You still want to go back?" asked Nix.

Benny said nothing.

"Look," Nix said, "Chong knows which direction Lilah took. He'll head that way, and if those machines chase him, then Lilah will hear it. She'll know what to do."

When Benny still said nothing, Nix touched his arm.

"Benny, let's find the others and see what they want to do, okay?"

He sighed and nodded, and kept to himself so many things that needed to be said.

Before Nix turned away, they shared a moment of silent eye contact. Benny ached to say so many things, and he was sure Nix did too. It was just that . . . he was afraid to hear what those things were. Her thoughts, and his.

He turned away first, and the ground seemed to be tilting under him, as if the world was no longer properly mounted on its axis and everything was tipping the wrong way.

I want to go home, he thought.

Deep inside his mind, Tom whispered, *Be careful, little brother, or you're going to lose Nix forever. Everything's hanging by a thread.*

They began walking, angling through a dry wash that was thick with tumbleweeds.

"I like the slingshot," observed Benny, half because it was true and half because he felt a peevish desire to score a point on Nix. "Quiet and nasty. We should get one. Chong used to be pretty good with one; maybe we could all learn."

"Slingshots are stupid," muttered Nix. "Something a kid would use."

"That girl was pretty tough," Benny said.

"You thought that cow looked pretty?"

"I said 'pretty tough,' Nix. Don't start, okay? She was tough and dangerous with that slingshot and the firecrackers and all. Saved us from the lions."

"Oh, please," sneered Nix. "And what kind of name is 'Riot' anyway?"

Suddenly there was movement behind them, deeper inside the forest. They spun around and saw another man standing a mere dozen paces away.

The stranger was tall, with dark eyes set so deep that they made his pale face look skeletal. His head was shaved, and his entire scalp was tattooed with a pattern of thorny vines. He wore black trousers and a billowy black shirt, and his legs and arms were wrapped with bloodred ribbons. On his shirtfront was a beautifully rendered chalk drawing of angel wings.

A reaper.

In Benny's mind, Tom's voice whispered, *Benny . . . run.*

31

CHONG DID NOT MOVE.

The reaper cut the air with the scythe again and again. With each pass he called out in a gravelly voice. "Hiding only makes it worse. The darkness wants to take you. Give in to it and there is only beauty. A touch is all, and then you are free. Free!"

Chong held his breath.

The reaper listened to the silence and shook his head. "Struggle against it and you beg for pain."

It was clear that the reaper did not know exactly where he was; he kept turning, shouting to different parts of the surrounding woods. It was a trick, and not a very good one, Chong mused. No one would be crazy enough to fall for it.

Then a second man stepped out of the woods on the far side of the clearing.

It was Carter. His clothes were torn and splashed with blood, and his hair and eyes were wild.

He looks like he's just been through hell, Chong thought. And he wondered where Sarah and Eve were. And that girl, Riot.

When the reaper saw Carter, he nodded approval. "Smart choice, brother. This reaper honors you and offers the gift of darkness to end your suffering and—"

"Skip the sales pitch, 'Brother' Andrew." Carter pointed his shotgun at the reaper's chest. "I'm not interested in anything you have to say. I'm going to give you one chance, because you used to be my friend. Drop the cutter and walk away. Leave me and mine in peace."

"Peace?" The reaper, Brother Andrew, shook his head, and Chong thought there was real regret in his face. "There is no peace left on earth, Carter. You of all people should know that. How many have you lost to the gray wanderers? Your first wife? Your son? Your sister? How many more do you have to see consumed before you understand that earth no longer belongs to mankind?"

"I don't want to hear it."

"We've been called home, brother," insisted Andrew. "Saint John and Mother Rose have shown us the way."

"They're murderers, and they've brainwashed the whole bunch of you into believing in some crazy made-up god and a bunch of lunatic ranting. They've blinded you with this darkness nonsense."

"No," said Andrew, "they've *opened* our eyes and our hearts to the truth."

"What truth? All you do is kill."

"No!" said Andrew, looking hurt and surprised. "We don't 'kill.' There is no 'murder' left in the world. Why can't you get it through your head that the gray plague was not a virus or an accident? It was the will of our god. Like the Death of the Firstborn in your own Bible, Carter. He has reached out his hand to erase the mistake of 'life.'"

"'Mistake'? Life is the only thing that matters."

Andrew shook his head. "No. God—the *true* god—meant

for mankind to leave the physical form and transition into the formlessness of the darkness. That was his will, his plan for the redemption of everyone."

Carter shook his head. "Horse crap. It was a plague, and it didn't kill everyone. There are a lot of people left and—"

"There are maggots crawling on the festering corpse of this world," countered Andrew. "Everyone who draws breath does so in defiance of the will of God."

"You still seem to be sucking air, Andrew."

The reaper placed one hand over the wings on his chest. "The reapers are the holy priests of our god. We have been asked to remain here and usher the last of the lost—the last of those like you who refuse to believe—into the darkness."

"Sure. By murder. Very compassionate of you."

"But it is compassion, Carter." He set the butt of his scythe down, and there was a slight shift in his body language and his phrasing. Less forced formality. "Listen to me, man; when the dead rose, I was right there in the thick of it with you. We brought all those people out of Omaha. We built Treetops and we started a life."

"Right, which is why—"

"Let me say my piece," interrupted Andrew. "Just hear me out."

Carter sighed and gestured with the barrel of his shotgun. "Make it quick."

Brother Andrew nodded. "You and I survived when a lot of other people fell because we were used to roughing it. All those weekends out hunting and fishing before things fell apart. The years we humped our battle-rattle over the Big Sand in Iraq and Afghanistan. We were survivors, Carter, and we did survive . . . and we helped a lot of other people survive."

Carter nodded.

"But for what?" demanded Andrew. "What have we really accomplished? What do we have to show for it? After that first season, after we holed up in that old shopping mall for all those weeks, we thought we'd slipped the punch. We thought that God smiled on us and we made it, right? But then what happened? That first winter we lost half the people we saved. Dysentery, three flu epidemics, tuberculosis . . . the list goes on and on. Disease killed more of us than the gray people ever did, and we've both traveled enough to know that this was happening all over. Remember Oshkosh? The whole city was dead from plague. Actual bubonic plague. Same with Bridgeport, and how many other cities? Same thing in Wyoming. Casper, Fort Washakie, Arapahoe—wiped out by the damn flu. That's where the whole second wave of the gray people came from. Not from them biting each other or the army dropping nukes. Millions of people died from bad water, bad food, infection, bacteria, parasites. By the time we reached Idaho, how many people did we still have? One out of every six who started out with us?"

The story Andrew was telling confirmed the worst of Chong's speculations about the world beyond Mountainside's chain-link fence. The nine towns in the Sierra Nevadas lucked out by having a good doctor and a biochemist who knew how to make antibiotics. Chong's father often said that those two men had saved more people than anyone who fired a gun or swung a sword. When Chong had told that to Tom, he agreed completely.

"What's your point, Andrew?" growled Carter. "Are you saying that we worked all these years for nothing?"

"That's exactly what I'm saying, brother," insisted Andrew. "Since we settled down and built Treetops, when have we had a year without a major flu epidemic? When have we ever had a really successful harvest? We're hunters, man, but we're not farmers. Sure, we put a lot of venison and wild pig on the table, but it was never enough. Not by half." He took a breath. "How long do you think people should keep pushing against things before they realize the truth?"

"What truth is that?"

"The only truth that matters," said Andrew. "We're dying off because we're supposed to. The gray plague, the famines, the other diseases, the wildfires, and the other stuff. These are like the plagues of ancient Egypt. The true god has revealed himself and is calling us home, Carter, he's offering us freedom from bondage."

"Through murder?" demanded Carter.

"It's not murder—it's euthanasia, and it's sanctioned by God. Look—before the plague, humanity, in its sinfulness and corruption, was like a cancer patient dying by inches, crying out for relief. Our god listened, Carter. Don't you see? *Our* god. When your god abandoned you, the true god listened. That's what Saint John and Mother Rose revealed to us. What the reapers are doing is holy work. This is God's merciful way to end all this pain, all this torment." Andrew shook his head. "How can you stand there and tell me that with everything out here—everything in nature—trying to kill us every single freaking day, we are meant to live on and suffer?"

"You're insane. All of you."

"Really? Think about it, Carter. Consider how many people have joined the reapers since Saint John began spreading the word. Thousands. Armies of them all over the west. There are probably more of us now than there are people like you. That's not a couple of people going crazy," said Andrew. "People already know that life on earth is over. They know. When they hear what Saint John has to say, they don't think that it's something bad. They're relieved. That's the truth of it, brother. People are just tired of struggling when there's no real way they can win. Not here, not while they're still trapped in the flesh."

But Carter shook his head. "I don't care how many people join you, Andrew, if your god tells you that it's right to hurt people, to kill them—to kill my little girl—then that god is a liar. That god is a lie."

Sadness darkened Brother Andrew's face. He let out a long, weary sigh. "I tried, Carter," he said sadly. "Because we have history, because we've been like brothers, I tried."

Carter pointed the shotgun at Andrew's face. "Sure, and because we were friends I'll give you a chance, Andrew. Drop the cutter and get your ass into the wind and we'll call it quits here."

The reaper gave a sad shake of his head. "I'll bet you don't have any shells left. Otherwise you'd have given me the gift of darkness."

Carter snugged the stock of the shotgun into his shoulder. "Want to find out?"

"Yes," replied the reaper earnestly. "I want to die. How can you still not get that? So either pull the trigger or put the gun down and join us."

"I'm taking my family away from here. You won't have to worry about us ever again."

"Away where?"

"Someplace where you can't touch us. Somewhere safe."

"Why not give it a name? Or are you afraid to say the name 'Sanctuary' out loud?"

Even from where he was hiding, Chong could hear Carter's shocked intake of breath.

"C'mon, man, did you really think we don't know you're looking for Sanctuary? We know that Sister Margaret is with you. Some of the scouts saw her. There's only one place she'd take you to try and keep you from us."

"No, you're wrong, we're heading south. Besides . . . there's no such place as Sanctuary," said Carter, but even to Chong his voice lacked conviction.

Brother Andrew snorted. "How can a smart guy like you trust someone like Sister Margaret? She betrayed her own mother, her own people. What makes you think she won't betray you?"

"We trust her. Riot's protected us this far."

Riot, thought Chong. *She's connected to the reapers?*

"Protected you?" Andrew laughed. "That's what you think she's doing? Tell me something, Carter, has she actually told you about Sanctuary? About what it really is? Or did she just recycle that old garbage about it being—oh, how's it go?—'a place for the weary to rest'?"

Carter said nothing.

"Well, let me tell you something—Sister Margaret is nuts. I mean really out of her mind." Andrew shook his head. "I know about Sanctuary. I know what goes on there, Carter, and believe me when I tell you that the darkness I'm offering you is a mercy. I'm giving you a chance to go out as a free man rather than spend the rest of your life in Sanctuary as a slave."

"You don't even know what you're talking about."

"The offer stands," said Andrew, "but the clock's ticking on my patience."

Carter studied him, and Chong could see doubt in the man's face, but there was anger, too. Much more of that.

"Go to hell," said Carter.

Brother Andrew sighed. "So be it," he said. "Such is the mercy of Thanatos that even with blasphemy on your lips the darkness welcomes you."

There was a sudden flash of silver from the woods, and Carter cried out and staggered forward. His finger jerked the trigger of the shotgun, and the hollow click told the story the reaper had already guessed. The weapon fell from Carter's hands as he thumped down hard on his knees.

That was when Chong saw what had struck the man.

An arrow.

It had flown out of the woods behind where Chong crouched and buried itself between Carter's shoulders.

"No . . . ," Carter gasped.

But the answer was a dreadful "yes" as a second arrow punched into Carter's back not a finger's breadth from the first.

The last word Carter managed to say was, "Eve."

Then he fell forward.

Despite everything Tom had taught him, Chong cried, "No!"

The reaper with the scythe turned his head sharply toward the spot where Chong crouched.

And smiled.

BENNY AND NIX REACTED IN THE SAME MOMENT: SHE PULLED HER pistol and Benny drew his sword. The reaper took a small step toward them. He did not appear to be armed, but Benny was taking no chances.

"Stay back, mister," warned Benny.

The man stopped and studied them with cold, penetrating eyes. "Nyx," he said.

Nix started. "What? How do you know my name?"

"Are you her?" asked the man. The smallest of smiles painted his face.

"Um . . ."

"Have you come to share with us?" asked the reaper. "Have you come to help your children share the darkness with the heretics?"

"Uhhh . . . ," Benny said, "what?"

"Have you given your gift to many?"

"What . . . gift?" asked Benny, though he was pretty sure he did not want an answer to the question.

The man frowned. "The gift of darkness. What other gift is there?"

"Benny . . . ," Nix warned. "Let's get out of here."

The man took another step toward them. He was still well out of attack range, but Benny kept his sword in a solid guard, ready to defend—or attack. "What beautiful children you are," said the man in a voice that was as soft as sand slithering through an hourglass. It made Benny's skin crawl. "You come bravely into the woods, bearing weapons from the old world, spreading the gift of darkness with the heretics."

"No . . . ," Nix said under her breath. Her face had gone white, and even her freckles were pale. The only color was the pink line of the scar that ran from hairline to jaw.

"Why are you people hunting Eve's family?" Benny asked.

"Eve?" asked the reaper, smiling faintly. "Eve died in the morning of the world, wrapped in the withered arms of Adam. Cain the betrayer buried them in the dust beyond the gates of Eden. Or so says the false bible."

"Ooo-kay," said Benny softly. "That's great. Exactly what we need while we're running for our lives. Big help. Thanks, man."

The man laid his palm flat over the angel wings on his chest. "Do you not know me, holy one? I am Saint John of the Knife, first of your reapers, guide and guardian of your flock. It was through me that you opened the first red mouth in the flesh of the infidel. It was with my hand, my blades, that you let the darkness flow from this world of pain and into the infinite peace of nothingness."

He turned and gestured toward the northern stretch of the woods, where the sound of the quads could still be heard faintly.

"We are abroad in this blighted land to offer priceless gifts to all the scattered children of a false and fallen god," said

Saint John. "We have been faithful and dutiful in our ministry. We have given the gift of darkness to so many . . . ah, so many. Soon we will sweep these lands clear of the last blasphemers. The physical world belongs to the gray wanderers. The children of flesh are called to join with the eternal darkness. Such is the will of the one true god, Thanatos—all praise to his darkness."

Benny and Nix just stared at him. Benny had no idea how to respond.

"How do you know my name?" Nix asked again.

Saint John continued, "Together we will watch the silence and the darkness wrap the world in the garments of purity and eternal peace. Tell me, holy one, is . . . that why you are here? Is that why you have taken physical form and come here with your knight? Are you here to walk among your sacred reapers?"

"Are . . . you crazy?" asked Benny reasonably. "Is that it? I just want to know so I can find some useful place to stand in this conversation."

"Look," said Nix, "I don't know how you know my name or who you think we are, but we are not a part of this. None of it. We're just a couple of kids traveling through. We only met Carter for a minute and—"

The man ignored her words. He took one more step closer, peering at them, looking into their eyes. "You are not with Carter, I can see that much. You say that you are children, and yet when I look into your eyes I see that darkness has already taken hold of you. You are angels of the darkness, even if you are still dressed like children of the heretics. You are reapers of the scattered fields. I can see it in your eyes. You have given the gift of darkness to others. Many others."

Benny felt something twist inside his heart. The gift of darkness. He had no idea what religion this man was supposed to belong to, but it was pretty clear what the 'darkness' was.

Death.

But how was death a gift? How did that make any sense, especially in a world where life was rare and so very precious?

At the same time, it unnerved him that this maniac could somehow tell that he and Nix had killed people. Since that terrible night when Mrs. Riley was murdered, Nix and Benny had been in several bloody confrontations, first with Charlie Pink-eye's gang and then with Preacher Jack's killers at Gameland. They had plenty of blood on their hands; and the fact that the men they'd killed were absolutely evil did very little to help either of them sleep at night. The fact remained that they had both taken human lives. That fact had gouged marks into each of their souls that no amount of justification could remove.

And this man could see that.

How? Who was he?

Run, warned Tom again, *get away from him. Go—now!*

"Have you come to let the darkness take you?" The man wore a strange little smile as he spoke those words, and he seemed oblivious to Nix's pistol and Benny's sword. "The darkness wants to take you. The darkness wants to take us all. Do you not agree?"

"Um . . . no?" replied Benny uncertainly. "Not today, thanks."

Saint John's eyes were filled with a strange light, as if he could read Benny's thoughts. Benny thought it might have been ordinary madness, but there was something else, too. Something he had never seen before, and it chilled him to the bone. It was a light of absolute fanatical belief. Not a simple faith, like Benny had seen in the eyes of way-station monks like Brother David, nor the desperate hope that was always present in the eyes of Pastor Kellogg back home. No, this was something else. This was a kind of insanity. And this man seemed to be engaged in his own inner conversation with things only he could see. Gods? Monsters?

Chong had quoted a passage to Benny after the Gameland affair was over. It was something a German philosopher named Nietzsche had written more than a century ago. "'He who fights with monsters should look to it that he himself does not become a monster,'" Chong recited as the four of them walked away from Tom's grave and the column of smoke that rose above the dust and fire and ash of Gameland. "'And when you gaze long into an abyss, the abyss also gazes into you.'"

The very thought of that had chilled Benny back then, and it returned now as a cold breath on the nape of his neck, because he was absolutely positive that it explained what he was seeing right now. This man—this complete stranger and utter wacko— was someone who had looked far too long into the abyss. Benny knew this with an intuitive flash, because looking into his eyes was like looking into the very same abyss. Into a bottomless well of horror and death. These thoughts, complex as they were, tumbled through his mind in less than a second.

Behind them, somewhere in the woods, Benny could hear more shouts. Riot's voice, and Sarah's. Then the roars of the quads as the reapers hunted them.

Saint John nodded gravely to Nix.

"Nyx," he said, his eyes taking on a dreamy quality, "daughter of Chaos, mother of Darkness and Light. Mother of the Fates, Sleep, Death, Strife, and Pain. Sweet mother of all shadows."

Out of the corner of his eye, Benny could see the gun trembling in Nix's hand.

Saint John said, "Please . . . forgive me my weakness, but I beg you to tell me—are you her? Did Mother Rose call you from the darkness in our hour of need?"

"Look, just back off," warned Nix, taking her pistol in two hands. "I don't know what you're talking about, but we don't want trouble."

"Trouble?" The man looked mystified. "You, of all that walk this earth, have nothing to fear from me—or any of our kindred." He suddenly smiled, and for a moment that smile seemed genuinely happy.

Nix cleared her throat. "Mister, I have no idea what you're talking about. Whoever you think we are—we're not. We're not part of whatever you're doing, and we don't want to be. We just want to leave, okay? Don't try anything and don't try to follow us or I swear to God that I'll shoot you."

The man who called himself Saint John of the Knife nodded, as if Nix had said something he both understood and liked. "Yes, yes, Goddess, I understand that the darkness is yours to give, and I welcome it with all my heart. I am a reaper, and I am yours body and soul until the darkness closes around us all!" His words, strange as they were, had the cadence of a church litany, and that made Benny's skin crawl. "Kill me now, or come with me to spread darkness to the heathens out there." He pointed to the field. "And then I would be so honored to kneel before you and accept your gift. A bullet, a knife . . . each is a path to glory."

"Nix," Benny said cautiously, "let's go."

They began backing away from Saint John. At first he smiled, apparently thinking that they were going to lead him in some kind of insane charge out onto the field, but when he saw that Nix and Benny were merely increasing the distance to go around him, his expression changed. At first it was lit by an expectant hopefulness, his smile lingering; and then his face grew confused.

"Holy one," called Saint John, "where are you going?"

"Far, far away from here," said Nix, "you incredible freak."

Even as she said it, Benny knew that it was a mistake.

A terrible mistake.

The reaper's expression changed once more; the confusion melted away to reveal harsh lines of an ice-cold rage.

"You are not her," growled Saint John in a low, feral voice. His pale face grew flushed, and his dark eyes filled with a dreadful light. "You steal the name of my goddess and you profane everything that is holy."

He spat onto the ground between them.

"I never said that I was."

Benny pulled her arm. "Nix, come on."

"And you, boy," growled Saint John, "you damn yourself by speaking her holy name, and you do it in the presence of a saint of her son's sacred Night Church. No fire exists in hell to burn that blasphemy from your soul."

"Hey, look, pal," snapped Benny, "we're not blaspheming anyone or anything. And if that's what it sounds like, then we're sorry. Like she said, we're not who you think we are, so we're just going to leave. Pretend you never saw us. You go ahead and do whatever it is you were doing, and we'll be out of your life and—"

Saint John spat again and took a threatening step forward, his fists balled. "Where are you from? Are you scouts from Sanctuary?" His eyes flared, and he bared his teeth. "That's it, isn't it? You think you can spy on the holy children of my god in order to lay a trap for us?"

"Still don't know what you're talking about, man," said Benny, "and we're still leaving. Adios."

"You pathetic maggots," sneered Saint John. "Do you think Sanctuary can hide from us? Do you think it can withstand us? We are the fists of God on earth."

"Whatever," said Benny.

"Sanctuary will fall, as every other town has fallen, as all evil must fall. The reapers will open every red door and wash its streets in blood. You cannot hope to defy the will of the only true god. Thanatos—all praise to the darkness."

Saint John reached into the billowy folds of his shirt and drew out two knives, and he did it so quickly and smoothly that they seemed to appear magically in his hands. Benny had seen enough skilled knife fighters—Tom, Solomon Jones, Sally Two-Knives, and others—to recognize that this man was a master of these blades.

Nix saw it too, and she stopped backing away and settled into a wide-legged shooter's stance. "Don't be stupid," she warned. Her voice did not sound like that of a fifteen-year-old girl. Benny knew that she was deadly serious.

The reaper held his ground but pointed one of the knives at them. "You are heretics and blasphemers, and in the name of Thanatos—praise be to the darkness—I curse you. Do you hear? Do you possess enough wit to know that the mouth of hell has opened to consume you? I curse you with pain and suffering, with loss and heartbreak. You will never know love and you will never know peace and you will live long years with no darkness to gather you in and give you rest. This I swear in the name of my god."

"I don't want to kill you," said Nix, "but if you try anything, I'll shoot you in the leg."

Her voice and her hands shook as she spoke, but Benny knew that she'd pull the trigger if she had to.

Saint John studied Nix's face.

"So be it," he said softly, and slowly resheathed his knives. Then he pushed up the sleeve to reveal his left forearm, and with his long right thumbnail he cut a deep red line in his flesh. Blood welled, nearly black in the shadows under the trees. The reaper smeared blood on his fingertips, spat on the blood, and then flicked it at them. It did not reach them, but that didn't seem to matter to the man in black. His face was alight with triumph, as if what he had just done sealed his threats into the fabric of reality. "May you live long," he snarled, as if that was the worst thing one person could wish upon another.

Then Saint John of the Knife turned and melted like a bad dream into the darkness that lurked under the tall trees.

Benny and Nix stood there, sword raised, gun pointing, mouths hanging open.

The birds and monkeys were silent in the trees, and the whole forest seemed to hold its breath. Drops of blood glistened on leaves that trembled and swayed. Nix lowered her pistol and began to tremble all over. Benny wrapped his arm around her, but he had his own case of the shakes and wasn't sure he was able to offer any real comfort.

"What just happened?" breathed Nix, her voice small and fragile. She used her thumb to gingerly uncock the pistol's hammer and lower it into place. "I mean, seriously . . . what just happened?"

"I—I don't know," Benny admitted.

"Did I provoke him? Did I just make it worse?"

"No," Benny lied. "I don't think so."

They backed away from the spot where the man—the reaper—had stood. Then, after five paces, they turned and ran as far and as fast as they could.

THE MAN CALLED SAINT JOHN STEPPED OUT FROM BEHIND A TREE AND watched the two teenagers run away.

When he'd left them, he'd gone into the woods and then circled around on their blind side, standing downwind of them so he could study them. He could have come up behind them and cut their throats, and his hands ached to do just that, but he was caught in a moment of indecision.

Before he had confronted them, Saint John had heard the boy call the girl "Nyx."

Nyx was the mother of his god.

He rubbed at the cut on his arm and frowned in doubt. His vexation with them had been righteous but hasty. Were they, in fact, heretics who profaned her holy name?

Or . . . was this some kind of test?

He chewed on that. It would not be the first such test laid before him. He remembered that night a few days after the gray plague started when he found a wretched woman being chased through the streets of a burning city by a pack of abusive men. Saint John had seen such horrors a thousand times as the world crumbled and died, but this one instance drew his attention. On some level too profound for him to fully grasp, the events were part of a test of his faith and his resolve. It was a subtle test, and even after all these years he could not understand every aspect of it; but what was important was that he recognized it as a test.

Against his habits and better judgment, Saint John had helped that woman. He saved her from the men by opening red mouths in their flesh. Their souls flowed into the darkness.

The woman appeared to flee from him, but soon Saint John found her hiding in a church. Hiding with twenty-seven angels. Twenty-seven celestial beings who had chosen to take human form, pretending to be orphaned children.

They had adopted Saint John, and he had adopted them.

Had he not accepted the challenge of that first test, Saint John would never have met the woman who would become the pope of his Night Church.

Mother Rose.

And the twenty-seven angels?

They were his first reapers.

Saint John raised his arm to his mouth and slowly, sensually licked up each drop of his own blood. It was hot and salty, smelling of copper and tasting like iron. Saint John's eyelids fluttered closed for a moment. Even his own blood was so delicious. All blood was delicious.

He wondered, not for the first time, if there were really vampires in the world, and if they were not merely men like him whose minds had been opened by God so they could appreciate the perfect taste of blood.

He decided that this was probably the case.

In the distance he heard a scream that rose louder than

the roar of the quads on which his reapers went about their sacred work. Was it male or female? It was hard to say, because there is a level of pain so pure that it strips away gender and identity, and that was what he heard now.

Saint John nodded his appreciation. Most of the reapers were ordinary folk—believers, true, but in no other way exceptional. They were blunt.

Whoever sculpted that scream was one of the special ones. One of his angels—of which only nine were left on this side of the darkness—or one of the recruits who had fully embraced the way of the blade and the glory of the red mouth.

He smiled and nodded to himself.

He began to walk through the woods, following the footprints of the girl who called herself Nyx and the boy who served as her knight. He did not hurry. The world's clock had run down, and haste was irrelevant.

In all it had been a good week's work. Twenty-five hundred of the heretics had gone into the darkness at Treetops. Only six hundred of them escaped the burning of their town. Of those, four hundred reached the mountains of southern Nevada. Barely two hundred made it to this patch of wild forestland in the arid Mojave.

Saint John doubted that a hundred heretics still remained on this side of the darkness.

Soon red doors would open for each of them. The reapers were doing everything he and Mother Rose had trained them to do, and they did it with the unquenchable diligence of true faith.

A quad motor growled behind him, and Saint John turned to wait as one of his reapers hurried to find him. When the machine came into view and Saint John saw who was riding it, he smiled.

Brother Peter.

Peter had been the first of the twenty-seven angels to embrace the way of the blade, and it had taken no urging at all. Peter was a natural, a prodigy. The number of heretics he had ushered into the darkness was legion, second only to Saint John himself.

The quad pulled up and Brother Peter turned off the engine, allowing a soothing quiet to settle over the woods. He placed a hand over the angel wings on his chest and gave a slight bow of the head.

"Honored One," he said softly.

Peter was in his early twenties and had grown up tall and powerful, but his face was unmarked because he had never, in all the years Saint John had known him, smiled. Not once. His scalp was tattooed with a tangle of thornbushes through which centipedes crawled.

"How goes the crusade?" asked Saint John.

"Carter split his people into six groups. He probably thought that would make it easier for them to escape, but it made it easier for us to hunt them. We opened the red doors of two of the groups. Brother Alan and Sister Gail are going to take the third in a pincer movement, because that group went into a valley, and Brother Andrew is hunting a fourth near the creek."

"And the other two?"

"Our people are looking."

"That is well." Saint John approved of Andrew, who was a recent convert and a former town guard from Treetops. It was he who had provided Brother Peter with a map to the tree-house city where Carter and his people had lived until a week ago. The knives of the reapers had been bloodied from tip to pommel that night, and every day since.

"I met Brother Simon a few minutes ago," said Peter. "He asked me to tell you that Mother Rose has called a meeting of the team leaders."

"Where?"

Brother Peter paused. "They are to meet her at the Shrine of the Fallen in two hours."

Saint John was a long time in responding. He folded his hands behind his back and seemed to be interested in the dance of a pair of dragonflies.

"I want you to be there," he said softly. "But don't be seen. I want to know everything that is said at that meeting."

"Yes, Honored One."

"And I want to know if anyone—anyone—enters the shrine itself."

"Mother Rose would never allow it. It's her shrine," said the young reaper. "Even I've never been inside."

"Nor have I," murmured Saint John.

The two reapers regarded each other for a silent moment.

Brother Peter frowned. "Why call a meeting there, of all places? Why a place she has expressly forbidden anyone to visit? I—don't understand."

Saint John's smile was small and cold. "God speaks to each of us in a different way. Who is to say what secrets he whispers to our beloved Rose?"

His smile was warm, but his tone was cold.

After a long silence, Brother Peter nodded. "There are

times I do not entirely . . . understand what Mother Rose does, Honored One."

"Oh?" said Saint John.

"Perhaps I am too simple a man, but sometimes I cannot connect her actions with the needs of our holy purpose."

A faint smile played over Saint John's lips. "I'm sure God forgives you for such doubts."

The younger man bowed. As he straightened he said, "There is another matter, Honored One."

"Oh?"

"I was patrolling the forest beyond the shrine, looking to see if Sister Margaret dared to lead any of the heretics that way . . ."

Saint John nodded encouragement.

". . . and I found five reapers who had red doors opened in them."

The saint spread his hands. "We knew that Carter would fight. He is stubborn in his heresy, and there are many like him in his group."

"No, Honored One, I do not believe that Carter or any of his people killed them. Whoever took them did it quietly and with great skill."

"What level of skill?"

Brother Peter's face was as bland as ever, but his eyes were alight. "Possibly as good as me. And around the bodies I found animal tracks."

"A dog?" asked Saint John.

"A very large dog."

"Ah," said Saint John, raising his eyebrows. "You think *he's* back? The ranger?"

"Yes, Honored One, I do . . . although that confuses me. Am I mistaken, or did not Brother Alexi swear that he killed the ranger? Did he not swear before God that he smashed the life out of him with his great hammer?"

"He did say so," agreed Saint John.

Brother Peter began to add something to that, but he bit it back. However, Saint John nodded as if the rest had been spoken.

Mother Rose had said she witnessed her pet giant kill this particular heretic. This mercenary who served the evil ones— the doctors and scientists; this killer who preyed on the reapers.

They studied each other for a long moment, each of them calculating the implications of that.

"Someday soon," murmured the saint, "we will have a discussion with Brother Alexi."

"Most assuredly," agreed Brother Peter, and his eyes were hard as metal. "But . . . if Brother Alexi has fallen from grace, what does that say about Mother Rose? They are inseparable. He does not scratch an itch without her say-so."

Saint John placed his hand on the younger man's shoulder. "We must be vigilant, but we must not leap to judgment. The truth always finds the light, you know this?"

"Yes."

"Then be patient. God has set many tasks before us. We have to find and end the rest of Carter's heretics and send them into the darkness. We must find Sister Margaret and make sure that she tells only us how to find Sanctuary . . . and not her mother. This is of paramount importance."

"Silencing her voice would be easy enough. . . ."

"Don't underestimate her," cautioned Saint John.

"Remember how talented she was. Had she not fallen from grace, her skill could have rivaled your own."

Brother Peter gave an elaborate shrug. "I welcome the opportunity to test that."

"Do not give her the slightest chance. As far as the ranger, Joe . . . we need to find him before he can do more harm. Every time he kills one of ours and is not punished for it, a seed of doubt is planted in the hearts of our reapers. This man must be found."

"Yes, Honored One."

Saint John nodded. "There are two other tasks at hand. First, I want you to select your most trusted reapers and have them join you when you go to observe Mother Rose's meeting at the shrine. Have some follow Her Holiness and Brother Alexi and send runners to me to report everything that is said at this meeting."

"Of course." Peter paused. "What is the other matter?"

Saint John looked at the line of footprints in the soft earth. He told Brother Peter about Nyx and her knight.

"Surely they are part of Carter's party," insisted Peter, but Saint John shook his head.

"I don't think so. Their eyes have looked upon the darkness, I'm sure of it." Saint John absently touched the cut on his forearm. "I will follow them and seek to discover the nature of this holy test." He took a breath. "Go now. The god of darkness calls us to our purpose."

"And we answer with joy," replied Brother Peter with his flat voice and unsmiling face.

He bowed low. Saint John kissed his head and blessed him.

The young man got back on his quad, fired up the engine, and roared off into the woods.

Saint John watched him go, nodding to himself with silent approval. Brother Peter was the best of the reapers. The best by far. A genius of the blade and a killer whose every breath was dedicated to giving the gift of darkness. Saint John had no doubts that Peter would find this man—this troublesome man—and do as he had promised. He would open the doors in the man's flesh and let the darkness in. It would be the greatest act of faith and devotion possible. Saint John almost envied him that pleasure.

He reached up and touched the silver whistle that hung around his neck. He stroked it contemplatively for a moment and then raised it to his lips. He blew into it, long and hard and with no apparent effect.

Soon, however, he heard the sound of clumsy feet crunching on dead leaves, and the swish of pine branches brushing against bodies that moved without delicacy but with the implacability of the stars themselves.

Then the saint of all the killers left on earth ran after Nix and Benny, and behind him an army of the living dead followed.

FROM NIX'S JOURNAL

Tom taught us that the samurai lived according to a code of ethics and behavior called Bushido. You'd think something that means "The Way of the Warrior" would be all about killing the enemy, but that's not how it was. There are seven "virtues" that true warriors had to live by.

1. Justice. This is about doing the right thing or making the right decision (even if it's the hardest choice at the time).

2. Bravery. We can't really be fearless, but we can act brave even when we're scared green.

3. Benevolence. Warriors should always show mercy, charity, and kindness.

4. Respect. Everyone deserves it. (I have to keep reminding myself of this one!)

5. Honesty. This includes trust and sincerity, too.

6. Loyalty. Yeah. This one's really important if we're going to survive out here in the Ruin.

7. Honor. Tom says this means that when you give your word, then that's set in stone. He said, "Honor isn't a convenience. It's a way of life."

34

An arrow thunked into the tree trunk an inch from Chong's face.

He screamed and threw himself down and away.

In the clearing, Brother Andrew shouted, "Danny! Did you get him?"

"He went right down," cried a second voice from well behind where Chong lay. "Go get him and I'll cover you."

Chong had no intention of waiting while the muscle-freak with the scythe came to kill him. He sprang to his feet and bolted for the crooked line of shrubs twenty yards away. He ran bent almost in half, sword clutched in one fist. Another arrow struck a tree directly in front of him, causing him to skid to a stop and dive down behind a thick pine. A third arrow hit the pine, and when he risked a look, a fourth cleaved the air so close to his head that it tugged at his hair. It tangled in a creosote bush and fell to the ground. Chong gave it a micro-second's glance. The arrow had an aluminum shaft, with black plastic fletching and a wicked barbed head that was smeared with some black goo. Poison? Either way, Chong did not want to touch it. He scuttled away as fast as he could.

"There he is," called the archer, Danny, as he stepped out of the woods. "It's just a kid with a toy sword."

Danny was a thin black man, dressed identically to Brother Andrew, shaved head and all. He had a leather quiver of arrows slung over his back, the fletched ends ready above his shoulder so all he had to do was reach up and slide an arrow out and down into his bow. Chong had seen plenty of hunters coming back from the Ruin with quivers identical to that. What struck him, though, was the bow this man carried. It was not one of the old-fashioned red-elm recurve bows made by the Gibson brothers in Haven; nor was it one of the sixty-two-inch plain longbows Chong and all his friends used in gym class. No, this was something from before First Night: a metal-and-fiberglass compound bow fitted with cables and pulleys to bend the limb, allowing the archer superior accuracy, velocity, and distance. Chong had seen only one like it before. A moody, scar-faced trade guard named Big Mike Sweeney gave a demonstration with one at the New Year Festival two years ago. He'd outshot every archer in the Nine Towns, and each of his arrows sank twice as deep as even the longbow arrows used by Cleveland Dave Wilcox. The Motor City Hammer had offered Big Mike a thousand ration dollars for the bow, but the scar-faced man had laughed and walked away.

Chong recognized and feared that weapon. His stomach clenched into a tiny knot of ice.

He ducked so low that he was almost on all fours and wormed his way into the densest tangle of brush he could find. He heard another arrow strike a tree, but the archer was aiming in the wrong direction. Chong felt a splinter of relief. If he could stay out of sight for another couple of minutes, then he could circle behind Danny and lose himself in the forest.

He risked one peek and saw that the archer was now between him and Andrew. Chong smiled grimly and kept moving.

"Hey! Where'd he go?" growled Brother Andrew. "Watch out, Danny, I can't see him—"

"Carter!" A woman's voice suddenly cried out in total horror, and everyone—Andrew, the archer, and Chong—turned to see a woman with an ax standing wide-eyed with shock at the edge of the clearing. Sarah. Eve clung to her mother's leg, face blank with incomprehension.

The archer smiled and drew another black-tipped arrow.

"Sarah," said Brother Andrew, and he actually looked relieved. "Looks like we'll get the whole family, praise be to the darkness. Carter won't have to go into the darkness alone."

The compassion in his voice chilled Chong. It was so weirdly inappropriate, and yet it seemed genuine.

"Carter!" Sarah's eyes blazed with madness, and she kept screaming her husband's name as if somehow the depth of her need could call him back from the dark place to which his soul had fled. Her body trembled as she fought between the desire to run to her husband and the need to protect her daughter.

"Sarah," said Andrew, "Carter is in the arms of Thanatos now—all praise his darkness."

"N-no . . ."

"He's waiting for you, sweetheart. He wants you and Evie to join him."

Tears streamed down Sarah's face. Eve began whimpering.

"I want my daddy," she wailed.

Brother Andrew smiled at the little girl. "You see? She

wants to be with him. The darkness offers peace and an end to suffering for all of you."

"You bastards killed my husband," growled Sarah, her voice made rough by the jagged pieces of her breaking heart. "And now you want to kill my baby?"

"We want to save Eve and all the other children," insisted Andrew. "Please, Sarah . . . don't fight this. Embrace it."

Chong knew that it was all hopeless. Sarah was on the edge of panic, and she could never defeat both reapers. She should never have come into the clearing, but Chong understood that she could not have done anything else. It was a terrible script written by an evil hand, and she and her daughter were going to become victims of their own drama.

The archer strung his arrow, the barbed head gleaming with black goo; Andrew hefted the scythe with its wicked three-foot-long curving blade.

Time seemed to have slowed for Chong, but this moment was stretched so taut that it was going to snap. He knew he could flee this encounter and head into the woods. Physically he could do that; but that was not possible on any other level. He also knew that he was no one's idea of a hero. Benny was, although his friend would laugh at the suggestion; and both Nix and Lilah were heroes. Chong was a self-admitted sidekick. No one should ever depend on him for anything heroic. He didn't have the mentality or the musculature for it. His bokken was clutched in his fists, and his teeth were clenched.

The reapers were distracted—Chong could simply run away.

"Move it, town boy," he snarled at himself; and then he was up and running.

Toward the tableau that was suddenly coming unstuck from time. Sarah screamed and rushed at Andrew; the reaper raised his scythe. The archer shifted his stance to take aim at Eve, who stood alone and confused in the dirt.

This is insane, Chong told himself. *I can't do this.*

"Danny!" yelled Brother Andrew. "Behind you!"

Chong was still too far away when the archer turned and fired.

35

A VOICE WHISPERED IN LILAH'S EAR.

Or perhaps in her mind.

If you don't stop the bleeding, you're going to die.

"I know that," she said irritably, and it was only when she heard the sound of her own voice that she realized the other voice had not spoken aloud.

Her eyes snapped open, and with a start she realized that she was awake. She remembered falling asleep, or at least she remembered the darkness folding around her. She liked the darkness; it was soft and gentle and sweet.

Waking was none of those things.

Pain seemed to be part of everything. Even opening her eyes hurt. The sun was directly overhead, and she squinted up through a gap in the trees.

You have to stop the bleeding.

The voice was a familiar one, but it was not one that had ever spoken to her before. Not when she was alone. Not out here in the Ruin.

George? Sure, she heard his voice all the time. Annie, too.

But not this. Not him.

"Tom—?" she asked.

The only answer was the soft rustle of the wind in the trees.

Her heart instantly began hammering as the full awareness of where she was flooded back into her mind with ugly clarity.

"Help me, Tom."

There was a reply to that, but it wasn't Tom's voice. It was the hungry grunt of the monster. Somehow it had found its way down from the cliff and was below her now.

The boar.

The impossible boar.

She looked down and gasped in horror. She was suspended in the interlocking boughs of two pine trees, but she wasn't sure how far off the ground she was. Below her was a wild boar that had somehow become infected with the zombie plague, but she did not know how to cope with it. She had no spear. That was lost, probably somewhere on the cliff or down there with the pig.

She heard a second grunt, and for a moment she strained to tell whether it was the same boar making shorter grunts or—

No, there it was again. Two grunts overlapping. Then a third. A fourth.

Then two more.

Six of them.

Somewhere below her was an entire pack of the dead boars.

She closed her eyes for a moment and listened inside her body. She could not feel any cuts, but she could feel the warmth of blood inside her clothes.

She gingerly wiggled her fingers. They worked fine. She tried her toes. Also fine. There was pain in the backs of her legs, but she was comforted by the fact that she could feel her legs. After the first boar had hit her and she landed on the rock, Lilah was sure she'd broken her back. Not so.

It was a comfort, but it was not the end of her troubles.

She lifted one leg. Only an inch, but it did move. Pain shot up the back of her thigh and into her hip joint. Had the boar torn her side open? If that was the case, then she knew that she was probably going to die.

Lilah took a breath and successfully moved hands and feet, and determined that her spine was not too badly damaged. That was something. A cut, even a bad one, was something she could deal with.

She opened her eyes and looked up at the branches above her. Several of them were cracked and broken from her fall. Directly above her was one that had snapped off, leaving a spike of wood nearly eight inches long. She reached for it, moving slowly and with great care. Her fingers wriggled for the branch, her fingertips brushing the bottom of it. Almost . . . almost.

But it was too far.

There was no way she could grab it without sitting up, and that meant that her angle to the boughs would radically change. By bending at the waist she would be placing a great deal of her upper body mass at an angle toward her middle. That V position of her body would concentrate her weight into a single point instead of spreading it out over the surface of the branches. She would slide right through and probably fall.

She looked up at the branch.

She had to make that bend, but she had to do it faster than gravity could pull her. Bend, reach, lunge, grab. Without knowing how badly she was hurt, it was a terrible risk.

The alternative was to lie there and bleed to death.

Lilah closed her eyes for a moment, conjuring the faces of the people she loved. Annie, George. Tom.

And Chong.

He was a town boy and not a good match for her in any way.

But she did love him, and she knew that Chong loved her . . . even though neither of them had ever spoken that word. Love. She smiled. Chong was probably too afraid to say it. But then again, so was she.

Afraid of all that the word meant.

As a result, they'd had so little between them. A few kisses, a few tender words. Nothing else. And if she did not move, that was all she would ever have.

That wasn't fair. She hadn't survived all those years in the wild only to be teased by the promise of love. In the thousands of books she'd read, love was the most important thing. It could move worlds.

Could it move her fast enough to grab that branch?

"Chong," she said, and this time it was his name she spoke. Not Tom's. Chong.

She opened her eyes and glared at the branch.

Then all at once she threw her weight upward, tightened her stomach muscles, stretched with her shoulder and back, and braced for the screaming pain. The branches under her creaked and cracked as she lunged.

The pain was . . . immense.

But her hand closed on the branch.

She took everything the pain could throw at her. She bit down on it, snarled at it, opened her mouth and howled it out of her as she pulled on that branch. Broken twigs slashed at her side and legs and arms, but she took that pain too.

Pain had never owned Lilah, and it did not own her now.

Screaming with agony and rage, she whipped her other hand up, pulling now with both arms, with the muscles of her shoulders and chest and back.

Suddenly she heard a sharp crack beneath her, and the main branch on which she lay collapsed away from her, leaving her hanging. The pain, clever and deceitful as it always was, revealed that it had so much more to give.

She screamed, but she took it.

The muscles all along her tanned arms stood taut against her skin. Hot wetness ran down from her torn side, and fat drops of blood fell down into the shadows. Below her the infected hogs sent up a squeal of hellish hunger.

"Damn you," she growled as she pulled herself up.

The whole tree swayed, tilting outward as if trying to shake her off.

Lilah pulled.

The pigs were in a frenzy, smashing themselves against the trunk.

Lilah pulled.

Pinecones rained down on her. Blood roared in her ears.

Lilah pulled.

She forced her knees up, forced her feet out to explore, forced them to find something solid.

And there it was. The stump of the branch that had just broken. Twenty inches of solid wood. Lilah stretched one foot out and shifted her weight onto it. The branch held.

With the last of her strength, she swung her body above the branch and settled her other foot on it.

Safe.

Gasping, bleeding, sweating, dizzy, and sick. But safe.

When she dared open her eyes, she looked down at the boars below her. Six of them. Dead pig eyes stared back up at her. They wanted her flesh. They had the patience of eternity to wait her out. Even with her pistol and spear she could never hope to defeat two of them, let alone a half dozen.

Nevertheless Lilah bent over so they could see her face.

And she smiled at them.

36

SAINT JOHN OF THE KNIFE RAN LIKE A GHOST, MAKING ONLY THOSE sounds he chose to make.

The children—the false Nyx and her knight—were clever, and they had some woodcraft, but they were not a tenth as silent as the man who followed them.

Behind and around Saint John there were other sounds. The distant roar of the quads as his reapers scoured the woods to hunt down the last of Carter's heretics. And, closer to hand, the artless footfalls of the following dead, coaxed in this direction by occasional blasts of his dog whistle.

Twice Saint John encountered reapers and twice he sent them away, declining their offer of help, ordering them to continue with the hunt for the heretics. By nightfall the last of that party should be accounted for, their bodies opened by sanctified blades so the darkness could enter. It had been a long chase from Treetops, the clever tree-house town in Wyoming. A thousand wooden houses built amid the boughs of the sturdy pines of the Bighorn National Forest.

He smiled at the thought. Wooden houses in wooden trees. Lovely to the eye, but so foolish, and ultimately no protection from torches and blades. No protection from the will of God.

The memories of that conflagration enchanted his mind as he ran. The graceful pines reaching like the arms of green titans into the endless star field of the night sky. The mingling of a hundred shades of yellow and orange and red as the trees caught fire. The screams of the blasphemers, crying out to a god who could not answer, for he did not exist. Saint John wished that he could be inside their minds at the moment when the darkness took them. How wonderful it must be to suddenly see and know the infinite truths.

It made him want to weep, as he had wept then. In the morning he had moved through the ashes, and his tears fell onto blackened bodies that now knew the glory of the eternal darkness.

Saint John had fallen to his knees, his arms red to the elbow with blood, his mouth smeared with it, his cheeks streaked with tears. There he had led the faithful in a prayer. Mercy for those who were too blind to see the truth. Grace for those who had embraced the darkness as the flames and the blades sanctified them. And patience to the reapers who each longed to step into that darkness, but whose sacred duty kept them here. In ugly, mortal flesh, attached to this world of hurt and misery until the work of their god was accomplished.

His wonderful memories were shattered by a gruff voice yelling from the woods. "There's one of them!"

Saint John slowed from a run to a walk and then stood still as three men emerged from the darkness of the forest. They were tough-looking. Big and muscular, each of them armed with a vicious farm tool. One man had a pitchfork, another had a sledgehammer that he held as if it were a tack hammer, and the third carried a pair of sickles.

Carter's people. Heretics. Their clothes were filthy and streaked with mud and blood. They were unshaven, and there was a desperate wildness in their eyes.

"Welcome, my friends," he said.

"Welcome, he says," growled the man with the sledge-hammer.

"I'll show him a welcome," laughed the man with the sickles.

"I offer the grace and blessings of Thanatos," said Saint John, "praise be to the darkness."

The man with the pitchfork pointed the wicked tines at him as the men closed in and spread out to form a loose ring. "You bastards killed Andy Harper's family, and the Millers and the Cohens and half the town."

"More than half, I assure you," murmured Saint John. "Many more than that."

The sledgehammer man gaped at him. "And you stand there and make jokes?"

Saint John shook his head. "No jokes, brother."

"My sister's husband is nothing but ashes because of you," said the sledgehammer man, "and her kids don't have their father. How is that anything but the devil's work?"

"If children grieve, then there is a path to release from all hurts and harms," replied Saint John. "We offered it to you. That offer still stands."

"Offer?" sneered the man with the pitchfork. "What kind of crap is that? You and your bunch are nothing but killers. You're no different from the walking dead."

"Oh, they're different," countered the man with the sickles. "The dead can't think. They're just mindless corpses, there ain't no evil in them, 'cept in what they do; but this scumbag and that psychotic witch Rose—they're pure evil." He glared at Saint John. "Evil to the core, and may you burn in hellfire forever for what you've done."

"There is no hellfire," murmured Saint John. "There is only the red doorway and the darkness."

"Red doorway?" demanded the sledgehammer man. "What the heck's that?"

Saint John drew his two knives, and in the shadows under the junipers, he showed them.

The screams of the three men chased all the birds from the trees.

37

So many things went wrong all at the same time.

Chong heard the twang of the bowstring.

He heard Sarah's inarticulate cry of grief and hatred.

He heard sounds of impact. Meaty and wet.

He heard Eve's shrill screech of horror.

He heard the laughter of the reaper named Brother Andrew.

Then all those separate sounds and all the disparate events snapped together into one terrible moment of action. Time whipped up and slammed into everyone, and suddenly the lives and fates of every person in that clearing changed forever.

Chong was no longer running.

He stood still, locked into a posture of attack, jerked to a sudden stop as surely as if he'd run into a wall. His bokken was in his hands, but the blade was shattered and the shock of a fading impact still trembled in his arms.

The woman, Eve's mother, was falling slowly, slowly to her knees, her protests silenced in the ugliest possible way.

Eve's face was covered with blood that was not her own, and her eyes danced with madness that was equal parts incomprehension and dreadful awareness.

Brother Andrew began to turn toward her.

But the archer.

The archer . . .

. . . was falling.

Danny looked at Chong with a challenging perplexity. His eyes met Chong's, then drifted down to the arrow he had just fired.

The arrow that stood out straight and immutable from Chong's torso. Chong looked down to see the feathered end of the arrow standing straight out from his stomach. He craned his neck and looked over his shoulder. The barbed tip of the arrow stuck out red and glistening behind him.

"Oh," said Chong.

The archer opened his mouth to speak, but instead of words, blood poured from between his lips. His skull looked wrong to Chong. Misshapen. Dented. Chong looked down at the broken wooden sword. The top half of the sword lay on the ground between him and the archer, shattered by the force of the blow he had just delivered.

"Oh," he said again.

With a wet gurgle, the archer dropped to his knees, then fell sideways, making no effort at all to catch his fall.

Brother Andrew turned away from the woman he had just murdered, and his grinning face went slack with shock.

"Danny . . . ?" he asked uncertainly.

Danny—the archer—was beyond answering.

Chong felt his legs beginning to tremble.

I'm shot, he thought.

The handle of the bokken tumbled from his rubbery fingers.

I'm in shock.

There was no pain. There was . . . nothing.

I'm dead.

And . . .

Well . . . that's what town boys get for trying to be heroes.

Brother Andrew took a step forward as he swung the scythe around to point at Chong. "You little piece of scum. Do you know what you've done?"

Chong wanted to explain. At the very least he wanted to ask why this man, this reaper, would be angry at the death of the archer. Clearly they were dedicated to death itself. It did not make sense that he would be angry at an incident that was part of his own beliefs. That was the thread of logic that was sewn through Chong's mind, and he wanted to discuss this philosophical point with Brother Andrew.

Chong found enough of his voice to croak out two words: "I'm sorry."

It was the wrong thing to say, and he really did not mean to give that apology to the reaper. He wanted Eve to hear it. Because her parents both lay dead on the sandy ground; but more so because Chong knew that he was not going to be able to save the little girl from this big brute.

He wanted to, though. He would even have accepted death as a price for saving her. That's what a samurai would do. There was justice in that. There was closure in that.

But to die with half the job done . . .

You're not a hero, he told himself, *but don't die a loser. Don't let them win.*

Chong took a step, but his knees buckled and he dropped down beside Danny's body. The bow was right there, inches away. The arrows were spilled all around him.

The universe is throwing you a bone, he told himself. *Take it.*

He reached for the bow with clumsy fingers. Picked it up. Picked up an arrow. The black goo smeared on the tip smelled horrible, like cadaverine or something worse.

But even as he fumbled it onto the string, Chong felt his strength pumping away. Flowing out of him.

He looked past Brother Andrew to where Eve stood.

"Run . . . ," he croaked.

The girl was frozen to the spot. Wide-eyed, voiceless with horrors so vast that she could do absolutely nothing but stand and stare.

And die. Chong knew that she was going to die. She'd stand there and be killed and never lift a hand because there just wasn't enough of her left for even that.

Brother Andrew seemed to snap out of his own daze. His lip curled in anger, and he adjusted his grip on his scythe as he began stalking across the clearing toward Chong.

"Run," begged Chong. He raised the bow and arrow, but his hands trembled with the palsy of shock and injury.

"I'll make you pay for what you've done," promised the reaper. "I'll make this last. I'll hear you scream and beg before I let you taste the darkness. By the god of death so I will."

"Will you please just shut up," Chong said between gritted teeth. Then, with the last energy he had, he pulled the string and released the arrow.

It flew straight and true and buried itself in the dirt between Andrew's feet.

The reaper laughed and raised his scythe, and its shadow painted a promise of darkness across his face.

FROM NIX'S JOURNAL

Before we left town, I did something nobody else knows about.

I went to the cemetery and dug a little hole next to where my mom's buried. I put two things in it.

The key to the house we used to live in and a drawing of me that Benny did. It looks just like I did before everything went bad.

I wanted to bury the me who used to live there, because that person was dead. It's a different person who left town.

38

Lilah steadied herself against the tree trunk and examined her wounds.

There were plenty of minor cuts and scrapes, but the real problem was a deep gash in her side that ran from just above the belt line on her left side to the middle of her thigh. The gash was uneven, deepest where the boar's tusk had struck her and going quickly shallow as it ran down her leg. Her gun belt had probably kept her from being impaled. The belt was gone, lying wherever it had landed, taking her gun with it. She still wore her vest, but all the pockets on the left had been ripped open, and the contents—including her first aid kit—were gone.

She had to stop the bleeding, though.

She patted her other pockets and found that she still had her folding knife, which had a sturdy three-inch blade. That was a relief. With a flick of her wrist she snapped the blade into place and used its razor edge to cut away both her trouser legs from mid-thigh down. The left side was useless, soaked with blood and smeared with some black goo that Lilah feared might have come from the boar's mouth. With a small grunt of disgust, she tossed it away. A moment later she heard squeals and furious grunts as the boars fought over the blood-soaked piece of cloth.

The other trouser leg was dirty but not as bad. She cut several long strips off it. She folded the remainder into a thick bandage and used the strips to lash it to her waist and thigh. Her canteen was lost, so she couldn't clean the wound, but right now it was more important to prevent further blood loss. She'd worry about infection later. If she got down from the tree, there were plenty of things she could find in a forest that were useful in combating infection. As George and Tom had each said, "Nature provides if you know how to ask." Lilah knew.

With the wound bandaged, Lilah felt her confidence returning.

However, along with the confidence came the full set of memories of everything that had happened before the boar attacked her.

Mother Rose and the reapers. The slaughter in the camp. The four-wheeled motorcycles.

And . . . the thing she had found by the cliff.

She had to get back to Chong and the others and tell them. They were in greater danger than she was, because as far as Lilah knew, the others had no idea what was happening in this stretch of desert forest. She needed to tell them, and then to get them all out of this place before . . .

Below her the boars grunted hungrily.

Lilah looked up, but there was no escape route there. The tree in which she stood reached all the way to the edge of the cliff, but long before it got there it narrowed to a slender wand that could never support her weight.

With the cold efficiency of a survivor, she dismissed it and looked down.

The hogs were there. If she landed among them, they'd close around her and tear her apart, of that she had no doubt.

However, if she were able to somehow avoid them and jump to the outside of their ring, then she might have a chance to use ground cover to help her effect an escape. There were boulders, thick bushes, and plenty of ravines and gullies in the landscape.

That left two questions.

If she climbed to a lower branch, could she manage to jump that far away from them? And if she did, did she simply have enough strength and stamina left to outrun and out-maneuver six tireless creatures?

The answer to both questions was almost certainly no.

But she had no other options. None. It was a bad choice or no choice.

So she took the bad choice.

However, before she made a move, a voice seemed to speak to her out of the shadows in her mind. Tom's voice. Just an echo.

"Warrior smart," she murmured. What was she missing that a smart warrior wouldn't?

Lilah examined the jagged branches that stuck out in all directions around her.

"Warrior smart," she said again. Then she took her knife and went to work.

CHONG TRIED TO RAISE THE BOW OVER HIS HEAD, AS IF IT COULD STOP THE reaper's killing blow.

"Don't fight it, boy," growled the reaper. "This is more mercy than you deserve—OWW!"

The reaper suddenly reeled back, the scythe falling to the dirt as he clapped his hands over his temple. Blood welled from between his fingers.

Chong did not understand what he was seeing. Death had been a heartbeat away.

Then he heard a *thwap* sound behind him, and something struck Brother Andrew in the cheek. The impact spun the reaper halfway around and opened a red gash beside his nose.

Chong saw something fall to the ground. Small and gray.

A stone?

He said, "What . . . ?"

There was another *thwap*, and another. More stones struck Brother Andrew. The big man howled in pain and tried to cover his face with his hands, but the next stone cracked against his fingers. Chong heard the bones break.

The world seemed to be going hazy and losing sense and clarity. Chong thought he heard a girl's voice, but Eve stood in front of him, her mouth shocked to silence.

Lilah, he thought. *God, here she is to rescue me. Again. She's going to be so mad at me.*

A female figure rushed out of the woods. Lithe and beautiful. Strong and alien. Wearing the fierce glare of a killer.

But it was not Lilah.

The figure raised her weapon and fired, and Brother Andrew howled in pain as another stone struck his forehead.

Chong spoke her name in a thin wheeze.

"Riot?"

The girl looked wild and terrible. Her face was bruised and crisscrossed with scratches. Blood trickled from one ear, and there was a shallow knife cut across the tanned flesh of her bare midsection.

She stood over Carter's body with tears streaming down her face as she drew and fired stone after stone from her slingshot.

The reaper bellowed and tried to fight through the barrage, dodging some of the shots, taking others on his huge forearms as he sought to protect his face. Riot kept shooting, though, and the sharp stones cut bloody lines in the reaper's skin.

And yet, the stones were not enough.

Brother Andrew was a monster of a man, with muscles packed onto his limbs. Riot was hurting him, but she wasn't stopping him, and with a bear's growl he waded into the attack, scythe clutched in powerful fists, head bowed to protect his face.

"No," whispered Chong. "No!"

He suddenly lunged for the reaper and grabbed a fistful of the red cloth streamers on the big man's ankle, yanking them with all the strength he had left. The sudden jerk made Brother Andrew stumble.

"Get off," snapped the reaper as he smashed Chong across the face with a brutal backhanded blow.

Fireworks exploded inside Chong's head and he sagged down, but his hand remained clamped around the red streamers. He distantly heard another *thwap* and Andrew's howl of pain, but Chong's vision was filled with black smoke. He collapsed down on his chest.

Andrew kicked free of his grip and raised a foot to stomp down on Chong's head. But there was a cry like a hunting hawk and the meaty thud of flesh on flesh, and Chong peered up in wonder to see the reaper and Riot fall together in a snarling and deadly embrace. Andrew had his hands on Riot's throat, but the young woman did not seem to care. She had a small knife in each hand, and as she crashed down and rolled over and over with the reaper, those blades did horrific work. Blood splashed the ground and spattered Chong's face as he watched, dumbfounded and appalled as Riot—a teenage girl—slaughtered the monstrous reaper.

There was no better word. No cleaner word.

It was slaughter.

Then it was over. Riot rose from the red ruin that had been Brother Andrew. Blood dripped from her knives, her arms, her face. Tears streamed down her cheeks. She looked across the clearing at Carter, then at Sarah, and finally at Eve—who stood as still and blank-eyed as a statue.

That was the last thing Chong saw before a massive wave of darkness rose up and then crashed down on him, washing everything else away.

BENNY AND NIX KEPT MOVING, HEADING EAST. WHEN THEY LOOKED BACK there was no sign of Saint John, and the sound of the quads had all but faded out. All that remained was a faint buzz far away. There were no more yells or gunshots, either. The forest became quiet, but it did not at all feel like a natural calm.

"I don't understand this," said Nix.

"Don't understand what? That guy back there or the whole freaking day?"

"People," she said angrily. "The world ended, most of the people on the whole planet died . . . there's no more reason for people to fight each other. There's so much farmland we can use that no one will ever need to go hungry again. Even out here in the desert there are berries and figs and streams of pure drinking water. There's no need to fight. But that's all we've done. First Charlie and the Hammer, then White Bear and Preacher Jack, and now all this. I don't understand it. When are we going to stop fighting? When are we going to actually want peace? When are we going to stop being so damn stupid?"

Benny shook his head. "I know, it's crazy."

"I mean," Nix went on, "are we being naive about this? Are we just a couple of stupid kids who think that the world should make some kind of sense?"

"I know," Benny said again. "I was kind of hoping we'd left that stuff behind with Gameland."

"It can't be everywhere," she growled softly. "It can't be."

As she said it, Benny noticed that she looked up at the sky, which was just visible through the canopy of juniper branches.

"They said they saw the jet," said Benny. "That's something."

She only grunted, and they walked in silence for several minutes.

Eventually Benny paused for a moment to use the sun and his wristwatch to orient himself. He squatted down and ran his fingers along the topsoil, which was darker than it had been when they'd first entered the forest.

"We should be pretty close to where Lilah went looking for Eve's parents," he said. "There's some moisture in this dirt. Maybe we're getting near to the creek Eve mentioned."

Nix nodded, but she studied the woods. "I wonder where Lilah is. Did Chong find her? And where are they both right now?"

"I don't know," admitted Benny. "There was a lot of fighting going on back at the field."

"I didn't hear Lilah's pistol anywhere," said Nix. "In fact, the only gun I heard was that guy Carter's shotgun. I don't think the reapers have guns."

Benny thought about that, and nodded. "I didn't see any either. That's something."

"Reapers," murmured Nix. "There's no way that name is going to be anything but bad."

"No kidding," he said as they started down the trail

again, angling more eastward to follow the richer soil mix. "That Saint John clown didn't make a lot of sense. Who's Thanatos?"

"One of the Greek gods of death," Nix said automatically.

Benny studied her. "How do you—?"

"We studied it in school."

"We did?"

"Of course. It's from Greek mythology."

"I don't remember anything about Thanatos or Nyx."

"Well," Nix said with a sniff, "while you and Morgie were trading Zombie Cards under your desks, some of us were actually paying attention."

"Okay, then explain to me why a bunch of freaks with knives are running around the woods talking about Greek gods. Did we have a Greek apocalypse, too?"

Nix grinned. "I think your new girlfriend is on Saint John's team."

"What?"

"Riot. She has the same tattoos on her head. So did all the reapers on the quads."

"First, she's not my girlfriend," said Benny. "My girlfriend is a crazy redhead with freckles."

That earned him a small smile from Nix.

"And second, Riot was with Carter. Besides, the woman I saw in the field was dressed like the reapers, and she had a full head of hair. So that doesn't prove anything."

"Maybe she wasn't with the reapers. I don't know, but the ones on the quads and Saint John had the same kind of skin art as Riot, so—"

"I don't care. Riot was with Eve's family."

A wide gully yawned before them, and they stopped to examine it, but there were no signs of lurking zoms or reapers with gleaming knives. Even so, they moved silently and with great caution, weapons ready, minds alert.

"Well, we have one thing going for us," Benny said as they left the gully behind them. "We should be safe from the reapers."

"How do you figure that?" Nix demanded.

"Aren't you supposed to be the mother of Thanksalot, the personification of death?"

"Thanatos," she corrected.

"Right. Praise be to the darkness."

"Ugh. Don't say that, it's freaky. Besides, Thanatos's mother was Nyx. With a y."

"Right, I'm sure that's going to make a world of difference," said Benny sourly. "If we're attacked, you can dazzle them with spelling and grammar."

She started to say something back, but Benny caught her wrist and pulled her down behind a tree. Nix started to ask what was wrong, but then she heard it too. The sound of motors coming their way.

Benny drew his sword but kept the blade in the shadow cast by the tree. Nix had her pistol out, the barrel pointed at the lead figure in a line of three quads that bumped and rocked along the forest path. Two men and a woman drove the machines. Reapers, without a doubt.

Benny was acutely aware that Nix had only two bullets left.

Nix thumbed the hammer back, but Benny whispered, "Don't. Not unless they see us."

Seconds burned away as the quads tore along the path,

the roar of the motors filling the air. Then, a hundred feet shy of where Benny and Nix crouched, the line of vehicles turned and headed due east. The motor sounds diminished quickly; soon the reapers were gone, and an uneasy silence draped itself over the forest once more.

Nix blew out her cheeks and leaned her forehead on her outstretched gun arm. She uncocked the pistol. Benny bent and kissed her on the shoulder.

"They're gone," he said as he slid the *katana* back into its sheath.

Without raising her head, Nix said, "You know, Benny, there was a time—was it only a day ago?—when the sound of a motor would have been like Christmas to us. It would have proved that the world wasn't dead, that there was something out here to find."

"I know." Benny sighed. "And I remember a time not that long ago when we were happy. When we used to laugh."

Nix raised her head and looked at him for a long moment, her lips parted as if she was going to reply. The look in her eyes was so deeply sad that Benny had to look away to hide the tears that suddenly formed in his eyes.

They got to their feet and continued moving toward the creek. Neither spoke for a long time. Then they found the stream and followed the muddy banks to a small clearing, and there they found the blood-spattered remains of several tents. They stood side by side at the edge of the creek, neither of them willing to take another step up the bank.

"God . . . ," whispered Nix in a voice that was filled with horror.

Benny spotted something and made himself climb the

slope to the camp. He bent and picked up a stuffed rabbit. It was smeared with blood. He held it out to Nix, but she just shook her head.

"There must have been an attack," he said. "That's why Eve ran. In the confusion she must have gotten separated from her family. From all this gear, it looks like there were a lot of people here. We only saw her parents and that girl, Riot."

"Benny, look," Nix said, pointing to the stream bed. Two bodies lay half-submerged right at the next bend. They walked cautiously down and saw that they were truly dead. Neither was a reaper. They were ordinary-looking folk, and savage blows to their heads and necks had probably killed them and prevented them from rising. An unintended mercy buried within a heinous crime.

A few yards away they found a third body, and they squatted down to examine it. It was a middle-aged woman, and it was clear that she had been stabbed in the chest. Nix tilted her head to one side and grunted.

"She wasn't quieted," she said. "No head wound, no incision at the brain stem."

Benny double-checked and then nodded. "It's happening here, too. Not all of the dead are reanimating."

"I wish I knew if that was a good thing," said Nix.

"It was for Tom."

She looked at the ground for a few seconds, then nodded. "I'm sorry."

He shook his head. In silence they rose and moved along the stream. They found other bodies. Many others.

This had been the scene of a terrible slaughter. Here and there they found dead reapers, too, and each of these had been quieted by knives to the base of their skulls. But most of the dead were not reapers. Benny stopped counting when the toll reached fifty. Men, women, and children.

No one had been spared.

No one.

Nix's lips curled back from her teeth in a feral grin. "Who are these freaks?"

Benny sat down on a rock and looked at his shoes. Then an idea struck him. "I think this is some kind of death cult," he said.

She turned sharply. "What?"

"Think about it," he said. "What else could it be? You said Thanatos was the Greek god of death, and Saint Jerk-o kept talking about the 'gift of darkness.' Seems kind of obvious."

Nix snorted. "I said Thanatos was one of the Greek gods of death. The nice one, the one that takes away suffering. These reapers don't seem like they're trying to alleviate suffering. Besides—I can't think of anything stupider than a death cult after an apocalypse."

"Maybe," Benny said dubiously.

"What's that supposed to mean?"

Benny looked at her, surprised. "Really? You're telling me that you can't see their point?"

"Their point?"

"Shh, keep your voice down."

Nix stepped closer. "Benny, what are you saying? That you agree with—?"

"What?" He almost laughed. "Agree? Are you nuts? I never said I agreed with anything. All I asked was whether you could understand their point."

"What possible point could there be to a death cult?"

Benny stared at her. "You're serious?"

She punched him on the arm. Hard. "Of course I'm serious."

"First . . . ow. Second, I thought you were the one who was always all torn up about people back home being so depressed and fatalistic. You were always going on about how people have just given up. That's why we're out here, isn't it? Trying to find some survivors who still believe that there is a future."

"That's my point," she snapped. "We need to focus on being alive."

"We do, sure, but that's you and me and Chong and Lilah. Maybe a few others. Everyone else is still acting like they're at a funeral for the human race."

"That's grief and depression," said Nix, "not a freaking death cult."

"Maybe those things aren't all that far apart. C'mon, you've heard all those stories about how many people committed suicide after First Night. Mayor Kirsch said that almost half the people who settled Mountainside killed themselves within eighteen months."

"It wasn't nearly that many," Nix said defensively, but it was a weak parry.

"Yes, it was. I heard Captain Strunk talking to Tom about it. Pastor Kellogg did a sermon about it."

Nix holstered her pistol. "I must have missed church that day."

"Okay, then what about the way-station monks? Some of them let themselves get bitten because they think it's what God wants. They think the zoms are the meek that are supposed to inherit the—"

"I know," she said bitterly.

Benny paused, studying her face. "Are you really going to sit there and tell me that you never thought about it?"

Nix's head whipped around so fast that her flying hair brushed across Benny's face. "I would never kill myself."

"Whoa! Whoa, now. Who said anything about—?"

"You did. You asked me if I thought about killing myself."

"No, I didn't," he insisted. "I asked if you ever thought about people in town killing themselves."

"That's not what you said."

"It's what I meant, and you know it."

Nix narrowed her eyes at him in an expression that was half a glare and half an inspection of his eyes.

"Whatever," she said, and turned away again. She drew her bokken, then stood there, pretending to study the landscape.

Benny stared at the back of her head and did not dare say anything else. Nix had been absolutely correct. He had asked her if she ever thought about killing herself.

The thing was . . . he did not know why he asked that.

He wondered if beating his head against the tree trunk would help the moment any. It seemed like the most reasonable option.

Nix abruptly walked into the woods, heading to an upslope that led away from this scene of carnage. "Let's go," she called over her shoulder.

"Where?"

She pointed toward a line of white rocks beyond the trees. "Up there. We can climb those rocks and see if we can spot Lilah and Chong."

She moved off, not looking back to see if he followed.

After several heavy seconds of indecision, Benny rose and ran after her.

They moved carefully through the brush, and the closer they got to the line of bright white rocks, the less certain Benny became that they were rocks at all.

Maybe it was a building, he thought. There had to be a ranger station or something out here.

Nix reached the edge of the woods first and suddenly stopped dead in her tracks.

"No . . . ," she said softly.

Her bokken dropped from her hand and clattered on the rocky ground. Benny hurried to catch up, and as he did Nix screamed out a single word.

"NO!"

She yelled it so loudly that birds erupted from the trees. The echo bounced off the surrounding rocks. It was loud enough to be heard a mile away.

Loud enough for everyone to hear them.

Chong. Lilah.

Riot.

The reapers.

The dead themselves.

Louder still than her scream was the thunder of Benny's heart as he saw what had torn that shout of denial out of her.

There was no ring of white rocks. There was no ranger station or a forgotten farmhouse.

It was a huge machine that had been smashed against the unforgiving landscape.

And it was heartbreakingly familiar.

It was an airplane.

PART TWO

BROKEN BIRDS

Shallow men believe in luck.
Strong men believe in cause and effect.

—RALPH WALDO EMERSON

"No!" cried Nix as she shoved past Benny and rushed forward, but he darted out a hand and caught her arm.

"Wait," he warned in a sharp whisper.

"Let me go," she said viciously, and tore her arm out of Benny's grasp, giving him a wild and murderous glare. "Don't you see what that is?"

"It's a jet—"

"It's *the* jet." Tears broke and fell down Nix's freckled cheeks. "Look at it. Everything's ruined. Oh God, Benny . . . everything's ruined."

Benny pushed back a low-hanging branch and stepped out of the woods so he could see the wreckage. His heart sank in his chest, and his fingertips were ice cold from shock.

Beyond the trees was a plateau. One side dropped away into a crevasse that was choked with tall pines; the other side leveled out into a section of flat forestland. A long trench was cut into the mud of the flatland, stretching back at least half a mile, and the nose of the craft was smashed into a mound of mud. Benny had slid into enough bases in rainy baseball games to understand the physics of that. The plane had not simply crashed; instead the pilot had tried to land it, coming in low and then sliding to a long, messy stop on the forest floor.

Because these woods were part of the Mojave Desert, the soil was loose and sandy, which had probably kept the plane from disintegrating on impact. The fuselage was almost intact, though there were jagged tears all along the side they could see. Both wings had been sheared clean off. One was wrapped like wet tissue around a tall finger of rock two hundred yards down the trench. The other wing had torn off closer to where the craft stopped its fatal slide, and it had twisted into an upright position, looking like the sail of an old-time vessel. The main fuselage was almost a hundred feet long and was cracked in two places, but the plane had not torn itself to pieces. Even so, bits of debris were littered behind it, some blackened from fire, others still gleaming white where they were visible against brown sand and green pinyons and junipers. Creeper vines clung to the metal skin of the plane and to each of the fractured wings. The vines were draped like spiderwebs between the blades of the four big, silent propellers.

The glass windows at the front of the craft were smashed in, and the creepers had intruded there, too. A metal hatch stood open a few yards aft of the crumpled nose, gaping like a black mouth in the whiteness of the plane. Plastic sheeting hung in tatters from the open hatch, and there were old bones in the grass below the ragged ends of the plastic. Benny had seen pictures of inflatable escape ramps that were used for emergency landings, and the plastic looked like it might be the remnants of one.

He pointed it out to Nix as he picked up her fallen bokken. "Look at that. Somebody survived the crash."

That thought edged down the panic in Nix's eyes by a couple of degrees. She accepted her wooden sword, but her hands gripped the handle with such white-knuckled force that Benny thought she was going to attack the dead aircraft. She took a couple of quick steps toward the plane.

"Be careful," he said, keeping his voice low in case there were reapers in the woods.

"I'm going to look," she said in a voice that was less confident than she probably wanted it to sound.

Benny began to follow and then stopped. He felt a frown pull down the corners of his mouth, but he did not consciously understand why. His eyes roved over the scene again. The trench, the plane, the foliage, the broken wings, the open door. His frown deepened.

Something was wrong. Very wrong.

"Nix, wait," he said. "Don't."

She paused and looked sharply at him. "Why not?"

Benny licked his lips. "I . . . don't think that's our jet."

"What are you talking about?"

"Nix, that's not the jet we saw."

She looked from the plane to Benny and back again, and there was such fury in her eyes that he made sure he wasn't in easy swinging range of her bokken. "You're crazy," she barked. "Of course it's the one we saw."

"No, it isn't, and keep your voice down." Benny came and stood beside her. "Look at it, Nix. This thing's been here for at least a year. Probably more."

"How would you know?"

Nix's harshness was beginning to grate on him, and he snapped back.

"Open your eyes," he said, his own tone growing sharp. He pointed to the small trees that had poked through the bottom of the trench. "Look at those saplings. Come on—they're at least a year old. At least that, and maybe older. Some of them look two years old."

"They're saplings, Benny. Saplings bend. They could have bent over and sprung back up."

"No way. They'd have been snapped off. Look, there are bigger trees that were torn right out of the ground."

It was true; the dead trunks of a hundred small pine trees lay in the trench, their limbs snapped, roots torn out of the sandy soil. Many of them were ripped completely apart, and there were dried sticks that could easily have been saplings that were killed during the crash. Benny pulled a few up and brought them over to Nix.

"See?" he said. "These were the saplings the plane hit. Those others could never have survived this big freaking thing crashing down on them."

"So what?" she demanded. Somehow, with her voice lowered to a whisper, she sounded even angrier and more annoyed with him. "Since when are you an expert on plant growth?"

"I'm not an expert, Nix, but I'm not stupid, either."

Nix started to say something, then thought better of it and instead said, "It could have crashed after we saw it. That's eight months. You don't know how fast juniper saplings grow, Benny. These could be only eight months old."

"Maybe," Benny conceded, "but I doubt it."

They moved forward together, cautiously, eyes searching the dead flying machine.

They were so riveted by the plane that they did not look into the surrounding woods and so did not see the dead zoms sprawled twenty yards down a crooked game trail; or the two bloody spots where a pair of reapers had died from Lilah's savage attack. Their bodies were gone, and bloody footprints trailed away into the shrubs.

Nix went over and stood by the draped plastic that hung from the open door. Benny continued walking until he was at the base of the upright section of wing, then he stared down the length of the trench at the other wing. He looked at the twisted blades of the propellers. Two six-bladed props had been attached to each wing, and one had fallen off. Benny went over to it and touched the tip of one of the propeller blades.

"I'll admit that I don't know everything about planes," he said, "but after we got back last year, I looked through every book we had in the library and in tons of magazines over at Chong's. This is definitely not the one we saw. I'm absolutely sure of it."

"Why?" she demanded, and there was mingled anger, fear, and hope in her eyes.

He was smiling as he turned.

"Nix, the thing we saw flying over the mountain was a jet . . . and this thing has propellers," he said. "Jets don't have propellers."

Nix's eyes flared and her mouth opened, but for the moment she was totally incapable of speech. Her eyes cut instantly from Benny's face to the blades of the massive propeller that lay in the dirt behind him.

"And that opens up a whole new can of worms," he added.

He patted the wing lightly. "Because no matter which one of us is right about when this crashed, it definitely crashed more than a dozen years after all the lights went out."

"God . . . ," breathed Nix.

"That means there were at least two planes in the air. And if there were two . . . how many more might be out there?"

FROM NIX'S JOURNAL

Just after Christmas I had a big fight with Benny. He found one of my notebooks. He swore that he didn't mean to read it. He said it was on the porch lying open, faceup. He saw what I'd written, and he flipped through the pages.

He had no right to do that. He had no right to make a big deal about it. So what if I wrote "We have to find the jet" a hundred times on every page? I told him it was a way to focus my mind and help me get ready for leaving town.

He didn't believe me, and we had a really bad fight.

I am NOT obsessed. Benny's a jerk sometimes.

SAINT JOHN CLEANED HIS KNIVES WITH A PIECE OF CLOTH HE KEPT IN HIS pocket. That cloth had cleaned those knives a hundred times.

He stepped around the red things that lay on the ground. Saint John did not disrespect them by stepping over their corpses. These heretics were in the darkness now, and their bodies were now holy relics, proof of the red doorway that opened between the world of flesh and the infinite realm of spirit.

"Thank you," he said to them. "Thank you."

He wept softly as he moved around the spot where the killing had been done. It was a shrine now, and anyone with eyes would be able to understand the beauty of what had happened here. That beauty coaxed tears from Saint John's eyes; but that was not the only reason he cried.

There were jealous tears on his face, and he lowered his head in shame, unable to look at these transformed ones. His envy of their freedom was nearly unbearable. Though they had been blasphemers mere moments ago, each of them—even the least of them—was more fully and truly connected to the darkness than he was. While he was clothed in flesh, while he lingered here on earth, he was an outsider to the purity of the darkness. An enabler, yes, a conduit, even a guide, but not a part of it.

For that, he wept.

He staggered over to a patch of unmarked grass and dropped heavily to his knees. He slid his knives into their sheaths and then bowed down, placing his forehead on the ground in abject humility.

"Please," he prayed, "let me come home. Please."

The darkness whispered inside his brain.

Not yet, my son. There is still so much work to do.

"How much longer, Lord? I have opened so many red doors, I have cleansed more heretics than I can count. How much longer?"

Until the world is silent. There are so few left, and you must save them all. You must guide each of them to the red door.

"Mother Rose and I are always in the service of—"

You, my child, are my trusted servant. You.

Tears fell like rain from Saint John's eyes, falling to the ground. His body shook with sobs, and he beat his fists upon the ground.

Last of all shall I bring you home, my believed son. Last and most treasured of all.

Saint John wept until his chest ached from it and his throat was raw.

Then, slowly, as if he lifted the entire world with him, he rose from the ground and climbed wearily to his feet.

He turned and looked at the crimson horrors behind him.

"Until the world is silent," he said thickly. He sniffed back the last of his tears. "Such is the will of Thanatos—praise be to the darkness."

Then he turned once more and followed the footprints of the two teenagers into the forest.

43

CHONG WAS HAVING THE WEIRDEST DREAM.

He felt as if he was flying.

Not happy flying, like in his dreams where he would rise up out of bed, swoop down the stairs, and zoom out into the streets of town and then soar up to dive and play with eagles and falcons. No, this was a bumpy, smelly, strangely loud kind of flying.

And it hurt.

He tried to move his hands and feet, but they seemed . . .

He fished for the proper way to describe it to himself.

They seemed . . . tied. Restrained.

Chong opened his eyes for just a moment and saw impossible things. He was moving across the ground at an incredible rate of speed. Faster than a horse could run. The ground was bumpy, and there was smoke in his nostrils.

He turned his head and saw the tanned back of a slim girl seated in front of him.

Her name was just beyond his reach.

The explanation to all this was just beyond his reach.

As he grabbed for it, the darkness came and took him again.

BENNY AND NIX STOOD IN SILENCE, LOST FOR THE MOMENT IN THE ENORMITY of what they now knew to be the truth.

Two planes.

Maybe more. Probably more.

Somebody was out there.

For Benny it was one of those moments in which he knew for sure that the world as he knew it had changed. No matter what he did, even if he turned around and went back to Mountainside, the world was never going to be the same again. It could not be.

We can't un-know this, he thought.

Nix stepped back and studied the plane. So far all they had seen was one side and the tail section. They would have to climb the mountain of impacted dirt to see the front and the other side. Above them, the dark mouth of the open hatch seemed to scream an invitation.

Or a warning, thought Benny.

Nix pointed to something on the side of the plane forward of the hatch.

"What's that?" she asked. "Is that writing?"

Benny squinted at it, mouthing the letters as he tried to

read them through a patina of dried mud. "'C-130J Super Hercules.'"

"What's that mean?"

"I . . . think it's the kind of plane this is. I half remember reading something about a plane called a C-130. I just can't remember what I read. Something about troop transports, maybe?"

"Troop transports?" Nix's eyes went wide. "Benny! Do you think that means there's an army someplace?"

He shook his head. "I don't know what it means. I can barely remember what it meant before First Night. Now . . . who knows?"

Nix's eyes roved over the dead machine, then she pointed again. "Look, on the tail. More writing."

They hurried closer to the big tail section, which also resembled a ship's sail. It was badly smudged with soot and grime. The sun glare reflecting off the white metal was so bright that they had to cup their hands around their eyes.

"I think that's a flag," Benny said.

"Not the American flag," corrected Nix. "Look, it only has a couple of stars. And there's something written below it. I can't make it out, though. American . . . something."

It took Benny a few seconds to piece it together. "'The . . . American . . . Nation.'"

Nix frowned. "Is that what they used to put on air force planes?"

"I'm not sure. I . . . don't ever remember seeing it put that way. Besides, I was mostly looking for commercial jetliners. That's what we saw."

They stood there for a moment. Benny could feel indecision gnawing at him. He turned and looked back at the woods. "I haven't heard anything for a while now."

"No," she agreed.

"I hope that's good news."

She nodded but said nothing; clearly she was more interested in the plane than in the welfare of Lilah and Chong. Benny found that profoundly disturbing.

"We need to look inside," said Nix.

"Yeah," Benny said, and headed to the front of the plane. The mound of dirt was so steep that he had to climb it on all fours. But as he reached the top, he saw that there was an easier path that emptied out from the woods. That wasn't what made him freeze in place, however. "Oh my God!"

"What?" demanded Nix, who was just behind him.

"Don't come up here," Benny warned, but it was already too late. Nix reached the top and cried out exactly as he had.

"Who . . . ?" she began, but shook her head and didn't finish.

The clearing in front of the plane was not at all clear.

There were several things placed just in front of the crumpled nose of the plane. They had been out of sight behind a row of twisted trees.

The first object was a small altar made from red stones scavenged from the arid ground. The altar was covered with bundles of dead flowers and small fire-blackened incense bowls. Set atop the altar was a row of human heads.

Not skulls. Heads.

Five of them. The oldest was withered and nearly picked clean by insects; the freshest could not have been more than a day old.

Nix gagged.

But the spectacle was worse than this pagan display.

Beyond the altar, standing in the shadow of the big plane, were three posts, more like T-bars than crosses, and lashed to each one was a body.

The bodies wore the faded and wind-torn rags of military uniforms.

The three bodies were withered, but they were not lifeless.

They were zoms.

FROM NIX'S JOURNAL

I remember one day when Tom got pretty cheesed at Benny. Benny was trying to impress Morgie, and he said something about having killed so many zoms that he could do it in his sleep.

Tom blew his stack.

He gave us all a big lecture about how we can never let down our guard, never rest on our laurels, never forget that every single zom is as much a danger now as they were the first time we faced them. He went on and on like that.

Benny apologized and all and said it was just a joke. But I don't think Tom really believes him.

45

LILAH WAS NOT AFRAID TO DIE.

Death was something she knew too well, too intimately, to fear. Annie and George were on the other side of death. So was Tom.

Only Chong was here, and in her heart Lilah believed that if she died today, then Chong would not survive very long. Not even with Benny and Nix. The Ruin was too hard for them. Too dangerous. They were all town kids.

Below her the boars grunted and milled around, agitated by the nearness of living flesh.

Lilah examined the thing she held in her tanned hands. It was not as powerful as the spear she'd lost; or as quick as the gun that lay somewhere in the gloom below, but she liked the heft of it.

Using her knife, she'd cut three of the straightest branches she could reach, then shaved off the twigs and smaller branches and trimmed the branches into four-foot-long poles. Then she removed her canvas vest, stowed the last useful items in her pants pockets, and cut the vest into many long strips. Once all the cutting and trimming was done, Lilah placed the crossbar of the knife between the poles and lashed it all together with turn after turn of canvas. Lilah knew a great deal about knots and binding. She preferred soft leather—deer hide was best—but a smart warrior used the resources at hand rather than wasting time longing for what she did not have.

It was a painstaking process, but Lilah did not hurry. A mistake in preparation would guarantee failure. The result of her work was a kind of long-handled ax. The blade of the knife protruded at a right angle from the tip of the ax, and a piece of hard, knotty wood was lashed to the back end to create a club. As long as the poles and bindings held, she could chop and smash.

The hogs crashed into the tree again.

Lilah climbed carefully down, limb by limb, until she stood on a stout branch seven feet above the circle of dead boars. They stopped ramming the tree and glared up at her, and Lilah's smile flickered. There was intelligence in those eyes. Not human intelligence, but the cold and calculating intelligence of a predator. Animal cunning. Animal hate.

Why? And . . . how? The zombie plague, whatever it was, erased all intelligence when it reanimated the dead body. Right?

It was a problem she would have to think about later. Now she needed her entire mind to be focused on what would happen in the next few seconds.

Lilah tested the bindings, looking for loose knots and weak points. There were none.

A vagary of wind brought sounds to her, and she lifted her head to listen. Were there voices? Yells? She listened and listened, but all she really heard was the white noise of the endlessly moving trees and the chatter of birds and monkeys.

"Warrior smart," she told herself.

And then she took her ax in both hands and jumped.

"ARE YOU DEAD?"

Chong heard the voice coming from somewhere beyond the darkness in which he floated. A girl's voice.

Nix? No, it was a harder voice.

Lilah? Definitely not. Lilah's voice was always a smoky whisper.

"Yo!" said the voice. "You in there, boy?" This time the voice was accompanied by a sharp poke in his shoulder.

He said, "Ow."

"Okay, then y'all's not dead."

She had a thick accent and pronounced it *dayud*.

Chong licked his lips. "Delighted to hear it," he said. There was a cool cloth across his eyes, and he had no desire to remove it. If he did, then he would have to face the reality of where he was, and he was not quite ready for that. He felt absolutely terrible. Weakness was the worst part, and it seemed to go all the way down to his bones. He wanted to sleep. Not here; at home. The best thing in the world would be to be curled up in his bed on the second floor of his family's A-frame house. Maybe Mom would come and tuck the blankets in around him and kiss him on the head in that way she always did, even when he was too big to be tucked in. Moms are moms, they did that sort of thing. It would be nice, too. Being tucked in by his mom would chase all the monsters away. A little kiss to make the pain go away too; to help him drift off to sleep.

That would be real nice.

But that was a different world. Mom probably thought that he was dead by now. Her skinny, bookish son lost out in the Rot and Ruin. Would she be sitting on the edge of his empty bed right now, crying, her heart broken? Would she be praying that her son wasn't a zom shambling forever through the decaying wasteland?

"Hey," said the girl, poking him a second time.

"Please stop doing that."

The cloth was whipped away, and Chong reluctantly opened his eyes.

Riot sat beside him. She had cleaned the blood from her face.

"You asked if I was dead," he said. His voice was thick. "Should I be dead? Am I dying?"

"Well," said the girl, "you got shot, boy, so put that in the pot and see if it's soup."

"Ah," he said, bracing himself for the return of his memories. Brother Andrew, the archer. Carter and Sarah.

The black-tipped arrow.

"Riot . . . ?" he said slowly. "That's your name, isn't it?"

"Well," she said, "look at you being sharp as a new blade of grass."

She studied him with eyes that were older than the face in which they were set. There was wisdom there, and a cunning that looked every bit as sharp as Lilah's, but there was something else, something that Chong always saw in Lilah's eyes. Sadness. Not new grief, but an older sadness that ran so deep it was as much a part of this girl as her skin. A sadness that was aware of itself and knew that it had nowhere to go.

They were inside what looked to be an old shack. Bare walls, a wood beam ceiling draped with spiderwebs.

"What else do y'all remember?" asked Riot.

"All of it, I suppose." Then he gasped. "Eve! What happened to her? Please, tell me that they—"

"She's here," said Riot quietly. "Keep your voice down. She's sleeping."

Chong turned his head and saw a tiny figure curled up under a thin blanket in the far corner. He made as if to sit up in order to see her better, but a meteor of pain slammed into him. He started to scream, but Riot instantly clapped a hand over his mouth, stifling the sound before it could escape. She bent close and whispered in his ear.

"If y'all wake that little girl yonder, I'll give you something to scream about, boy. We clear on that?"

Chong took in a ragged breath through his nose. Even that was an effort. He felt thin, hollow, like he was more ghost than person. He stared into her eyes and saw that there was more fear than threat there.

He nodded.

Riot studied him for a moment, returned his nod, and slowly removed her hand. She sat back on her heels.

Chong very carefully gasped in a lungful of air. The pain subsided slowly.

"Poor kid saw her mommy and daddy cut down in front

of her," murmured Riot. "Hasn't said a word since. Not a peep. She ain't ever gonna be right after something like that, but at least we can let her sleep some. It'll be a mite easier trying to grapple hold of things when she's not dead-dog tired."

Chong nodded. "She's still young . . . maybe she won't remember all of it."

Riot gave him a strange, sad look. "Nobody's that young."

"You see something like that too?"

She shrugged. "I've seen some things."

He waited, but she didn't elaborate. He looked around. "Where are we?"

"Old ranger station, I think. Brought you here on a quad I filched from one of the reapers who clear don't need it no more."

He cleared his throat. He was bare-chested, and he glanced down at the feathered end of the arrow that stood up straight from his flesh. It was low, just inside the hip bone. He touched the feathers ever so lightly. "What do we do about . . . um . . . this?"

"Unless you like the look of it, we's going to have to git 'er out. Your shirt was all bloody so I cut it off ya."

"Ah."

"Wound's a funny color and it smells, which bothers me 'cause that's too fast for ordinary infection. So I packed some stuff around the entry and exit holes—spiderwebs and moss and suchlike. Keeps it from going septic."

Chong nodded; he knew something about natural medicines. These days everyone did, and he'd read several survival manuals during the Warrior Smart training. Sphagnum moss had acidic and antibacterial properties; spiderwebs, apart from also being antibacterial, were rich in vitamin K and helped blood to clot. Chong found it comforting that this girl knew her natural medicines. Out in the Ruin, infection was every bit as dangerous as zoms and wild animals.

Over in one corner was a small fire, and some herbs were steeping in a shallow pan of water. The bow and quiver of arrows that had once belonged to Brother Danny lay on the floor. Souvenirs of an encounter Chong would rather have forgotten.

"How . . . how bad is it?" he asked cautiously. "How bad am I hurt?"

"You ain't dead, so that's something. Arrow missed most of the good stuff, and you ain't spittin' blood or nuthin'."

"Hooray?" he muttered weakly, making it almost a question.

"On the downside, you lost about a bucket of blood, boy, and you didn't do yourself any favors when you grappled hold of Andrew back there. I wouldn'ta bet a dead possum on you making it this long, you being such a skinny boy an' all. But there's some pepper in your grits."

"Thanks. I think." He closed his eyes for a second as a wave of nausea swept through him. His skin felt greasy and clammy. "Can you just pull it out?"

Riot snorted and bent down to pick up Brother Danny's quiver of arrows. She fished one of the arrows out and held up the point. "That arrow's got the same barbed point as this. Big bear tip. I'd tear a flank steak offa you if I tried to pull it out. That what you want, boy?"

"No. And will you please stop calling me 'boy'?"

"What do you want me to call you?" she asked, her eyes filled with challenge and amusement.

"My name is Louis Chong. Most people just call me Chong."

"Chong, huh. That Korean?"

"Chinese."

"Okay. Well, t'other thing is that I don't know what this black stuff is that's smeared all over the tip. Smells like death, and that's generally not good news."

"Poison?"

"Or something," she said. "Either way, we have to be smart about how we take it out and what we do about infection."

He cocked his head at her and licked his lips. "Why are you helping me? Back there at the field, you and your friends seemed pretty determined to . . . you know."

"Yeah, I do know, and we'd have done it too."

"I believe you. So . . . why the change of heart? Not that I'm looking to make you question your decisions."

Riot glanced at Eve for a moment. "Evie told me that you and your friends—the cute boy with the sword and that red-headed witch—saved her from the gray people. That earned you some real points."

"It didn't look that way back on the field. I remember you trying to take our weapons and supplies."

Riot shrugged. "Times is tough, ain't you heard? Apocalypse an' all." She rubbed her face. "You also tried to save Sarah and Eve from Brother Andrew. Almost died doing it. Cartin' you here and plucking out an arrow seems the least I can do."

"Brother Andrew," Chong repeated with a confused shake

of the head. "Who the heck are these reapers and why are they doing all this?" he asked. "I mean, I heard Andrew and Carter talking, so I think I understand some of it. Is it some kind of cult thing? Some religious cult?"

Riot considered the questions. "It's religious," she admitted. "Don't know much about 'cults.' But this is something real, and it's big."

She explained about Saint John and his belief that the Gray Plague had been a kind of "rapture," and that anyone left behind was a sinner. Saint John formed the reapers to usher those left behind into the darkness.

"Darkness? What's that? Heaven?"

"Don't rightly know. Saint John says that it's the place where pain and sufferin' don't exist no more. He never said anything about pearly gates or none of that stuff."

"And people join him?"

A strange light kindled in her eyes. "Oh, yes they do. By the hundreds and by the thousands."

Chong thought about it. "Brother Andrew said a lot of things about how hard it is to survive out here. All the disease and hunger, not to mention the zoms."

"Zoms? Oh, you mean the zees. Nobody much calls 'em zoms, 'cept the odd trader or ranger. Mostly it's 'gray people,' 'gray wanderers.' All the same."

"So . . . let me see if I understand this," said Chong. "People are eager to join the reapers and embrace the 'darkness' because this world is too hard to live in? Is that about it?"

She nodded. "It ain't as simple as that, but you got the bones of it. If all you know is suffering and fear, and next year looks to be just as bad, and the year after that and the year after that . . . who wouldn't take a hard look at an offer of no pain, no suffering?"

Chong sighed. "I'd say it was the craziest thing I ever heard of, but it's actually not. Those who want to go see God can do it right now, and those who want to find some kind of redemption—or maybe some kind of important purpose—can join the reapers and do God's work before they head off to join their loved ones."

Riot gave him a long, appraising look. "Ain't stupid, are ya?"

"I try not to be."

He suddenly swayed as another wave of nausea churned through him. He fought to control the urge to vomit.

"You okay?"

"I've felt better. Little woozy. Sick to my stomach."

Riot placed her palm on his forehead. "You're sweatin' up a storm, but I don't feel no fever. You're sick as a dog."

"Arrows in my body tend to do that to me," Chong said.

"Ah," she said. "So I heard."

Riot bent close and studied the arrowhead. "That is a beaut."

"Swell." Chong could actually feel his body turn cold. "Since we can't, um, yank it out . . . what are our options?"

"It's an aluminum arrow," she said, nodding toward the shaft. "So I'll try and unscrew the head, and then we can pull it out backwards-like. Might jostle a bit, which is why I wanted you awake 'fore I try. Can't have you waking up screaming."

"No, we can't have that."

She nodded at his bare shoulder. "What's that?"

Chong did not need to look to see what she meant. There was a fresh scar from where a zombie had tried to take a bite out of him in one of the fighting pits at Gameland. He explained that to Riot.

"You was a pit fighter?'

"Not by choice."

"And you got bit and healed?" She looked dubious.

"The zom's teeth just pinched, and I pulled away at the same time. I lost some skin, but I didn't get infected."

"You got the luck. Bit by a gray wanderer and lived to brag on it, and now shot by a reaper and you'll have that scar to use to charm the ladies. Is . . . there a lady, by the way? Maybe that little redhead with the freckles?"

"That's Nix, and she's with Benny."

"And you all alone?" she asked, a smile touching the corners of her mouth.

"I . . . I'm kind of seeing someone."

"Oh?" she asked casually as she knelt over the small fire and placed the tip of a knife in the flames. Chong did not ask her why. He already had a bad idea about what that burning metal would be used for.

"Tell me about her."

Chong told Riot an abbreviated version of Lilah's story.

Riot turned and stared at him. "The Lost Girl? You're joshing me."

"No . . . why? Don't tell me you've heard of her?"

"Oh, dang, son, I heard ten different versions of that tall tale." She laughed and shook her head. "Boys are funny. They'll make up any dang story just to impress a gal."

"You think I'm making this up?"

"Oh, no. Not at all. But when we're done here I'll introduce you to my uncle, Daniel Boone. He keeps a chupacabra for a pet and has a fresh-raised gray man as his personal butler."

Chong tried to argue, to explain that Lilah was real and that he knew her, but Riot kept laughing and shaking her head. Finally he gave it up.

Riot gave him a wicked little grin and ticked her chin toward the arrow. "So, unless you got more tall tales to tell . . . let's give 'er a go, shall we?"

BENNY AND NIX STARED AT THE ZOMBIES ON THE T-BARS. THE CREATURES twisted and reached for them, their moans softer than the desert breeze. Red streamers were tied around their ankles.

Around the neck of each was hung a small plank of whitewashed wood. The message on each was the same.

I DIED A SINNER

DARKNESS IS DENIED TO ME

"What's it supposed to mean?" asked Nix in a hushed and frightened voice.

"I don't know and I don't want to know."

Nix nervously touched one of the streamers tied to the nearest zom's ankle. "That looks like what Saint John was wearing."

"Yeah. Let me rephrase what I said. I really do not freaking want to know what this means. Actually, this whole thing is really scaring the crap out of me. We need to find Lilah and—"

"We need to look inside that plane."

He smiled at her. "You're actually nuts, aren't you? The desert sun's baked your brains and—"

Nix just looked at him. Benny felt suddenly detached from the moment. Here was Nix, the girl he loved, the girl he'd risked his life for, the girl he'd left his home for. Nix, with her wild red hair and explosions of freckles and brilliant green eyes. Nix, who had a scar on her face that Benny actually thought looked sexy. Nix, who was everything to him. But she was also the Nix he did not know. The girl he'd come to know less and less ever since they'd seen that jet.

This Nix laughed less often. This Nix was less kind, less . . . Soft?

He considered that word and its implications.

Soft could mean weak, or it could mean gentle, open, receptive. The Nix he'd known all his life was soft, but was she ever weak? No, absolutely not. Not before and not after the jet. Okay, then what about the other meaning of soft? Was this new Nix gentle?

Mostly no. Life had been so hard on her that she had become hardened.

Was she open?

Again, mostly no. Where once they could spend hours discussing or even debating points as trivial and varied as the species of a butterfly or the politics of the Nine Towns, this new Nix seldom let him inside her thoughts.

Was this Nix receptive?

That was the hardest call. She seemed open to new experiences, and would readily listen to advice or information about the best ways to do things, the best routes, safety in the Ruin, all sorts of things. But that was only receptivity along the lines of a file cabinet—information was stored, but Benny had no idea of how it was being processed.

Was this the Nix he'd fallen in love with?

No. That Nix was gone. If not forever, then at least for now. There was hardly any trace of her left.

That left a final and dreadful question. One that he had been debating for a couple of weeks now.

Was he in love with this Nix?

Benny searched and searched inside his head and heart, and he just simply did not know. The only consolation was that he didn't understand this Nix. Maybe when he did, things would get better.

He knew that Nix had always wanted to leave Mountainside. He and Chong both considered her a visionary; she had big, but practical, dreams about going beyond the fence line to make a new home out here in the Ruin. But that was before her mother was murdered and Nix was abducted. It was before Nix had been forced to fight in the zombie pits at Gameland, where she'd encountered the reanimated zombie of Charlie Pink-eye. It was before Tom died.

After all those things, Nix had changed.

Now, standing in front of the crashed plane, with proof of ugliness and madness out here in the Ruin, Benny looked into those emerald eyes and did not see anyone he recognized.

All this, all these jumbled thoughts, crashed through his mind in the space of a second or two. Most of the thoughts were rehashes of issues that had been hanging unresolved on the walls of his brain.

Benny turned away from her stare, unable to look into her eyes any longer. The Nix he knew was not there, and he didn't want this new Nix to see the agony that must be in his own eyes.

He walked to the base of the T-bars and looked up at the zoms.

He cleared his throat. "I think they were the pilots," he said.

"Why?"

"The uniforms. There were pictures in some of the books."

"Should we . . . quiet them?"

Benny looked up at the dead, who looked down at him with empty eyes and hungry mouths. Their hands pawed at the air, gray hands opening and closing on nothing.

"No," he said. "They're not hurting anyone."

Benny felt her come to stand beside him.

"I'm going to climb up into the plane," she said.

Benny cleared his throat. "It's not safe."

"Safe?" Nix echoed faintly. "When are we ever going to be safe?"

"I—"

"I'm serious, Benny. Unless we find where this plane came from, all we're ever going to do is keep running for our lives. Is that what you want? Is that why you came out here?"

He looked up at the cloudless blue sky and did not look at her. "Nix, you know exactly why I came out here."

"Look, Benny . . . ," she said in the softest voice he'd heard her use in weeks. "I know things have been bad."

He dared not turn. This was hardly the first time she'd tuned into what he was thinking, or perhaps what he was feeling. Nix was always empathic. Benny said nothing.

"Give me time," she said.

She did not wait for him to answer. She turned away and walked down the slope to the piece of plastic sheeting that hung from the open hatch. Benny turned his head ever so slightly and watched as she began to climb.

LILAH DID NOT SCREAM A WAR CRY AS SHE JUMPED DOWN TO FACE THE boars. She did not need to hype herself up for the fight; every nerve in her body was already blazing with the anticipation of battle and pain.

The pain in her side was a searing white-hot inferno, but she swallowed it, using the pain as fuel, knowing it would shotgun adrenaline into her system. It would make her faster, more aggressive, more vicious. It would keep the fear under control. And there was a lot of fear. She never pretended to be fearless, not to others and never to herself.

She did not fear her own death. Not really.

She feared not living, and to her that wasn't the same thing.

Death ended thought, ended knowing.

Not living meant that she would never see Chong's face again. She would never see the exasperation he tried so hard to hide whenever she did or said something that wasn't "acceptable" to the people in town. She would never hear his soft voice as he recited poetry. Dickinson, Rossetti, Keats. She would never feel the warmth of his hand in hers. Chong's hands were always warm, even when it was snowing outside.

She would never kiss him again.

She would never get to say the words that she ached to say.

So she said them now, just in case. Just to have them out there, to put them on the wind. To make them real.

"Chong," she murmured quietly, "I love you."

It was unlikely that he would ever get to hear her say those words. The thought of these monsters taking all that away from her made Lilah mad.

Very mad.

Killing mad.

With a feral snarl that would probably have scared the life out of Chong, Lilah dropped from the branch.

She fell with all the silence and speed of gravity. Her snow-white hair whipped away from her face as she plummeted.

She struck the closest boar feetfirst with a dead-weight impact that staggered the beast even though it was nearly five times her weight and mass. The heels of her shoes struck it on the right shoulder, and the impact sent shock waves through her shins and through the gash in her side. However, Lilah bent her knees as she struck, letting the big muscles of her thighs absorb the shock rather than her fragile knee joints.

The impact knocked the boar sideways into a second animal, and Lilah fell backward away from the pack. Despite the pain, she hit the ground the right way, tucked, rolled, and came up onto the balls of her feet.

All the boars squealed in a killing frenzy. Lilah wasted no time; there was none to waste. She rushed in and swung her ax in a high overhand blow that whistled through the air. The blade smashed into the first hog's skull and punched through right into its brain. The creature cried out and then instantly collapsed, dead for gone and forever.

Lilah went with its fall, letting the creature's own weight tear the blade free.

She'd timed it right. The first boar was down between her and the others. That bought her two seconds of time. She needed one.

Lilah whipped the ax over and around her head just as a second boar scrabbled over the dead one, and the blade struck it square in the eye socket. The steel stabbed through one eye and out the other side.

But the boar kept charging.

The puncture had missed the brain.

What had been perfect timing a moment ago was now fatal. The boar tossed its head and tore the ax handle from her hands as easily as she could have taken a toy away from little Eve. Lilah staggered back and nearly fell. Her ax went flying into the weeds on the far side of the clearing. It might as well have been on the far side of the moon for all the good it would do her now.

The boars that had fallen were back on their feet, and the whole pack charged at her.

Lilah screamed and dove away, rolling again, feeling more of her wound open up as she rose once more to her feet. She ran, and the pain chased her as surely as did the pack of boars.

The clearing was covered in short, dry grass that had withered to a lusterless brown. As Lilah ran across it, heading for the shelter of a boulder, she saw a darker brown amid the grass, and a half pace later the gleam of steel.

Her torn gun belt and the big Sig Sauer pistol were right there!

But the boars were too close.

Lilah ran past her gun and reached the boulder a split second before the pigs caught up. She slapped the curve of the rock and launched her body onto it and then over it. The boars slammed into the stone, one after another, their dead brains too damaged to correct the angle of their charge. They rebounded from the impact, and as Lilah ran around the far side of the rock, she saw that one of them had shattered its big front tusks. Far from reducing it as a threat, the damage resulted in dagger-sharp jagged stumps.

She piled on the speed, bent almost double even though her whole left side burned with fresh blood, then scooped up the holster, grabbed the butt of the pistol, racked the slide, skidded to a stop, whirled, and brought the gun up as the boars barreled straight toward her.

And then everything went a little crazy.

As she pulled the trigger there were two blasts.

Not one.

The lead boar pitched down and tumbled over and over, its head blown to fragments. The boars behind it squealed and stumbled, colliding with their fellows, crashing into and over one another in a massive pile. Only one boar remained on its feet, and it drove straight at Lilah.

Then something huge and gray came flying out of the woods and struck the third boar like a missile, knocking it sideways and down. The new creature rattled with the sound of metal, and Lilah had a surreal glimpse of spiked steel bands, chain mail, and a great horned helmet. It was a dog, but it was like nothing Lilah had ever seen. A monstrous mastiff, armored like a tank. It dragged down the much heavier boar and began systematically slashing the undead creature to pieces. It did not bite at all but instead smashed and tore with the blades welded to its armor.

The last three boars rose from where they had fallen over the one Lilah had shot. One took a single lurching step toward her, paused for a moment, and then fell over dead.

As it landed, Lilah saw the black dime-size bullet hole in its temple.

The two others glared at her. They grunted with awful hunger and charged.

Lilah brought her gun up, but a voice yelled, "No!"

And a second figure came rushing from the woods. Not a dog this time, but a man.

He leaped over the dead hogs and landed right in the path of the charging boars. The pale sunlight that slanted down through the trees glittered on the edge of a long sword the man raised above his head.

Not just any kind of sword.

A *katana*.

The man stepped into the charge of the hogs and slashed low, left and right, and suddenly the animals were falling forward, one leg on each sheared clean away. The man spun and slashed, the blade moving with incredible speed and precision so that it appeared as if the boars merely disintegrated. Then he pivoted and made two massive downward stabs, ramming the point of his sword through the weakest parts of the creatures' skulls and destroying the spark of unnatural life that burned in their zombie brains.

Behind him, the dog rose from the destroyed hulk of the other boar.

Lilah froze, her pistol clamped in hands that now trembled.

The pain in her side was screaming through her nerve endings, and shadows were piling up inside her mind.

But for all that, she could not help staring at the man who stood ten feet away, his face and body hidden by deep shadows, the *katana* held in his powerful hands.

She stared in uncomprehending shock.

The last thing she said before blood loss and damage dragged her down into the darkness was, *"Tom . . . ?"*

"Y'ALL READY?" ASKED RIOT. SHE WAS CROUCHED BEHIND CHONG, HER fingers lightly touching the barbed head of the arrow.

"No," he said through clenched teeth. Then a moment later he croaked, "Go ahead."

"Take hold of that other end, and don't you let it turn. Otherwise we'll be doing nothing but reaming the hole."

"Well," he said as conversationally as he could, "we wouldn't want that now, would we?"

"Here," she said, handing him a thick piece of leather strapping she'd cut from her belt, "take this. Put it between your teeth."

"I don't need that."

"Yeah," she said, "you do."

Chong took it with great trepidation and placed it between his strong white teeth. Then he reached down and wrapped his fingers around the shaft just below the dark feathers. "O-okay."

Riot took a deep breath; so did Chong.

"Here goes."

She gripped the end that protruded from his back, closing her left fist around it; then pinched the flat of the barb between thumb and fingers and . . . turned.

The whole arrow turned. Blood suddenly welled from both sides of the wound, darkening the strips of Chong's shirt that Riot had used to pack the wound.

The pain was . . . exquisite. It was pain on a level Chong had never imagined before, and in the last month he had been beaten, kicked, stomped, and punched by full-grown bounty hunters. Memories of that other pain lined the shelves in his mind. This pain was on a much higher shelf. It was worse than when he'd gotten shot by the arrow in the first place. When the arrow hit him, the shock of it blunted his nerve endings and slammed his mind and body into a weird kind of traumatic numbness.

That was then, this was now.

He could feel every single nerve ending as the arrow turned despite their grips.

As it turned out, he did indeed need that leather strap. Instead of throwing his mouth wide to scream, he bit down on the pain, and the scream echoed around within his body. He could feel his scream burning through him.

Riot straightened and craned her neck to see how he was holding the arrow.

"Dang it, son, don't grab the shaft, grab the feathers. You need friction to hold it steady. Hold it tight." She chuckled and added, "Pretend you're holding the Lost Girl's hand."

Several biting remarks occurred to Chong, but he did not have the breath to speak them. Instead he shifted his hand position, clamped down harder on the leather strap, and waited for her to try again.

She gritted her teeth and channeled her strength into her fingers.

The arrowhead did not turn. The whole shaft shifted inside the tunnel of flesh. The pain was every bit as bad. Chong screamed a muffled scream of torment, sucking in the sound, feeling tears and sweat burst from him. Feeling the heat of fresh blood on his stomach and back.

"It's stuck like a boot in mud," growled Riot needlessly. She tried again. And again.

Chong could feel nausea washing around in his stomach, but he did not dare give in to it. If he started vomiting now, it would make everything worse.

"Y'all want me to stop?" asked Riot.

Chong did. He really did. He wanted to tell her that. Maybe beg for her to stop. Stopping was the only sane choice.

"N-no . . . ," he wheezed, forcing the word past the leather strap.

Riot leaned over and looked at him for a moment, studying his eyes. There was a strange expression on her face that Chong could not interpret. She gave him the smallest of smiles and a tiny nod, then bent back to her work.

Riot tried again. And again. Over and over, and each time it was worse than the time before. Chong wept unashamedly.

Then . . .

"It's turning!"

Suddenly the pain and the awkward, terrible shifting of the arrow in his body changed. The arrow became almost still except for a faint tremor as the arrowhead turned and turned on its threads.

"Got 'er done!" cried Riot.

Chong closed his eyes and collapsed back, soaked with sweat and exhausted. The arrowhead was one step.

It was the easy step.

There were two more.

Riot got up and ran to the fire. She wrapped a piece of cloth around the knife and removed it from the fire. Three inches of the blade glowed yellow-white. She hurried back to Chong and knelt in front of him.

"Okay," she said, and Chong could see that she, too, was sweating heavily, "here's the fun part. I got to pull this puppy out and then cauterize the wounds. Both sides. You're bleeding, so we got to do it right quick. You ready?"

"Stop asking me that," he mumbled around the leather strap. "Just do it!"

Riot did something else first.

She quickly bent forward and kissed Chong on the tip of his nose.

"For luck," she said.

Then she took the arrow in her left hand, took a breath, and pulled.

It came out with a dreadful sucking sound that Chong knew he would never forget. Blood welled hot and red from the wound.

"Bite down," she ordered, and then she moved in with the white-hot blade.

The pain went off the scale, but still Chong held on. He screamed into the strap and bit the leather so hard he tasted blood in his mouth, but he held on.

And then he caught the smell of his own burning flesh.

That was when he passed out.

Benny came down the hill and watched Nix climb. Then, with a sigh and a certain knowledge that this was a bad idea, he took hold of one of the rents in the plastic and began climbing too.

The plastic was strong, and though it swayed with their weight, the climb was easy, and there were enough holes to provide easy purchase for hands and feet. Nix scrambled up ahead of him, nimble as a monkey.

"Slow down," Benny warned.

"Catch up," she fired back, and gave him a second's worth of a smile.

Almost like the old Nix.

Benny scrambled up after her, and they reached the open hatch shoulder-to-shoulder. Very carefully, as if they were peering in through the window of an old abandoned house from which ghosts might peer back, they raised their heads above the deck and looked inside.

There was a lot of debris. Broken fittings and equipment from the plane that must have torn loose during the crash, pieces of shattered pine branches, and last fall's dried leaves. And bones. Lots of bones. Leg and arm bones, the slender curves of ribs, and part of a skull.

Benny heard Nix's sharp intake of breath.

"No," he said in a hushed voice, "I think it's a monkey."

"Are you sure?"

Benny climbed the rest of the way up and crouched inside the hatch. He lifted the skull fragment and examined it. "Monkey," he said with relief, as much to himself as to her.

"Any, um, people bones?"

"No."

But as Nix climbed in she froze. Benny followed the line of her gaze and saw that there were more bundles of dried flowers and incense bowls. And another sign, the writing small and feminine, painted in red on white wood.

THIS SHRINE SPEAKS TO THE FOLLY OF THE WORLD THAT WAS.

EVEN THEIR STEEL ANGELS FELL FROM GRACE.

TO DISTURB THIS PLACE IS TO INVITE DAMNATION.

They were both quiet for a moment.

Finally Benny said, "Well, that's comforting."

Nix said nothing.

They looked around. The hatch opened into a narrow compartment that seemed to divide the airplane into two parts: the cockpit to their left and a huge cargo bay to their right.

Both doors were closed, and there were painted warnings on each, and white wax had been poured over the door handles. Red ribbon had been pressed into the wax.

Nix used her palm to wipe away a film of grime that obscured the message on the cockpit door. It was a single word:

LIES

"That's interesting," she said. "Let's see what's on the other door."

She crossed to the cargo bay door and tore away some creeper vines. Again the message was a single word.

DEATH

"Charming," observed Benny. "Take your pick."

Nix crossed back to the cockpit door. "This one first."

"Sure." Benny bent and examined the seal and found it untouched. "Looks like nobody has been here. Open these doors and that wax will crack right off."

Nix touched the door to the cockpit. "Open it."

"You sure this is such a smart idea?"

She made a disgusted sound. "Don't be such a girl."

Benny bit back four or five vile and wildly inappropriate comments and reached for the door. The wax seal was thick, and he had to use both hands to turn the metal handle; then with a crack the wax broke apart and the lock clicked open.

Nix, for all her bravado, pushed Benny's shoulder. "You first."

51

SAINT JOHN CAME SLOWLY OUT OF THE FOREST AND STOOD AT THE EDGE of the plateau. The crashed steel angel lay where it had died two years ago. The gray wanderers who had been the crew of the plane still hung from their posts.

Everything was as it should be.

He bent and studied the ground, but there was no easy story to read. The top shelf of the plateau was mostly flat rock, baked hard by the sun and unable to take a footprint. The tracks of the two teenagers had petered out a quarter mile back, and now Saint John was unsure if he had come the right way.

He looked up at the open hatch. Had they gone up into the thing?

He smiled and shook his head, dismissing that level of heresy in children so young. They would not remember airplanes anyway—they'd grown up in a world without such machines. Or . . . mostly without them.

He walked to the base of the plastic sheeting and gave it an experimental tug.

It was solid enough, and he debated climbing up, but he dismissed the idea. There was nowhere to go in there, no reason to try. If the children had been real flesh and bone, then they would surely die up there. If they were, as Saint John suspected, merely spiritual beings pretending to be human teenagers, then they would have no need to enter the shrine.

What would be the upshot if he were to go up and look for himself?

Apart from the direct insult to Mother Rose, whose shrine this was, it would surely be viewed as a lack of faith on his part.

These children had tried to tempt him into an act of transgression. A sin. He smiled.

It was a clever trap, but his faith was stronger than his curiosity. His faith was his armor and his sword.

A sound distracted him—the roar as a quad motor started—and he walked to the edge of the cliff and looked down to see which of his reapers was down there.

Saint John froze, his breath catching in his throat.

What he saw was not any of his people.

Instead he saw a big man buckling a girl—another teenager—onto the back of an idling quad. The girl was a complete stranger.

The man, however, was not.

Nor was the monstrous mastiff who stood wide-legged beside the machine, its body clad in chain mail and spikes.

Oh, he certainly knew this man.

This sinner.

This kind of heretic.

He mouthed the man's name. "Joe."

Saint John's hand strayed to the handle of his favorite knife, hidden as it was beneath the folds of his shirt.

And then he understood.

The two teenagers he had followed had manifested on

earth only partly to test his faith, and he had passed that test here at the Shrine of the Fallen. But they had a higher purpose, and one that was of great importance to the reapers and their cause.

Saint John now knew where Joe was.

Joe, however, did not know that Saint John of the Knife, the man he had tried to kill so many times, crouched on the edge of a cliff not a hundred feet above where he stood.

Joe knew the secrets of Sanctuary. If those secrets could be wrested from him, then they could be used to destroy Sanctuary. And oh how it needed to be destroyed. Not just for the evil that it represented, but also because of the temptation it offered to the corrupt.

Like Mother Rose.

Saint John knew full well that if his dear Mother Rose were to reach Sanctuary first—reach it and take it—then she would become a great and terrible threat. To him, to the will of God. She would become the dark queen of this world, and if Saint John could not prevent that, then God would turn his back on him and close the pathway to darkness forever.

The key to all of it was the ranger named Joe.

Joe would soon beg to reveal the secrets of Sanctuary. The sinner would tell Saint John everything and anything he wanted to know.

And Saint John would not mind at all if Joe had to scream his answers.

52

LILAH WOKE WITH A START AND IMMEDIATELY GRABBED FOR HER GUN, DREW it, raised it, and pointed it, all in a fraction of a second.

"No," said the man who sat across from her.

Beside him a monster of a dog growled a deep-chested warning.

"Who are you?"

Before the man could answer, a wave of nausea struck Lilah, and she turned away to throw up.

There was a small pit in the ground already there in case she needed to throw up. Lilah quickly bent over it. The retching and spasming hurt. A lot.

But strangely, not as much as she'd expected it to.

She clutched the pistol, still pointing it in the general direction of the stranger. When her stomach had nothing left, she sagged back and gasped.

"There's a canteen with clean water and a cloth to wipe your face," said the man.

She studied him warily. He was a big man, lean but muscular, with blond hair shot through with gray and a face that was cut by laugh lines and scars. Deep blue eyes and very white teeth. He wore jeans and a camouflage T-shirt. There was an automatic pistol holstered on his right hip and a sheathed *katana* placed within easy reach on the ground.

"You're not Tom Imura."

"Ah," he said. "That's what you meant."

"What?"

"Before you passed out, you called me Tom."

Lilah said nothing. Instead she appraised the dog. She had seen mastiffs before—they were popular among the bounty hunters. The dogs were fierce, powerful, and able to take down anyone—man, zom, or apparently, a full grown wild boar. This dog was one of the biggest she'd ever seen. Easily two hundred fifty pounds. Probably more. His body was wrapped in a coat of light chain mail, and long bands of segmented metal ran from shoulders to flanks. Metal spikes stood up along the bands. A horned war helmet sat unbuckled by the dog's feet.

The dog had dark eyes that were filled with intelligence and controlled hostility.

"Who are you?" Lilah demanded again as she shifted her aim from heart to head.

"Before you pull that trigger, let me ask you something," said the stranger casually. "Does that gun feel right to you? I mean, does it feel like it's fully loaded? 'Cause I'm thinking it doesn't." He held up the slender magazine. "Bullets are kind of heavy, don't you think?"

Lilah glared at him and then turned the pistol over. The slot at the base of the grip was empty.

"I may be getting old," mused the man, "but I'm not senile. Not yet, at least."

She cursed.

"Jeez, they teach you those words in school? What is the world coming to?"

He balanced the magazine atop a small rock that lay between them. Lilah knew that even without her injuries she could never get it, slap it into place, rack the slide, and fire before the man and the dog were on her.

She lowered the gun.

The man smiled and picked up a metal spoon to stir a small pot of soup that hung over a tiny fire. The soup smelled wonderful.

"Who are you?" she asked again.

"Well, I'm not Tom Imura, that's for sure, I think we can both agree on that. Maybe you don't know the man, but he's Japanese and I'm a blond-haired, blue-eyed all-American boy from Baltimore."

"When I first saw you . . . you were in shadows," she said. "And you have the same sword."

The man nodded at the sword slung on the ground. "Similar sword," he corrected. "Tom carries a Paul Chen *kami katana*, or he did last time I saw him. And he slings his over his shoulder."

Lilah said nothing.

"My name's Joe," he said, then jerked a thumb over his shoulder at the dog. "That's Grimm. He's the brains of this outfit, and he's made it pretty clear that I exist to fetch and carry for him."

Grimm made a wet, glopping sound with his mouth. Perhaps it was an agreement.

"We're in a safe place," Joe continued. "No bad guys, no walkers."

Lilah looked around. They were in a natural shelter formed by two massive red boulders. A quad motorcycle was parked in the shade. Joe noticed her looking at it.

"Before you ask," he said, "no—I'm not a reaper."

"Then who *are* you?" she said once more. "And why did you help me back there?"

"Is that a serious question?"

"Of course."

"Well, let's see. Girl. Hurt girl, actually. Bunch of freaking zombie pigs that want to eat hurt girl. Hmmm, why'd I step in? Truth is, I slept badly last night, woke with a kink in my shoulder, and as everyone knows, there's no better way to loosen up old joints than to go chop-socky on a couple of zombie pigs. Well-known fact."

She glowered at him. "That's a stupid answer."

"No," he corrected, "it's a silly answer. The question was pretty silly too, don't you think?" Before Lilah could organize a comeback, Joe dipped a tin cup into the steaming pot. "Have some soup."

She tried to think of a really good reason to refuse his offer. She wanted to smash it out of his hand and use the confusion to run, but she was positive that her injuries would slow her down. The dog would catch her and tear her apart.

Joe smiled at her as if reading her thoughts.

So Lilah took the cup. While Joe watched, she sniffed it suspiciously and finally took an experimental sip. She waited to see if there was any ill effect.

"It's chicken soup," explained Joe. "For some reason there's a lot of wild chickens out here. Wacky postapocalyptic landscape, right? Threw a few herbs in. Might be a little spicy."

Joe handed her a piece of clean cloth to use as a napkin.

Lilah noticed that he made no attempt to touch her. She knew that she was more than a little naive when it came to people, but at the same time she knew a lot about men. Or rather, about some kinds of men. She and Annie had been treated roughly at Gameland. Even though none of the bounty hunters had ever sexually abused them, Lilah had heard their rough jokes, and she believed that if they had stayed at that horrible place the jokes might have changed into something far worse.

During their Warrior Smart training, Tom had been very frank with them about the realities of the world. Death was not the only harm that could come to a person out in the Ruin. Especially a girl. Tom warned about strangers. The truth was often ugly, he said, and predators preyed on the unaware and uninformed.

Even so, this man seemed different. He appeared to be considerate and was making an exaggerated show of propriety. Why? To lull her off guard, or to allay her fears?

She brooded on that as she drank the soup. It was very spicy, but it was delicious.

If this man had wanted to assault her, he could have done it while she was unconscious. If he had, then dog or no, she would have found a way to make him pay. But she knew her own body. The only pain was from her wounds. She could feel the familiar tightness of stitches along her hip and thigh, but she still wore her clothes. When she probed the area, she saw that he'd cut slits in the side of her pants in order to dress the wounds. He had not removed her pants.

She eyed him over the rim of the cup.

Joe was a strange man; and once again Lilah had the sense that she was looking at Tom, even though this man was bigger, older, and of an entirely different ethnicity. There was a sameness, a kinship between him and Tom that she could not yet identify. She had seen similar qualities in Sally Two-Knives, Solomon Jones, and a few of the other bounty hunters who had fought alongside Tom at Gameland. She wasn't sure if it was a sign of moral goodness or merely a lack of obvious corruption. It was too soon to tell.

Joe watched her as she studied him, and he allowed it. He even gave what appeared to be an encouraging nod. Strange, strange man.

The dog, Grimm, suddenly got up and walked over to sniff her. Before he actually did so, he cut a look at Joe. The man gave a small gesture with one finger. A signal of some kind. The dog whuffed and bent close to sniff Lilah.

"Is he safe?" she asked.

"Safe as I want him to be," said Joe. "Pet him if you want."

As he said that, Joe made a small clicking sound with his tongue. Another signal.

Lilah tentatively reached out and touched the dog's head. His fur was dark and coarse, but very soft. She ran her fingers along the top of his head, tracing the skull, and then gently rubbed one of his ears between thumb and forefinger.

Grimm turned his head and licked her fingers.

"You made a friend," said Joe. "Grimm's not easy to charm."

"He's a war dog," she said, intending that to explain why the dog would understand her. Joe nodded and sipped his soup. Grimm flopped down next to Lilah, and she continued to stroke his head. The dog's eyes rolled up as if he was in heaven.

"Who are you?" Lilah asked again. "I mean . . . what are you?"

"I'm a ranger," he said after a short pause. "It's a group of scouts. Most of us are former soldiers or SpecOps and—"

"SpecOps?"

"Special Operators," he explained. "Soldiers who did special missions."

"Oh," she said, "like Delta Force and the SEALs. I read about them in books. Novels, mostly."

"Like that. Our outfit's been around for a few years now, working the southern states mostly, but a couple of us started going north and west to see how things had fallen out. I even spent a little time up your way."

"My way? How do you know—?"

"You mentioned Tom Imura."

"You knew him?"

There was the slightest pause before the man said, "Once upon a time."

They sipped their soup and studied each other.

"Why are you here?" she said, indicating the forest.

He shrugged. "I poke my nose in here and there. Guess you could call me a professional troublemaker."

As Lilah set her cup down, the injury throbbed and she hissed between clenched teeth. "How badly am I hurt?"

"Nothing that won't heal if you take care of yourself," he said. "You have a world-class collection of bruises and scrapes, and your left knee is puffy, so we might be looking at a sprain. You got thirty stitches down your side. Looks like you got clipped by the boar's tusk. Wound's clean, though, no sign of infection."

Lilah chewed on a word for a few moments before she said it. "Thanks."

"My pleasure. And I saw the way you handled yourself out there. You are one tough kid."

"I'm not a kid," she said.

"Fair enough. No offense meant."

She let it go and changed subjects. "That boar was a zom."

"Yup," agreed Joe.

"How?"

"Darned if I know," he admitted. "Only seen a few of those critters around these last few months, and I don't mind saying that it scares the bejesus out of me."

"You've seen this before?"

"Yup. First one I saw was around Jericho Junction over in Utah. Then last week I saw a small pack of them chasing a bunch of other hogs. There's been a population explosion of wild boars down south, all uninfected, at least as far as I know; but these were definitely walkers. Haven't had a really good night's sleep since. The thought that this plague has crossed the species barrier is . . ." He shook his head, unable or unwilling to quantify the potential danger.

Lilah nodded. "It doesn't make sense. Zoms are zoms. They're people. The plague was never in the animals."

"It is now." He rubbed his eyes. "The plague's been changing. Diseases do that. They've always done that. Before First Night there were new viruses every year, some of which were new strains of diseases we thought we'd beaten. It was simply good luck that most of the diseases of animals didn't jump to humans, and that most human diseases didn't jump to animals. That's all past tense, though. The zombie plague, whatever it was, wiped out humanity, and now it's moving into animals."

"Other animals?"

He shrugged. "Let's hope not. So far it's only a small percentage of the boar population, and pig biology is pretty close to humans. That might account for it. If it gets into flies or insects, or birds, then we're really screwed. We can't build a fence to keep them out. Even so, those pigs . . . man, they give me the creeps."

Lilah could tell that he was trying to keep his tone light, but the horror was in his eyes. "That's not the only thing that's changed," she said. "Some of the zoms are faster."

"Yeah, that's old news. I've seen some real Olympic sprinters in the last year. Mostly in the Pacific Northwest. Not so much here, though."

"We saw some today."

He narrowed his blue eyes. "You're sure?"

"I killed two of them today. One of them picked up a stick and tried to hit me with it."

That news seemed to jolt Joe, and he stared at her for a moment. Several times his mouth began to form questions, but he left them unsaid. They ate their soup in silence, each of them contemplating the implications of faster and perhaps smarter zoms.

Lilah held out her cup for more soup. "You haven't asked me my name."

"Don't need to," he said as he ladled more into her cup. He was smiling, but the smile held secrets. "You're the Lost Girl, aren't you?"

53

THE COCKPIT WAS A SMALL COMPARTMENT WITH TWO BIG CHAIRS FACING the smashed-out front windows and one chair set to one side, facing a wall of controls the like of which they had only ever seen in books. Computers and scanners. Things that belonged to a world that might as well have been ancient Rome or the Dark Ages for all that these devices related to Benny and Nix's experience.

Light streamed in through the gaping windows.

There were three chairs, all empty, which reinforced Benny's guess that the zoms outside had once been the crew.

"What do you think happened?" asked Nix. "Why'd it crash?"

"I have no idea," he said. They spoke in hushed voices even though they were alone. The altar outside and the painted warning inside made them both feel like something was about to jump out at them.

There was a discarded jacket on the floor, and Benny picked it up. A small version of the same flag that was on the plane's tail had been sewn onto one pocket, and below that was embroidered THE AMERICAN NATION.

"I don't get it," said Nix. "Shouldn't it read 'United States of America'?"

Benny thought about it. "Maybe not. This plane is definitely something from after First Night. Built before, maybe, but flown out here long afterward."

"So?"

"There is no United States of America anymore. Not like it used to be." He folded the jacket over the back of the pilot's chair. "You know, I read in one book that the president and Congress were supposed to have a bunker or some kind of underground place they could go to during a national disaster or war. Maybe that's what happened. Maybe some part of the government survived and, I don't know, kind of rebuilt things after First Night. Not the same kind of country, of course, but some kind of country."

"The American Nation," she said, nodding. "Maybe."

54

LILAH TENSED.

Joe's comment still hung in the air.

You're the Lost Girl.

"How do you . . . ?" Her words trailed off, and she looked wildly around, then bared her teeth. Her fingers tensed around the cup of soup as she prepared to hurl it in his face. "This is all about collecting a bounty, isn't it? Try it and I'll paint these rocks with your blood—"

Grimm suddenly sat up and in the process transformed from a friendly dog being petted to the war hound that he truly was.

"Whoa," said Joe, "slow down."

Lilah growled low in her throat. So did Grimm.

But Joe chuckled and shook his head. "I'm a lot of things, kid, but I'm not a bounty hunter. Never felt the calling. That's more Tom Imura's gig than mine."

He clicked his tongue. "Grimm, down and easy."

The dog's attitude instantly changed, this time reverting back to lazy dog. He sat and pretended to look as innocent as a puppy.

"I guessed who you are because I've lived out in the Ruin since everything went to hell, kid, and I spent a fair amount of time in central California. Everyone round those parts knows the story of the Lost Girl. Tom Imura spent some time looking for you. Guess he found you."

"How did you know Tom?" Lilah asked suspiciously.

"We've known each other off and on for eight, ten years. We had some friends in common, once upon a time. And back before First Night I even knew his uncle, Sam. We worked together for a bit. Tom takes after him. Same kind of cool smarts, same kind of integrity. After the zoms rose, I was back and forth between the Nine Towns for a while. This was early on, when they were just getting settled, but I got bored and moved on. Haven't been back there in years now."

"Was Tom a friend of yours?"

Then Joe narrowed his eyes. "You keep putting Tom in the past tense. Why? Has something happened to him?"

Lilah said nothing, but she could feel her eyes filling with tears.

"What happened to Tom?" asked Joe. Then understanding and pain flickered in his eyes. "Ah . . . jeez. How'd it happen? Walkers finally get him?"

"No," she said. "He was murdered."

Lilah told him about Tom's fight with the Matthias clan. About the destruction of Gameland, and about the murder of Tom Imura by the madman Preacher Jack. When she was done, Joe got up and walked over to a small table and leaned on it, his shoulders slumping. Grimm caught the sudden shift in mood and whined a little.

"You know," said Joe thickly, "after all the death I've seen—before and after First Night—after all the times I've pulled a trigger, after all the comrades I've buried, and all the people

I've seen go down in blood and pain, you'd think that another death wouldn't mean a thing to me. You'd think that I'd have too many calluses." He shook his head. "But . . . Tom Imura. Damn."

When he turned back to her, Joe looked ten years older. His face was drawn, his eyes dark with loss.

"Long time ago," he said, "Tom talked about uniting the Nine Towns. He wanted to create a group like my rangers. He wanted to bring in some people he trusted, people who didn't run with Charlie's bunch. Guys like Solomon Jones, Hector Mexico, and Sally Two-Knives. That ever happen?"

"No," said Lilah. "Those people were there at Gameland, they helped Tom, but the people in the towns never wanted an army like that. It made Tom angry, because it left the Nine Towns so vulnerable."

"Tom had the right idea. He usually did. People should have listened to him."

"There are a lot of stupid people," said Lilah harshly.

Joe snapped his fingers. "Hey—Tom had a little brother. Benny. What happened to him?"

Lilah told him the rest of the story. When she got to the part about the ravine and the rescue of the little girl, Joe stiffened.

"Wait! You mean that Tom's kid brother is out there right now? In these woods?"

"Yes," she said. "Benny, Nix, Chong . . . but they're safe. We have a camp near—"

"Well, isn't that just swell?" growled Joe. "Why didn't you tell me that before?"

She looked at him. "Why would you think I'd trust you so fast?"

"Because I saved your life and sewed up your wounds?"

Lilah gave him a stony look. "You could have been pretending to help me for some reasons of your own. If you know who I am, and if you knew Tom, then you probably know that people have taken advantage of me before. Why should I trust you or anyone?"

Joe nodded. "Good point."

He looked over his shoulder, as if he could see the whole forest. Then he doused the fire with the remains of his soup and stood up. Grimm instantly got to his feet as well.

"Listen to me," he said. "You have a choice—you can stay here or come with me, but I've got to go find Tom's kid brother and your other friends, and I mean right now."

"Why?"

Joe pointed with his empty soup cup. "Out there? Did you happen to see a bunch of Froot Loops running around? Bald heads, tattoos, angel wings on their chests?"

"The reapers. But who are—?"

"They are the bad guys, sweetie. They call themselves a religious movement, but that's crap. They don't want to save anyone. They want to kill everyone. The Night Church, the Church of Thanatos, is run by a total wack job called Saint John and a conniving, malicious witch named Mother Rose. They came out of nowhere about ten years ago, and since then they've converted thousands of people to their cause."

"What cause?"

Joe handed Lilah the magazine to her pistol, then knelt to buckle the horned helmet onto Grimm's massive head.

"They have a pretty simple agenda," he said. "The total extinction of the human race."

55

HER NAME WAS SISTER AMY. FIFTEEN YEARS AGO, BEFORE THE GRAY PLAGUE, she had been a bodyguard in the entertainment industry. Before that she had been a soldier. During the plague Amy had lost everyone she loved. Two sisters, a brother, parents, and grandparents. Friends. Everyone who made her life worth living. The gray plague had taken everything from her except her awareness of her own loss, her own pain.

For years afterward she was a ghost. She drifted from town to town, looking for something to believe in, looking for proof that the whole world wasn't going to die. She found famine and disease. She found whole settlements that had starved to death, and settlements that had survived for years before finally falling to the gray wanderers.

She found nothing to believe in. Nothing she could save, and to someone like her, protecting and saving people was all that mattered. But she hadn't been able to save her family, and in the wastelands of what had once been America she found nothing else worth saving. Nothing that would last if saved.

And then she met Saint John, and all that changed.

Now she was one of the most trusted reapers of the Night

Church. A true believer who worshipped Saint John as much as she worshipped Thanatos and the darkness. The saint had promised her—actually sworn to her—that when her time came, he would take his own sacred knives and open a red mouth in her flesh. With his own sanctified hands he would guide her into the darkness.

That was something she could believe in. A guaranteed end to pain, and a pathway to the sea of darkness in which the spirits of her family swam.

It was beautiful.

She would do anything for Saint John.

Sister Amy lay on the ground, her body totally hidden by a thick line of shrubs, her scent masked by the chemicals into which her red ribbons had been dipped. Those chemicals fooled more than the gray people. Even dogs avoided the smell. It did not trigger their aggression. It just made her scent . . . uninteresting, and that was the genius of it.

She lay in the hot darkness, her body utterly still, her breathing controlled, her mind quiet and receptive.

Listening.

To the ranger and the Lost Girl.

To strange tales of how, in the terrible days after First Night, the lost and lonely survivors found one another and built fences against the dead. How they built nine towns in central California. And how, behind the fences, they survived.

Nine towns, filled with heretics whose every heartbeat was an affront to God.

Nine towns that did not even know that the army of the Night Church existed.

Yet.

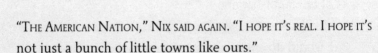

56

"The American Nation," Nix said again. "I hope it's real. I hope it's not just a bunch of little towns like ours."

"It has to be more than that," said Benny. "They have planes. This one and the jet. Maybe more. They even made a flag. It sounds . . . I don't know . . . *big*. Bigger than anything we've ever seen."

Nix turned away from him and stared out through the broken windows into the hot desert outside. Her back was as stiff as a board, and she gripped the back of the pilot's chair so ferociously that her fingers dug into the cracked leather.

"Hey," said Benny, "what's wrong? We did it, we found proof that there's something out there. I know things are crazy right at the moment, with those freaks out there and all, but I thought you'd be—"

She cut a sharp look at him. "Be what? Be happy? Is that what you want, Benny? For me to be *happy*? God, you really don't know who I am, do you? You have no idea why I want to find that jet, or why finding all this is so . . . so . . . ." She gave the pilot's chair a vicious kick and didn't finish her sentence. Instead she glared out the window, muttering "God" under her breath.

"Maybe I *do* understand," Benny said, and as he said it he was aware that he was stepping way out on a limb. But he was tired of being careful all the time.

Nix didn't look at him. "*What* do you understand?"

"You even said it once," Benny said. "You said that Mountainside wasn't your home anymore. With your mom gone, and now Tom . . . you don't feel like you belong there anymore."

She still didn't look at him.

Benny said, "Hey, I know that you think I'm just some dumb boy who doesn't *get* you. Chong thinks I'm halfway to being a moron, and Lilah . . . well, I doubt Lilah thinks about me at all. But I'm not stupid and I'm not blind. Since Tom died I've had a lot of time to think things over. I've seen you drift away more and more ever since we left and—"

"This isn't *about* us, Benny."

"I'm not *talking* about us. I'm not talking about our relationship falling apart. When I say that I see you drifting away, I mean from everything. You don't try to relate to anyone. Well . . . I guess Eve was the only one, and that was only for a few minutes. You've gone inside your own head, Nix, and I'm pretty sure you don't like what's in there."

"You don't know what you're talking about," she snapped.

"Yeah, I do. Just like I know that every time I want to talk about something, you snap at me. It's a defense mechanism. You keep me and everyone else at arm's length that way. And that way no one can get in." He took a step toward her. "You really think I don't understand? You lost your whole family when your mom died. You and I started when you were emotionally screwed up, I know that. I know that Tom and your mom were in love. They were probably going to get married, but that was taken away from you too. You think you're all alone, so you need—really need—to find another place. A place that isn't Mountainside and isn't the Rot and Ruin. I get that, I really do. That's why you've been so obsessed about the jet. It's like a . . . like a lifeline, I guess."

"It's not that simple," she said bitterly.

"I know that, too," Benny said.

Nix turned away again and continued to stare out at the desert forest.

Benny summoned all the courage he could find. He braced himself to say what he knew he had to say next.

"Nix," he began softly, "it's okay if you don't love me anymore. It's okay if you don't want to be my girlfriend anymore. It's okay if you just want to be you."

She stiffened.

"I love you," he said. "I really do, and I guess what I'm trying to say is that whatever you need to do to figure out who you are and what you want . . . I've got your back, but I'll never get in your way."

His mouth hurt to say those words, and inside his chest it felt as if a huge, icy fist was squeezing his heart into pulp. But Benny stood his ground and forced his eyes to stay dry. Tears now would be of no help to anyone.

Nix did not turn, she did not say a word. She stared out at the day, and Benny watched her and tried to remember how to breathe.

Then Nix gasped and said, "Oh my God!" She stumbled backward in horror, pointing out into the desert.

"What—?" asked Benny.

But as he rushed to her side, he saw what it was. Outside, near where the three zombies hung on their T-bars, were three people. Reapers.

Two men and a tall woman with masses of dark brown hair.

"Nix!" cried Benny in a strangled whisper, "that's *her*. That's the woman I saw today in the field right before the zoms chased me."

57

"YOU'RE SURE?" ASKED NIX. "SHE'S THE ONE FROM THE FIELD?"

"Positive."

They studied her. She was tall and beautiful, and she stood with a grace that spoke of great confidence. Benny recalled the word he had thought of when he first saw her: regal. Queenly. But queen of what?

There were other reapers around her. Men and women, all of them dressed in black with angel wings and red tassels. They all carried weapons. Swords, axes, knives.

"I don't see any guns," whispered Benny.

"Not much of a comfort," replied Nix sourly.

Then they gaped at a man who came out of the woods to take up a very protective post just behind the queenly woman. He was a giant, and he carried a massive long-handled sledge-hammer.

"What is he?" asked Nix. "A troll?"

"Close enough."

The air was split by the roar of quads as more reapers appeared from the forest until there were at least two dozen of them gathered around the woman. Except for her, all of them had shaved and tattooed heads like Saint John. *And Riot,* thought Benny.

None of them stood very close to her, though every eye was fixed on her. None of them paid much attention to the plane, and it was clear that they had all seen it before, or did not care about it. The woman ignored it completely.

She beckoned over a grim-faced young man, and for several moments they stood apart, their heads bowed together in an intense discussion while the giant guarded them.

"I can't hear anything," complained Benny. "Can you?"

Nix's face was screwed up with concentration. "No."

That changed a moment later. The young man bowed deeply to the woman, turned, and melted into the forest. The woman stepped onto a small, flat rock, and the other reapers clustered around her. She raised her arms out to the sides and stood for a moment in silence, the wind making the red streamers snap and pop.

Then, in a loud, clear voice she addressed the reapers. "You are the blessed of Thanatos!"

"All praise to the darkness," they cried.

"In you he is well pleased. As I am pleased."

"All praise to Mother Rose!"

Nix turned to Benny and mouthed the name. "Mother Rose."

It was the name Saint John had mentioned.

"My children," said Mother Rose, "you have all done exceedingly well. Your faith and devotion lifts my heart."

They smiled, and a few even dabbed at wet eyes.

"Look at where we stand, my beloved ones." She gestured to the plane, and for a moment Benny's heart froze, thinking that she was pointing at them. But he and Nix were in shadows, invisible from outside. Even so his heart hammered. "The

Shrine of the Fallen. A symbol of the corrupt world that was lies here, broken and empty. This once-mighty war machine and every heretic aboard have been given the gift of darkness. All the war machines of the old, corrupt world are silenced now. The world itself is falling silent. A silence decreed by our god. A silence that is proof of the eternal darkness that waits for us all."

"Praise be to the darkness!"

"Saint John and his prophet, Brother Peter, have told you many times that we are coming to the end of our long road, that the darkness is a heartbeat away for us all."

The crowd grew silent, attentive.

"But I tell you that there is much still to do."

Even in the plane Benny could hear the crowd sigh. It was a sad sound. But Mother Rose held up a hand.

"Do not be afraid, my children. Our god has not abandoned you, and he has not foresworn his holy promise to lift you up and grant you peace. No, I say now, in your hearing, that Lord Thanatos will deliver one hundredfold on his promises. You will have peace and so much more."

She waited as the crowd milled, the reapers murmuring to one another in confusion, but now Benny could hear a note of hope in their sounds.

"Where once the family of the reapers was weak, now we are strong," said Mother Rose. "Where once we were scattered like sheep, now we are part of a great family. A community of saints for whom the heavens themselves are ours to sow."

There were definite frowns on many of the faces, but Mother Rose's beatific smile never wavered.

"What's she doing?" asked Nix.

Benny shook his head.

"You all know that the last of Carter's heretics are in these woods," said Mother Rose. "What most of you do not know is that she who was my daughter intends to lead them to Sanctuary."

The collected reapers gasped in horror.

"Saint John and Brother Peter are hunting them now," continued Mother Rose. "It is their desire that every one of the heretics be sent into the darkness."

A few of the reapers gave rousing shouts of approval, but Mother Rose looked at them with unblinking eyes until they fell silent. The reapers shuffled like naughty schoolboys.

"Saint John, beloved of Thanatos—"

"Praise be to his darkness."

"—wants to find and destroy Sanctuary. He wants to open red mouths in the flesh of everyone there. He wants to end the heartbeat of all heresy."

No one cheered, though it seemed clear to Benny that many of them agreed with what Saint John wanted to do. Confusion and doubt was written on every face except that of Mother Rose and the giant with the hammer.

"But," said Mother Rose, her voice becoming quieter, almost a whisper, "this is not what our god wants."

No one even blinked. They stared, stock-still.

"I have had a vision, my beloved children. In a sacred trance, Lord Thanatos himself spoke to me."

"Oh brother," growled Nix. "Do you believe this crap?"

"They seem to," said Benny.

It was true; many of the reapers touched their hands to the angel designs on their chests.

"The lord of the darkness has tested us so many times and

in so many ways. Those of you who have been with the Night Church since Wichita remember how many tests have been put before us."

Several heads nodded.

"There have been failures and setbacks and defeats . . . and yet each time, no matter how devastating each new calamity appeared, we found the holy path through the fire and the smoke. We passed each test, no matter how difficult. We did this. Each of us, serving the will of our god even when God has made the path uncertain and the way forward choked with thorns and fog."

More heads nodded now.

"And what has this done? All along the way we have seen many of our fellows fall, and while their spirits have gone on into the darkness we have stayed behind, weeping and tearing at our garments, crying out, Why? Why them and not us? Why has the lord of the night punished us so many times when others whose will and whose faith were not as strong as ours were allowed to go into the sacred darkness?"

"Tell us why, Mother!" cried out one of the reapers. It was a thin man with a beaky nose. He fell to his knees and clapped his hands together. "Tell us, please!"

Another reaper dropped to her knees. "What sins have we committed that bar our way to paradise?"

Nix and Benny looked at each other.

"Is it me, or did that look planned?" asked Nix.

"Yeah," agreed Benny, "I think she seeded the crowd like Mr. Hopewell does when he's running the Sunday auction."

Mother Rose stepped forward and touched the bowed head of the kneeling woman.

"Sins, my daughter?" she said. "Did I say that you have sinned?"

She paused a beat and looked at the others.

"Did I say that any of you have sinned?" She drew the kneeling woman to her feet and kissed her on both cheeks. "No, my beloved, we have all passed through that fire together, and in its heat we have been purified."

The last word hung in the air like the clear note of a church bell. Even Benny felt a chill.

"Each of us here in this sacred place has passed through the fire many times. Each of us has stayed true even when we thought that our god had withdrawn his grace from us. Each of us has proven our faith beyond all doubt. And thus, the lord of the darkness has revealed to me that this—all of this, our struggles, our doubts, our pain, our longing, our faith—has made us the chosen of Thanatos."

There was another beat.

"Henceforth we will rise to be worthy of that choice. We will sing out in joy for the glory of God's grace. We will no longer fear life and flee like sheep into the darkness of the grave." Mother Rose raised her arms in triumph. "We have been reapers at work in the fields of the Lord. This task we have done well and faithfully. The fields are clear of vermin and pests. They are clean, and they welcome us to put down our tools of reaping and set about our new work."

The woman who had been kissed cried out, "What is our purpose, Mother Rose, beloved of Thanatos?"

Mother Rose turned so that her upraised hands indicated everything. Not just this field, Benny knew . . . but everything.

"The chosen will go out into the world and reclaim it."

Although Benny didn't really understand the nature of this church, he thought he had the gist of it. It felt like a weird slant on something Charlie Pink-eye used to say: *Kill 'em all and let God sort 'em out.*

Except that now this woman seemed to be changing the rules.

"Is she talking about double-crossing Saint John?" asked Nix, once more proving that she was reading his thoughts.

"I think so."

"Better her than me," said Nix. "That guy freaked me out."

"Yeah, well, I'm not having fuzzy puppy love about Mother Nut Job down there."

"How many sides are there in this fight? I thought it was Eve's family against these reapers."

Benny nodded. "Sorry to make a bad joke, but from what we just heard, I think there's trouble in paradise."

"Ugh." Nix looked around the cockpit. "Whose side do you think they were on?"

"I haven't the slightest idea. The good guys' side, I hope."

"Okay, but who are the good guys? Eve's dad tried to shoot us."

"Wait, something's happening," Benny said.

Down in the clearing, the reapers were arguing among themselves. However, one by one they broke from the group and knelt before Mother Rose.

"Praise be to the mother of us all," yelled one man. "Praise be to the mother of the chosen!"

Suddenly they were all kneeling and crying out, repeating those words like a chant as Mother Rose stood above them, arms up and out, drinking in their cries. The reapers crawled forward to kiss the bloodred streamers tied to Mother Rose's clothes. Benny saw, however, that one of the reapers hesitated longer than the others before joining the group. He was a barrel-chested Latino with twin knives thrust through his belt. And Benny saw Mother Rose flick a covert glance to the giant and then to that reaper.

"He's a dead man," said Nix before Benny could say it. "He's not buying any of this, and he's freaking dead."

"Sucks to be him," agreed Benny.

As they watched, the gathering broke up. Mother Rose said a few words to each of them, mostly telling them to spread the word to the other reapers. At no point did she tell them to keep Saint John out of the loop, but it was the impression Benny got.

The man who had been the first to drop to his knees lingered for a moment, as did a few others, and Benny noted that these reapers were the ones who had first "seen the light." It confirmed his suspicions that they were plants in the gathering, just like the friends of Mr. Hopewell who yelled out the first bids and kept driving up the sale price. These people clustered around Mother Rose and received additional instructions that Benny and Nix could not hear. When Mother Rose nodded in the direction the Latino man had taken, one of the reapers smiled, nodded, and hurried silently into the woods to follow.

Afterward, Mother Rose and the giant stood in silence until the sounds of the quads and the shouts of the "chosen" faded into silence.

The big man shook his head and laughed with a rumble from deep in his chest.

"Well, Rosie," he said, "you really did it now. There's no coming back from this."

"I don't intend to come back, Alexi," she said with

cold amusement. "It's all about moving forward. Besides, if we waited any longer, Saint John might actually destroy Sanctuary. And we can't have that, can we?"

"No, ma'am. But . . . Saint John's going to be pissed. He has his heart set on seeing that place burn."

"He can take it up with God. It's his own fault. He made me the head of this crazy church. Besides," she said with a smile, "I had a holy vision."

They laughed and began to walk away.

Then the woman did something that absolutely mystified Nix and Benny while at the same time freezing the blood in their veins. Mother Rose turned, raised her fingers to her lips, and blew a kiss into the air.

Directly toward the plane.

Then she and the giant smiled at each other. They turned away and walked without haste into the forest.

Half a minute later another reaper appeared. He stepped out of a pocket of dense shadows where no one had apparently noticed him. He was a tough, unsmiling young man with intense dark eyes. He walked to the spot where Mother Rose and Brother Alexi had stood. Even from all the way up in the plane, Benny could see the muscles bunch at the corners of his jaw and the rigid lines of muscle definition that stood out on his arms as he clenched his fists. Benny wasn't sure if he had ever seen anyone that totally and utterly furious.

The man spat on the ground where Mother Rose had stood, then turned and melted like the specter of murder into the forest.

Benny and Nix stared for a long time at the empty clearing.

"What the hell was that all about?" breathed Nix.

Benny shook his head. "I don't have the slightest idea."

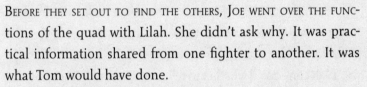

58

Before they set out to find the others, Joe went over the functions of the quad with Lilah. She didn't ask why. It was practical information shared from one fighter to another. It was what Tom would have done.

"This thing will go all day long without much fuel," he explained. "Runs on ethanol, and the reapers had a tanker of the stuff."

"Had?"

"I, um, borrowed it from them," he explained. "Got it hid in an arroyo a few miles from here. When we find your friends, we'll see about borrowing a few more quads. Beats the heck out of walking everywhere."

"How come these machines work? I thought the EMPs . . . ?"

"They blew out a lot of stuff, but not everything. I've been to places where people have cars—well, had cars. Gasoline wasn't made to last more than a year or two, and by now it's all bad. Only things still running are vehicles that used to run on ethanol. There are plenty of cornfields left. Saw a couple of junkers powered by hand-crank generators, solar panels, and even a few with little mini wind turbines. They only get up to about ten miles an hour, but that still beats walking."

Lilah drove the machine around the big boulders a few times while Joe watched, nodding his approval. Grimm gave a single deep bark to show that he, too, was impressed.

Joe waved her to a stop and switched off the machine. "Okay, you're good to go, and your bandages aren't leaking, so that's good too. I won't ask if you feel fit enough to pull a trigger. Already know that answer."

She nodded. "I don't want to have to fight these people," she said. "I want to find my friends and continue on our way."

"Yeah, about that," Joe said. "You never really told me why four teenagers are way the heck out in the Ruin. It's not the place for a class trip."

Lilah considered whether to tell him. She couldn't see how the information could be used to hurt her or the others. So she told Joe about the jet. And about the plane she'd seen on the plateau.

"Hold on, hold on," said Joe, suddenly excited. "You saw the transport?"

"What?"

"Big C-130J Super Hercules. Prop job, not a jet. You saw that plane somewhere out here?"

"I saw the jet and—"

Joe cut her off and explained the difference between a jumbo jet and a propeller-driven military transport plane. When he described the latter, she began nodding.

"Yes, that is what I found. It was on the plateau right by the cliff I fell off of. Where we fought the pigs."

"Did you see any people? Pilots, crew? They'd be in uniforms. . . ."

"There were three zoms there, hung up on posts." She described the uniforms.

"Flight crew. Damn it. I knew those guys." Joe made a pained face. "We've been looking for that plane for over a year. Nobody thought it was this close, though. With all the reapers around here, it's probably been stripped clean. And that's a real shame. Dr. Monica McReady was aboard that plane. Losing her was a damn hard setback."

"Setback for whom?"

Joe said, "The human race. She was one of the best epidemiologists we had. One of only a handful who made it through First Night and the plague years. She was worth more than you and me and any five thousand people you can name, and that's no joke." He paused. "I guess we were all hoping she was alive somewhere. We kept expecting her to come banging on the door one of these days. I've got rangers out everywhere looking for her. The work she was doing . . . I can't begin to tell you how important it is."

"Try," she said frankly.

Joe laughed. "Doc McReady set up the first lab during the outbreak and later moved it to North Carolina, which is where people are trying to build a new America. Lots of people there now, and they even have the lights back on. Later, after we got some reports of possible mutations to the plague in Oregon, Washington, and southern Canada, McReady took a field team up to Joint Base Lewis-McChord, which is a few miles southwest of Tacoma. They had to clean up the base first, since everyone was zommed out. McReady established a research camp up there that she called Hope One. Sixty people—scientists, support staff, and a small platoon to guard them. And it was up there that McReady figured out what caused the plague."

"People think it was radiation from a—"

"Oh, please. No one really believes that."

"A virus, then?"

"Yes . . . and no. McReady discovered that it's actually a combination of several diseases and a few nasty little parasites, all of them working together like a microscopic terrorist cabal. Most people call it the Gray Plague, but the official designation is Reaper, and, yes, that's where the reapers got their name. Bunch of freaks. Anyway, the Reaper Plague is genuine mad science, and everyone's pretty sure that Mother Nature did not snort this out because she was feeling cranky."

"What does that mean?"

"It means that someone made this thing," said Joe, "and somehow it got out of the lab. Or maybe it was deliberately released. No one knows that part, and we probably never will. Whoever launched it is probably dead or shuffling around as a walker. Doesn't matter. What matters is that McReady's last report indicated that she was on the verge of some major breakthrough. The problem is that we don't know what that breakthrough was or even could be, because no one down here has a clue. The only hint we have is a cryptic reference in her last report of the plan to field-test a counter-plague."

"A counter-plague . . . ? You mean a disease that would stop the Reaper Plague?"

"That's exactly what I mean. Problem is, McReady sent a distress call from Hope One, saying that the walker activity was spiking. They sent the C-130 up to evac her, the staff, and all the research notes. When the plane never showed, I sent a team of my rangers up. They found Hope One deserted. No staff, no research, so we know that the transport plane at least accomplished the evacuation, but no one ever saw that plane. There were a couple of places where the C-130 could have made an emergency landing, so the decision was made to send a heavy transport to do flyovers of the route. We hoped they'd find the plane down on some airfield and McReady's people waiting for a new ride. The bird they sent to look was a mother of a C-5 Galaxy, and my guess is that's the jet your friends saw. The timing would be about right. It did a zig-zag search, looking for any sign of McReady's plane, but they never found it. And it turns out the darn thing is right here! Made it almost all the way home. Holy crap."

Lilah stared at him. "You know about the jet? You know what it is? Where it is?"

"Sure. Been on it half a dozen times."

Lilah felt suddenly strange, as if she had stepped out of the real world and into a dream. When she'd seen the crashed plane, she thought that the whole purpose of their journey into the Ruin had come to a dead end. She was sure that the knowledge of its destruction would devastate Nix and Benny. Chong, she knew, didn't really care one way or the other; he was along because he was in love with her.

Now . . . Nix would be so happy.

Joe interrupted her thoughts. "You said that the flight crew was zommed out and hung on posts? Anything else around them? Incense bowls, bunches of flowers, anything like that?"

"Yes. And signs around their necks saying that they were sinners."

"Reapers," growled Joe. Grimm must have recognized the

word, because he gave his own low growl, full of menace and promise.

"These reapers . . . will you please tell me who they are?"

"We don't have time to go into the whole history of the reapers," said Joe. "The short version is this. Prior to First Night, Saint John was what the police used to call a serial killer. He was a psychopathic mass murderer, and one of almost legendary status. There were books and movies made about him. No real surprise that he survived the Reaper Plague. About ten years ago, Saint John showed up at a settlement north of Topeka. Set himself up as a kind of preacher, talking about how man did not need to suffer, how there was an end to pain, yada, yada. Long story short, at first his message got no traction because people were still busy surviving the end of everything. They were in full-blown survival mode, and nobody wanted to hear about just giving up and giving in." He removed the magazine from his gun, checked that it was fully loaded, and slapped it back into place. "But as time went on, things got worse out there."

He told her about the rampant diseases that swept through a lot of the communities, and the resulting death toll.

"Plus there was radiation in spots from reactor meltdowns, and more radiation from the cities they nuked on First Night. Cancer rates are probably up a thousand percent. For a lot of people in a lot of places it pretty much looked like suffering was all there was and all there was ever going to be."

"And that's when they started listening to Saint John?"

"Yup. By then he'd managed to recruit a hundred or so followers. His reapers. They'd go into a town, and at first there were a lot of discussions and sermons about embracing the nonphysical and letting go of the struggle to hold on to a dying world. Crap like that. Saint John presided over mass suicides in one town after another."

"That's stupid."

"It's people," said Joe as he began filling the gas tank from a red plastic bottle.

"But . . . how can the reapers convince people to commit suicide when—?"

"When they're still sucking air? Yeah, well, this whole enchilada gets crazier and crazier. When they've wiped out all the heretics and blasphemers, they intend to kill each other, and the last man standing will hang himself. Delightful, huh?"

"Really stupid," Lilah insisted.

"Not everyone is suited for survival, especially the way people were in the early twenty-first century. People had gotten really soft, really addicted to machines, electronics, and specialists who would come in and do everything from fixing the plumbing to pulling a tooth. Nobody knew how to do things for themselves. It was kind of pathetic."

"You sound like you agree with Saint John."

He set down the plastic container and replaced the quad's gas cap. "No freaking way, darlin'. Just because there are a lot of sheep doesn't mean everyone's a sheep. There are a lot—a whole lot—of cases where people really rose to the challenge. They learned what they didn't know, they built shelters, they rediscovered hunting and farming, they reclaimed those qualities that put man at the top of the food chain in the first place. And they became the leaders who gathered everyone else around them. Your own town, and the other eight there in central California, are examples of that. People pitching in together to make a better life for everyone."

"How many towns did Saint John attack?"

"Too many," said Joe bitterly. "Way too many."

"Is there anyone left?"

He nodded. "Sure. Saint John never made it to North Carolina, and that's where the real heartbeat of this country is. It's the new capital. Granted, it's a small start compared to what we lost, but it is a start. And there are a lot of scattered towns and settlements. It's a big country, and Saint John hasn't had time to kill everyone." He paused. "If his army keeps growing at the rate it's been going . . . then nowhere's going to be safe."

"You make him sound as dangerous as the plague."

Joe nodded again. "Yeah . . . I guess he is. He uses Mother Rose to recruit people into the reapers so he has a big enough force to destroy any town that won't simply roll over for him. It's a useful model for conquest. Genghis Khan and Alexander the Great did the same thing, though their motives were different."

"I don't understand it, though," said Lilah. "Why do so many people join him?"

Joe helped her onto the back of the quad. "Too many people have simply lost hope. As long as the Gray Plague is still happening and the zoms are still out there, it's going to be hard for most people not to think Saint John has the only answer worth hearing."

"But you said that Dr. McReady and the others were working on a cure. . . ."

"They are, sure." Joe sighed. "But most people don't know that. McReady's breakthrough, whatever it is, is new science.

We don't even know what it is yet, or whether it'll really change things. And without McReady's research, we're still stuck on the same sinking ship."

Lilah said, "Have you given up hope too?"

Joe adjusted the seat belts carefully around Lilah's wound. "Not a chance."

"You're going to fight back?"

"Honey, I never stopped fighting." He slid his *katana* into a slot on the quad. "So here's the plan. We're going to find your friends, and then you kids are going to help me search every inch of that plane. If there's any chance that even some of McReady's research survived the crash, then I need to secure it and get it into the hands of the rest of the research team."

"Where are they?"

"Close," said Joe. "McReady only took a small team with her to Hope One. The rest of the science geeks are split between a new lab in North Carolina and one they set up in a military base out here. They had to reclaim the base from the zoms, but that was no problem, and it was in great shape. It was what they called a 'hardened' facility, meaning that the EMPs didn't knock out the power. Once they reclaimed it, the geek squad were able to repurpose the base from military research and development to a biological research facility."

"A laboratory?" asked Lilah. "Out here?"

"Yup," said Joe. "Really well-hidden but closer than you'd think. McReady named it Sanctuary."

And he told Lilah where it was.

As the sound of the ranger's quad faded, Sister Amy rolled out from under the line of shrubs. Her mind burned with the things she wanted to tell Saint John. Needed to tell him.

Sanctuary.

And . . . nine towns.

Towns with no organized defenses.

As she ran through the woods she could not keep the smile off her face.

BROTHER PETER KNELT IN THE DIRT BEFORE SAINT JOHN. HE RESTED HIS weight on his fists, his head was bowed, and he waited for the storm of the saint's wrath to tear the world apart.

But there was silence.

After almost three excruciating minutes, Brother Peter raised his head and looked at the man who he worshipped more than the Lord Thanatos. His friend, his mentor, and in every way that mattered, his father.

Saint John stood there, hands clasped behind his back, head tilted to one side as he watched monkeys frolic in the trees. No storms of rage burned across the saint's face. There were no tears.

There was nothing.

"Honored One?" ventured Brother Peter. "Did you hear what I—?"

Saint John spoke, his quiet voice overriding the younger man's.

"When the world burned down," he said, "I was alone. For many months before that, I was in a hospital, in a psychiatric ward—did you know that?" He did not wait for an answer. "They thought I was sick . . . mentally unstable . . . because

I said that the god of darkness spoke to me inside my head. There are people with such sickness, you know; before the Fall and since. Some of them have joined us. Others have joined the way-station monks. After all, God speaks in so many different ways, and in the end he speaks to everyone."

"Even heretics?"

"Even them," agreed Saint John. "Although the heretics hear the voice of God and refuse to listen. Others—the lost ones—hear the voice and don't, or can't, recognize it for what it is. They are to be pitied. When we usher them into the darkness, it is always with kindness, with a gentler touch of the knife."

The saint began walking, and Brother Peter rose and fell into step beside him.

"After the Fall, I wandered the streets of my city, watching it burn, watching the darkness grow. The Gray People never touched me. Not once."

"A miracle, Honored One."

"Yes. It was proof, you see. It showed others that I was indeed the first saint of this church." They walked through the forest as casually as if the day had not been filled with screams and murder. Two scholars idly discussing a point of philosophy on a lovely afternoon. "And then I found Mother Rose. She was . . . merely 'Rose' then. A woman who had lost herself even before the world fell down around her. I rescued her from savage men, heretics who saw the coming of the darkness as an invitation to hurt and humiliate those weaker than themselves."

"I remember," said Brother Peter faintly.

"I know you do. And you remember the years that

followed, as Rose accepted the darkness into her heart and became elevated as the mother of all."

"Yes." Brother Peter could not keep the bitterness out of his voice.

"Those were good days. You were so young and yet so bright. So eager to learn the ways of the blade and the purity that is the darkness. Pride is a sin, but I will accept whatever rebuke is due me for the pride I felt in you. Then and now. You have been the rock on which I built the Night Church." They walked a few paces. "You, Peter. Not her."

Brother Peter bowed his head in humility.

"Tell me," said Saint John, "when you look inside your head and your heart . . . at those times when you are in the depths of prayer and meditation . . . what does paradise look like?"

"Look like?" asked Peter.

"Yes. If you were to paint a picture of what waits for us— what you want to be on the other side of the doorway, what you truly believe is beyond this world—what is that picture? Describe it to me."

They walked for half a dozen paces before Peter said, "It is the darkness."

"And—?"

"The darkness is all. The darkness is enough. The darkness is everything."

Saint John nodded. "That is what I see. That is what I believe is there."

"But I—"

"And when you think about this world—when you imagine what this planet will be when the last of the heretics is gone, and when the last of us communes with our own blades so that our darkness joins with eternity—tell me, Brother Peter, what does this world look like?"

They were at the edge of the forest now, and they looked out on the vast desert that stretched away before them and vanished into the shimmering horizon. Brother Peter nodded toward the endless sand. "That is what I see, Honored One."

"The desert?"

"The peacefulness. Empty of human pain and misery. Empty of struggle. Restored to the perfection of nature."

"And all that man has made and built?"

"It will turn to dust. This world will heal of the infection that is man. The world will be whole and perfect again."

They stood there for many minutes as they each considered this.

"Do you know," asked Saint John at length, "that I always knew this day was coming?"

Brother Peter turned and stared at him.

"Mother Rose," said the saint. "It was inevitable that she would betray me. It was ordained that it happen. Like in the Christian story of Jesus and Judas. The betrayal was always part of the plan. Judas was a good and righteous man for most of his life, but in a moment of weakness, or perhaps pride, he stepped off the path."

Brother Peter nodded.

"For ordinary people," the saint continued, "such a thing can be forgiven. It can be ascribed to human weakness. As with Thomas, who doubted, and Peter, who denied. Those are momentary weaknesses, forgivable sins."

"But not Judas?"

"Not him for the Christians, and not Mother Rose for us. She is not an ordinary person. Neither are you, and neither am I. Why? We have looked into our minds and have seen the true face of our god."

"The darkness," said Brother Peter.

"The darkness," said Saint John. "I fear that Mother Rose has turned away from the darkness and allowed herself to become seduced by the light. By this world. Not the pure world that will come, but the corrupt and infected world that existed before the Fall. I have long suspected that she enjoyed being in the flesh. She has become seduced by its illusion of power."

"Yes."

"It is why she has worked so hard to recruit new reapers."

"But we need—"

"No. We have more than we will ever need. We have reapers in the thousands, and we have the Gray People in their millions. Mother Rose has never quite grasped that. Or rather, she has purposely ignored it. She wants people to stay alive."

"Why?" asked Brother Peter, appalled by the very thought of it.

"For the same reason she has recruited so very many reapers."

"And . . . why?"

Saint John smiled. "She wants to conquer the world, my son," he said, "and then she intends to rule it."

Brother Peter shook his head. "But she knows the darkness. She believes—"

"Don't you think that Judas believed in the son of his god? Don't you think that those people who flew planes into towers or strapped on vests of explosives believed in their god? There are misguided people in all faiths, and there always have been." Saint John sighed. "Mother Rose has been very quietly recruiting from within the reapers. Brother Alexi, Brother Simon . . . others. The weak ones who think they are strong, but who long to be here rather than to truly be with the darkness. She will use them as her generals. They probably believe in her with their whole hearts. Some of them are quite lost. Others . . . well, there has always been corruption in any organized religion. Insidious people who exploit the honest faith of the masses. Mother Rose will use all that—faith, belief, greed, whatever tools she can find—and with those she will very likely conquer every settlement, town, and city in this country. She will make a kingdom for herself here on earth."

He pointed into the desert.

"And I suspect she wants to make Sanctuary her Camelot, the seat of her power."

Brother Peter felt stricken. "Then . . . we have failed?"

The saint turned toward him, his face filled with love but also with a passionate light. "No, my son, and do not fall to doubt now. Mother Rose does not know that we know. In her pride, she opens her throat to us."

FROM NIX'S JOURNAL

Warrior Smart

Tom wasn't one for he-man war quotes,
but there were two that he liked.

"Si vis pacem, para bellum," which was
a quote from De Re Militari by fourth-
century Roman author Publius Flavius
Vegetius Renatus. It translates as: "If
you wish for peace, prepare for war."

Tom said that the best way to ensure that
you won't be attacked is to be too strong
to make it worth the other guy's while.
Or something like that. I mean,
I never read much about samurai
or armed soldiers getting mugged.

The other phrase was one from the
samurai: "We train ten thousand hours to
prepare for a single moment that we pray
never comes."

I get that.

61

For a long time Chong floated in an infinite ocean of pain.

For hours, days, weeks . . . maybe years.

Time was meaningless.

Then he heard a voice.

"You in there, boy?"

"Don't . . . call me 'boy,'" Chong said thickly.

"I need y'all to wake up," said Riot. "We need to have us a talk."

Chong slowly opened his eyes. He was lying on his uninjured side and had to look over his shoulder to see Riot, who knelt behind him. She appeared to be studying the exit wound. When Chong looked down at the entry wound, all he saw was a red-black burn.

He expected it to hurt, and it did. The area around the burn was puffy and red. Chong felt hot, as if the heat of the cauterizing blade had infused his entire body. Sweat ran down his torso and pooled under him.

"I don't feel too great," he said.

Riot breathed in and out through her nose for a moment. "Yeah, well, that's the thing," she said. "We maybe got us a problem."

"Really? A problem?" He arched an eyebrow. "Beyond arrows, burned flesh, an army of killers, and the end of the world?"

She did not smile.

"Riot—?"

Instead of answering, she picked up the arrowhead she'd unscrewed. She sniffed it, and her frown deepened. Then she picked up the quiver of arrows and studied the blackened tips of each.

"Oh, man . . . ," she breathed.

"What is it?" asked Chong. "What's wrong? Is it poison?"

Riot got up and walked around so she faced him. There was a haunted look in her eyes, and her mouth was drawn and tight.

"Is it poison?" Chong repeated.

"No," she said faintly. "No, I don't think we're going to catch that kind of a break."

"What's that supposed to mean? It doesn't look that bad."

"You ain't seein' it from t'other side. Skin around the wound looks funny. It's turning black, and there are some crooked dark lines creeping out from it."

"God," said Chong, feeling panic leap up in his chest. "That's blood poisoning! You're telling me I have blood poisoning?"

After a long pause, Riot said, "I don't think that's what we got here. The lines are black, not red."

"But—"

"You're running a fever . . . but the skin back here's cool to the touch."

"Then we need to treat me for shock. Do you have any-thing we can use as a blanket or—"

"No," she said. "Ain't shock, neither. I think we got our-selves somethin' else. Something we maybe can't fix."

"What's that mean?"

"That black goo on the tips?" Riot held one of the arrows under his nose. "Tell me what it smells like to you."

Chong studied her eyes for a long moment. There was a bleak, defeated look in them that made him hesitate before he took an arrow from her. Even then he didn't immediately raise the arrow to his nose.

"You already know what it is," he asked quietly, "don't you?"

Riot nodded.

Chong closed his eyes for a moment. Instead of it being dark behind his eyelids, he saw twisted threads of bright red forking like lightning inside his personal darkness.

Then he opened his eyes and took a tentative sniff. He smelled what she had smelled.

"No," he said, and his denial matched frequency with hers. This wasn't something you just could refuse to accept.

Riot said nothing.

"Why . . . why would anyone *do* something like that?" demanded Chong.

"Why do you think?"

The answer was obvious, but it took all his courage to say it. "So . . . even if he just wounded someone …they'd … they'd …"

Words failed him.

Riot sighed and sat down on the floor, placing the arrows well away from Eve.

However, the smell lingered in Chong's nose. He knew exactly what it was, and why it smelled like cadaverine.

The archer had dipped his arrows in the infected flesh of the living dead.

And now that infection was burning its way through Chong's flesh.

"HONORED ONE!" CRIED SISTER AMY AS SHE DASHED OUT OF THE WOODS.

The saint and Brother Peter turned and waited for her to catch up with them. Amy was badly winded, and she dropped to her knees before them, bending to kiss the red tassels on their legs.

When she could speak without panting, Sister Amy told them about finding the ranger named Joe, and watching as he rescued a white-haired girl, tended to her wounds, and spoke with her. She told the saint everything and saved the choicest bit for last.

Saint John listened, and when she was finished, his eyes blazed with inner light.

"Nine towns," he murmured. "In central California?"

"No militia," mused Brother Peter. "Living up there in the mountains, they probably think they have nothing to fear except wandering gray people."

"From what the girl said," added Sister Amy, "they seem to believe that everything beyond their fence lines is wasteland."

"How naive," said Saint John. "How arrogant."

He turned and looked toward the northwest as if he could see across all those miles.

"Nine towns," he said softly.

63

"WE BETTER NOT STAY HERE LONG," SAID BENNY. "LET'S TAKE A QUICK look through this stuff, then get the heck out of here before those reapers come back. And we have to find Lilah and Chong. They don't know about all this crazy stuff."

Nix gave a noncommittal grunt as she set to work searching the cabinets and closets in the cockpit.

A few seconds later Nix opened one cabinet and jumped back as papers, maps, and other items came tumbling out. A mouse squeaked and dropped to the floor before scurrying into a tiny opening in the control panel. Benny squatted down and began poking through the papers. Nix picked up the maps and began unfolding them.

Benny saw a sheaf of papers on a clipboard hanging from a hook inside the cabinet. He pulled it down and began leafing through the pages in hopes of finding something that might provide answers to the mysteries that were stacking up all around them.

What he found instead dried the spit in his mouth and made his heart begin pounding like the hooves of a galloping horse.

"Nix!" he hissed. "My God . . . look at this."

"What is . . . ?" She trailed off as she began reading.

What they read changed their world.

McREADY, MONICA A., M.D. / FIELD NOTES

Hope 1 / Maj. Sancho Ruiz commanding

Date: December 2, 14 A.R.

Observation: The specimens collected
in the Pacific Northwest represent
reanimates displaying both general and
acute behavioral qualities. They have been
categorized into the following subgroups:

R1: Reanimates consistent with all known
examples prior to 7/22/13. These are the
standard "slow walkers." All field-tested
subjects scored in the expected range of 2.1
to 3.6 on the Seldon Scale.

Specimens: 26 (coded yellow)

R2: Moderately mobile reanimates ("fast
walkers") matching the behavior first
recorded by Colonel G. Dietrich in Tulsa,
Oklahoma, in July of last year. Tissue
samples are in dry ice, bin #101. Limited
field-testing tentatively places these
subjects in the 4.4 to 5.1 range of the
Seldon Scale.

Specimens: 4 (coded blue)

R3: Acutely mobile reanimates ("runners"). This is an entirely new classification; however, it verifies reports by independent witnesses dating 9/14/14 and later. Subjects display a marked increase in walking speed and the capability of coordinated running over short distances. Sensory acuity appears to be correspondingly increased. Limited field-testing and observation places this group generally in the 6.5 to 7.5 range on the Seldon Scale. If this is verified, then we are seeing the first incidents of reanimates exceeding the 5.3 ceiling.

Specimens: 2 (coded green)

Addendum: The two collected specimens are the only survivors of at least seven observed cases. Other specimens were destroyed during attempts to capture them. From (as yet) unverified observation, it appears that there may be as many as four distinct subgroups within the R3's.

R3/A: These reanimates appear to be capable of running over/around obstacles, including random objects, hallways, stairs, etc., as long as the obstacles are stationary. They did not, however, display competence in avoiding obstacles introduced into their paths.

There appears to be some disconnect with perception and reaction time.

R3/B: These reanimates were not only able to run over/around obstacles, but they demonstrated a marked ability to avoid additional obstacles introduced at varying speeds. NOTE: One such specimen avoided a rock thrown at its head and attempted to leap over a shopping cart shoved at it by one of the soldiers in our detail. It failed in its attempt, however, and was subsequently put down by the soldier.

R3/C: One observed specimen presented the greatest number of radical behavioral changes. It was able to negotiate obstacles and avoid many of the objects thrown at it or tossed into its path; and it demonstrated a shocking tendency to use simple tools. At various times during a running fight, it used rocks and sticks as clubs and even threw (ineffectually) a stone at one of the soldiers.

R3/D: It is this specimen that most disturbs me. In the absence of formal study, this reanimate appeared to be able to grasp certain concepts, particularly stealth and subterfuge. It appeared to hide behind an overturned car and wait until a soldier walked past, at which point it attacked the soldier, inflicting a serious bite. While other soldiers pursued it, the specimen twice hid, and twice changed its gait to imitate the slow walkers. As a result, two additional soldiers received bites. Though both wounds were superficial, the infection did take hold. In light of secondhand observation only and no formal investigation, I hesitate to rate this subspecies according to the Seldon Scale. However, Dr. Han and Maj. Dietrich both suggested that it would probably rate in the high 8's. If they are correct, and if this is anything more than a regional fluke, this is a potential disaster.

NOTE D.1: All three of the soldiers who were bitten expired within seventy-two hours.

NOTE D.2: Two of the three soldiers reanimated.

NOTE D.3: One of the reanimated soldiers (Lance Corporal Herschel Cohen) displayed all the behavior patterns of the classic slow walker.

NOTE D.4: One of the reanimated soldiers (Private Zachery Bloom) displayed characteristics typical of the R2's.

NOTE D.5: Staff Sergeant Linda Czerkowski
did not reanimate, even though she was
observed continuously for forty-eight hours.
Samples of her blood, tissue, and brain matter
were collected and are in dry ice, bin #119.

Conclusions:

I think we can put to rest the debate as to
whether the Reaper pathogen has mutated.

We have been able to isolate fairly pure
examples of the parasite, and we can
begin studying them once we get back to
Sanctuary.

The sequencer at Hope 1 is on the fritz
again, so we have been unable to sequence
the DNA, either of the parasite or these
new mutations; however, it seems clear that
Reaper is continuing to mutate. There is no
way at this point to know how many new
strains of the disease are active within the
reanimate population.

I would like to again strongly urge the lifting
of the communication ban. Without open
discussions with colonies of survivors, we
will never be able to amass a reliable body of
information. We simply do not know enough,

and it is imperative that we establish the
location and spread of new Reaper strains.

I am gravely concerned about the R3
variations. Does this mutation occur only in
new reanimates? If not, is there a possibility
it could spread to the existing population
of R1's? It's doubtful we could survive a
catastrophe of that magnitude.

I believe we should put five to ten more field
teams in play before the end of January. The
sooner we can verify this information and
collect data, the better.

Postscript: There are reports, as yet unverified
by our teams, of reanimates moving in
clusters. This seems improbable, but in light
of other radical changes I believe it would be
prudent to investigate this. Perhaps Captain
Ledger and his rangers would be best suited
for this.

There was more of it, but what they had just read was
almost too much to grasp.

"Captain Ledger?" echoed Benny. "Hey, I know him . . . I
mean, I have a Zombie Card with him on it."

Nix said nothing. Her eyes were closed and she swayed
for a moment, and then suddenly her knees buckled and she

sagged to the floor. Benny caught her under the arm and steadied her.

"Whoa! Nix, what's wrong?"

She shook her head. Tears rolled down her cheeks. "It's all real," she murmured. "The jet . . . other people. The world isn't . . . isn't . . ."

She threw her arms around Benny's neck, buried her face against his chest, and began to cry.

Dumbfounded and confused, Benny wrapped his arms around her as she wept.

All the time Nix kept saying, "It's real . . . it's real."

SAINT JOHN AND BROTHER PETER SQUATTED IN THE DIRT ON EITHER SIDE
of a burly man with a bushy brown beard and the iron-hard
muscles of the steelworker he had been in his youth.

Now that man lay screaming, and with each scream he
yielded up more and more of his power to the saint and
the high priest of the Night Church. Red mouths had been
opened by the score in his trembling flesh. Every bit of bravado and contempt and resistance had flowed out of him.

This man, Brother Eric, was one of Mother Rose's most
trusted team leaders. A deacon of great power among the
reapers. Close friend to Brother Simon and Brother Alexi. A
confidant of Her Holiness.

And sadly for him, he was intimately aware of what Mother
Rose was planning.

Where once he had thought himself too committed to her
and too powerful in himself to be forced to betray even the most
casual secret, now he could not scream enough of the truth.

Saint John rose and turned away from the screaming man.

"He has told us everything of use," he said quietly. "He
has paid for his sins and now the darkness wants him. Send
him on."

Brother Peter looked down at the blade in his hand and

stifled a disappointed sigh. He would never question an order from the saint, however. With a deft flick of his wrist, the screaming stopped.

"Praise be to the darkness," he murmured as he wiped his knife clean with a handful of grass. He rose and stood with the saint. "I am sorry for your pain."

Saint John shook his head.

"I knew about this betrayal long ago. I have already shed my tears."

Even so, Brother Peter could see the glisten in the saint's eyes. It filled him with a red rage that howled in his head. That anyone would bring harm to this beloved servant of their god was unbearable. There was nothing he would not do to remove that hurt from this holy man.

However, he was also filled with doubts.

"Honored One," he began, "the infection within the Night Church runs so deep."

"Yes. To its very heart."

"How can it be purged?"

Saint John looked at the bloody knife in his own hand. He watched a drop of red fall and splatter on a green leaf.

"Mother Rose believes that her victory lies beyond the walls of Sanctuary." He gestured as if shooing away a fly. "Let her have it."

"But—"

"Let her take her 'chosen ones,' Peter. Let her carve the infection out of our army. Whoever is left . . . well, we know we can trust them."

"We won't help her attack Sanctuary?"

"No."

"Honored One . . . we've spent so much time preparing for this, searching for this place. Our people fear it as a citadel of evil. We can't just walk away."

Saint John said, "That is exactly what we will do. We will leave this place of evil to Mother Rose."

"But—"

The saint turned and looked toward the northwest. "I feel that we are called elsewhere, Peter. I feel that call with all my heart and soul."

"California? Those nine towns?"

"Those nine towns."

"May I ask why?"

"Mother Rose will attack Sanctuary. The ranger, Joe, may warn Sanctuary before she does so. We will watch what happens. If Mother Rose takes it, then we will come back and take it from her. She is not as wise a general as she believes."

"And if Sanctuary defeats her?"

"You can learn much about an enemy when you watch him win. We will watch and learn . . . and plan. Either way, Sanctuary will wait for us."

"So . . . that's it?" asked Chong in a hollow voice. "I just die? I become a zom?"

His eyes burned with tears, but the rest of him felt cold.

Riot sat with her back to the wall. "I don't . . . " She let it trail off and merely shook her head.

"No, damn it," protested Chong. "That's not how this works."

His statement made no sense, and he knew it. But what else could he say? The arrow had gone all the way through him, pushing the infected matter deep into his flesh, into his bloodstream. The sickness was already at work within him. His skin was cool and clammy to the touch and yet sweat poured down his face. In his chest, his heart was beating with all the urgent frenzy of a trapped rabbit.

He was infected.

He was dying.

He was, by any standard of life here in the Rot and Ruin, already dead.

It was too real, too big, too wrong.

"No," Chong said again.

Riot sniffed back some tears. "I'm sorry."

She got up and walked to the open doorway of the old shack and stood there, staring silently out at the desert, fists balled tightly at her sides.

Chong turned away and put his face in his hands. Even when the first sob broke in his chest, the arrow wounds, which should have screamed with pain, merely ached. Even his pain was dying.

Sorry.

So small a word for so enormous a thing.

Lilah.

He cried out her name in his mind, and he saw her, standing tall and beautiful, leaning on her spear, her honey-colored eyes always aware. If she saw him right here and now, would she even wait before quieting him? Would her feelings for him make her pause even for a second before she drove her spear into the back of his neck? Would she grieve afterward? Would the unsurprising death of a clumsy town boy break her heart, or merely add another layer of callus to it?

I'm so sorry, he thought. *Oh, Lilah, I'm so sorry.*

He squeezed his eyes shut in pain that was deeper than his physical wounds. He thought about his parents. The last time they'd seen him, he was heading out with Tom for a simple overnight camping trip in the Ruin. It had been allowed only because Tom and Lilah would both be there, and they were the most experienced zombie hunters anyone knew. And they'd allowed it because his folks knew that Chong needed to say good-bye to Benny and Nix. And Lilah.

I'm sorry, Mom. I'm sorry, Pop.

I'm sorry for everything.

Chong heard a small, soft sound and turned to see Eve in

the middle of the room. She was pink-faced from sleep and jumpy-eyed from bad dreams and waking realities.

Chong sniffed and hastily wiped away his tears.

"Hello, sweetheart," he said, and he even conjured a smile. "How are you?"

Eve came over and stood in front of him. The trauma of everything she'd experienced had regressed her. The child she had become was younger still, and Chong could see that so little of her was left—and that was hanging by a thread.

She reached out a finger and almost touched the burn on Chong's stomach. The flesh around it was livid and veined with black lines.

"Hurt?" she asked in the tiniest of voices. Looking into her eyes was like looking into a haunted house.

"No, honey . . . it's not bad," lied Chong. "Hardly hurts at all."

He reached out and gently stroked Eve's tangled blond hair. She flinched at first, but he waited, showed her that his hand was empty, and tried again. This time Eve allowed it. Then she knelt down and laid her head against his chest.

"I had a bad dream," she murmured.

That thought—that Eve believed this was a dream she would or could wake up from—came close to breaking Chong's heart. He continued to stroke her hair while he lay there and tried not to be afraid of what he was becoming.

He hoped Lilah would never find him.

PART THREE

SANCTUARY

The act of dying is one of the acts of life.

—MARCUS AURELIUS

FROM NIX'S JOURNAL

Tom once asked us each if we knew what we would fight for. What we would kill for. What we would die for.

He said if a person didn't know the answers to those questions, then they should never go to war. He also said that if a person did know the answers to those questions, they should never want to go to war.

I don't know if I can answer any of those questions yet, but I feel like I'm already living inside a war.

66

"NIX?" ASKED BENNY GENTLY. "ARE YOU ALL RIGHT?"

She kept crying and didn't answer.

"Look . . . Tom was right," said Benny, "the plague is changing, and maybe that's good news. Those papers said that it was mutating. Maybe it's mutating into something that won't be as bad."

"Oh sure, and when's the last time something changed for the better?" she sobbed. "Everything is wrong. This isn't how it's supposed to be. This isn't how any of this is supposed to be. It's all wrong, Benny. God, I'm so stupid."

"Wait—what? Nix, what are you talking about? How's any of this your fault?"

"You don't understand." She was crying so hard those were the only words he could understand. "You just don't understand."

"Nix . . . I want to understand . . . just tell me what's wrong."

Benny felt his own tears running in lines down his face and falling onto her hair.

What storms raged inside Nix? Benny could make a list, but he was achingly positive that any list he could make would not be complete.

"I'm sorry," he said, because he had nothing better to say. "It'll be okay."

"No," she said. "It's not going to be okay."

He pushed her gently back and studied her face. "What do you mean?"

There was a strange light in her beautiful green eyes, and an even stranger half smile on her lips. The smile was crooked and filled with self-loathing and self-mockery.

"Oh, Benny," she said in a terrible whisper, "I think I'm in trouble."

"Trouble?"

"I think I'm going crazy."

He smiled. "You're not going crazy."

"How would you know?"

"Nix, don't you think I'd know?"

She shook her head. "No one knows. No one understands."

"Try me, Nix. If something's wrong, then tell me. Let me in."

"God, if you knew what was going on in my head, you'd run so fast. . . ."

"No."

"Yes, you would."

"No," he said firmly, leaning all his weight into the word, "I wouldn't. You can tell me anything."

She continued to shake her head.

So Benny said, "I hear voices."

He dropped it on her, and for a moment she stopped crying, stopped shaking her head, and stared at him. A twisted half smile kept trying to form on her lips.

"Yup," said Benny, tapping his temple. "Sometimes I have a real party in here."

"This isn't a joke. . . ."

"Do I look like I'm laughing?" He did smile, though, and he knew that smile was probably every bit as crooked as hers.

"Why haven't you said anything?"

"Why haven't you?" Benny sighed. "It's not like we've been communicating that well lately, Nix."

She sighed. "A lot's happened."

"I know, but we haven't talked about it. I think that's the whole problem."

"It's not that simple."

"Okay, so if it's not the whole problem, then it's the doorway to the problem. C'mon, Nix, it's been a month since Gameland. Since then, what have we talked about? Hunting for food. Cooking. Routes on the map. Which leaves are safe to use as toilet paper. Jeez, Nix, we talk about stuff that just gets us through the day, but we don't talk about what happened."

Nix said nothing.

"We killed people, Nix."

"I know. We killed people seven months ago at Charlie's camp, too."

"Yeah, but we didn't really talk about it. Not in any way that made sense of it, or cleared it. Don't you think that's a little weird?"

She shrugged. "Everything's weird."

"After everything that's happened, Nix, I really don't think either of us has a chance of being totally sane. I guess 'normal' was last year."

She thought about that and gave a grudging nod.

"Okay," Benny continued, "but it can't be good that we don't talk about this stuff. We never really talked about your mom and what happened."

Nix turned away.

"And . . . that's exactly what I mean," he said. "I even start to mention it and you lock up. That can't be the best way of dealing with—"

"What kind of voices?" Nix interrupted.

"It . . . used to be what I guess you could call my 'inner voice,'" he began slowly. "It was like me, but not me. It was smarter, you know? It knew about stuff. It's hard to explain."

"What kind of stuff?"

"All kinds of stuff. Even how to talk to you."

The ghost of a smile flitted across her lips.

"But that's not what really has me scared," Benny continued. He took a breath and then blurted it. "I think Tom's talking to me too."

"Oh."

"At first I thought I was just remembering things he said. But lately . . . I don't know. I think he's actually talking to me. Like, maybe it's his ghost."

"Ghost?"

Benny nodded. "God, this is why I don't talk about this stuff, because you're definitely going to think I'm totally monkey-bat crazy."

"You always have been," she said with another small smile.

"Since Tom died . . . I knew that I had to keep him alive somehow. I know it sounds crazy, but it makes sense to me. I have to remember everything Tom ever said. Every lesson he gave us. Everything. God, Nix, he was the very last samurai, do you realize that? The last one. Think about everything that . . . died . . . with him. Everything he knew. Everything he could have taught us is gone. Do you get how bad that is? All that knowledge. How to fight, how to do things. Gone. Just—gone."

"I know, Benny. My mom knew a lot of things too."

"Look, Nix, I didn't mean—"

"I know what you meant. It's okay."

Benny licked his lips, which had gone completely dry. "I can't stand it, Nix. I can't stand that it's all gone. I can't stand that he's gone." His nose was starting to run, and he dug a handkerchief out of his pocket and wiped it.

"I know," she said.

"But," Benny said, "maybe he's not. That's what I'm trying to say. Today, when I was down in the ravine . . . he actually spoke to me. It wasn't a memory. It was like he was right there."

"You were surrounded by zoms, Benny. You were probably in shock."

"No kidding. Doesn't change anything. Tom started speaking to me, and I could hear him as clear as I'm hearing you now."

"Why are you scared of that? He's your brother."

"Um . . . hello? He's a ghost?"

"You only think you're hearing Tom's ghost."

"Yes."

"Is he here now?" Nix asked. "Can you ask him a question? Ask him what my mom's middle name was."

"He's a ghost, not a carnival magician."

"Tom knew her middle name," said Nix. "Ask him. If it's really him, then he'll know."

"That's stupid—"

"Ask him!" she yelled.

"I can't!" he yelled back.

"Why not?"

"Because it doesn't work like that."

"How do you know how it works? Come on, Benny, we've been on the run since we got up this morning. Exactly when did you have time to process everything and come to the unshakable conclusion that you're the expert on all things spiritual?"

"Why are you getting mad at me? I'm trying to get some help here 'cause I think I'm really screwed up, and you're giving me crap."

"Benny, how do you know this is Tom?"

"I just know."

"No," she snapped, "that's not good enough. How do you know?"

"I just do. He was my brother. I think I'd know my brother's voice. This is him."

"Then ask him my mother's middle name. What are you afraid of?"

"I'm not afraid of that."

When Nix didn't say anything, Benny sighed.

"Look," he said, "why are you badgering me about this? You think I want to hear my dead brother's voice?"

"Why not? I'd give anything to hear my mother speak to me," said Nix in a voice that was filled with fragile cracks.

"Why?" he asked.

"Because," shouted Nix, "I can't even remember what she sounded like."

After a long moment, Benny said, "What?"

"God . . . I'd give anything for her to start talking to me." A sob hitched in her chest. "Benny . . . I can't even remember what my mother looked like."

Sitting with Eve steadied Chong. He understood why. It was harder to let yourself sink if someone else needed you to be their rock. He saw Benny and Nix do that for each other, even though he was positive they weren't aware of it.

It did not mean that Chong was less terrified, but the girl's terror and trauma were worse than his own. Even if he died, what she was going through was worse. She'd seen her parents murdered right in front of her. When Chong died, his fear would end; Eve would have to live with those memories.

Everything's relative.

Eve sat close to him, sucking her thumb, occasionally humming disjointed pieces of lullabies.

Riot went outside to make sure they were still safe, then came back and sat down. Chong studied Riot's face. She was a puzzle to him. She reminded him of Tom's bounty hunter friend, Sally Two-Knives. Tough, fiercely individual, violent, and clearly with a heart.

"Talk to me," said Chong.

"About what?" she asked. "I've been racking my brain trying to come up with some smart way out of this bear trap, but every which way I look there's just more traps."

"Yeah, let's not talk about that," said Chong. "Why don't you tell me your story? I mean . . . are you a reaper?"

She looked away for a moment. "Not as such," she said.

"Okay, that was evasive."

She shrugged. "I was a reaper once upon a time. Ain't now. End of story."

"No," said Chong. "I'm dying, I get to be nosy. You're a walking contradiction. You have the same skin art as the reapers, but you went after Brother Andrew like you owed him for a lot of hurt."

Riot ran a hand thoughtfully over her scalp, then sighed. "I was no more'n two years old when the plague hit," she said slowly. "My dad was raising me. He was a country doctor down in North Carolina. He'd divorced my ma 'cause she was a drunk and a bum and no damn good."

"I'm sorry," Chong began, but she waved it away.

"That's the nice part of the story. Y'all want to hear it or not?"

He nodded. His skin was cold and clammy, and he had an incredibly bad headache. He sat cross-legged with his back to the wall.

"I could use the distraction," he admitted.

"Well, when the whole world turned into an all-you-can-eat buffet, Pa packed me in his car and drove northwest. Got as far as Jefferson City, Missouri, before the EMPs killed the car. After that we joined up with a buncha folks who was running from the dead. I don't remember nothin' about that. All kind of a blur. We was always running, always hiding, and always hungry. People came and went. Then we met up with a bigger bunch of folks, and when they found out Pa was a doc, they made sure that he was always safe. Me too.

"My pa was always trying to steer over toward Topeka, which was the last place he knew my mom to be living. And sure enough, she was there and she was alive. My pa said it was like a miracle. Only thing was, Ma was hooked up with a group that was calling itself the Night Church, and she was keeping company with its leader, a man named Saint John."

Eve wormed closer to Chong, her thumb still socketed in her mouth. It frightened Chong that the child was barely talking. She'd said a few words after she woke up, but then she seemed to shut down. It was so sad.

"Saint John said that it really was a miracle that my ma found me," continued Riot, "and he said that it made me special. Like I was some kind of holy person." She gave a bitter laugh. "Me. Holy. Right."

"This Night Church," asked Chong, "they're the reapers?"

She nodded. "They didn't start calling themselves that until much later. By then I was being trained to be a fighter. Saint John knows every kind of evil move there is. Karate and all that. Dirty fighting. Hands, feet, knives, strangle wires. He taught me all that stuff, and I was the head of my class. Hooray for me." She touched her scalp. "This stuff was actually a health thing first. We all came down with the worst case of lice in the history of bugs. Couldn't shake 'em, couldn't wash 'em out, so Pa suggested everybody shave all their hair off. Worked, too. But while we was all bald, somebody took it in their head to go and get tattooed. Not sure who started it, but everyone in the Night Church did it. Saint John, too, and he called it the mark in flesh of our devotion. Some crap like that."

"Why don't you grow your hair back?"

She ran her fingers lightly over her scalp. "I tried, but it don't grow in right. Comes in all patchy and nasty. Better to keep it like this. Besides, the reapers can't stand that I have the mark and I ain't one of 'em. Drives Ma nuts too."

"Your mother is still with them?"

"My dear old ma," said Riot acidly, "is the high holy muck-a-muck of the Night Church. Calls herself Mother Rose. An' she's the only one who didn't get her head tattooed. Grew her hair back, and Saint John somehow spun that as it was a special mark that only she could have. No, don't look too close at it, 'cause you'll hurt yourself. It don't make a lick of sense."

"Why did you leave?"

"I wised up," she said. "I guess I kind of had what you might call a 'moment.' I was fourteen by then and leadin' my own team of reapers. All girls, daughters of the inner circle of the church. We were getting ready to hit this little walled-in town in Idaho—and the thing is, I never even found out its name—and the night before the raid, I was on recon with a couple of the other girls when I heard something from over the walls."

"What?" asked Chong.

"Weren't much, just a lady singing a lullaby to her baby." She paused as if looking into that memory with perfect clarity. "I was up in a tree where I could see over the wall. The guards don't watch trees because the gray people can't climb."

Chong nodded.

"I could see into a lighted window, and there's this gal, maybe twenty years old, holding a little baby in her arms as she rocked in a chair. Just a single candle lit on a table. It was the strangest thing I'd ever seen. The woman was so . . . happy. She had her baby, and she was in a safe town, and there was music and laughter in the streets. The world outside might be full of monsters and the whole world might have gone to hell, but here she was, rocking her baby and singing a song."

"What happened?"

Riot sniffed and shook her head. "When I came back to give my report . . . I couldn't do it. I just couldn't. So I lied. I spun a yarn about the whole town being filled with armed men and lots of guns and suchlike. I said that we'd get ourselves killed sure as God made little green apples."

"Did they believe you?"

She looked at Eve and smiled sadly. "No. Saint John had other people scoutin' too, and they saw the truth, that the town was wide open, that the defenses were only good against gray people."

"What happened?"

"They came in and killed 'em all. Every last man, woman . . . and child . . . in that town. Saint John sent his pet goon, Brother Peter, to drag me in for a talk, but I read the writing on the wall and cut bait. I was gone before sunup. Just up and went."

"They let you just leave?"

"'Let'? No. I had to muss a few of them 'up some, but I got away." She sniffed again. "After that I fell in with a gang of scavengers. That's where I got the nickname. Riot. Did a bunch of bad stuff and raised a lot of Cain. Then . . . I got real sick, and a way-station monk took me to a place called Sanctuary. They fixed me up right and proper. They wanted me to stay there, but I snuck out of that place like I did from my mom's camp. Didn't hurt nobody, though. After that I knocked around a bit, got into some more trouble. But . . . a year ago I found a bunch of refugees on the run from some reapers. I helped 'em slip away, but there were a lot of sick and injured, including a bunch of kids, so I took 'em to Sanctuary. Kind of dropped 'em at the door and ran. Done that a few times now. The folks at Sanctuary don't mind people coming in for help, but they really don't like people leaving. I think they'd as soon put a leash on me if they had the chance. I don't give them no chance. I drop and run, drop and run. That's what I was trying to do with Carter and his crew. Guess I kind of made it my calling."

"Why?"

She shrugged. "I don't know. Maybe it's penance."

"But . . . the stuff you did while you were with the reapers, that wasn't your fault. You didn't know any better, and when you did, you left."

"Maybe. That don't make me sleep any better at night."

She reached over and stroked Eve's hair.

"I got wind of the reapers planning on making a move on her town. Treetops it was called. I'd been there a few times with the scavengers. Nice folks, so I tried to get there in time to warn people, but I was about four hours too late. All I could do was offer to lead the survivors to Sanctuary."

"You left out one part," said Chong. "What happened to your dad?"

She shook her head. "I don't know. Saint John and Mama said he up and left one night. Just took off . . . but I don't believe that. I think they killed him."

"Why?"

Riot gave him a hard look. "If you're running a church

based on killing everyone who's still sucking air, do you really want a doctor around? Pa was all about some oath when he was in medical school. He was all about saving lives . . . so I guess he had to go."

"I'm sorry," said Chong, and he meant it. "It . . . it must be lonely for you."

"Well, it's the end of the world, you know? Kinda sucks for everyone."

Chong smiled a bitter little smile. "Yeah, I really get that."

Riot studied his face for several thoughtful seconds. "I don't know much about medicine," she admitted, "'cept how to patch a busted leg or stitch a knife cut, take out the occasional arrow. Point is, I know where we might be able to get some help."

"Help? Come on, Riot, we both know how this ends. I get sicker and sicker and then I die. And then you . . . well, then you take care of me. There's no variation on that story. Everyone who gets infected dies."

At that last word, Eve gave a soft whimper of protest and buried her head against his chest. Chong stroked her hair. He wanted to do the same thing she was doing—curl up in a fetal position and hope the world would just go away.

"Chong, listen to me," insisted Riot. "I think I should take you to Sanctuary."

"And what exactly *is* Sanctuary? Is it just a bunch of way-station monks or . . . ?"

Riot looked away for a moment, debating with herself about something. When she turned back, her face was even more tense. "Sanctuary is a lot of different things to different people," she said. "For some—people like . . ." Instead of naming Carter, she nodded to Eve, and Chong understood. "For folks runnin' from the reapers, Sanctuary's just that. A safe place. It's squirreled away pretty good, and it's got some natural defenses. Mountains and suchlike. Hard as all get-out to find."

"It's a settlement?"

"To some," she said. "Mostly it's a kind of hospital, and I want to take little Evie there. I'm not going to be any good taking care of her, and she's going to be hurtin' for a long spell. There's a bunch of monks who look after people."

"Way-station monks? I've met some. The call themselves the Children of God, and they refer to the gray people as the Children of Lazarus."

"Right, right. Well, they made Sanctuary their own place, and they take in the sick and injured and tend to them."

"Are they actual doctors?"

"They're not," she said, but Chong caught the slight emphasis on "they're."

"Are . . . there other doctors there?"

"Kind of."

"And you think they could help me?"

"I don't know," she admitted. "But if anyone can, they's the ones."

"Okay, then let's go."

"Well, there's a bit of a hitch," she said slowly, looking almost pained.

"What hitch?"

"If they let you into that other place . . . not the part with the monks, but the part where they can maybe help you . . ."

"Yes?"

"You won't be allowed to leave."

"Until—?"

"Ever," she said. "They don't like strangers wandering around who know where Sanctuary is. They won't kill you or nothing, but you won't ever leave."

Chong closed his eyes and looked into his own future. All he could see was a blank wall.

"What choice do I have?"

FROM NIX'S JOURNAL

Last night I dreamed that the zombie plague never started. But the dream was weird; there were no details. I suppose it's because I never knew the world before First Night.

All I know is town and the Ruin.

"I . . . I'M SORRY, NIX," SAID BENNY.

She glared at him through her tears. "Yeah, well, sorry doesn't do much. I lost my mom. I lost everything, and it's all that damn town's fault."

"What?"

"God, I couldn't stand to be there another minute. It was like living in a graveyard. No one ever talked about what happened to the world. No one ever talked about the future. You know why? Because no one believed there was a future. Everyone in Mountainside was just sitting around, waiting to die. They act like they're dead already."

"I—"

She angrily fisted tears out of her eyes. "My mom was murdered by Charlie Pink-eye, and I was kidnapped. You'd think people would at least react to that, but they didn't. Not really. After we destroyed Charlie's camp and came back to town, people acted like I'd never been away. Except for Captain Strunk, Mayor Kirsch, and Leroy Williams, no one even asked where I'd been or what it was like out in the Ruin. People didn't want to know. And at Mom's funeral, you know what people said to me? They said stuff like 'she's in a better place' and 'at least she's not suffering anymore.' Suffering? She wasn't sick, she was beaten to death!"

"Nix, I—"

"No one ever—ever—said anything about the fact that I was kidnapped and taken to Gameland. No one. I don't think people even believed it. There were people in town who said they were sorry my mom had some problems with Charlie. Some problems. Problems? Like she died because they had a fricking argument. They wrote her off, because to pay any real attention to what happened would mean that they would have to accept that Gameland was real, and if they did that, they'd have to accept what goes on there, which means they'd have to talk about zoms. And people don't. God! Remember what Preacher Jack called town? He said it was limbo . . . that the people there were just waiting to die. And I wonder why I'm going crazy? That town made me crazy, and if we'd stayed there any longer, it would have killed me. That's no joke, Benny. I would have died."

There was a very dangerous light in her eyes when she said that.

"Whoa, now," said Benny. "Let's not—"

Nix grabbed a fistful of Benny's shirt. "I'm not exaggerating, Benny, and I'm not joking. That town is limbo. It's nothing, it isn't real. The people there, they're no different from the zoms. They think they're alive because they can talk, but they don't talk about anything. They chatter. They make small talk and pretend that's the same as engaging with one another. Going through the motions of life is not the same thing as living."

"Nix, I know this stuff. It's why I left too."

"No," she said fiercely, shaking him. "God, please don't lie to me, Benny. Not now. Not out here. You left because of me. I know it. Tom knew it too. Tom left because of me too."

"No way."

"Yes. He was going to marry my mom, but my mom died. He would have stayed in town and raised you and maybe helped raise me, but I wanted to leave. He knew—knew—that no matter what happened, even if he tried to stop me, I would leave town. So he created our big Road Trip so he could watch over me. For my mom, maybe. And because you were in love with me. Benny—you left town because of me, and Tom left town because of you and me . . . and now Tom's dead. If we don't find that jet and find something real, a place that shows that we're all still alive, then Tom will have died for nothing. And it will be all my fault."

Benny stared into her eyes, and now he understood.

The size of it, the jagged edges of it, the skewed and destructive logic of it.

That knowledge gouged out a massive hole in his chest.

"Nix," Benny said gently, "you can't do this to yourself."

"It's true!"

"No," he said, "it isn't. Listen to me. Tom didn't leave Mountainside because of you. Or me. He left because your mom wasn't there anymore, and he couldn't stand that. He left because he wanted to find the same kind of place you want to find. A place where people are alive. He wanted that for me and for you and for himself. There was no chance in hell that Tom wouldn't leave town. Remember what he said after Danny Houser's funeral? He said, 'I can't stand this damn town anymore.' He said that, and he moved up the time we were scheduled to leave. Tom needed to escape that town."

"But he died!"

Benny bent forward and pressed his forehead against Nix's. "He died, Nix, but you didn't kill him and neither did I. Even though I think I did almost every night. I think about all the things I've done wrong and how if I'd done this or done that, you and I would never have wound up at Gameland. And yeah, I can make myself crazy too. But we didn't kill Tom. An evil man did that. Preacher Jack shot Tom in the back and that is the truth."

Nix sniffed but said nothing.

"Nix . . . what would Tom tell us if he could hear this conversation?"

She shook her head.

"No . . . tell me," Benny insisted.

She sat back and wiped at her eyes. "He—he'd say what you just said. That Preacher Jack . . ."

"Right. Preacher Jack. An evil man who did an evil thing."

Nix looked at the broken windows. "And now we have Saint John and Mother Rose. Is that all there is, Benny? Just corruption and evil?"

Fifty conciliatory lies rose to Benny's lips. But this was not the time to placate Nix.

"I don't know," he admitted.

Panic flared in her eyes, but he smiled.

"I don't know what's out here," Benny said, "but I can't believe that there's nothing left worth finding. I won't believe it. I don't. We met Eve, Nix. She has a family."

"Who tried to kill us."

"No. I don't see it that way, not anymore. Think about it.

They were out of their minds worrying about Eve, and then they find her with us. They don't know us from a can of paint, and I think it's pretty clear that they're on the run. They see us and they're terrified that we're reapers. In their places we might have made the same mistake. But look at it another way—they're running from evil. They aren't the reapers. They were willing to fight and kill to protect their little girl. What does that tell you? And there's all that talk about Sanctuary. Despite what Mother Rose and those other freak jobs said, it doesn't exactly sound like an abode of evil, does it?"

"No," she admitted hesitantly.

"No," he agreed.

"And the people who flew this plane. They were scientists working to understand the plague and maybe cure it. Again, not the definition of evil."

"No."

"The American Nation," Benny said, testing the name and nodding approval. "I say we gather up some of these papers, check out the rest of the plane, then get out of here and find Lilah and Chong."

"And then what?"

"I'm working on that," he admitted.

They looked at each other for a long moment.

"I do love you, Benny," she said.

"I love you, too."

"Even though I'm a nut?"

"Like I'm well-balanced? Hearing voices, remember?" He grinned at her.

She shook her head in exasperation, but she was smiling, too.

Riot helped Chong to his feet and steadied him as he took a couple of shaky steps. Eve trailed along behind, silent as a ghost. She stayed close, though, as if unwilling to be more than a few feet from Chong's side.

Chong insisted on taking the bow and arrows with him.

"Why?"

"Well," he said weakly, "I can shoot. I'm pretty good. And . . . if there are really doctors at Sanctuary, they might want to look at the stuff on the arrowheads."

"Okay," she said, and helped him sling the bow and quiver over his shoulder. "How are ya feelin'?"

"I've been better," he admitted. "My legs feel funny, like they fell asleep, but there's no pins and needles. Funny thing is that the arrow wound doesn't seem to hurt much."

"Oh."

"Yes," he said dryly, "I'm pretty sure that's not a good sign."

They walked toward the door of the shack. With each step Chong felt his balance improve, but he was not all that encouraged. It was more of a matter of getting used to his condition rather than there being any actual improvement.

"I don't know if y'all want to hear this," said Riot, "but I heard once about a feller who got the gray sickness and didn't die."

Chong swiveled his head around and stared at her. "I'm pretty sure I do want to hear about that."

She looked pained. "Well . . . it ain't like things worked out too great for him."

"Tell me anyway."

Together they walked out of the shack toward her quad.

Riot sucked her teeth for a moment. "Well," she began reluctantly, "this was a feller name of Hiram, a corn farmer up from Arkansas who hired out as a hunter for small settlements. He'd go out with a wagon covered in sheet metal and some horses dressed in coats made from license plates bolted onto leather covers. He'd kill him some deer and whatever else he could draw a bead on, then he'd bring it all back to the settlement and sell it out of the back of his wagon. Well, one time he comes back and he's looking mighty poorly."

"Like I am?"

She glanced at him and offered a fragile smile. "Near enough as makes no never mind."

"What happened?"

"Well, it turns out that he ate himself a leg of wild mutton he'd shot and got sick. He asked my pa to take a look at him, and Pa asked to see the rest of the sheep he'd cut the leg off of." She paused while she helped Chong step over the back of the quad. There was no seat belt, but she lashed him in place with some rope she took from a gear bag.

When he was settled in, he said, "I think I can guess what your father found when he examined the sheep."

Riot nodded, but said it anyway. "There was a small bite on its shoulder. Not bad, and not fatal, but a bite. One of them had tried to chow down on it and the critter scampered."

"So what happened to Hiram?"

"That's the funny part. And I mean—"

"Funny weird, not funny ha-ha, I get it."

She nodded. "Hiram got sick as a hound dog. Lay in bed for ten, twelve days, and they posted a guard on him in case he needed seeing to."

"But . . . ?"

Riot picked up Eve, kissed her, hugged her, and then placed her in the seat. "Hold on to her."

"Don't worry," said Chong, "I won't let her go. But what happened to Hiram? Did he get better?"

A few strange expressions wandered across Riot's features. "Not 'better' as you'd like to hear. He didn't die, though. Not exactly. Old Hiram got better enough to get out of bed. He could talk to people and all, and he even went back to hunting after a time."

"But . . . ?" Chong urged. He wanted to kick her.

"He never did get all the way right again. And every once in a while he'd come down all bitey."

"'Bitey'?"

"Yeah. He'd get riled and go all weird and try to take a chomp outta someone. Did it more than once."

"He bit people?"

Riot looked away. "Might even have eaten some people, but that was just a rumor. He run off after a while, 'bout a half step before people did something permanent about him."

"What—I mean—what was he?"

"Don't know what science would call that feller. We kids gave him a nickname, though."

"I can't wait to hear this," said Chong.

"We called him a half-zee," she said. "Hiram Half-Zee."

"Swell," he said, and thought, *Lilah will just love that. Right up until she quiets me.*

"Hold on, boy," said Riot. She perched on the very front of the crowded seat, then fired up the quad, and a moment later they were zooming through the forest, the four fat tires kicking up plumes of sandy soil behind them.

70

"Nix, I think we need to find this 'Sanctuary' place. You read that report, you saw the notes. Whoever this Dr. McReady was, she thought she was really onto something important. Faster zoms? Smarter zoms? If there are scientists and some kind of military at Sanctuary, then they *have* to be told about this. We can't just let this stuff rot here."

Nix chewed her lip thoughtfully.

"And we have to warn the people at Sanctuary about the reapers. I didn't understand everything that went on out there, but that woman, Mother Rose, and those reaper freaks are going to attack that place."

"I don't want to get in the middle of another big fight," Nix said. "After Charlie and White Bear and Preacher Jack, I don't know if I can . . ."

Her voice trailed off, and she closed her eyes.

"Nix," he said softly, "I'm not going to make any stupid speeches about destiny, but . . ."

"But you are anyway," she said, looking at him now. "You're going to say that something—destiny, fate, or Tom's ghost—steered us here, and now we have to make some huge decision about what to do with this information. Right?"

He said nothing.

"You're going to say that this is one of those 'it's up to us or no one' things, like all those heroic stories you and Morgie used to read. The hero on the journey who faces a challenge only he can handle, blah, blah, blah."

Benny held his tongue.

"And you're going to say that the tough thing to do is the right thing to do. That it's the samurai thing to do. That it's the warrior smart thing to do. That if we have information that could save lives, then it's our responsibility to do exactly that. Right? Isn't that what you were going to say?"

He cleared his throat. "Something like that."

Nix leaned on the back of the pilot's chair and stared out of the window. She let out a long sigh and in a voice that was odd and distant said, "Tom taught us a lot more than how to fight. More than the Warrior Smart stuff. Being able to fight is never going to be enough. Not in this world. Charlie learned that. So did White Bear and Preacher Jack."

"No."

"Sometimes it's easy to forget what the word 'samurai' means."

"'To serve,'" said Benny.

"'To serve,'" she agreed. "To do the honorable thing. The right thing, even when it's hard. Even when it hurts."

She bent and picked up her bokken, which had fallen to the floor. Nix looked at it for a long moment, then turned slowly toward Benny. She looked tired, frightened, and stressed, but beneath all that an old, familiar green fire burned in her eyes. She took a breath and gave Benny a single, decisive nod.

"Then let's do it," she said. "Let's go be samurai."

71

"HOW FAR IS IT BACK TO THE PLATEAU?" ASKED LILAH. SHE HAD TO LEAN close to Joe's ear and yell.

"Two miles," he said. "We'll be there in . . . oh crap."

He jammed on the brakes, and the quad skidded to a dusty halt. Grimm, who had been loping along beside the quad, stopped dead and uttered a low growl.

Lilah looked past Joe's muscular shoulder.

"Oh," she said.

The path through the forest was blocked with reapers. An even dozen of the killers. They had all turned at the sound of the quad, and their expressions quickly changed from curiosity, to confusion, to an ugly delight. The rasp of steel as they all drew their weapons was louder than the idling motor.

"Can we go around?" asked Lilah.

"We can," said Joe, "but we'd lose a lot of time, and from what you said, this is the route your friends would most likely have taken. If we go around, we could miss them entirely, and that crowd of bozos might find them."

Lilah grunted.

"Then we fight," she said.

He turned and grinned at her. "I admire your spunk, dar-lin', but you're in no shape for a brawl."

"I can shoot."

"There's that." Joe dismounted. "Tell you what," he said, "you can play target practice with anyone who gets past me and the fuzz-monster."

"There are too many for you," she said. "Even with Grimm."

The dog looked from her to the advancing knot of reap-ers and back again and almost seemed to smile. He gave a discreet *whuff* and held his ground.

"Just watch our backs," said Joe, and began walking toward the reapers. Lilah watched him. The man sauntered down the path as if he was taking a leisurely stroll on a spring evening. Grimm walked beside him. Joe's sword was still slot-ted into its rack on the quad and his gun was in its holster. The man was insane.

The reapers thought so too. They grinned at one another and puffed out their chests as they strode forward to share the darkness with this sinner.

Joe stopped when he was twenty feet away and held up a hand, palm out. Grimm sat down next to him.

"Okay, kids," he said loud enough for the reapers and Lilah to hear, "before you go all wrath-of-God on me, let's chat for a bit."

The reapers slowed and stopped, looking wary. Their eyes darted from Joe to the dog and back again. One of them, a tall man with a head tattoo of hummingbirds and flowers, stepped out in front of the others.

"Who are you?" he demanded.

"Doesn't matter who I am," said Joe.

"Have you come to accept the darkness?"

"Not as such, no."

"Then what do we have to talk about?"

Joe shrugged. "Oh, I don't know. How about we see how devoted you guys are to the whole joy-of-dying thing."

The leader of the reapers snorted. "We are reapers of the Night Church, servants of God and purifiers of this infected world."

"Okay," said Joe. "And . . . ?"

"And we do not fear dying. To die is to become one with the darkness, and that is the greatest joy of all."

"Really?" asked Joe, seemingly incredulous. "You guys actually believe that?"

"Yes!" declared the man with the hummingbird tattoos, and the other reapers roared in agreement.

"No fear of death at all, is that what I'm hearing? I mean, is that the gist?"

"Death is a pathway to glory and oneness with the infinite."

"So . . . if I shot one of you, everyone here would be good with that?"

"You think like someone from the old world," sneered the leader. "You still think that we fear death and—"

Joe drew his pistol and shot the man through the heart. The draw was lightning fast—faster than anything Lilah had ever seen, faster even than Tom—and the leader pitched backward without even a cry.

The echo bounced around the woods and then vanished, leaving a stunned silence behind.

"Now the funny thing is," said Joe into the silence, "there's more than a couple of you who look pretty damn scared right now."

They gaped at him and cut uncertain looks at one another.

Joe holstered his pistol, reached into his pocket, and removed a round metal object. It was squat and green, with a single metal arm and a round ring. He held it up.

"This is an M67 fragmentation grenade. Yeah, I know it's from the old world, but let's pretend that it still has relevance to the moment. It has a casualty radius of fifteen meters, with a fatality radius of five meters. That covers all of you cats. Now, I'm willing to bet a brand-new ration dollar that not one of you is going to bravely stand there while I throw this. In fact, I'm willing to bet you're all going to run away as if you really are afraid for your own lives. What do you think about that?"

The reapers stared at him.

Joe grinned at them.

He pulled the pin. He kept his fingers tight around the metal arm, holding it in place.

And the reapers scattered. They flew away from the path as fast as they could run.

Joe held his ground. Beside him Grimm yawned.

The sound of the reapers crashing through the forest eventually faded into silence. Joe sighed, replaced the pin in the grenade, and dropped it into his pocket. Then he turned and strolled back to Lilah.

"Call me cynical," he said, "but I've come to believe that most people who follow a total wack job aren't always true believers. They just like to follow. They like the perks. Makes them feel strong. Kind of weakens your faith in fruitcake fanatics."

Lilah goggled at him. "Would you have really thrown the grenade?"

Joe grinned. "What do you think?"

Lilah nodded, then asked, "If we meet more reapers, will they all do that?"

He shook his head. "Sadly . . . no. Some of them are true believers, and those you have to deal with." He paused. "And there are a few of them who are way past simply believing. There are some who really won't care if you shoot them or maim them, and they will crawl on broken knees through hell itself to take you with them. Saint John's like that. And Brother Peter. You don't talk with them, you don't screw around. If you are ever unfortunate enough to be face-to-face with either of them—you take your shot before you take your next breath. 'Cause otherwise it will be your last breath."

She frowned. "You're afraid of Saint John?"

Joe put his hands on her shoulders. "Lilah, there's not a living soul on this planet who shouldn't be afraid of Saint John."

He got back on the quad, and they roared off toward the plateau.

72

MOTHER ROSE STOOD IN THE SHADE OF A MASSIVE COTTONWOOD TREE. Brother Alexi stood behind her, his massive hammer standing on its head, the handle leaning against the tree trunk. Other reapers—all trusted members of her inner circle, her chosen ones—stood in a loose ring around them. In the middle of this ring was a ragged prisoner, a stocky man with a Hawaiian face and curly black hair. He knelt directly in front of Mother Rose, and she towered over him, dominating him with her personal power as well as the evident control she held over his life.

The Hawaiian bowed his head.

"—and this girl who was leading you," said Mother Rose, "her name was Riot?"

"Yes, ma'am," mumbled the prisoner.

"She was leading all of Carter's people through the woods?"

There was a pause before the man said, "Carter wasn't our leader. We're *all* from Treetops. No one elected him 'king.' We all fought our way out."

Mother Rose flicked a glance at Alexi, who mouthed the word "Bingo."

"What is your name?" she asked.

"Mako," said the Hawaiian. "Like the shark."

"It is my belief, Brother Mako," said Mother Rose, "that Carter presumed leadership of your group only because he had a relationship with Riot."

"I guess. Carter's always been an arrogant . . ." Mako let the rest go. "The two of them were thick as thieves, ever since we met her."

"They are both sinners," said Mother Rose.

Mako hesitated, then nodded. "I guess so."

"I know so. Sinners and heretics who care only for themselves. Tell me what happened."

Mako glanced at the reapers, then risked a look up at Mother Rose, who gave him an encouraging smile.

"I don't want to die," said Mako. Fear and defiance warred on his face. "I don't owe a damn thing to Carter. I . . . don't want to die."

"Death waits for all sinners," said Mother Rose. "But for those who serve the will of God . . . there is always a chance for a new life."

Mako blinked in confusion. "But . . . I thought . . . the reapers . . ."

Mother Rose bent and caressed the man's bruised cheek. "The world is full of mysteries, and the Lord Thanatos moves in such unexpected ways."

"Wait . . . I . . ."

She bent closer still and whispered in Mako's ear. "A new world is waiting to be born. If there is something you know—a word, a name—something you ache to tell me . . . then that name will buy your way into a new paradise. And no, my friend, I am not talking about the darkness. This is no trick. This new world will be right here. This world. *Our* world."

"You promise?"

"On my life," she assured him. "Now . . . tell me."

Mako leaned back and studied her face, looking for the lie. Finding none.

"I know where Riot was taking Carter and . . . the rest of us. A place called Sanctuary."

"I already know that she was taking them to Sanctuary," said Mother Rose with a sigh. "Is that all you know?"

The big Hawaiian man shook his head. "There were four of us. Carter, his wife, Riot, and me. Two nights ago, Riot drew a map in the dirt to show us the best routes in case we ran into trouble. In case we got separated from her."

Mother Rose waited, holding her breath.

"I know how to *find* Sanctuary," said Mako. "I can take you there."

FROM NIX'S JOURNAL

When we left town, no one came to see us off.

No one.

How screwed up is that?

73

THEY GATHERED UP AS MANY OF THE PAPERS AND MAPS AS THEY COULD and shoved them into the largest pockets of their canvas vests. Maybe Chong could make sense of the science stuff, and perhaps they'd eventually find someone who needed to have this information.

Someone from the American Nation, perhaps.

The door to the cargo bay was heavier than the cockpit door, but there was the same kind of unbroken wax seal over the lever-style metal handle.

Above it, the word DEATH seemed to glare at Benny.

"So encouraging," he said.

He placed his fingers lightly on the handle and arched an inquiring eyebrow at Nix.

"We have to," she said.

"I guess we do."

He gripped the handle, took a breath, and turned it. The wax snapped and fell away. The big lock went *clunk*, and then the door shifted in his hand. Nix rested her hand on her pistol, and Benny drew his sword. It was too big a weapon for practical indoor use, but he'd rather have a clumsy weapon than none at all when going through any doorway marked DEATH.

I'm crazy, he told himself, *but not that crazy.*

Benny nudged the door open with his foot. "I'll go first," he said.

In truth he'd rather go first out of the hatchway and down to the desert floor. Then all the way back to Mountainside. Hopefully no one would be living in his old house yet. Maybe his bed would even still be there.

"Okay," said Nix. No argument, no tussle over who was pack leader.

Nix's quick agreement did absolutely nothing to bolster Benny's confidence as he stared into the ominous darkness of the big plane's cargo bay.

Faint light from the hatchway reached tentatively into the bay but failed to reveal anything. He took a cautious step inside. The air smelled heavily of industrial grease—the old stuff, made from oil, not the stuff they mostly used in town that was made from animal fat; and there were other smells. Dust, animal dung, and some sharp chemical smells that reminded him of the kind of booze that Charlie Pink-eye and his crew drank. Stuff Mr. Lafferty at the general store sold as whiskey but that Morgie Mitchell's dad used to call "rotgut." And the ever-present stink of death. It wasn't as strong as the other smells, but it was there.

All they could see were dozens of crates lashed together with nylon bands and secured to metal rings set in the floor. Most of the crates were made from some tough-looking plastic; but a few were metal and the biggest were wooden.

"What can you see?" whispered Nix.

"Nothing much. Bunch of big crates and boxes."

"Boxes of what?"

"Don't know. Probably not puppies, apple pie, and new baseball gloves. Pretty much bet on that."

He took a few steps inside, listening for sounds and hearing only his own nervous breathing. The cargo bay stretched past the stacks of crates and vanished into the gloom. He had all-weather matches in his vest, but he didn't really want to put down his sword long enough to fish one out and light it. Not yet.

The floor creaked under his weight, and Benny remembered all the cracks he'd seen in the plane's crippled body.

A soft scuff behind him told him that Nix had entered the bay.

"You have your gun out?" he asked very quietly.

"Yes."

"Put it away. I don't want to get a bullet in the back because another mouse jumps out at us."

She muttered something, but he heard the scrape of metal on leather as she holstered it.

Benny's night vision was kicking in, and he was able to make out some details. There were words stenciled in black on some of the cases, and Benny mouthed them as he read the closest ones. The wooden boxes had labels like:

MRE

LAB EQUIP

MED RECS

HAZMAT SUITS

The metal cases were labeled:

RPG

CLAYMORE MINES

LAW RKTS

M-249 SAW

M24 SWS

"What is this stuff?" Benny asked.

"I have no idea. It must all be lab equipment and science stuff."

Benny nodded and moved a few steps deeper into the darkness.

"Do you hear anything?" whispered Nix.

"No. You?"

"No."

"That's good," said Benny, and mentally added, *I think*.

He moved a few steps forward, trying to sort out and identify the shapes of things he saw. The pale light was too weak, and the shadows of the bay seemed impenetrable.

Benny leaned toward Nix and spoke softly into her ear. "Listen, I'm going to walk down the center aisle. Wait for me here. If there's something hinky, I don't want to have to run you down to get out of here. This place gives me the super-creeps."

There was a faint rattle and then the scrape of a sulfur match. Light blinded him, and the sulfur stung his nostrils. He winced and peered through the glare to see Nix holding out a match.

In the intense darkness of the cargo bay, even the pale light of the match revealed so much that was hidden.

Vehicles chained to the floor.

Banks of computer equipment standing inert against the walls.

Gleaming loading hooks on chains attached to the ceiling.

And beyond the rows of crates were row after row of metal chairs.

Benny and Nix both froze in shock.

People sat in the chairs. They were dressed identically in one-piece jumpsuits. At least two dozen of them wore yellow jumpsuits, four were in blue jumpsuits, and two wore green.

They were all dead.

But all of them stared with hungry eyes at Benny and Nix.

Nix screamed.

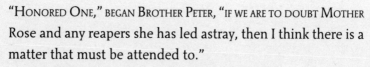

74

"HONORED ONE," BEGAN BROTHER PETER, "IF WE ARE TO DOUBT MOTHER Rose and any reapers she has led astray, then I think there is a matter that must be attended to."

Saint John's face was bland. "Which matter?"

"The Shrine of the Fallen."

"What about it?"

"The way Mother Rose protects it, denying everyone— even your own holy self—to enter it, there must be something of great value hidden there."

"Value is relative," said the saint. "A man with his house on fire and a man dying of thirst each place a different value on a glass of water."

Brother Peter nodded, accepting the point, but doubt still chewed at him. "She can't possibly hope to take Sanctuary with only a few reapers. What does she have—a hundred or two who will follow her? No, she must have some resource we don't know about. It *has* to be inside the shrine. It was a military plane. Surely there are some weapons aboard. . . ."

"I have no doubt."

"Then, Honored One, shouldn't *we* take it instead?"

Saint John shook his head sadly. "Even you, Peter? Even you?"

"I don't—"

"You think there are weapons aboard that crashed airplane. So do I. Mother Rose knows it for sure. She has done everything short of building a wall around the shrine to make sure no one ever looks inside. For a time I even agreed with her. The plane represents the world that was. Whether it is filled to its rafters with scientific research on how to *cure* the gray plague, or medical supplies to treat all the many diseases that have been with us since the Fall, or a battle tank, it doesn't matter what is in that plane. All of it is evil. All of it is polluted."

"I understand that, Honored One," insisted Brother Peter, "but surely if we used such weapons, their nature would change. As Mother Rose is so fond of saying, it is the *intention* that matters when picking up a sword and not the sword itself. After all, you allowed us to use the quads, and they are from the old world."

"They are not weapons of war."

"Even so—"

Saint John held up a hand. "I know what you would advise me, Peter, and it would sound like wisdom to both of us. It would even sound like a victory—to take something forged with ill intent and turn it to a holy purpose."

"Yes, I—"

"But that is a pathway that would lead us from the purity of who we are back to the pollution of what we were."

75

MOTHER ROSE WALKED THROUGH THE FOREST WITH BROTHER ALEXI by her side. A hundred reapers followed forty paces behind them. Their newest "chosen one," Brother Mako, walked in the midst of the crowd. He looked slightly dazed but very happy to still be alive. The other chosen talked and laughed with him, clapping him on the back, sharing stories with him. They treated him like a hero, like a brother or cousin who had just done something amazing that benefited the family. And it all drew Mako further into his new role as a chosen of Mother Rose.

This was how it worked, and Mother Rose was pleased. This kind of con was always her gift. Alexi, who had been a highly successful drug dealer for the Russian Mafia before the Fall, was also pleased. The best cons were always those in which the mark felt like he had made all the important choices, and that those choices were the only good ones to make. The world as it was might have ended, but a sucker was a sucker was a sucker.

The process was simple. Invite and include so a person feels like they are a part of something. Like they belong. It was the cement of loyalty; and on some level everyone in the

Night Church understood this. It was never spoken about, but because each of them had been brought in this way, every one of them reinforced it with new recruits. Mother Rose knew that it allowed each person to justify their own decision to join. It was an infection of self-justification, and that was how it all worked.

"What do you want to do about the rest of Carter's crew?" asked Alexi. "They're hiding like rabbits around here somewhere."

She waved a hand. "Who cares about them? If we have time later, we'll see about recruiting some of them. Forget the rest. We're past that now."

"Hey, a runner's coming in," said Alexi, nodding at the woods to their left. They slowed their pace but did not stop, and Sister Caitlyn came out of the forest and fell into step beside them.

"Holiness," she said, a little breathlessly, "we got a problem."

"Tell me."

"Saint John and Brother Peter just had a long chat with Brother Eric."

"What kind of 'chat'?"

"The bad kind. They hung parts of Eric from the trees," said Caitlyn, her color bad. "The way they do when they're serious about finding out stuff."

They walked a few paces in silence.

Brother Alexi ground his teeth. "Eric knew damn near everything."

"He knew a lot," agreed Mother Rose. "But not everything."

"How'd they tumble to us so fast?" asked the giant.

Sister Caitlyn shook her head. "I don't think any of us went to him."

"They could have had someone watching from the woods when we met at the shrine," said Alexi. "Plenty of places to hide and—"

"It doesn't matter," said Mother Rose. "What does matter is that Saint John knows."

"This sucks," grumped Alexi. "I had a nice little timetable for working the new agenda into the army. Real subtle, too. I have a list of all the right people to talk to. The ones who could influence whole groups within the army. Damn."

Mother Rose said nothing as they continued to walk toward the edge of the forest. Alexi and Caitlyn fell silent, but both of them looked disappointed and nervous.

Rebellion was fine, even imperative, unless they wanted to die young, which neither of them did, but going up against Saint John, Brother Peter, and the main body of the reaper army too soon . . . that promised a short and ugly future. Mother Rose's insurrection was barely two hours old.

"We really screwed the pooch here," said Alexi.

"No," said Mother Rose. "We don't need the army to take Sanctuary."

"I'm not just worried about taking Sanctuary, Rose," said Alexi. "But I have to admit that I'm more than a little concerned about Saint John hunting us with the main force of the reaper army. We have less than three hundred. Even without pulling in all of the legions from Wyoming and Utah, Saint John can chase us down with forty thousand knives."

"Let him try."

Caitlyn and Alexi stared at her. Mother Rose smiled as she let seconds fall all around them.

"But . . . ," began Alexi, but Mother Rose cut him off.

"He has numbers," she said, "but we have something else. Don't you think it's time that the Shrine of the Fallen yields up its mysteries?"

A big, ugly grin bloomed on Alexi's dark face. "Oh . . . yes. Long past time."

Mother Rose placed her fingertips on his chest over his heart. "You know what to do, my love. Caitlyn and I will gather the rest of our chosen ones and march on Sanctuary. Take a dozen fighters and go to the shrine. Follow as quick as you can."

Alexi took her hand and kissed it. Then he turned and began growling orders to twelve of the toughest chosen. Together they vanished into the woods.

Confused, Caitlyn asked, "Mother . . . what's at the shrine?"

Mother Rose's smile was small and cold. "A power that not even Saint John, with all of his power, can hope to withstand."

With that she turned and signaled to her chosen, who followed her on the way to Sanctuary.

"Nix!" yelled Benny. "Get back!"

He shoved her out of the way and brought his sword up in a two-handed grip.

As Nix fell, the match winked out, plunging the room into total darkness.

"Match—match—MATCH!" shrieked Benny.

Suddenly another match flared, and Benny crouched in the corridor between the stacks of crates, sword raised, feet braced, ready to fight to the death to buy Nix enough time to get out and climb down to safety.

The zoms stared at Nix and Benny.

Benny backed up a pace, edging toward the hatch.

Gray eyes, milky and dead, were focused on the two teenagers. They moaned with aching hunger. A strange moan, muted and low.

And they did not attack.

Nix screamed once more and then stopped.

Benny stopped trying to back away.

The zoms stared at them with unyielding need, but they did not move.

And the moment held.

"Benny—?"

All Benny could do was stare.

"Benny," demanded Nix. "What is—what is—?"

She fell silent too.

The zoms were still seated in their chairs.

Benny licked his dry lips and took a tentative step forward. Toward the zoms. Their eyes shifted to follow him.

The zoms themselves, however, did not.

They could not.

And now Benny could see why. They were all secured to the chairs by rope looped around their ankles, wrists, waists, and throats.

And every mouth had been sewn shut with silver wire.

"Are you seeing this?" Benny whispered.

Nix nodded mutely.

Benny sagged back, sick and disgusted down to a level he could not frame into words. This was so . . . weird, so wrong. So horrible.

On one level he understood the logic of it. Zoms that can't move or bite are safer. They can be handled without as much fear of the contagion.

But this was . . . awful.

Benny heard Nix retch. Then she spun away and threw up behind the packing cases. When she was done, she leaned heavily against the crates, eyes closed, chest heaving. Beads of sweat like tiny diamond chips glistened on her face. She pushed roughly away from him and then turned warily back toward the ghastly scene before them.

"What," she gasped, "is this? This is crazy. This is wrong."

"I know," Benny said weakly. He stared at the zoms. Each of them had a network of thin wires wrapped around their heads, with sockets drilled into their sinuses, ears, and fore-heads. God only knew what that was for.

Nix found a blank writing tablet on one of the crates, rolled it up, and lit it. It was a small torch, but better than holding a match. She held it up as they moved carefully down the corridor, looking at every zom, making sure each one was securely lashed in place.

"If any of them as much as twitches, I'm going to punch a Benny-shaped hole right through the wall," he said.

"Just don't get in my way," said Nix.

The muted moan of the zoms followed them.

"God," she said, "I can't stand to look at them."

"I know."

Benny saw a row of blue boxes against one wall and sidled past the front row of seated zoms. Each box was labeled:

HOPE 1

AMERICAN NATION BIOLOGICAL RESEARCH AND TESTING FACILITY

FIELD RESEARCH & RECORDS

There were over eighty boxes.

"Lot of research," he murmured.

"What?" asked Nix from across the bay.

Benny turned away. "Nothing," he said. "Just junk. Let's get the heck out of here."

They crept past the zoms again, hurried down the corridor, and stepped into the hatch. Nix dropped the torch and stamped it out as Benny pulled the door shut.

They peered over the edge of the hatch, saw only empty

desert and the sparse forest, and climbed down the plastic sheeting.

"Let's go," said Nix as she swung her leg over the edge.

"I'll be down in a sec," said Benny as he fished his matches out of his vest pocket. "There's plenty of wax here. I'm going to reseal the doors. Maybe they won't know we've been in here."

Nix nodded and began climbing down. "Don't take too long."

It wasn't difficult work. Benny used some dried twigs from among the debris to hold the flame, and he picked up all the wax he could find and dribbled it over the handles, then pressed the red ribbons back in place. The original job had been thorough but not neat, and his finished product looked about the same. He nodded, satisfied, then ground the burning twig underfoot and moved to the open hatch.

He was just about to call Nix's name when he heard her scream.

Benny saw why.

She stood in the clearing near where they had exited the forest earlier, but she was not alone.

She was surrounded by a dozen reapers.

SAINT JOHN STOOD ON A ROCKY OUTCROP THAT OFFERED AN EXCELLENT view of the forest, the plateau, and the surrounding desert. Brother Peter and other trusted reapers had come and gone a dozen times over the last hour, bringing him information on everything that happened inside the forest.

"Observe only," Saint John had instructed them. "Do not be seen, and do not interfere until you have talked to me."

These reapers were his, heart and soul, and they obeyed without question. They were also very smart and highly trained. They moved like ghosts and they watched like owls. For some of them it was hard not to take action. It was as if the knives at their belts ached to open red mouths in every person who moved under the desert sun.

As his reapers brought him pieces of the strange puzzle, Saint John assembled them into a picture whose image did not entirely surprise him, though it saddened him, threatening to break his heart.

So many things happening at once.

Riot had been spotted. Carter's daughter, Eve, and an unknown heretic—a Chinese boy whose body was wrapped in bandages—were with Riot, sharing a quad with her. They were heading by a circuitous route toward the Shrine of the Fallen.

The ranger, Joe, had also been seen. A dozen reapers had fled from him rather than lay down their own lives to send that sinner into the darkness. Saint John would have Brother Peter re-educate them in some matters of faith.

The ranger, it seemed, was also heading toward the shrine.

And two children had been seen climbing into the shrine itself. A red-haired girl with a scarred face and a boy with Japanese eyes.

Nyx and her knight.

That was a piece of the puzzle Saint John did not yet understand. Several intriguing possibilities occurred to him, each of them dependent on whether this Nyx was a true manifestation of Thanatos's mother on earth. If she was something false, perhaps a demon of one of the old religions, then things could turn against God's will. Saint John would send Brother Peter to learn the truth.

Brother Peter came to join him.

"Honored One, I sent a hundred runners out," he said. "It will take at least a week to gather everyone from Utah and the other states."

"That is good. We will leave coded signs so they may follow us."

The young man nodded toward the line of red mountains that separated the forest from the vast desert.

"Sanctuary is so close," he said, amazed. "All this time, so close."

"We were not meant to find it sooner than now."

Brother Peter glanced at him. "We've looked for it so long. . . ."

"And in doing so we've put our own desires before the will of our god. The fact that its location was withheld from us is proof that God had other work for us."

"But . . . we can take it. We have the numbers."

"All things in their time," said the saint with mild reproof in his voice.

Brother Peter placed his hand on his wings and bowed. "Forgive a sinner, Honored One."

Saint John patted his shoulder.

They both looked off toward the northeast.

"Nine towns," murmured Saint John.

"Nine towns," agreed Peter.

"When we come back this way," said the saint, "our army will have grown. Remember, we are not seeking a battle—the lord of the darkness simply wants a victory. A knife will accomplish this, but a tsunami will do it more surely."

"Ah," said Brother Peter, getting it now. "And what of Mother Rose?"

"She craves Sanctuary. The thought of it has corrupted her." He sighed. "The darkness does not know her anymore."

BENNY FROZE. HE WAS UP IN THE HATCHWAY OF THE AIRPLANE, AND NIX was down on the ground. She had a pistol with two bullets, he had a sword.

There were at least a dozen reapers, not to mention Brother Alexi. Nix had her pistol out in a flash, the hammer thumbed back, barrel pointed down at her side.

"You lose your way, missy?" asked the giant. "Can't find your friend Carter in all these big, bad woods?"

"Look, mister," replied Nix, "I don't know who you are or what you want. Just leave me alone."

"I think we're already past that. You're where you shouldn't be, maybe seeing things you shouldn't see, and that's a real problem for me."

"I didn't touch anything of yours," Nix said. She kept the pistol pointing down, but Benny could tell that everyone in the clearing was aware of it. None of them made a move toward her.

The giant grinned. "And I suppose all those papers stickin' out of your pockets are just homework? Or maybe notes to your boyfriend?"

"Just leave me alone."

Alexi shook his head. He hoisted his hammer and laid it

across one massive shoulder. "Two ways we can play this. You be nice and hand me those papers, or I take them off of you. You won't like it the second way."

Even up in the plane Benny could hear the other reapers laugh. Benny couldn't tell whether that was because these reapers were different or because the woman, Mother Rose, wasn't here. At the moment, the people with Brother Alexi just seemed like a group of thugs.

Nix suddenly raised the pistol and pointed it at the giant's chest.

"If anyone tries to touch me, I'll kill you," she said.

"Won't stop us from getting the papers, missy," Alexi said. "Go ahead and pull the trigger, sweet cheeks. My chosen ones will leave pieces of you along thirty miles of road."

"You won't be there to see it," growled Nix, and the giant gave an appreciative laugh.

Benny knew that this situation was going to fall apart any second. Even if Nix shot the giant, she had only two bullets left, and then it would be her with a bokken against a dozen killers with knives and swords. He almost swung his leg out to start climbing down.

Almost.

But an idea stopped him.

Knives and swords.

He reached up and touched the sword he carried, thought about it, shook his head, and instead drew his knife.

This is the stupidest thing you've ever done, he told himself.

Then Benny turned his back on Nix and the reapers and lunged for the handle to the cargo bay.

79

THAT'S IT, THOUGHT NIX RILEY. *I'M GOING TO DIE. RIGHT HERE, RIGHT NOW.*

Brother Alexi was like something out of a nightmare. Seven feet tall, his body packed with muscle, his skin reeking from whatever chemical the reapers used to fend off the living dead. He leered down at her, the big sledgehammer resting with false idleness. Nix could see the tension in the man's arm—he was ready to smash her flat.

She wished Benny were there with her.

She wished Benny would stay hidden and stay alive.

She wished Tom weren't dead.

The reapers began to close in around her. The afternoon sun was beginning to fall behind the trees, and the slanting light struck yellow fire from the edges of all those knives and axes.

Mom, she thought, *I hope you're waiting for me.*

Please.

Be there to bring me home.

"Now," said Alexi, and he suddenly grabbed the closest reaper and flung him at Nix.

Nix screamed.

And fired.

80

Joe skidded the quad to a stop.

"Did you hear that?" he barked.

"A shot," said Lilah, nodding. "Up ahead, by the crashed plane. Reapers?"

"No."

"How do you know?"

"Reapers don't use guns."

There was a second shot. With the engine idling low, they could hear it better.

"Handgun," said Joe. "Wheel gun, not an automatic."

Lilah grabbed Joe's sleeve. "Nix!"

Joe stared at her for one shaved fragment of a second.

"Grimm! Reapers! Hit-hit-HIT!"

The powerful mastiff gave a single howl of dark intent, and then he went racing away at a speed Lilah would never have thought possible for so massive a beast. The armor rattled along Grimm's sides as he crashed into the brush, cutting off the path to take the straightest line of attack.

"Lock and load, little darlin'," bellowed Joe as he gunned the engine.

THE FIRST REAPER FELL WITH A RED POPPY BLOSSOMING IN THE CENTER OF his chest. That stalled the others for a short second, and Nix stole her chance. She whirled and ran for the mound of dirt near the front of the wrecked plane. She knew from her training that if she could gain the high ground, she might have a slim chance.

It was bravado, she knew. A delusion, because there was nowhere to go once she made the high ground. The reapers could catch her.

Or she could lead them away from the plane and give Benny a chance.

If only Benny would do the smart thing and take it. If only he would stop thinking that he had to be Tom now that Tom was dead.

She ran.

Months of hard training in Tom's Warrior Smart program had made Nix lean, toned her muscles, made her cat quick. She outpaced the reapers and was halfway up the slope before they were organized. Then the whole mass of them was racing along the length of the plane in murderous pursuit.

Nix climbed and climbed.

One of the reapers, faster than the others, came flying up the slope after her and dove to grab her ankles. Nix fell hard, but as she landed she twisted around and fired.

The reaper pitched backward down the slope and crashed into two others.

Nix scrambled on all fours to the top of the slope and flopped over the rim of hard-packed dirt. She rolled to her knees and clawed her bokken from its sling. She rose, turning to meet the charge.

She froze and stared.

In absolute horror.

The reapers gaped in horror too.

They screamed.

They tried to run.

But it was already too late.

From the open hatch of the airplane came a horde of zombies. Dozens of them in colored jumpsuits, boiling out of the broken plane like cockroaches, leaping down onto the reapers, heedless of whatever bones they broke in the fall. The reapers tried to turn, tried to flee, but they were in one another's way. The zoms dove at them.

Most of them were lumbering monsters.

But not all.

Some were fast.

Some were very fast.

Brother Alexi roared in annoyance. "They can't hurt you, you silly buggers. You're all wearing the tassels. Get a damn grip."

He strode toward the reapers, who were wrestling on the

ground with the living dead. His look of annoyance lasted three steps. Then he saw blood geyser up.

The screams stopped him in his tracks.

The high-pitched, awful screams.

Nix saw the way doubt carved itself onto the giant's face, and then those lines instantly eroded into outright fear.

These dead were not stopped by the chemical on the red streamers. They did not react to it at all.

Alexi snatched up the silver dog whistle he wore around his neck and blew fiercely. The dead—a few of them—looked up briefly. Then they returned to the meat that was fresh and close at hand.

The slaughter was appalling.

Nix, alone at the top of the slope, realized with sudden clarity what had happened. She whispered a single, shocked word. "Benny."

And as if by magic, she heard him call her name.

"NIX!"

82

BENNY LEANED OUT THROUGH THE BROKEN WINDOWS OF THE COCKPIT.

"Nix!" he yelled.

Twenty feet away Nix Riley whirled and stared in all the wrong places first. Then she spotted Benny, and the smile that bloomed on her face was the brightest and most beautiful thing he'd ever seen.

"Come on!" he cried.

She ran along the top of the mound toward him, cutting through the shadows cast by the three dead pilots writhing on their T-bars.

"Try to climb up," he said.

Nix turned to watch the carnage at the bottom of the slope. She winced and turned away in disgust.

"No . . . we'll be trapped in there. See if you can climb down here."

Benny climbed onto the control panel, kicked out the last jagged shards of the shattered windows, and wriggled out into the fresh air. He slid awkwardly down the crumpled nose and dropped nine feet to the top of the slope, landing with a grunt. Nix caught him, but they lost their balance and fell backward. Benny caught something out of the corner of his eye, and before he could twist out of the way, he struck his head on one of the T-bars. The zoms moaned down at him, and snakes of fire writhed through the air all around him.

"Benny! Are you all right?" asked Nix.

He cursed and groaned as Nix pulled him to his feet.

"You're bleeding," she said.

Benny dragged his forearm across his face, and it came away with a bright red smear.

"Swell."

They looked down the slope at the mayhem. There was so much blood and movement that it was almost impossible to tell the living dead from the dying. They backed away and peered out from behind the nose of the plane.

"Did you let the zoms out?" she asked.

"Yeah," he said.

"How?"

Benny said nothing. He closed his eyes and was back in that darkened cabin, a new makeshift torch in one hand, his quieting knife in the other. The idea had been insane then, and it felt much crazier now.

He had to free the zom farthest from the door first, and for a terrible moment he had crouched there, staring into those dead eyes, trapped between the need to help Nix and his own horror. The zom's eyes were milky, and even though Benny knew that there was no mind behind them—no personality, no humanity left—he felt like he was committing some awful sin.

"Nix," he whispered as he slipped the point of the knife into the silver wire that held the zom's mouth shut. The wire was thin and the blade was strong. The wire parted easily. All Benny had to do was cut a couple of loops, and the zom did the rest as it fought to open its mouth. And bite.

He debated pulling out the network of wires that covered its head, but decided not to. He had no idea what its purpose was, and this didn't seem like the time to find out.

Benny quickly slashed the bindings on hands and feet, but even in his panic he was no fool. His training was right there, burning like a beacon as he worked. He cut the ropes almost all the way through, leaving only threads.

He did this over and over again, working with a pace that crossed the line into frenzy. Terror was the whip that drove him. His knife slashed and cut, and sometimes it gouged chunks of dry flesh from the zoms.

As he went along row after row, the cabin filled with the dry rustle of zoms fighting to break the last threads.

The first ones tore free before Benny was done. They began shuffling toward him.

Benny bit back a scream and slashed at the nylon straps holding a stack of metal cases in place, and suddenly hundreds of pounds of dead weight crashed down on the zoms. One of them collapsed with a broken neck, but for the others the cases were nothing more than an obstacle to climb over to get to their meal.

In the flickering torchlight, Benny saw that there was a second row of cases behind the stack he'd toppled. They were made of heavy-duty blue plastic and marked with a design that everyone who had survived First Night knew all too well: a biohazard symbol. The cases were stenciled in white letters:

REAPER PLAGUE

MUTATION SAMPLES

HANDLE WITH EXTREME CAUTION

The zoms kept coming, and Benny heard himself whimpering, making small cries and yelps, as he cut the last zoms free.

He scuttled backward, knocking over more crates.

The big stack of metal boxes fell next. A zom closed in on Benny, and he shoved one labeled LAW RKTS in its face. The zom flew backward into others. The container case slid off the stack and crashed down on its corner. The impact popped the hinges so the case flopped open. Benny glanced at it and saw something that vaguely resembled a gun, but it wasn't anything he understood how to use. He ignored it and kept scrambling backward.

That was when Benny almost died.

He heard a sudden growl. Not a moan—a growl—and he looked up to see a zom climbing over the other zoms. Climbing fast. It was one of two zoms dressed in green jumpsuits—and Benny remembered too late the notations he and Nix had read on the clipboard, about the zoms in green.

This is an entirely new classification . . . able to negotiate obstacles . . . avoid many of the objects thrown at it . . . use simple tools. This reanimate appeared to be able to grasp certain concepts, particularly stealth and subterfuge.

The zom snarled at him. Its eyes were not dead eyes. They were more like those of the lions who had surrounded the camp. There was intelligence in them. If not human, then some new order of primitive intelligence.

A hateful intelligence.

The zom came clawing and scrambling its way over the others, howling out its hunger, racing straight at Benny.

Behind it, the second green-jumpsuited zom tore free of its bindings and hissed like a snake.

Benny backed away, his torch falling from his hand.

He spun and ran as fast as he could.

The zoms crawled over the others, dropped onto the metal deck, and ran after him.

Benny dove through the cargo bay hatch, across the narrow corridor, slammed into the cockpit door, jerked the handle hard, shoved his weight against it, jumped inside, slammed the door shut, and shot the handle back into place.

Then Tom spoke in his head for the first time in hours.

Some zoms can turn door handles.

Benny thought it was a slice of memory served up in a moment of need, but it still sounded like Tom was right there behind him.

He looked down at the handle.

It began to turn.

With a cry, Benny grabbed it and shoved it to the locked position. There was a shallow well around the handle so the whole door was flush.

The handle jerked and rattled with incredible force. This was not the fumbling of a zom, not according to everything Benny had seen. This was coordinated. This was powerful.

Benny thought he had already reached the limit of how high his terror could soar.

He was wrong.

He held on with one hand while he desperately scrabbled

in his pockets for something he could use to wedge the handle in place. The only thing he had that was strong enough was his quieting knife.

Outside he heard the first screams as the freed zoms attacked the reapers.

With no choice left to him, Benny jammed the knife into the narrow slot between the handle and the steel door. He jammed it in hard until there was no give at all.

Instantly the zom gave up on the handle and began pounding on the door with insane fury.

Then nothing.

These memories replayed in Benny's head in a second, and he heard the echo of Nix's question.

"How?"

How had he let them out?

"Don't ask," he said, drawing his sword. "Come on . . . we have to get out of here and get these papers to Sanctuary."

Together they edged away from the fight. They turned to make a dash for the safety of the woods.

Safety, however, was not theirs to have.

There was a zombie in the way.

He wore a bloody and torn green jumpsuit.

RIOT DROVE THE QUAD LIKE SHE HAD A DEATH WISH.

The machine bounced and jounced and bucked as she pushed it to the limits of speed and maneuverability. Even belted in, Chong and Eve had to hold on for dear life.

Chong kept praying that they would pass through some kind of veil and cross from a day that could only be part of some mad nightmare and into yesterday, when the worst problem was knowing which berries wouldn't give him diarrhea.

Then he heard the strangest sound.

A small burble of happy laughter.

He looked down at the child who clung to him. Her face was alight with sheer joy as the quad banged over fallen branches and leaped channels cut by rainwater.

Eve grinned up at him, and for the first time since he had first met her, Chong saw the uncomplicated purity of happiness. It was so odd, so totally out of keeping with everything that was happening, that even though he smiled back at her, Chong was deeply afraid for this child.

He did not for a moment believe that a kid who was borderline catatonic could simply "snap out of it." No way. Chong kept his smile in place, but he felt that he was looking at the beautiful face of a horror deeper than his own infection.

God, don't let her be all the way over the edge, he silently prayed. *If I have any grace coming to me, then let's agree that I don't really need it anymore. Give it to the kid. Give Eve a chance.*

Even his prayers were orderly, and Chong was good with it. He meant every word.

He closed his eyes for a moment as a fresh wave of motion-induced nausea wormed through his guts.

Lilah, he thought. *Lilah . . .*

Riot's quad burst out of the forest and into the desert. "We'll be in Sanctuary in less than—"

She screamed and slammed on the brakes.

Chong opened his eyes.

The desert was filled with reapers. More than a hundred of them.

One of them, a tall woman who—unlike the other reapers—had long flowing hair, drew a slender knife and pointed it at Riot.

Riot groaned and spoke a word that Chong knew would burn like acid on her tongue.

"Ma!"

She immediately spun the quad and plunged back into the forest.

Even over the roar of the engine, Chong could hear a hundred voices howl as the reapers gave chase.

84

"I GOT THIS," SAID NIX, RAISING HER BOKKEN.

"No!" warned Benny as he moved away from it, using his body to push Nix back. "It's one of those smart fast ones from that scientist's report."

The zombie began stalking them, and immediately Nix and Benny knew they were in dangerously unknown territory. This wasn't the slow, relentless shuffle of the zoms they knew. The creature in the green jumpsuit seemed to be assessing them as it stalked slowly forward. Its milky eyes flicked from Nix's bokken to Benny's *katana*.

The creature—and Benny could no longer think of this thing as a zombie—bent forward and bared its teeth, its face wrinkling with feral animal hate.

"Oh God," whispered Nix.

The creature snarled in pure fury and rushed at them.

Benny was caught in a dreadful moment of indecision.

Run or fight?

He could feel Nix's whole body trembling beside him.

The fight and the slope were behind them.

The choice was made for him, because the creature raced at them far too fast for any chance of escape.

BROTHER ALEXI SWUNG HIS HAMMER AND THE HEAVY WEAPON, POWERED by the giant's massive muscles and all his mounting terror, slammed into the first zombie to reach him.

The zom's head exploded, and the lifeless body flopped to the ground.

Alexi used the force of the blow to turn his body in a pirouette, and as the hammer came around again he smashed it into the second zom. The blow caught the dead thing on the shoulder, but the force shattered its spine.

Alexi checked the swing and brought the hammer over and down onto a third zombie, and a fourth.

He laughed out loud, and his fear melted away to become diluted in battle joy.

"Come on, you rotting buggers!" he bellowed.

The zoms rose from the twitching bodies of the chosen ones, their empty eyes seeking out the author of that challenge, their mouths dripping red.

"Come on!"

They came.

Eighteen of them came.

His laughter died in his chest.

Some of them were in jumpsuits, some were in blood-stained black—with angel wings on their chests.

Something small and round sailed past Alexi's face, and he flinched reflexively away from it. It looked like a metal baseball, and it hit the ground in front of the leading wave of zoms, bounced once, and exploded.

The blast was huge.

Pieces of zoms were flung in every direction. Blood splashed against the white plane.

Alexi spun around, shielding his eyes.

Then the air was fractured by gunfire and the combat howl of a huge dog.

BENNY HAD NO CHOICE.

He and Nix were too close to each other to swing their swords—they were breaking one of Tom's cardinal rules about battlefield combat.

But she seemed frozen in place.

"I'm sorry!" Benny said, and shoved her backward as he jumped forward to meet the creature.

He heard Nix's scream as she hit the edge of the slope—and fell.

Benny had no time to process that.

The creature was on him, and Benny lunged in low and to the left, swinging the sword in as powerful a lateral cut as he could manage. The shock of impact jolted him, but the *katana* was sharper than a razor. It sliced through dead flesh and brittle bone.

The creature fell past him and Benny turned, controlling the erratic postimpact swing of his blade. As he pivoted, he saw the zom scramble to a stop at the top of the slope and wheel around. The sword had cut completely through the right side of its chest, from front to back. Muscle and bone were destroyed, and the monster's right arm sagged down. It did not even pause. There was no reaction to damage; there was no pain.

It growled and came charging again, and Benny tried the same trick, aiming lower this time, trying to catch the leg.

The creature dodged out of the way.

Dodged.

It . . .

Benny's brain almost froze. Even with the warning on Dr. McReady's document, it was—it seemed—impossible.

The zom grabbed Benny's vest with its good left hand and jerked him forward, toward its mouth full of rotting gray teeth.

Benny had no angle for a cut, so he punched the zom across the mouth with the hand that held the sword. The blow was awkward but powerful, and teeth flew from the open mouth.

The zom ignored the damage and lunged forward to take a bite.

Benny threw himself backward, and the zom's shattered teeth closed around a pocket of the vest instead. Benny heard a bottle of cadaverine crunch to stinking fragments inside the pocket.

The creature did not notice or care, and Benny was positive now that the network of wires bolted to its face somehow cut off its sense of smell. Maybe the scientists had done it as part of some experiment, or maybe smell was really a zombie's primary hunting sense. Not that it mattered right now . . . the zom could see and it could still bite.

Benny fell backward with the creature, and as he fell he brought his knee up between its legs, hitting it square on the bottom of the pelvis. The fall and the kick gave Benny the power he needed to hurl the monster completely over him. It landed with a bone-rattling thud and immediately scrambled to its feet.

Benny brought his sword around into a two-hand grip but only got as far as his knees before he realized that he was in worse trouble than he thought.

As the zom raced toward him again, it snatched up a broken branch from the ground and swung it full force at Benny's head.

There was a moment of red-black blankness. Benny never actually felt the blow. One second it was about to hit him, and then he was falling.

Then he saw something inexplicable.

The zom was falling too.

It crashed down a yard away face-to-face with Benny. The milky eyes stared at him, but now there was nothing there. No animal rage. Nothing.

But the strangest part of all was that there seemed to be an arrow sticking out of its temple.

Then a shadow fell over him, and Benny tried to bring up his sword in a last desperate defense against some new terror. Maybe the other green-jumpsuited zom?

"Hey, monkey-banger," said a familiar voice. "You pick the strangest times to lie down for a nap."

Benny blinked and stared. "Chong?"

It was Chong, but as Benny struggled to get to his feet, he saw his friend's face. And froze.

Chong's skin was gray, and a pale film of white covered his eyes.

Chong was a zom.

87

Alexi turned to see two strangers—a man and a teenage girl—climb off a quad, guns in their hands, barrels raised. He saw a monster of a dog dressed in spiked armor race past him and heard it crunch into the oncoming zoms. Bullets burned past him on either side.

He heard the teenage girl yell, "NIX!"

And he heard the voice of the red-haired girl yell, "LILAH!"

Then zoms piled onto him and he staggered backward.

Alexi roared and shook his body like an angry bear, flinging the dead off him. He swung his hammer to crush heads and chests.

Out of the corner of his eye, he saw the little redhead swinging her toy sword like she actually knew something. Shattering legs, crushing skulls, dodging and twisting.

She'd make a great reaper, he thought as he fought. *If she lives through this, I'm going to recruit that little witch.*

Zombies were falling dead around him, from those he smashed, from the wooden blade of the redhead, from the gunshots, and from the dog.

Alexi really liked the dog.

He'd never seen anything fight like that, and he wondered

why it had never occurred to him to train dogs to work with the reapers. This one was a cunning fighter, clearly trained to fight the dead. It did not bite at all, but instead used its horned helmet and spiked armor to rend and smash and dismember. The dead had no chance against it. Those who tried to bite it shattered their teeth on its chain mail. It was like a pack of lions trying to tear down an armored personnel carrier.

Suddenly Alexi realized that everyone in the clearing was engaged in fighting the dead except him. The gray people who had attacked him were all dead. He glanced at the man and girl with the guns. They were totally absorbed in their own personal wars.

He hefted his hammer.

"Screw this," he said, and ran away as fast as his long legs could carry him.

He vanished into the woods to find Mother Rose.

"CHONG—?" BENNY GASPED.

The dead-pale face split in a rueful grin. "What's left of him."

"But—but—your face. What happened?"

Chong stood bare-chested, wrapped in bandages. He held a sophisticated bow in his hands, and there was a quiver of arrows slung low across his hips. He did not meet Benny's eyes, though; he gaped at something above them. When Benny reached up to touch his forehead, he felt swollen flesh. Blood dripped like red rain across his eyes.

The pain caught up to him then.

Immense, crashing, like a giant bell ringing an inch from his ears.

Chong said something, but the words didn't seem to make sense.

Benny asked him to repeat it, but he heard his own words.

They were meaningless gibberish.

The fading sunlight flared too white and too bright, and then the hinges fell off the world and Benny was falling.

Falling.

Falling.

BENNY COULD NOT MOVE. HE COULD BARELY BREATHE. HIS HEAD FELT LIKE it was actually on fire.

He heard several sounds happen all at once, colliding into one another so hard and fast that it was hard to separate them out and assign meaning.

He heard a girl scream in fear. Nix?

Did she say his name? Was she the one shouting it over and over?

He heard a dog barking.

So weird. He didn't have a dog.

He heard the moans of the living dead.

He heard gunshots.

He closed his eyes for a moment, and when he opened them the light had changed. And now there was a ring of faces around him. Benny raised a hand and touched one of them; he traced the line of a pink scar down through a field of freckles.

"I love you," he said.

The face, grave with concern, flushed, and that made Benny smile.

"Benny," said Nix, "you're hurt. You hit your head."

"A zom hit my head," he said. "I was hit in the head by a zom." He thought that was funny and laughed, but laughing hurt, so he stopped.

The other faces swam in and out of focus. Lilah. Chong.

"Are you dead?" he asked Chong.

Chong tried to smile, but it didn't suit his face. "That's open to debate," he said.

Nix said, "What's that supposed to mean?"

Chong said something, but Benny didn't understand it. Thinking was so hard. His head felt like it was in a hollow metal box and someone kept banging on it.

He thought he heard Nix scream. Or cry. Or maybe she was laughing.

"Are you sleeping?" asked a tiny voice, and Benny realized that his eyes had closed. He open them to see a lovely little face.

"Eve?"

"You found me in a hole in the ground," she said. At first Benny thought it didn't make sense, but then he realized it did.

"Yeah, just like a bunny rabbit." He touched the tip of her nose. "You're a little bunny."

She giggled.

That sound seemed to screw one of the world's hinges back into place.

A strange voice said, "Kid's a mess. Skull fracture, concussion . . ."

Benny looked toward the sound of the voice. A big man smiled down at him. One of those tight smiles people give when they don't want you to know how bad things look through their eyes. It was almost a wince.

"I'm Joe," he said.

"I know you," said Benny as he raised a bloody finger and touched Joe's face. "You're on a Zombie Card. Captain Ledger, Hero of First Night. You're number two-eighty-four. I have two of you. I was going to trade one of you to Morgie for his Sheriff Rick card."

Riot's face swam into view. "What the heck are Zombie Cards?"

"Kid's delirious."

Chong said, "The reapers are coming. We saw them."

"Where and how many?" demanded Joe.

"Reaper, reaper . . . ," Benny began, and tried to work it into a rhyme, but he couldn't.

"There are a couple of hundred of them out on the desert, heading toward the hills," said Riot. "But a bunch came running after us."

"On foot or on quad?"

"Both. I lost them, but they'll find us."

Benny wondered what they were talking about. It began to occur to him that his head was not working properly, that his thoughts were silly. The word "delirious" triggered a response that went deeper than his understanding. A voice spoke inside his head.

Think, Benny, it said. *You saw something.*

But he did not understand what the voice meant.

Joe said, "Then we have to go now. Get to Sanctuary . . ."

"We can't move Benny," insisted Nix. "His head . . ."

"What's an MRE?" Benny asked. They ignored him. He frowned, because he was sure that was important. He'd read it somewhere.

"We can't fight off an army of reapers. Not here."

"We can't let 'em get to Sanctuary," growled Riot. "They'll slaughter the monks and refugees and all them scientists and—"

Joe looked stricken. "I know. They have a few soldiers there, but they can't stop an army. And my rangers are scattered all over the place. We have to warn them. That means either we go without this kid, in which case the reapers'll carve him into lunch meat; or we put him on a quad and let the ride out there do the job for them."

In the distance they heard the faint buzz of quads. They all looked that way and then at one another.

"Oh God," breathed Nix.

Benny, whispered Tom, *you know what you saw. Tell them. Tell them. . . .*

"What I wouldn't give for a minigun or an—"

Benny asked dazedly, "What's a LAW rickett?"

Joe froze and stared down at him.

"What did you say?"

"That's what it said. L-A-W-R-K-T. LAW rickett. I read it. M-R-E. R-P-G and—"

Joe suddenly bent close to Benny, his face inches away.

"A LAW rocket? God almighty, kid . . . where did you see that?" he asked in a fierce whisper.

Benny smiled and winked. "I can't tell you," he said. "It's a secret."

And then he passed out.

BENNY FELT A LOT OF HANDS ON HIM. HE FELT HIMSELF MOVING. WHEN he opened his eyes, though, the movement had already stopped and he was back inside the airplane.

"Zoms!" he cried.

But no one reacted.

Nothing tried to bite him.

Maybe I'm wrong about that, he decided, and went back to sleep.

The sound of quads woke him up. Quads and shouts and a dog barking.

Benny still hadn't seen any dog. He just heard one. A big one too.

"They're coming," said Riot. "God—Brother Alexi's back with a slew of reapers. Gotta be fifty, sixty of them."

"Oh God," Nix said, "there's too many!"

Someone laughed. Joe? Was Benny's Zombie Card laughing? Silly.

He opened his eyes and saw Joe carrying something that looked like a big toy gun. Like one of those big plastic toys from before First Night. A Super Soaker. Mayor Kirsch bought one for his kids. Cost three hundred ration dollars. That was more than Mrs. Riley made in a whole season doing sewing.

"Nix?" he asked.

A small, warm hand took his, and Benny tried to turn toward her, but his head wouldn't move. His whole body felt weird, like it was tied to a board. How crazy was that?

Nix leaned over, and he saw her face. She was so pretty.

"Nix, is your mom here?"

Pain flickered in her green eyes.

"Mama's dead, Benny. You know that."

"Oh. I thought I heard her laughing. She was baking muffins."

Something hot and wet fell on his cheek.

A tear.

Where did that come from?

The roar of quads filled the whole cabin. Benny thought it sounded like a zillion of them. People were yelling. Roaring. Cursing, too.

"They're coming!" shrieked Nix. "They're climbing up!"

Joe's voice roared: "Fire in the hole!"

There was big hissing sound, and then the whole plane shook with a gigantic rolling *booooom!*

The sound was too big for Benny, and he went back down in the darkness. He was sure Nix's mom was baking muffins.

Nix and Chong stood at the edge of the hatch and stared down at horror.

The air was thick with smoke from the LAW rockets and rocket-propelled grenades that the ranger had fired. The air tasted of gunpowder and wrongness.

The clearing and the whole edge of the plateau was a slaughterhouse. Burned and blasted bodies lay everywhere. Even the trees at the edge of the forest had died in the barrage as the weapons of the old world wrought their carnage.

They were both crying.

"One man," whispered Nix.

Chong nodded, unable to speak. Sick in body, sick in soul. One man.

The ranger, Joe, had used those terrible weapons. The reapers, the chosen ones, the elite of Mother Rose's army, had poured out of the forest, brought back by Alexi to claim the weapons hidden in the shrine. They thought themselves to be the most powerful force left on earth. They thought themselves to be unstoppable—those among them who believed in God and those who only believed in Mother Rose—they surged forward to slaughter the pitiful handful of people who stood against them.

And they all died.

Every last one of them. More than half of Mother Rose's army. Gone.

Nix and Chong had not fired a shot.

Nor had Lilah.

Or Riot.

Even Grimm had only watched.

One man.

Now Joe walked among the bodies, looking for signs of reanimation. Every now and then a hollow crack broke the silence. As he reloaded, he looked around, and his eyes met those of Chong and Nix. The ranger's face was totally without expression as he pocketed the empty magazine and slapped a new one into place. His eyes were not bright with battle lust or dark with emotion. His eyes were . . . nothing. They were as dead in their way as the zoms. Joe stood for a moment, watching them watching him, then turned without a word and went about his grotesque but necessary work.

Chong found his voice, but it was thin and fragile. "When we fought Preacher Jack and his people at Gameland," he began slowly, "I thought I understood what war was really like. But . . ."

"This is war," said Nix. "This is what it really looks like. God . . . there has to be something better than this."

Chong nodded and turned away.

But then a new sound intruded into the moment. A motor sound, but not the sound of quads. It was bigger. Much, much bigger.

They leaned out.

The sound was massive, rolling out over the tops of the trees.

They turned and looked upward.

"Oh my God!" cried Nix.

Even Chong, despite everything, smiled.

The thing was enormous and white, with massive wings stretching on either side. It flew directly over the clearing, and its shadow caressed their faces as they watched. It flew low and descended toward the red desert mountains in a graceful line.

Down among the dead, Joe stopped and shielded his eyes as he looked up. Stained with soot and blood, he smiled.

The jet.

IN THE LAST GLOW OF THE DYING SUN, MOTHER ROSE STOOD AT THE EDGE of the forest. She watched the jet descend toward Sanctuary. Once, long ago, she had seen it flying high in the sky, and she'd thought it was a passenger liner. How foolish a thought that had been. She knew what it was now; her daughter had told her. A C-5 Galaxy. A cargo jet that brought staff and supplies to Sanctuary.

Even if Mako hadn't revealed the location of the place, the landing jet would have been a beacon.

Not that it mattered anymore. Mother Rose had less than one hundred reapers left. A fraction of her force. All the rest . . . ?

Alexi had come running from the shrine, bloody and furious, claiming that children and a ranger were trying to take the weapons from the fallen plane. Mother Rose had sent so many of her reapers back with him. Too many.

And all of them . . . gone. Dead. Torn to rags by the weapons she had hidden and protected from Saint John and the rest of the Night Church.

Her weapons. The tools that would have made her the queen of this world.

Gone. The weapons, her reapers, her dreams . . . gone.

Only Alexi returned. Bloodier still. Defeated. A general without an army.

Her remaining reapers milled in the darkness. Not enough to take Sanctuary away from the monks and scientists who worked there.

Not enough.

"We're done," said Alexi.

Mother Rose almost stabbed him. Her hand was on her knife, but her heart was breaking and she simply could not do it. It was over.

"We were so close," she said.

Alexi leaned on his hammer and hung his head. "One day," he said. "If we'd jumped on this yesterday. One damn day." He let the handle of his hammer fall away to thump into the sand. "Now what? How the hell do we come back from this?"

Mother Rose shook her head. "I don't know. I . . . I'll think of something."

"No," said a voice, soft as a shadow.

Mother Rose whipped her head around.

"Saint John," she said in a whisper.

"Get back!" barked Brother Alexi, lunging for his hammer. A shadow rose up from behind a bush as the giant stretched out for his weapon, and then Alexi simply sagged forward and collapsed onto the ground. Mother Rose stared in incomprehension as the sand beneath Alexi darkened and glistened wetly. Alexi tried to speak, but there was no possibility of that. Not with what was left of his throat. He blinked once, twice, and then stared at the darkening sky.

The shadow moved into the light.

Brother Peter wore no expression at all on his face. The fading sunlight gleamed on the bloody knife in his hand.

Saint John walked slowly toward Mother Rose. He had no weapon in his hand, but she wasn't fooled. Saint John himself was a weapon, and every fold and pocket of his clothes hid blades. He was, after all, Saint John of the Knife. How many times had she seen this man reach out in the most casual fashion, his hand seemingly empty at the beginning of a gesture and filled with steel at the end, and between start and finish the air bloomed with red. He was the greatest killer the world had ever known; she believed that with her whole heart, even if she had never believed in the saint's God or the Night Church.

To her, it was all a scam. A means to an end.

And this was an end.

Not the one she dreamed of. Not the one she wanted.

Saint John stopped inches away. His face, though not handsome, was beautiful, the way the carved faces of saints in churches are beautiful. Cold and remote and inhuman.

Tears dropped from Mother Rose's eyes. She knew they would do nothing to change the shape of this day. Nor would anything she could say.

If her reapers were closer, if Alexi was alive, if they had the weapons from the shrine, then she would have tried to manage this moment. To shape it, to try and work a con on the saint.

But those possibilities had set with the burning sun.

She said, "I'm sorry."

Strangely, surprisingly, she meant it.

Saint John bent close and kissed her on the lips. Without

passion, but with love. With the kind of love only he understood.

"I know," he said.

"Please don't let it hurt," she whispered.

"No," he said.

And it did not.

Mother Rose fell into his arms, and Saint John lowered her to the ground. Then he stepped back, turned, and with Brother Peter at his side, walked away.

She lay there as the sun set. Time was dancing away from her.

There was movement somewhere to her right, and she managed to turn her head, just a little. Brother Alexi was stirring, crawling across the grass toward her.

Alive, she thought, her heart filling with joy. *My love is alive.*

Except that he wasn't.

The giant was as pale as the distant stars, and as he bent toward her she could see the darkness. It was in his eyes and in his open mouth.

It's real, she thought. Her last thought. *The darkness is real.*

93

When Benny opened his eyes once more, the world had changed.

It wasn't the inside of the plane. It was daytime.

There was a motor roar, and even though he could not turn his head, he could cut his eyes left and right. There were quads. Riot and Chong on one. Nix and Eve on another. A big dog galloping along with them.

Is that a dog barking? wondered Benny. The dog was all in armor, and Benny thought that was cool.

He heard the motors slow.

"Sanctuary," said a voice.

Nix?

He thought so.

"We have to hurry," said another voice. Joe. "He's slipping fast."

Benny wondered if they were talking about him.

Or Chong?

The quads moved forward, and Benny looked up to see a big chain-link fence.

We're home, he thought. We made it all the way back to Mountainside.

But there was a sign beside the gate he'd never seen on the fence back home. It read:

SANCTUARY

GIVE ME YOUR TIRED, YOUR POOR

YOUR HUDDLED MASSES YEARNING TO BREATHE FREE

But below that the original words were still visible, though sand-blasted to pale ghosts of letters by the unrelenting desert winds. As Benny passed the sign he read it:

AREA 51

UNITED STATES AIR FORCE

THIS IS A RESTRICTED AREA

TRESPASSERS WILL BE PROSECUTED

He closed his eyes again and the world went away, taking all its puzzles and mysteries with it.

EPILOGUE

-1-

BENNY SAW TOM THERE IN THE DARKNESS.

His brother stood halfway down a long hallway that vanished into soft gray light. Tom was dressed for the Ruin, with his leather jacket and the *kami katana* slung over his shoulder.

"Tom?"

His brother turned slowly toward him.

He looked younger than Benny remembered. There were fewer shadows in Tom's eyes.

"Hey, kiddo," said Tom. "You have any idea what happened?"

"Yeah, a zombie hit me with a stick."

"Crazy, huh? Bet you didn't think that could happen."

"Guess not." Benny touched his head. It hurt, but it was all in one piece. That surprised him. In most of his dreams his head was in a thousand pieces and he was crawling around looking for the important ones.

"How come you never told me that zoms could do that?" Benny asked.

Tom shrugged. "World's a big, strange place, Benny. What makes you think I know everything?"

"Oh."

"Next time somebody swings something at your head, you might want to think about ducking."

"Hilarious. Remind me to smother you in your sleep."

"Little too late for that, kiddo."

Even though Tom wasn't moving, he seemed to be a little farther away. For the first time Benny realized that there were other people in the hallways. They were indistinct, more of a sense of movement in the gray light rather than specific shapes. He thought he recognized one of them, though.

"Chong?"

The figure stopped moving, but he stood with his back to Benny.

"Tom—is that Chong?"

His brother turned and looked at the figure. Then he bent and spoke quietly to him, but Benny couldn't hear what was said.

"Is that Chong?" Benny asked again. "Is . . . is he going with you?"

Tom patted the other figure on the shoulder and then walked toward Benny. The other person remained back in the shadows.

Tom stopped a few feet away. He looked older now, more like he did that day they all left town.

"Can I come with you too?" asked Benny.

Sadness flickered in Tom's eyes, but he still made a joke. "No, kiddo . . . you got other places to mess up, other people to annoy."

"Tom . . . I really miss you, man."

"I know. Me too."

"Is it wrong that I want to go home?"

Tom touched Benny's face. His palm was warm. "Where's home now?" asked Tom.

Benny shook his head. "This isn't what we expected."

"What did you expect?" asked Tom.

"I don't know. I thought we'd . . . I mean, I thought that it would be . . ."

"Easier? Benny, I wish I could tell you that the world was a better place than it is," Tom said quietly. "Or that it's all going to be easier. But you know it isn't, and I think you knew that before you walked through the fence back home. Nix is looking for something perfect."

"I know. And we keep not finding it."

"Perfect doesn't exist. Not like she thinks. There's a lot of hurt out here. A lot of pain, and a lot of people doing bad things."

"Is that all there is? Hard times and bad people?"

Tom smiled. "I didn't say that everyone was bad. I said that there are people doing bad things. Some of them, but not all of them. You met some good ones too. You know that, right?"

"I know."

"This is the world, Benny. It's seldom what we expect it to be." He took his hand away. "But here's the secret, here's the thing I wanted to say."

"What?"

Tom smiled. "You can fix the world. You, Nix . . . your generation. You can fix the world and make it right."

"You mean put it back the way it was?"

"Was it right the way it was?"

"No."

"Then there's your answer." He cocked his head. "You already know this, though. Don't you?"

Benny thought about it.

"I guess so." He looked up at Tom. "Does that mean you're not really here and that this is some kind of coma thing? Like I'm having one of those vision thingies they talk about in books?"

Tom gave an elaborate shrug. "How would I know, little brother? You're the hero with the magic sword. I'm just a ghost—who is considerably better-looking than you."

"Hey!"

"I'm just saying."

They stood there, grinning at each other.

"I love you, Tom."

"Love you too, Benny."

Tom turned and walked away, and Benny let him go.

2

"WELCOME BACK TO THE WORLD," SAID PHOENIX RILEY.

Benny cranked open one eyelid and saw her perched on a chair a few feet away. "Nix," he said, his voice as weak as a whisper. He lay on a cot surrounded by a screen of sheets hung from metal poles.

"Benny!" Nix flew to him, but her hands were so gentle and tentative. She covered his face with a hundred quick kisses.

He tried to raise his head, to kiss her, but that was impossible. His head hurt too much, and his muscles felt like limp spaghetti. Nix looked worn thin, her face pale, her red hair hanging limp.

"How . . . bad is it . . . ?" he asked, not really wanting to know.

"You . . . almost slipped away from us," she said, and her smile was a little too bright, her laugh a bit too forced. "God . . . this was the longest week of my life!"

"Week?"

"Benny, we've been here for eight days."

He gaped at her.

"I thought I lost you, Benny," she said, and she held his hand with all her strength. She bent and kissed his knuckles.

"Where are we?" he asked "This place . . . is this Sanctuary?"

She nodded, sniffed, and dabbed at her eyes, but she kept her smile bolted in place.

"It's on an old military base," she said as she helped him sit up. She was very careful with him, as if he were made of glass. "It's run by the way-station monks. There are a couple hundred of them here."

All Benny could see was the curtain. "Where is everybody?"

"They're here," she said, but her eyes darted away for a moment. "We're all here."

"I want to see Lilah and Chong."

Nix hesitated. "Okay," she said eventually. "Let me get your robe and mask."

"Mask?"

"Everyone has to wear them in the houses. It's confusing . . . it's easier if you see it."

Nix helped him stand and put on a robe made of heavy wool. Then she took a blue cotton mask and tied it around his mouth and nose. She put one on too.

"Sanctuary isn't exactly what we thought it was," she said, and her voice sounded ready to crack.

Nix slowly pushed back the curtains, and Benny stared wide-eyed.

They were in a vast room, hundreds of feet long, with a massive arched ceiling and huge windows at either end.

"It used to be an airplane hangar," she explained. "There are eight like this one. And more on the other side of the compound."

Benny hardly heard her. He stared numbly at the rows of cots that stretched from one end of the hangar to the other. Every bed was filled. Some of the beds were screened off, as his had been. Most were not, and most of the figures lay as still as death. Farther down the row, separated by a line of sawhorse barricades, was a larger screened-off area. Benny heard continuous coughs coming from there. Everywhere there were soft cries, the sound of weeping, moans of pain. Way-station monks in their simple tunics moved from bed to bed, washing the patients, hand-feeding them, talking to them. A few sat reading to people who seemed to stare up at the nothingness above their beds.

"Oh my God."

"There are a thousand people in each hangar. All the hangars are full."

Benny was appalled. "What is this place? Nix, this isn't right. I thought there was a lab where they were studying the plague, trying to cure it."

"That's the other Sanctuary," said Nix. "The labs are on the other side of the compound. I'll show you."

They walked slowly between the rows. Benny's balance was bad and his legs weak, but Nix supported him and they walked with great care. Some of the patients looked at them, their eyes glazed with pain or bleak with despair.

"Who are these people?"

"Refugees from all over. The way-station monks bring a lot of them here. Some find their own way. Riot brings some."

"Did the reapers do all this?"

Nix shook her head. "Benny, after First Night, there were no real hospitals left. No factories to mass-produce drugs. No local doctors to prescribe them. Everything broke down. Diseases just went wild. Everything, even simple infections, went crazy. It's like this everywhere. People are dying everywhere faster than the zoms can kill them. The monks can't help everyone. They aren't real doctors . . . they're just monks. They have a few places like this."

"Hospitals?"

She gave another sad shake of her head. They paused to look at an old man who lay curled into a fetal position, his skin mottled with dark blisters.

"It's a hospice, Benny. This hangar is a healing place, but not the others. The monks call those transition houses. They bring people here to take care of them while they're dying."

"Where are the doctors and nurses?"

"There are no doctors on this side of the compound. The doctors and the scientists are all in a different hangar. In what they call a clean facility. Almost no one's allowed in except for the research field teams. And a few special patients." She paused. "The thing is . . . once a patient goes into the clean facility, they're not allowed out again."

"Why not?"

"Because most of them die, and the ones that don't are being studied. They're trying to cure the Reaper Plague . . . what we've always called the zombie plague. Not just that, though . . . they're trying to cure all these diseases. They've even come up with some treatments, and when they do, they give them to the monks. Not everyone who comes here dies."

"But most do?"

She nodded sadly. "By the time most people come here, they're already so sick. All the monks can do is make them comfortable."

"It's—it's—" Benny had no word bad enough to hang on it.

"They're doing what they can."

They walked toward the exit doors. One or two of the patients nodded to him and he nodded back, though he wasn't sure what that silent communication signified. Maybe, *We're not dead yet.*

It was horrible.

"I'm remembering things in bits and pieces. I remember a big dog and some strange guy. Joe, maybe? I have this weird memory about a Zombie Card. . . ."

"That's him." Nix told him about Lilah finding Joe, and about Joe being the head of a team of wilderness scouts called the rangers. "He used to be a bounty hunter up around our way, which is how he knew Tom and why he's on a Zombie Card, but he left a long time ago and went south. Benny . . . there's a kind of government. It's small, but it's there. They call it—"

"—the American Nation. We saw it on the plane."

"It's real," she said. "They only have about a hundred thousand people so far, mostly in North Carolina, and they've been looking for more. People are trying to put it back together."

Benny thought about his dream, about what Tom had said.

"I hope not," he said. "They need to make something else, something new. Something better."

Nix's green eyes glittered as she studied him; then she nodded.

They walked on until they reached the end of the big hangar. The sadness of it all was a crushing weight on Benny. His heart hurt worse than his head, and he wanted to go back to his cot, pull the blankets over his head, and let all this go away. That was impossible, though, and he knew it.

Nix opened the door, and they stepped out into the sunlight.

Benny blinked and held a hand up to shade his eyes. As he adjusted to the glare, he saw that they stood outside the first in a row of massive hangars. Monks walked slowly in and out of the buildings. The grounds outside were planted with herbs, and there were rock gardens with benches for meditation. It looked peaceful out here, but the hangars held horrors inside.

Nix pointed at the other buildings, each of which had a large number painted above the door. "Building One is for patients they think will recover. Mostly injuries, animal bites, or people wounded by reaper attacks."

"What about the other buildings?"

Nix pulled off her mask. "We're not allowed to go in there. That's where they keep the people with communicable diseases. Pneumonia, tuberculosis, cholera, bubonic plague. The monks who work in there never come outside."

"What happens to them?"

Nix did not answer. She didn't have to. Instead she said, "There are always new monks going in."

"That's horrible!"

She sniffed back tears. "But the monks keep volunteering. I spoke to one, a woman about my mom's age. She said that it didn't matter if she got sick. When it was her time to go into one of the other buildings, then at least in her last days, caring for people, she would know that her life mattered."

Benny stared at her. "That's what it's come to? Is that all there is out here? Just this?"

"No," she said, and he saw a steadiness in her eyes that he had not seen for a long time. More like the old Nix. More like the one he fell in love with. And yet there was sadness, too. Something deep and terrible. She took his hand and led him around the corner of the hangar.

Nix pointed to a spot beyond the herb garden. There was a small playground with a swing set, some monkey bars, a slide, and a big sandbox. A dozen children laughed and played and ran, their faces as bright as the sun, their laughter cleaner than anything in the world.

A little blond girl was with them, playing a game of tag in and around the legs of the monkey bars as three female monks watched with patient smiles. She wore a white tunic, and there were flowers in her hair.

"Eve," said Benny.

He made to call out to her, but Nix shook her head. "Not yet. This is only the second day that she's been playing."

"She looks happy," he said.

"More each day."

Benny nodded. Even though he knew that there would be a long uphill road for Eve, seeing her smile put a smile on his lips. He saw another figure sitting cross-legged on the ground in the shade of a palm tree that overhung the playground.

"Is that Riot?" he asked.

"Yes. She won't let Eve out of her sight."

"You still think she's a freak?"

Nix shook her head. "She's been through a lot." She told Benny about Riot's past, about her being a reaper and about how she'd rebelled against that lifestyle and spent the years since helping people.

"Her mom is Mother Rose?" gasped Benny.

"Was," corrected Nix. "Mother Rose died that day we found the wrecked plane. Riot's been dealing with that, and I think it hit her harder than she expected."

"How could it not?" asked Benny. "She was still her mother."

Nix nodded. "I guess . . . she's one of us. And she did everything she could to help Eve's family. She knows now that we were only trying to help Eve too."

"Well," Benny said, "Eve's still here. We accomplished something. We saved a kid. That's got to count for something, even in this world."

Shadows moved in Nix's eyes. Not the dangerous ones that had been there so often since her mother was killed; but shadows nonetheless. Was it because their trip had failed so badly in almost every way, or because this harsh world out here in no way matched Nix's expectations? Benny was afraid to ask for fear of breaking what resolve she had managed to put in place.

Nix sniffed back some more tears and said, "Listen, Benny, there are some things I have to tell you. Good and bad things, okay?"

"I don't know how much more I want to hear," he said, pitching it as a joke and watching it fall flat.

Nix said, "Do you remember seeing the jet?"

Benny brightened. "I—think so. Was it real?"

"It's real, and it's here. It's in one of the hangars on the other side of the compound. But before I show you, I have to warn you about something. I need you to understand how this place works."

"You're scaring me here, Nix."

"I don't mean to." She took a ragged breath. "Benny, people have been coming here for years. A lot of them. Long before the American Nation set up the lab. Before they had any kind of treatments for anything. People came here to die in peace, Benny. They came here because this place is run by way-station monks. Do you understand what that means?"

"Yes," Benny said, though his voice was a hoarse croak. "Way-station monks think the zoms are the meek who are supposed to inherit the earth."

"Have inherited the earth, Benny. Have."

He studied her, but her eyes were hard. She seemed to be waiting for him to ask, so he asked. A terrible thought crept into his mind.

"Nix," he asked, "what happened to all those people?"

Nix nodded and took him gently by the hand and guided him around the corner of the hangar.

Benny stopped dead in his tracks. Just beyond the hangar was a trench that was twenty feet wide and twenty feet deep. Beyond that was a set of runways for a military airport. Benny had seen pictures of places like this. The flat ground stretched all the way to the range of red rocks in one direction and into a heat haze on the far horizon. A second set of hangars—four in all—stood a thousand yards beyond the trench, and in front of those was a six-story concrete building. Surrounding these buildings was a ten-foot-high cinder-block wall. On the far side of the landing field, well beyond the runways, there was a line of slender towers, like lampposts but with bell-shaped devices mounted atop each one.

Outside the cinder-block wall, filling the desert and stretching off into the shimmering horizon, were zoms. Thousands upon thousands of them. There were more lining the edge of the trench, and when Benny looked toward the back of the building, he saw many more.

Nix said, "Joe says that there are probably two or three hundred thousand of them now. When people die, they are taken across the trench and allowed to roam free. The monks pray for them several times a day."

"But the jet? The lab?"

Nix reached into the V of her blouse and pulled out a silver whistle on a chain. "Recognize this? It's a reaper's dog whistle. It's ultrasonic. The zoms follow it every time." She pointed. "See those towers? When the jet is ready to take off or land, they blast an ultrasonic call through those. The zoms follow the call to the towers, and it clears the runway. I've seen it work twice now. It's amazing."

"Dog whistles," said Benny. "It's warrior smart. Tom would approve."

Nix nodded.

"What goes on over there?" asked Benny, pointing to the concrete buildings.

Nix started to answer, but the brave front she had been putting up collapsed, and she crumpled into grief. She put her face in her hands, and her body shook with sobs.

"Hey . . . hey . . . Nix—what's wrong?"

Nix turned and wrapped her arms around him, sobbing as hard now as she had back on the crashed plane. But through her sobs she forced herself to speak.

"They're working on the cure over there, Benny. They really are. With the stuff we found, the stuff on the plane, they think that maybe they really will cure it. They think that they'll be able to stop the plague . . . to stop the infection . . ."

"That's great, Nix," Benny said, stroking her back.

But she shook her head and kept shaking it.

"Nix? What is it . . . what's wrong?"

And then he understood.

Then he remembered.

The memory was a knife in his heart.

"Nix," he whispered, and his voice broke on that single word. "Nix . . . where's Chong?"

She clung to him. "They're trying, Benny. They're trying everything. But . . . he's so sick. He's already so . . ."

Nix couldn't say another word.

Benny wouldn't have been able to hear her anyway.

They clung to each other, and together they dropped brokenly to their knees.

3

IT WOULD BE HELL.

Lilah knew that.

Hell was something the Lost Girl knew. She had lived it all her life.

She was a toddler on First Night, but she remembered the panic and flight. The endless screams. The blood and the dying.

She saw her pregnant mother die as Lilah's sister, Annie, came screaming into the world. She remembered the other refugees, filled with terror and confusion, at first recoil from her mother as she came back from that place where all souls go and only the soulless return from. She remembered what they did—what they had to do. Lilah had screamed herself raw. Those screams had smashed down the doorway into hell.

She remembered Charlie Pink-eye and the Hammer brutalizing George and then laying rough hands on her and Annie. Dragging them to Gameland.

To the zombie pits.

She remembered coming back to Gameland to rescue Annie, but Annie was not there. A thing was, wearing the disguise of beautiful little Annie.

Lilah remembered what she had been forced to do.

And she remembered every moment of every day of every month of the lonely years that followed.

Hell?

Lilah knew hell.

It had nothing to teach her, no new tricks it could play on her.

She sat on the edge of Chong's bed and watched the strange machines beep and ping. But each beep was farther apart, each ping closer to a whisper.

Lilah held Chong's icy hand in hers. His eyes stared up at the ceiling, but they were milky, the irises transformed into a polluted mix of brown and green and black. The pupils were pinpricks, the whites veined with black lines as thin as sewing thread.

Bags of chemicals and medicines hung pendulously from the metal bed frame, dripping their mysteries into Chong's veins. His arm was covered with the black marks from needles. So many needles.

Lilah had refused to wear a hazmat suit. The doctors had warned her that if she didn't put one on, she could never leave this building. Even they couldn't guarantee that she wouldn't carry a disease out with her that would do what the Reaper Plague and all the other plagues had failed to do. Wipe everyone and everything out. The people inside the labs lived in isolation, never touching flesh to flesh, not even a handshake. They wore their hazmat suits all day until they sealed themselves into their private bedroom cells.

Lilah didn't care about any of that.

If she got sick and died, so what?

She would not be alone in death's kingdom. She knew that.

She listened to the beeps and willed Chong to fight.

To fight.

Fight.

"You damn well fight, you stupid town boy," she growled.

But with every minute those beeps, those electronic signs of life, grew fainter and fainter.

Until all she could hear was a long, continuous scream from the heart monitor.

It was almost the loudest sound in the world.

Only her own, endless keening cry of grief was louder.

Hell, it seemed, had one last trick to play.

4

BENNY AND NIX STOOD BY THE EDGE OF THE TRENCH AS THE SUN FELL behind the world and the stars ignited overhead. The trench was twenty feet across. It might as well have been ten miles. Ten thousand miles.

They stared at the tall building with its electric lights glowing against the shadows on the walls.

Stared at one window, high and to the left.

An hour ago they had seen Lilah's silhouette there.

There had been no sign of her since.

They didn't even turn when Joe's quad rumbled to a stop. They heard him switch it off, heard Grimm's soft *whuff* and the crunch of Joe's shoes on the gravel, but they never took their eyes from that lighted window.

"Listen," said Joe softly, "I just brought back the last of the stuff from the plane. The scientists are going over it now. It was exactly what they needed. It . . ." His voice trailed off.

"Go away," said Benny. His voice was crushed flat and empty.

Joe walked around and stood in front of them, forcing them to see him, to react to him. He squatted down, resting his elbows on his knees. Grimm stood beside him, his eyes dark and liquid.

"I want you two to listen to me," Joe said. "Straight talk here, okay? I know you're hurting. I know why you left Mountainside. I understand why you've been searching for the jet. I know what it means to you. A better place than your little town. A chance at a real future. I get that. I'd have done the same. Tom must have thought so too, or he'd have never left and never taken you with him."

"You don't know anything," said Nix.

"No? Well, I know this much," said Joe. "You left a place that was dying on its feet. Mountainside and the rest of the Nine Towns are just going through the motions of being alive. Everybody knows that. You knew it and you got the hell out. You wanted to find a place to start something new and fresh."

Benny glanced at him. It was almost the same thing Tom had said.

"You have," said Joe.

"No," said Nix.

Somewhere far away a coyote whined at the rising moon.

"You found the stuff in the jet," said Joe. "You kids might have actually helped saved the world."

"It's not worth it," Benny said. "It cost too much."

Joe sighed and stood up. He looked up at the endless stars.

"It's been a long night," he said softly, "and there are still a lot of hours of darkness left. But . . ."

He started to turn away, and Benny said, "But what?"

Joe gave him a small, sad smile. "No matter how long the night is, the sun always comes up."

He nodded to them, clicked his tongue for Grimm, and walked slowly away. He climbed onto his quad and started the engine.

They watched him drive away.

After a while Nix turned to Benny. "Is he right?" she asked.

Benny shook his head. "I don't know."

He wrapped his arm around her, and they looked up at the lighted window.

The stars burned their way across the sackcloth that covered the sky.

5

SAINT JOHN STOOD ON A CLIFF THAT LOOKED DOWN ON A BLACK ROAD. Brother Peter stood beside him, hands clasped behind his back, head bowed in thought. It was a beautiful night, with a billion stars and a fingernail moon. Crickets chirped in the grass, and owls hunted in the air.

The saint enjoyed being out here in the wild. The desert had reclaimed much of the road over the years, but it was there, and it ran straight and true to the line of mountains that formed the border of Nevada and California.

"Nine towns," murmured Saint John. "And a place called Mountainside."

"Praise be to the darkness," said Brother Peter.

Saint John raised his hand, held it high in the moonlight for a long moment, and pointed a slender finger toward the road. Toward the northwest.

The desert behind him was like a sea of roiling black. The reapers came first, flowing out of the dark, and as they reached Brother Peter they formed into orderly lines, seven across. Then they followed Brother Peter down the road. Some of them prayed, some of them sang. It took twenty minutes for all the reapers to file past where the saint stood.

Thousands upon thousands of reapers.

Those who had thought themselves lost when the world ended, who now knew that all roads led through pain and into the healing darkness. Those who had lost faith in this world of disease and death and endless struggle, who now thrived with a purpose—God's purpose. Many of them had once fought against the reapers and then, in their defeat, beheld the truth and took up their weapons again in the service of Thanatos, all praise his darkness.

The lost who had been found.

The blind who now saw.

The last army of the world, marching to fight the last war. The only war that ever mattered. The war to save mankind from its own sinful ways.

Saint John lingered a moment after the last of them was on the road. He closed his eyes and lifted a silver dog whistle to his lips, kissed it, and then blew into it, long and hard.

Behind him a second wave—ten times larger than the mass of reapers—moved forward. If the reapers were a sea, then this was an ocean, moving in a tidal surge under the watching moon. All the crickets were shocked to silence by the moan that rose from tens of thousands of dead throats.

Saint John smiled.

Nine towns waiting.

All those godless souls waiting, aching to be shown the way.

His reapers would open red mouths in the flesh of every man, woman, and child.

And then the gray people would consume them all, flesh and bone.

HEROES OF FIRST NIGHT

Nº 284

CAPTAIN LEDGER

This former Special Ops agent leads a team of rangers on hazardous missions into the most distant and dangerous parts of the Ruin. Even the toughest bounty hunters say, "Don't cross Captain Ledger and his ward dog, Grimm. You won't do it twice."

WILD CARD

No 193

RIOT

Legends abound in the Rot & Ruin, but one of the most persistent speaks of a teenage girl who is as wild as she is beautiful. When Riot is on the scene, armed with a slingshot and running from a dark past, something bad is probably happening.

WILD CARD
(REAPERS SUBSET)

No 194

SAINT JOHN OF THE KNIFE

Little is known for sure about the man called Saint John of the Knife. Is he a saint or a killer? The leader of the Night Church comes out of the east at the head of an army of devoted followers called reapers. Beware Saint John!

WILD CARD
(REAPERS SUBSET)

№ 197

MOTHER ROSE

Mysterious and beautiful, charismatic Mother Rose is the spiritual leader of the Night Church. Her followers are willing to die for her. Or kill for her.

WILD CARD

No 190

HIRAM HALF-ZEE

Legends say that ol' Hiram got himself infected by the zombie plague but he didn't quite die from it. Nor did he quite recover. Now he's half-human and half-zombie. Don't invite Hiram Half-Zee over for a bite!

Don't miss the final book in the gripping Rot & Ruin series!

Benny Imura and his friends have found what they were searching for: the jet and Sanctuary. But their victory is short-lived. Sanctuary isn't what they expected, and Chong is hovering between life and death, battling a strain of zom virus that's eating him alive. The only person who can save him is a doctor who may have discovered the holy grail: a cure for the zombie plague. But the reapers are hunting for her too, and if the doctor—and her cure—fall into the wrong hands, Chong will be only the first casualty. . . .

BENNY IMURA SAT IN THE DARK AND SPOKE WITH MONSTERS.

It was like that every day.

It had become the pattern of his life. Shadows and blood.
And monsters.

Everywhere.

Monsters.

THE THING CROUCHED IN THE DARKNESS.

It stank of raw meat and decay. A metal collar was bolted around its neck and a steel chain lay coiled on the bottom of the cage, looking like the discarded skin of some great snake.

The thing raised its head and glared through the bars. Greasy black hair hung in filthy strings, half hiding the gray face. The skin looked diseased, dead. But the eyes . . .

The eyes.

They watched with a malevolent intensity that spoke of a dreadful awareness. Pale hands gripped the bars with such force that the knuckles were white with tension. The thing's teeth were caked with pieces of meat.

Benny Imura sat crossed-legged on the floor.

Sick to his stomach.

Sick at heart.

Sick in the depths of his soul.

Benny leaned forward. His voice was thick and soft when he spoke.

"Can you hear me?"

The creature's lips curled.

"Yes, you can hear me," said Benny. "Good . . . can you understand me? Do you know who I am?"

A fat drop of bloody spit oozed from between the creature's teeth, rolled over its bottom lip, hung for a moment, and then dropped with a faint *plash* to the floor.

Benny leaned closer still. "Do you recognize me?"

After a long moment, the thing in the cage leaned forward too. Its face underwent a slow process of change. Doubt flickered in its eyes; the lips relaxed over the teeth. It sniffed the air as if trying to identify Benny's scent. The doubt in its eyes deepened. It bent closer still, and now the lips seemed like they were trying to shape a word.

Benny pushed himself even closer, trying to hear what sound that word carried.

"Huh," murmured the creature in a rasping croak, ". . . huh . . . hun . . ."

"Go on," Benny encouraged. "Go ahead. You can do it. Say something. . . ."

The creature rested its forehead against the inside of the bars, and Benny leaned all the way forward.

". . . hunh . . . hunh . . ."

"What is it?" whispered Benny. "What are you trying to say?"

The creature spoke the word. It came out as a whisper. A full word. Two syllables.

"Hungry!"

Suddenly it lunged at Benny; gray hands shot between the bars and grabbed Benny's shirt. The creature howled with triumph.

"HUNGRY!"

Wet teeth snapped at him. It jammed its face between the bars, trying to bite him, to tear him.

To feed its hunger.

Benny screamed and flung himself backward, but the creature had him in its powerful hands. The teeth snapped. Saliva that was as cold and dirty as gutter water splashed Benny's face.

"Hungry . . . hungry . . . hungry!" screamed the thing.

Behind Benny a voice shouted in anger. The soldier, moving too slow and too late. Something whistled through the air above Benny's head and rang off the bars. A baton, swung by the soldier with crippling force.

The creature jerked backward from a blow that would have smashed its jaw and shattered its teeth.

"No!" bellowed Benny, still caught by the thing's hands, but squirming, fighting it and swinging his arms up to block the soldier.

"Move, kid!" snarled the guard.

The baton hit the bars again with a deafening *caroooom!*

Benny bent his knees and forced his foot into the narrow gap between him and the bars, then kicked himself backward. The creature lost one handhold on his shirt, but it grabbed the bar to brace itself so it could pull even harder with the other. Benny kicked out, once, twice, again, slamming his heel into the hand holding the bar, hitting knuckles every time. The creature howled and whipped its hand back from the bars. Its screech of agony tore the air.

Benny's mind reeled. *It can still feel pain.*

It was the strangest feeling for Benny. That thought, that bit of truth, was a comfort to him.

If it could still feel pain . . .

It was still alive.

"Out of the way, kid," roared the soldier, raising his stick again. "I got the son of a—"

Benny kicked once more, and the whole front of his shirt tore away. He collapsed backward against the soldier, hitting his legs so hard the man fell against the concrete wall. Benny sank onto the cold floor, gasping, shuddering with terror.

Inside the cage, the creature clutched its hands to its gray flesh and let out a high, keening cry of pain and frustration.

And of hunger.

The soldier pushed himself angrily off the wall, hooked Benny under the armpit, hauled him to his feet, and flung him toward the door. "That's it. You're out of here. And I'm going to teach this monster some damn manners."

"No!" shouted Benny. He slapped the soldier's hands aside and shoved the man in the chest with both hands. The move was backed by all of Benny's hurt and rage; the soldier flew backward, skidded on the damp concrete, and fell. The baton clattered from his hand and rolled away.

The creature in the cage howled and once more lunged through the bars, trying this time to grab the fallen soldier's outflung arm. The guard snatched it out of the way with a cry of disgust. Spitting in fury, the soldier rolled sideways onto his knees and reached for the baton.

"You made a big damn mistake, boy. I'm going to kick your ass, and then you're going to watch me beat some manners into—"

There was a sudden rasp of steel and something silver

flashed through the air and the moment froze. The soldier was on his knees, one hand braced on the ground, the other holding the baton. His eyes bugged wide as he tried to look down at the thing that pressed into the soft flesh of his throat. The soldier could see his own reflection in the long, slender blade of Benny Imura's *katana*.

"Listen to me," said Benny, and he didn't care that his voice was thick with emotion or that it broke with a sob. "You're not going to do anything to me, and you're not going to do anything to—"

"To *what*? It's a monster. It's an abomination."

Benny pressed the tip of the sword into the man's skin. A single tiny bead of hot blood popped onto the edge of the steel and ran along the mirror-bright surface in a crooked line.

"It's not a monster," said Benny. "And he has a name."

The soldier said nothing.

Benny increased the pressure. "Say his name."

The soldier's face flushed red with fury.

"*Say it*," snarled Benny in a voice he had never heard himself use before. Harsh, cruel, vicious. Uncompromising.

The soldier said the name.

He spat it out of his mouth like a bad taste.

"*Chong.*"

Benny removed the sword and the soldier started to turn, but the blade flashed through the shadows and came to rest again, with the razor-sharp edge right across the man's throat.

"I'm going to come back tomorrow," said Benny in that same ugly voice. "And the day after that, and the day after that. If I find even a single bruise on my friend, if you or any of your friends hurt him in any way . . . then you're going to have a lot more to worry about than monsters in cages."

The soldier glared at Benny, his intent lethal.

"You're out of your mind, boy."

Benny could feel his mouth twist into a smile, but from the look in the soldier's eyes it could not have been a nice smile.

"Out of my mind? Yeah," said Benny. "I probably am."

Benny stepped back and lowered the sword. He turned his back on the soldier and went over to the cage. He stood well out of reach this time.

"I'm sorry, Chong," he said.

Tears ran down Benny's face. He looked into those dark eyes, searching for some trace of the person he'd known all his life. The quick wit, the deep intelligence, the gentle humor. If Chong was alive, then those things had to still be in there. Somewhere. Benny leaned closer still, needing to catch the slightest glimpse of his friend. He could bear this horror if there was the slightest chance that Chong was only detached from conscious control, if he was like a prisoner inside a boarded-up house. As horrible as that was, it suggested that a solution, some kind of rescue, was possible.

"C'mon, you monkey-banger," Benny whispered. "Give me something here. You're smarter than me . . . *you* find *me*. Say something. Anything . . ."

The thing's gray lips curled back from wet teeth.

". . . hungry . . ."

That was all the creature could say. Drool ran down its chin and dropped to the straw-covered floor of its cage.

"He's not dead, you know," Benny said to the soldier.

The soldier wiped at the trickle of blood on his throat. "He ain't alive."

"He's. Not. Dead." Benny spaced and emphasized each word.

"Yeah. Sure. Whatever you want, kid."

Benny resheathed his sword, turned, and walked past the guard, out through the iron door, up the stone stairs, and out into the brutal heat of the Nevada morning.

FROM NIX'S JOURNAL

Three weeks ago we were in a war.

I guess it was a religious war. Sort of. A holy war, though it seems weird to even write those words.

A crazy woman named Mother Rose and an even crazier man named Saint John started a religion called the Night Church. They worshipped one of the old Greek gods of death, Thanatos. Somehow they got it into their heads that the zombie plague was their god's deliberate attempt to wipe out all of humanity. They considered anyone who didn't die to be a blasphemer going against their god's will.

So, the people in the Night Church decided that they needed to complete Thanatos's plan by killing everyone who's left. They trained all the people in the church to be really good fighters. They call themselves the reapers.

When that's done, they plan to kill themselves.

Crazy, right?

According to our new friend, Riot, who is (no joke) Mother Rose's daughter, the reapers have killed about ten thousand people.

Ten thousand.

A lot of reapers were killed in a big battle. Joe killed them with rocket launchers and other weapons we found on a crashed plane. Joe's a good guy, but seeing him kill all those killers . . . that was nuts. It was wrong no matter what side I look at it from.

But then . . . what choice did he have?

I wish the world still made sense.

Jonathan Maberry is a *New York Times* best-selling author, multiple Bram Stoker Award winner, and Marvel Comics writer. He's the author of many novels, including *Assassin's Code*, *Dead of Night*, *Patient Zero*, *Rot & Ruin*, and *Dust & Decay*. The topics of his nonfiction books range from martial arts to zombie pop culture. Since 1978 he has sold more than 1,200 magazine feature articles, 3,000 columns, two plays, greeting cards, song lyrics, poetry, and textbooks. Jonathan continues to teach the celebrated Experimental Writing for Teens class, which he created. He founded the Writers Coffeehouse, cofounded the Liars Club, and is a frequent speaker at schools and libraries, as well as a keynote speaker and guest of honor at major writers' and genre conferences. Jonathan lives in Bucks County, Pennsylvania, with his wife, Sara, and their son, Sam. Visit him online at www.jonathanmaberry.com and on Twitter (@jonathanmaberry) and Facebook.